CW01499631

THE MIDDLE YEARS
AND OTHER TALES

THE MIDDLE YEARS AND OTHER TALES

Henry James

Selected and with a preface by
Frances Wilson

riverrun

This paperback edition first published in Great Britain in 2025 by riverrun

an imprint of Quercus
Part of John Murray Group

1

Preface copyright © 2025 Frances Wilson

A CIP catalogue record for this book is available from the British Library

Paperback ISBN 978 1 52943 114 8
eBook ISBN 978 1 52943 114 8

Typeset by Fournier MT Std by Hewer Text UK Ltd, Edinburgh
Printed and bound in Great Britain by Clays Ltd, Elcograf S.p.A.

Papers used by Quercus are from well-managed forests and other responsible sources.

Quercus
Carmelite House
50 Victoria Embankment
London EC4Y 0DZ

John Murray Group
Part of Hodder & Stoughton Limited
An Hachette UK company

The authorized representative in the EEA is Hachette Ireland, 8 Castlecourt
Centre, Dublin 15, D15 XTP3, Ireland (email: info@hbgi.ie)

Contents

Preface

THESE TALES represent Henry James's middle years. They open with 'The Author of *Beltraffio*' (1884), a reflection on literary lions written when James was forty-one and himself the author of seven novels including *The Portrait of a Lady* (1881), and close with his elegy, 'The Altar of the Dead' (1895). At the heart of the volume is 'The Middle Years' (1893), about a disappointed and dying author called Dencombe, whose most recent, and final, novel is also called 'The Middle Years'. The mood of James's own middle years was what he called 'misanthropic, melancholy, morbid, morose', following the 'inexplicable injury' wrought on his 'situation' by the reception of *The Bostonians* (1885) and *The Princess Casamassima* (1886), 'from which', he told William Dean Howells in 1888, 'I expected so much and derived so little'. He had 'entered upon evil days'; the 'desire and demand' for his fiction was 'zero', and his forthcoming novel, *The Tragic Muse* (1891), would therefore, he (wrongly) believed, be his last.

'The Middle Years' is James's public statement as an artist and a private reflection on his craft. 'We work in the dark —' says

Dencombe, the author's alter ego, 'we do what we can – we give what we have. Our doubt is our passion and our passion is our task. The rest is the madness of art.' Convalescing from a serious illness in Bournemouth, Dencombe is reading an advance copy of 'The Middle Years' when, by a quirk of fate, he meets a young acolyte called Dr Hugh who is absorbed in the same book (the words 'chance', 'accident' and 'coincidence' recur throughout the tale). 'Dr Hugh was an apparition,' Dencombe feels, and so apparitional is his admirer, and so like his former self, that he belongs in one of James's ghost stories (three of which, 'Sir Edmund Orme', 'Nona Vincent' and 'Owen Wingrave', are also included in this volume), or explorations of duality such as 'The Private Life' or 'The Jolly Corner'. As he reads, Dencombe instinctively starts to 'alter' his earlier writing, giving it the varnish of his second thoughts. Like James, he is 'a passionate corrector, a fingerer of style; the last thing he ever arrived at was a form final for himself. His ideal would have been to publish secretly, and then, on the published text, treat himself to the terrified revise.' The correction of his sentences, which involves making them longer, is aligned to Dencombe's sense that his life has been 'too short', that he has 'ripened too late'; the art came but in order 'to fructify, to use the material, one must have a second age, an extension . . . "Ah for another go! – ah for a better chance!"' What Dencombe means by 'a better chance' is the kind of 'terrified revise' James later allowed himself in the twenty-four volume New York Edition of his novels and tales (1907–1909), whose extensive alterations to the original texts conform to the verbosity of his late style (the average length of one of James's late sentences being 55½ words).

The following tales, concerned with artists, audiences and afterlives, have been selected less for subject than for size: none, apart from 'The Author of *Beltraffio*' (19,000 words) is over 15,000 words ('The Aspern Papers', also from James's middle period but weighing in at 26,500 words, is therefore excluded). We know what he could do with expansion, but how did James manage the demands of brevity? He wrote his stories 'for gold', as he put it, selling them to the magazines whose required length – which he struggled to achieve – was between 7,000 and 10,000 words. The illustrated quarterly *The Yellow Book* (with Aubrey Beardsley as art editor) was the only magazine where no word-length was required, so when the editor accepted 'The Death of the Lion' – in which a novelist is lionized to death – the tale could become what Leon Edel describes as 'a 'length proper to itself' '.

Brevity was one of James's preoccupations during these years (few writers have been more aware of word-counts), and he returned to the subject repeatedly in the Notebooks, where he geared up for the work ahead. 'I must hammer away at the effort to do, successfully and triumphantly, a large number of very short things,' he confided in July 1891: 'It takes time and practice to get into the trick of it. I have never attempted before to deal with such extreme brevity. However, the extreme brevity is a necessary condition only for some of them – the others may be of varying kinds and degrees of shortness.'

What did he mean by 'kinds and degrees of shortness'? How long could shortness afford to be? Only the Anglo-Saxons, James said, took the 'dull view' that 'a "short story" was a "short story", and that was the end of it. Shades and differences, varieties and styles, the value above all of the idea happily developed, languished, to extinction, under the hard-and-fast rule of the "from six to eight thousand words".' James compared his 'very short things' to a family, 'quite organized as such, with its proper representatives, its "heads", its subdivisions and branches, its poor relations perhaps not least'. Included in the subdivisions were 'the concise anecdote', passed on to him, usually at a dinner party, and consisting of 'something that has oddly happened to someone'; the 'picture', a composition with the minimum dramatic action ('I rejoice in the anecdote but I revel in the picture'); the 'little idea' ('It must be an idea. It can't be a story in the vulgar sense of the word. It must illustrate something'); the 'single incident' ('I know what I mean by the single incident. The Real Thing, The Middle Years, Brooksmith, even, The Private Life, Owen Wingrave, are what I call single incidents'); and 'the beautiful and blest *nouvelle*', a French term because it was a French form, practised by 'the heirs of Balzac'. *Nouvelles*, such as 'The Turn of the Screw' (42,000 words), were anecdotes in which 'the subject treated would perhaps seem one comparatively demanding "developments"'. But everything he wrote, James felt, demanded developments, 'my temptation and my joy'. The challenge he faced was to let his 'things' alone, to prevent the anecdote or picture or single incident or idea from becoming a *nouvelle*, and the *nouvelle* from becoming a novel.

'I've lost sight too much of the necessary smallness, necessary singleness of the subject,' James wrote of 'The Real Thing' (1892). 'Suffice it that I'm simply face to face with the little question, "*can* I do the thing in 10,000 words or can I not?"' 'The Real Thing' (10,000 words exactly) is a lesson in art for the ignorant. Major and Mrs Monarch – a smart couple down on their luck – believe that, being the 'real thing', they would make good models for smart couples in book illustrations. The real thing, however, is of less interest to the illustrator/narrator, to whom they introduce themselves, than the 'unreal' thing, such as Miss Churm, 'a freckled cockney' who can 'represent everything', including a Russian princess. Miss Churm is 'makeable' while the Monarchs are 'already made'. She may appear 'shabby', the illustrator concedes, 'but you must allow for the alchemy of art'. The alchemy of art is what the Monarchs, for whom art is a copy of life, do not understand. Alchemy was James's art too: transforming an anecdote made of metal into something he sold for gold required a similar trick, which he compared to the reduction of ingredients in a cauldron. The 'boilings and reboilings' he went through in order to fit 'The Middle Years' into the word-length required by *Scribner's Magazine* were recalled in one of his New York Edition Prefaces:

To get it right was to squeeze my subject into the five or six thousand words I had been invited to make it consist of – it consists, in fact, should the curious care to know, of some 5550 – and I scarce perhaps recall another case . . . in which my struggle to keep compression rich, if not, better still, to keep accretions compressed, betrayed for me such community with the anxious effort of some warden of the insane engaged at a critical moment in making fast a victim's straitjacket . . . I well remember finding the whole process and act (which, to the exclusion of everything else, dragged itself out for a month) one of the most expensive of its sort in which I had ever engaged.

The straitjacketed tale (8,170 words rather than 5,550) was mercifully not subjected to the expansions executed on other texts included the New York Edition. James's 'better chances' were rarely improvements.

The tales that are squeezed into shortness begin their lives in littleness. Or rather, each tale 'begin[s] and end[s] in its little self', as James put it in his Notebooks in September 1895. Little things appear harmless, and James repeatedly used the word to ward off his fear of the work ahead, whose dimension threatened to overwhelm him. 'My little story has grown upon my hands,' he said of 'The House Beautiful', 'and will make a thing of 30,000 words. But though I have been scared at the dimensions it was taking – scared in view of the meagreness of the little subject – yet I think I see the way to make it fill out its skin and be very fairly solid and fine.' ('The House Beautiful' became the *The Spoils of Poynton*: 71,500 words.) He also describes in his Notebooks his 'little *donnée*', 'little chapter', 'little drama', 'little sketch', 'little tale', 'little question', and 'little anecdote'. 'I don't see why this shouldn't be a little masterpiece of concision,' James wrote of 'Louisa Pallant', another tale he struggled to keep within length.

James published twenty little masterpieces between 1890 and 1895; six of those in the following pages appeared in 1892, the year that his much-loved sister Alice died of breast cancer. His production of tales increased in the early nineties so he could finance his 'sustained attack on the theatre': if the novels were unappreciated, he would offer the public his dramas. His first performed play, *The American*, opened in September 1891 and 'died an honourable death', as Alice put it, five months later. *Guy Domville*, his final play, was performed in January 1895 and greeted by what James described as 'the hoots and jeers and catcalls of the roughs'. Writing again to Howells, he repeated the image of having 'fallen upon evil days – every sign or symbol of one's being in the least wanted, anywhere or by anyone, having so utterly failed'. One reason he failed as a dramatist was because his dialogue was too indirect, and in 'The Visits', the most daring of the 1892 tales, the brief encounter between Louisa Chantry and Jack Brandon is so unspeakable that it remains unspoken, unknown to the narrator herself (for whom Louisa is experiencing 'a nameless pain') and unmentioned even by James in his Notebooks.

'She says it's *horrible*,' my poor friend murmured, with tears in her eyes and tragic speculation in her mild maternal face.

'But in what way? Does she give you no facts, no clue?'

'It was something she did.'

We looked at each other a moment. 'Did?' I echoed. 'Did to whom?'

'She won't tell me – she says she *can't*. She tries to bring it out, but it sticks in her throat.'

James's Notebooks now filled with plans for tales about 'living death', which he compares to a 'deep humiliation' in which 'the pride, the passion, the idea of greatness . . . has been smothered and defeated by circumstances'. He explores the idea of un-appreciated authors 'galvanized' by the sympathy of a friend and admirer: a writer's greatest achievement, James suggests in 'The Author of *Beltraffio*', 'The Death of the Lion' and 'The Middle Years', lies not in the quantity of his sales, but the 'transference' he achieves with one sympathetic reader.

The author similarly, however, galvanizes his acolyte by casting, as Dencombe calls it, 'our little spell'. The relationship between the artist and his sympathetic reader is in this sense a collaboration, and collaboration – or what James called 'the intense desire of being to get itself shared' – was another pre-occupation of his middle years. The theme recurs in various forms throughout the following tales: unlike the models who lend themselves to the artist's imagination in 'The Real Thing', Major and Mrs Monarch have no idea how collaboration works, while the butler in 'Brooksmith' cannot survive without his master. Collaboration in 'The Private Life' takes the form of a split self, a necessity for all authors. Based on James's impression of Robert Browning, Clare Vawdrey – 'the greatest (in the opinion of many) of our literary glories' – bores the dinner guests downstairs with his commonplace opinions while also sitting upstairs at the desk, writing works of genius. 'The Private Life' is seen as a parody of Browning, but it was James's tribute to an artist who had, as he put it, 'arrived somehow, for his own deep purposes, at the enjoyment of a double identity'. Browning had built a wall around his public self, which he could live either side of. 'It contained an invisible door,' James observed in *William Wetmore Story and His Friends*,

> through which, working the lock at will, he could softly pass and of which he kept the golden key – carrying the same about with him even in the pocket of his dinner-waistcoat, yet even in his most splendid expansions showing it, happy man, to none. Such at least was the appearance he could repeatedly conjure up to a deep and mystified admirer.

In 'Collaboration' (1892), a German composer and a French poet form a creative partnership which so horrifies Parisian society that the pair make their art 'on alien soil, at a little place on the Genoese Riviera where sunshine is cheap and tobacco bad, and they live (the two together) for five francs a day, which is all they can muster between them'. Their collaboration is considered by the xenophobes to be 'monstrous', and while James's little point is that art exceeds boundaries, he too distrusted the idea of collaboration ('we work in the dark'), having experienced a version of it first hand in his relations with his siblings, Alice and William. In the James family theatricals, every production was a joint effort and the real drama of his middle years was going on behind the scenes.

'Within the last year', Alice wrote in her diary at the end of 1890, '[Henry] has published *The Tragic Muse*, brought out The American, and written a play, Mrs Vibert . . . and his admirable comedy: combined with William's [*The Principles of*] *Psychology* not a bad show for one family! especially if I can get myself dead, the hardest job of all.' Alice had herself been galvanized by the *The American*, a play so identified with her that Henry called it 'the other invalid'. 'Our absorbing interest just now is of course Harry's dramatic debut at the end of the month', Alice wrote to William's wife in September 1890. 'The American', she told her diary, was 'the great family event, over which I have been palpitating for the last 18 months'; her anticipated death, however, might make 'a sad complication, as I don't want to immerse [Henry] in a deathbed scene on his "first night".'

Meanwhile William James, like Dr Hugh in 'The Middle Years', was involved in 'the new psychology' of telepathy and hypnotism, in which he tried to interest his siblings. On the first night of *Guy Domville*, Henry asked William to send him a telepathic message – 'this is really the time to show your stuff'. Five years earlier, in October 1890, William had asked Henry to act as his medium and read to the newly formed Society for Psychical Research his own paper on the clairvoyant Mrs Piper. 'You were very easy and interesting to read and were altogether the "feature" of the entertainment,' Henry reported. In James's supernatural tale 'Nona Vincent', written immediately after the Mrs Piper episode, the dramatist Allan Wayworth bases the heroine of his play *Nona Vincent* on his friend, Mrs Alsager. The part of Nona Vincent is performed, however, by an actress called Violet Grey who cannot 'possess' the character any more than Mrs Monarch can possess the character of a lady of fashion for a book illustration. Miss Grey reads the part and no more: she simply 'isn't *in it*', the critics say; 'she doesn't *see* Nona Vincent . . . She's out of it – she gives you a different person.' The collaboration between the actors and the playwright should, in a successful production, be a form of thought transference, and in the tale's denouement this is what takes place when Wayworth has an occult vision of Nona Vincent at the same moment as Violet Grey, visiting Mrs Alsager, imbibes the energy of her inspiration, thus changing the fortunes of the play.

'The Altar of the Dead' (1895), in which decades of slow time are compressed into 14,700 words, was James's homage to the friends and family who died in the early nineties. Mourning his fiancée, George Stransom lights candles to her memory in a Catholic church which he visits every day: the belief that absence can become presence is his art and his religion. Stransom meets in the church another mourner, the name of whom we – and for many years he – never learns; the communication between the two is largely unspoken, but she becomes a collaborator of sorts. James's 'little thing' was rejected by the magazine editors who considered it distasteful; 'The Altar of the Dead' was therefore first published alongside 'The Death of the Lion' and 'The Middle Years' in *Terminations* (1895), James's aptly named latest collection of stories.

Twenty-one years after 'The Middle Years' was published in *Scribner's Magazine*, James gave the same title to a volume of (unfinished) autobiography – to accompany *A Small Boy and Others* and *Notes of a Son and Brother* – which he dictated in 1914 when he, like Dencombe, was dying. 'The Middle Years' is therefore the name of a tale by Henry James, of the 'little book' by Dencombe within that tale, and of a posthumously published fragment in which James recalls his arrival in London in 1879 and his first meetings with the literary lions of the day. Both the fictional and autobiographical versions of 'The Middle Years' are concerned with authors, acolytes, and endings rather than the middle of things. Or rather they are about, as are all the tales of James's middle years, the recognition of one's own extreme brevity.

Frances Wilson

The Middle Years
and Other Tales

The Author of Beltraffio

I

MUCH AS I WISHED to see him, I had kept my letter of introduction for three weeks in my pocket-book. I was nervous and timid about meeting him – conscious of youth and ignorance, convinced that he was tormented by strangers, and especially by my country-people, and not exempt from the suspicion that he had the irritability as well as the brilliancy of genius. Moreover, the pleasure, if it should occur (for I could scarcely believe it was really at hand), would be so great that I wished to think of it in advance, to feel that it was in my pocket, not to mix it with satisfactions more superficial and usual. In the little game of new sensations that I was playing with my ingenuous mind, I wished to keep my visit to the author of *Beltraffio* as a trump-card. It was three years after the publication of that fascinating work, which I had read over five times, and which now, with my riper judgement, I admire on the whole as much as ever. This will give you about the date of my first visit (of any duration) to England; for you will not have forgotten the commotion – I may even say the scandal – produced by Mark Ambient's masterpiece. It was the most complete presentation that had yet been made of the gospel of art; it was a kind of aesthetic war-cry. People had endeavoured to sail nearer to 'truth' in the cut of their sleeves and the shape of their sideboards; but there had not as yet been, among English novels, such an example of beauty of execution and value of subject. Nothing had been done in that line from the point of view of art for art. This was my own point of view, I may mention, when I was twenty-five; whether it is altered now I won't take upon myself to say – especially as the discerning reader will be able to judge for himself. I had been in England a twelvemonth before the time to which I began by alluding, and had learned then that Mr Ambient was in distant lands – was making a considerable tour in the East. So there was nothing to do but to keep my letter till I should be in London again. It was of little use to me to hear that his wife had not left England and, with her little boy, their only child, was spending the period of her husband's absence – a good many months – at a small place they had down in Surrey. They had a house in London which was let. All this I learned, and also that Mrs Ambient was charming (my friend, the American poet, from whom I had my introduction, had never seen her, his relations with the great man being only epistolary); but she was not, after all, though she had lived so near the rose, the author of *Beltraffio*, and I did not go down into Surrey to call on her. I went to the Continent, spent the following winter in Italy, and returned to London in May. My visit to Italy opened my eyes to a good many things, but to nothing more than the beauty of certain pages in the works of Mark Ambient. I had every one of his productions in my portmanteau – they are not, as you know, very numerous, but he had preluded to *Beltraffio* by some exquisite things – and I used to read them over in the evening at the inn. I used to say to myself that the man who drew those characters and wrote that style understood what he saw and knew what he was doing. This is my only reason for mentioning my winter in Italy. He had been there much in former years, and he was saturated with what painters call the 'feeling' of that classic land. He expressed the charm of the old hill-cities of Tuscany, the look of certain lonely grass-grown places which, in the past, had echoed with life; he understood the great artists, he understood the spirit of the Renaissance, he understood everything. The scene of one of his earlier novels was laid in Rome, the scene of another in Florence, and I moved through these cities in company with the figures whom Mark Ambient had set so firmly upon their feet. This is why I was now so much happier even than before in the prospect of making his acquaintance.

At last, when I had dallied with this privilege long enough, I despatched to him the missive of the American poet. He had already gone out of town; he shrank from the rigour of the London season, and it was his habit to migrate on the first of June. Moreover, I had heard that this year he was hard at work on a new book, into which some of his impressions of the East were to be wrought, so that he desired nothing so much as quiet days. This knowledge, however, did not prevent me – *cet âge est sans pitié* – from sending with my friend's letter a note of my own, in which I asked Mr Ambient's leave to come down and see him for an hour or two, on a day to be designated by himself. My proposal was accompanied with a very frank expression of my sentiments, and the effect of the whole projectile was to elicit from the great man the kindest possible invitation. He would be delighted to see me, especially if I should turn up on the following Saturday and could remain till the Monday morning. We would take a walk over the Surrey commons, and I should tell him all about the other great man, the one in America. He indicated to me the best train, and it may be imagined whether on the Saturday afternoon I was punctual at Waterloo. He carried his benevolence to the point of coming to meet me at the little station at which I was to alight, and my heart beat very fast as I saw his handsome face, surmounted with a soft wide-awake, and which I knew by a photograph long since enshrined upon my mantel-shelf, scanning the carriage-windows as the train rolled up. He recognized me as infallibly as I had recognized him; he appeared to know by instinct how a young American of an aesthetic turn would look when much divided between eagerness and modesty. He took me by the hand, and smiled at me, and said, 'You must be – a – *you*, I think!' and asked if I should mind going on foot to his house, which would take but a few minutes. I remember thinking it a piece of extraordinary affability that he should give directions about the conveyance of my bag, and feeling altogether very happy and rosy, in fact quite transported, when he laid his hand on my shoulder as we came out of the station. I surveyed him, askance, as we walked together; I had already – I had indeed instantly – seen that he was a delightful creature. His face is so well known that I needn't describe it; he looked to me at once an English gentleman and a man of genius, and I thought that a happy combination. There was just a little of the Bohemian in his appearance; you would easily have guessed that he belonged to the guild of artists and men of letters. He was addicted to velvet jackets, to cigarettes, to loose shirt-collars, to looking a little dishevelled. His features, which were fine but not perfectly regular, are fairly enough represented in his portraits; but no portrait that I have seen gives any idea of his expression. There were so many things in it, and they chased each other in and out of his face. I have seen people who were grave and gay in quick alternation; but Mark Ambient was grave and gay at one and the same moment. There were other strange oppositions and contradictions in his slightly faded and fatigued countenance. He seemed both young and old, both anxious and indifferent. He had evidently had an active past, which inspired one with curiosity, and yet it was impossible not to be more curious still about his future. He was just enough above middle height to be spoken of as tall, and rather lean and long in the flank. He had the friendliest, frankest manner possible, and yet I could see that he was shy. He was thirty-eight years old at the time *Beltraffio* was published. He asked me about his friend in America, about the length of my stay in England, about the last news in London and the people I had seen there; and I remember looking for the signs of genius in the very form of his questions – and thinking I found it. I liked his voice. There was genius in his house, too, I thought, when we got there; there was imagination in the carpets and curtains, in the pictures and books, in the garden behind it, where certain old brown walls were muffled in creepers that appeared to me to have been copied from a masterpiece of one of the pre-Raphaelites. That was the way many things struck me at that time, in England; as if they were reproductions of something that existed primarily in art or literature. It was not the picture, the poem, the fictive page, that seemed to me a copy; these things were the originals, and the life of happy and distinguished people was fashioned in their image. Mark Ambient called his house a cottage, and I perceived afterwards that he was right; for if it had not been a cottage it must have been a villa, and a villa, in England at least, was not a place in which one could fancy him at home. But it was, to my vision, a cottage glorified and translated; it was a palace of art, on a slightly reduced scale – it was an old English demesne. It nestled under a cluster of magnificent beeches, it had little creaking lattices that opened out of, or into, pendent mats of ivy, and gables, and old red tiles, as well as a general aspect of being painted in water-colours and inhabited by people whose lives would go on in chapters and volumes. The lawn seemed to me of extraordinary extent, the garden-walls of incalculable height, the whole air of the place delightfully still, and private, and proper to itself. 'My wife must be somewhere about,' Mark Ambient said, as we went in. 'We shall find her perhaps; we have got about an hour before dinner. She may be in the garden. I will show you my little place.'

We passed through the house, and into the grounds, as I should have called them, which extended into the rear. They covered but three or four acres, but, like the house, they were very old and crooked, and full of traces of long habitation, with inequalities of level and little steps – mossy and cracked were these – which connected the different parts with each other. The limits of the place, cleverly dissimulated, were muffled in the deepest verdure. They made, as I remember, a kind of curtain at the farther end, in one of the folds of which, as it were, we presently perceived, from afar, a little group. 'Ah, there she is!' said Mark Ambient; 'and she has got the boy.' He made this last remark in a tone slightly different from any in which he yet had spoken. I was not fully aware of it at the time, but it lingered in my ear and I afterwards understood it.

'Is it your son?' I inquired, feeling the question not to be brilliant.

'Yes, my only child. He is always in his mother's pocket. She coddles him too much.' It came back to me afterwards, too – the manner in which he spoke these words. They were not petulant; they expressed rather a sudden coldness, a kind of mechanical submission. We went a few steps further, and then he stopped short, and called the boy, beckoning to him repeatedly.

'Dolcino, come and see your daddy!' There was something in the way he stood still and waited that made me think he did it for a purpose. Mrs Ambient had her arm round the child's waist, and he was leaning against her knee; but though he looked up at the sound of his father's voice, she gave no sign of releasing him. A lady, apparently a neighbour, was seated near her, and before them was a garden-table, on which a tea-service had been placed.

Mark Ambient called again, and Dolcino struggled in the maternal embrace, but he was too tightly held, and after two or three fruitless efforts he suddenly turned round and buried his head deep in his mother's lap. There was a certain awkwardness in the scene; I thought it rather odd that Mrs Ambient should pay so little attention to her husband. But I would not for the world have betrayed my thought, and, to conceal it, I observed that it must be such a pleasant thing to have tea in the garden. 'Ah, she won't let him come!' said Mark Ambient, with a sigh; and we went our way till we reached the two ladies. He mentioned my name to his wife, and I noticed that he addressed her as 'My dear', very genially, without any trace of resentment at her detention of the child. The quickness of the transition made me vaguely ask myself whether he were henpecked – a shocking conjecture, which I instantly dismissed. Mrs Ambient was quite such a wife as I should have expected him to have; slim and fair, with a long neck and pretty eyes and an air of great refinement. She was a little cold, and a little shy; but she was very sweet, and she had a certain look of race, justified by my afterwards learning that she was 'connected' with two or three great families. I have seen poets married to women of whom it was difficult to conceive that they should gratify the poetic fancy – women with dull faces and glutinous minds, who were none the less, however, excellent wives. But there was no obvious incongruity in Mark Ambient's union. Mrs Ambient, delicate and quiet, in a white dress, with her beautiful child at her side, was worthy of the author of a work so distinguished as *Beltraffio*. Round her neck she wore a black velvet ribbon, of which the long ends, tied behind, hung down her back, and to which, in front, was attached a miniature portrait of her little boy. Her smooth, shining hair was confined in a net. She gave me a very pleasant greeting, and Dolcino – I thought this little name of endearment delightful – took advantage of her getting up to slip away from her and go to his father, who said nothing to him, but simply seized him and held him high in his arms for a moment, kissing him several times. I had lost no time in observing that the child, who was not more than seven years old, was extraordinarily beautiful. He had the face of an angel – the eyes, the hair, the more than mortal bloom, the smile of innocence. There was something touching, almost alarming, in his beauty, which seemed to be composed of elements too fine and pure for the breath of this world. When I spoke to him, and he came and held out his hand and smiled at me, I felt a sudden pity for him, as if he had been an orphan, or a changeling, or stamped with some social stigma. It was impossible to be, in fact, more exempt from these misfortunes, and yet, as one kissed him, it was hard to keep from murmuring 'Poor little devil!' though why one should have applied this epithet to a living cherub is more than I can say. Afterwards, indeed, I knew a little better; I simply discovered that he was too charming to live, wondering at the same time that his parents should not have perceived it, and should not be in proportionate grief and despair. For myself, I had no doubt of his evanescence, having already noticed that there is a kind of charm which is like a death-warrant. The lady who had been sitting with Mrs Ambient was a jolly, ruddy personage, dressed in velveteen and rather limp feathers, whom I guessed to be the vicar's wife – our hostess did not introduce me – and who immediately began to talk to Ambient about chrysanthemums. This was a safe subject, and yet there was a certain surprise for me in seeing the author of *Beltraffio* even in such superficial communion with the Church of England. His writings implied so much detachment from that institution, expressed a view of life so profane, as it were, so independent, and so little likely, in general, to be thought edifying, that I should have expected to find him an object of horror to vicars and their ladies – of horror repaid on his own part by good-natured but brilliant mockery. This proves how little I knew as yet of the English people and their extraordinary talent for keeping up their forms, as well as of some of the mysteries of Mark Ambient's hearth and home. I found afterwards that he had, in his study, between smiles and cigar-smoke, some wonderful comparisons for his clerical neighbours; but meanwhile the chrysanthemums were a source of harmony, for he and the vicaress were equally fond of them, and I was surprised at the knowledge they exhibited of this interesting plant. The lady's visit, however, had presumably already been long, and she presently got up, saying she must go, and kissed Mrs Ambient. Mark started to walk with her to the gate of the grounds, holding Dolcino by the hand.

'Stay with me, my darling,' Mrs Ambient said to the boy, who was wandering away with his father.

Mark Ambient paid no attention to the summons, but Dolcino turned round and looked with eyes of shy entreaty at his mother. 'Can't I go with papa?'

'Not when I ask you to stay with me.'

'But please don't ask me, mamma,' said the child, in his little clear, new voice.

'I must ask you when I want you. Come to me, my darling.' And Mrs Ambient, who had seated herself again, held out her long, slender hands.

Her husband stopped, with his back turned to her, but without releasing the child. He was still talking to the vicaress, but this good lady, I think, had lost the thread of her attention. She looked at Mrs Ambient and at Dolcino, and then she looked at me, smiling very hard, in an extremely fixed, cheerful manner.

'Papa,' said the child, 'mamma wants me not to go with you.'

'He's very tired – he has run about all day. He ought to be quiet till he goes to bed. Otherwise he won't sleep.' These declarations fell successively and gravely from Mrs Ambient's lips.

Her husband, still without turning round, bent over the boy and looked at him in silence. The vicaress gave a genial, irrelevant laugh, and observed that he was a precious little pet. 'Let him choose,' said Mark Ambient. 'My dear little boy, will you go with me or will you stay with your mother?'

'Oh, it's a shame!' cried the vicar's lady, with increased hilarity.

'Papa, I don't think I can choose,' the child answered, making his voice very low and confidential. 'But I have been a great deal with mamma today,' he added in a moment.

'And very little with papa! My dear fellow, I think you have chosen!' And Mark Ambient walked off with his son, accompanied by re-echoing but inarticulate comments from my fellow-visitor.

His wife had seated herself again, and her fixed eyes, bent upon the ground, expressed for a few moments so much mute agitation that I felt as if almost any remark from my own lips would be a false note. But Mrs Ambient quickly recovered herself, and said to me civilly enough that she hoped I didn't mind having had to walk from the station. I reassured her on this point, and she went on, 'We have got a thing that might have gone for you, but my husband wouldn't order it.'

'That gave me the pleasure of a walk with him,' I rejoined.

She was silent a minute, and then she said, 'I believe the Americans walk very little.'

'Yes, we always run,' I answered, laughingly.

She looked at me seriously, and I began to perceive a certain coldness in her pretty eyes. 'I suppose your distances are so great.'

'Yes; but we break our marches! I can't tell you what a pleasure it is for me to find myself here,' I added. 'I have the greatest admiration for Mr Ambient.'

'He will like that. He likes being admired.'

'He must have a very happy life, then. He has many worshippers.'

'Oh yes, I have seen some of them,' said Mrs Ambient, looking away, very far from me, rather as if such a vision were before her at the moment. Something in her tone seemed to indicate that the vision was scarcely edifying, and I guessed very quickly that she was not in sympathy with the author of *Beltraffio*. I thought the fact strange, but, somehow, in the glow of my own enthusiasm, I didn't think it important; it only made me wish to be rather explicit about that enthusiasm.

'For me, you know,' I remarked, 'he is quite the greatest of living writers.'

'Of course I can't judge. Of course he's very clever,' said Mrs Ambient, smiling a little.

'He's magnificent, Mrs Ambient! There are pages in each of his books that have a perfection that classes them with the greatest things. Therefore, for me to see him in this familiar way – in his habit as he lives – and to find, apparently, the man as delightful as the artist, I can't tell you how much too good to be true it seems, and how great a privilege I think it.' I knew that I was gushing, but I couldn't help it, and what I said was a good deal less than what I felt. I was by no means sure that I should dare to say even so much as this to Ambient himself, and there was a kind of rapture in speaking it out to his wife, which was not affected by the fact that, as a wife, she appeared peculiar. She listened to me with her face grave again, and with her lips a little compressed, as if there were no doubt, of course, that her husband was remarkable, but at the same time she had heard all this before and couldn't be expected to be particularly interested in it. There was even in her manner an intimation that I was rather young, and that people usually got over that sort of thing. 'I assure you that for me this is a red-letter day,' I added.

She made no response, until after a pause, looking round her, she said abruptly, though gently, 'We are very much afraid about the fruit this year.'

My eyes wandered to the mossy, mottled garden-walls, where plum-trees and pear-trees, flattened and fastened upon the rusty bricks, looked like crucified figures with many arms. 'Doesn't it promise well?' I inquired.

'No, the trees look very dull. We had such late frosts.'

Then there was another pause. Mrs Ambient kept her eyes fixed on the opposite end of the grounds, as if she were watching for her husband's return with the child. 'Is Mr Ambient fond of gardening?' it occurred to me to inquire, irresistibly impelled as I felt myself, moreover, to bring the conversation constantly back to him.

'He is very fond of plums,' said his wife.

'Ah, well then, I hope your crop will be better than you fear. It's a lovely old place,' I continued. 'The whole character of it is that of certain places that he describes. Your house is like one of his pictures.'

'It's a pleasant little place. There are hundreds like it.'

'Oh, it has got his tone,' I said laughing, and insisting on my point the more that Mrs Ambient appeared to see in my appreciation of her simple establishment a sign of limited experience.

It was evident that I insisted too much. 'His tone?' she repeated, with a quick look at me and a slightly heightened colour.

'Surely he has a tone, Mrs Ambient.'

'Oh yes, he has indeed! But I don't in the least consider that I am living in one of his books; I shouldn't care for that, at all,' she went on, with a smile which had in some degree the effect of converting my slightly sharp protest into a joke deficient in point. 'I am afraid I am not very literary,' said Mrs Ambient. 'And I am not artistic.'

'I am very sure you are not stupid nor *bornée*,' I ventured to reply, with the accompaniment of feeling immediately afterwards that I had been both familiar and patronizing. My only consolation was in the reflection that it was she, and not I, who had begun it. She had brought her idiosyncrasies into the discussion.

'Well, whatever I am, I am very different from my husband. If you like him, you won't like me. You needn't say anything. Your liking me isn't in the least necessary.'

'Don't defy me!' I exclaimed.

She looked as if she had not heard me, which was the best thing she could do; and we sat some time without further speech. Mrs Ambient had evidently the enviable English quality of being able to be silent without being restless. But at last she spoke; she asked me if there seemed to be many people in town. I gave her what satisfaction I could on this point, and we talked a little about London and of some pictures it presented at that time of the year. At the end of this I came back, irrepressibly, to Mark Ambient.

'Doesn't he like to be there now? I suppose he doesn't find the proper quiet for his work. I should think his things had been written, for the most part, in a very still place. They suggest a great stillness, following on a kind of tumult – don't you think so? I suppose London is a tremendous place to collect impressions, but a refuge like this, in the country, must be much better for working them up. Does he get many of his impressions in London, do you think?' I proceeded from point to point, in this malign inquiry, simply because my hostess, who probably thought me a very pushing and talkative young man, gave me time; for when I paused – I have not represented my pauses – she simply continued to let her eyes wander, and, with her long fair fingers, played with the medallion on her neck. When I stopped altogether, however, she was obliged to say something, and what she said was that she had not the least idea where her husband got his impressions. This made me think her, for a moment, positively disagreeable; delicate and proper and rather aristocratically dry as she sat there. But I must either have lost the impression a moment later, or been goaded by it to further aggression, for I remember asking her whether Mr Ambient was in a good vein of work, and when we might look for the appearance of the book on which he was engaged. I have every reason now to know that she thought me an odious person.

She gave a strange, small laugh as she said, 'I'm afraid you think I know a great deal more about my husband's work than I do. I haven't the least idea what he is doing,' she added presently, in a slightly different, that is, a more explanatory, tone; as if she recognized in some degree the enormity of her confession. 'I don't read what he writes!'

She did not succeed (and would not, even had she tried much harder) in making it seem to me anything less than monstrous. I stared at her, and I think I blushed. 'Don't you admire his genius? Don't you admire *Beltraffio*?'

She hesitated a moment, and I wondered what she could possibly say. She did not speak – I could see – the first words that rose to her lips; she repeated what she had said a few minutes before. 'Oh, of course he's very clever!' And with this she got up; her husband and little boy had reappeared. Mrs Ambient left me and went to meet them; she stopped and had a few words with her husband, which I did not hear, and which ended in her taking the child by the hand and returning to the house with him. Her husband joined me in a moment, looking, I thought, the least bit conscious and constrained, and said that if I would come in with him he would show me my room. In looking back upon these first moments of my visit to him, I find it important to avoid the error of appearing to have understood his situation from the first, and to have seen in him the signs of things which I learned only afterwards. This later knowledge throws a backward light, and makes me forget that at least on the occasion of which I am speaking now (I mean that first afternoon), Mark Ambient struck me as a fortunate man. Allowing for this, I think he was rather silent and irresponsive as we walked back to the house – though I remember well the answer he made to a remark of mine in relation to his child.

'That's an extraordinary little boy of yours,' I said. 'I have never seen such a child.'

'Why do you call him extraordinary?'

'He's so beautiful – so fascinating. He's like a little work of art.'

He turned quickly, grasping my arm an instant. 'Oh, don't call him that, or you'll – you'll—!' And in his hesitation he broke off, suddenly, laughing at my surprise. But immediately afterwards he added, 'You will make his little future very difficult.'

I declared that I wouldn't for the world take any liberties with his little future – it seemed to me to hang by threads of such delicacy. I should only be highly interested in watching it. 'You Americans are very sharp,' said Ambient. 'You notice more things than we do.'

'Ah, if you want visitors who are not struck with you, you shouldn't ask me down here!'

He showed me my room, a little bower of chintz, with open windows where the light was green, and before he left me he

said irrelevantly, 'As for my little boy, you know, we shall probably kill him between us, before we have done with him!' And
he made this assertion as if he really believed it, without any
appearance of jest, with his fine, near-sighted, expressive eyes
looking straight into mine.

'Do you mean by spoiling him?'

'No – by fighting for him!'

'You had better give him to me to keep for you,' I said. 'Let
me remove the apple of discord.'

I laughed, of course, but he had the air of being perfectly
serious. 'It would be quite the best thing we could do. I should
be quite ready to do it.'

'I am greatly obliged to you for your confidence.'

Mark Ambient lingered there, with his hands in his pockets. I
felt, within a few moments, as if I had, morally speaking, taken
several steps nearer to him. He looked weary, just as he faced me
then, looked preoccupied, and as if there were something one
might do for him. I was terribly conscious of the limits of my own
ability, but I wondered what such a service might be – feeling at
bottom, however, that the only thing I could do for him was to
like him. I suppose he guessed this, and was grateful for what was
in my mind; for he went on presently, 'I haven't the advantage of
being an American. But I also notice a little, and I have an idea
that – a –' here he smiled and laid his hand on my shoulder – 'that
even apart from your nationality, you are not destitute of
intelligence! I have only known you half an hour, but – a—' And
here he hesitated again. 'You are very young, after all.'

'But you may treat me as if I could understand you!' I said; and before he left me to dress for dinner he had virtually given me a promise that he would.

When I went down into the drawing-room – I was very punctual – I found that neither my hostess nor my host had appeared. A lady rose from a sofa, however, and inclined her head as I rather surprisedly gazed at her. 'I daresay you don't know me,' she said, with a modern laugh. 'I am Mark Ambient's sister.' Whereupon I shook hands with her – saluting her very low. Her laugh was modern – by which I mean that it consisted of the vocal agitation which, between people who meet in drawing-rooms, serves as the solvent of social mysteries, the medium of transitions; but her appearance was – what shall I call it? – mediaeval. She was pale and angular, with a long, thin face, inhabited by sad, dark eyes, and black hair intertwined with golden fillets and curious chains. She wore a faded velvet robe, which clung to her when she moved, fashioned, as to the neck and sleeves, like the garments of old Venetians and Florentines. She looked pictorial and melancholy, and was so perfect an image of a type which I – in my ignorance – supposed to be extinct, that while she rose before me I was almost as much startled as if I had seen a ghost. I afterwards perceived that Miss Ambient was not incapable of deriving pleasure from the effect she produced, and I think this sentiment had something to do with her sinking again into her seat, with her long, lean, but not ungraceful arms locked together in an archaic manner on her knees, and her mournful eyes addressing themselves to me with

22

an intentness which was an earnest of what they were destined subsequently to inflict upon me. She was a singular, self-conscious, artificial creature, and I never, subsequently, more than half penetrated her motives and mysteries. Of one thing I am sure, however: that they were considerably less extraordinary than her appearance announced. Miss Ambient was a restless, yearning spinster, consumed with the love of Michael-Angelesque attitudes and mystical robes; but I am pretty sure she had not in her nature those depths of unutterable thought which, when you first knew her, seemed to look out from her eyes and to prompt her complicated gestures. Those features, in especial, had a misleading eloquence; they rested upon you with a far-off dimness, an air of obstructed sympathy, which was certainly not always a key to the spirit of their owner; and I suspect that a young lady could not really have been so dejected and disillusioned as Miss Ambient looked, without having committed a crime for which she was consumed with remorse or parted with a hope which she could not sanely have entertained. She had, I believe, the usual allowance of vulgar impulses; she wished to be looked at, she wished to be married, she wished to be thought original. It costs me something to speak in this irreverent manner of Mark Ambient's sister, but I shall have still more disagreeable things to say before I have finished my little anecdote, and moreover – I confess it – I owe the young lady a sort of grudge. Putting aside the curious cast of her face, she had no natural aptitude for an artistic development – she had little real intelligence. But her affections rubbed off on her brother's renown, and as there were plenty of people who disapproved of him totally, they could easily point to his sister as a person formed by his influence. It was quite possible to regard her as a warning, and she had done him but little good with the world at large. He was the original, and she was the inevitable imitation. I think he was scarcely aware of the impression she produced – beyond having a general idea that she made up very well as a Rossetti; he was used to her, and he was sorry for her – wishing she would marry and observing that she didn't. Doubtless I take her too seriously, for she did me no harm – though I am bound to add that I feel I can only half account for her. She was not so mystical as she looked, but she was a strange, indirect, uncomfortable, embarrassing woman. My story will give the reader at best so very small a knot to untie that I need not hope to excite his curiosity by delaying to remark that Mrs Ambient hated her sister-in-law. This I only found out afterwards, when I found out some other things. But I mention it at once, for I shall perhaps not seem to count too much on having enlisted the imagination of the reader if I say that he will already have guessed it. Mrs Ambient was a person of conscience, and she endeavoured to behave properly to her kinswoman, who spent a month with her twice a year; but it required no great insight to discover that the two ladies were made of a very different paste, and that the usual feminine hypocrisies must have cost them, on either side, much more than the usual effort. Mrs Ambient, smooth-haired, thin-lipped, perpetually fresh, must have regarded her crumpled and dishevelled visitor as a very stale joke; she herself was not a Rossetti, but a Gainsborough or a Lawrence, and she had in her appearance no elements more romantic than a cold, ladylike candour, and a well-starched muslin dress. It was in a garment, and with an expression, of this kind, that she made her entrance, after I had exchanged a few words with Miss Ambient. Her husband presently followed her, and there being no other company we went to dinner. The impression I received from that repast is present to me still. There were elements of oddity in my companions, but they were vague and latent, and didn't interfere with my delight. It came mainly, of course, from Ambient's talk, which was the most brilliant and interesting I had ever heard. I know not whether he laid himself out to dazzle a rather juvenile pilgrim from over the sea; but it matters little, for it was very easy for him to shine. He was almost better as a talker than as a writer; that is, if the extraordinary finish of his written prose be really, as some people have maintained, a fault. There was such a kindness in him, however, that I have no doubt it gave him ideas to see me sit open-mouthed, as I suppose I did. Not so the two ladies, who not only were very nearly dumb from beginning to the end of the meal, but who had not the air of being struck with such an exhibition of wit and knowledge. Mrs Ambient, placid and detached, met neither my eye nor her husband's; she attended to her dinner, watched the servants, arranged the puckers in her dress, exchanged at wide intervals a remark with her sister-in-law, and while she slowly rubbed her white hands, between the courses, looked out of the window at the first signs of twilight – the long June day allowing us to dine without candles. Miss Ambient appeared to give little direct heed to her brother's discourse; but, on the other hand, she was much engaged in watching its effect upon me. Her lustreless pupils continued to attach themselves to my countenance, and it was only her air of belonging to another century that kept them from being importunate. She seemed to look at me across the ages, and the interval of time diminished the realism of the performance. It was as if she knew in a general way that her brother must be talking very well, but she herself was so rich in ideas that she had no need to pick them up, and was at liberty to see what would become of a young American when subjected to a high aesthetic temperature. The temperature was aesthetic, certainly, but it was less so than I could have desired, for I was unsuccessful in certain little attempts to make Mark Ambient talk about himself. I tried to put him on the ground of his own writings, but he slipped through my fingers every time and shifted the saddle to one of his contemporaries. He talked about Balzac and Browning, and what was being done in foreign countries, and about his recent tour in the East, and the extraordinary forms of life that one saw in that part of the world. I perceived that he had reasons for not wishing to descant upon literature, and suffered him without protest to deliver himself on certain social topics, which he treated with extraordinary humour and with constant revelations of that power of ironical portraiture of which his books are full. He had a great deal to say about London, as London appears to the observer who doesn't fear the accusation of cynicism, during the high-pressure time – from April to July – of its peculiarities. He flashed his faculty of making the fanciful real and the real fanciful over the perfunctory pleasures and desperate exertions of so many of his compatriots, among whom there were evidently not a few types for which he had little love. London bored him, and he made capital sport of it; his only allusion, that I can remember, to his own work was his saying that he meant some day to write an immense grotesque epic of London society. Miss Ambient's perpetual gaze seemed to say to me, 'Do you perceive how artistic we are? Frankly now, is it possible to be more artistic than this? You surely won't deny that we are remarkable.' I was irritated by her use of the plural pronoun, for she had no right to pair herself with her brother; and moreover, of course, I could not see my way to include Mrs Ambient. But there was no doubt that (for that matter) they were all remarkable, and, with all allowances, I had never heard anything so artistic. Mark Ambient's conversation seemed to play over the whole field of knowledge and taste; it made me feel that this at last was real talk, that this was distinction, culture, experience.

After the ladies had left us he took me into his study, to smoke, and here I led him on to gossip freely enough about himself. I was bent upon proving to him that I was worthy to listen to him, upon repaying him (for what he had said to me before dinner) by showing him how perfectly I understood. He liked to talk, he liked to defend his ideas (not that I attacked them), he liked a little perhaps – it was a pardonable weakness

– to astonish the youthful mind and to feel its admiration and sympathy. I confess that my own youthful mind was considerably astonished at some of his speeches; he startled me and he made me wince. He could not help forgetting, or rather he couldn't know, how little personal contact I had had with the school in which he was master; and he promoted me at a jump, as it were, to the study of its innermost mysteries. My trepidations, however, were delightful; they were just what I had hoped for, and their only fault was that they passed away too quickly, for I found that, as regards most things, I very soon seized Mark Ambient's point of view. It was the point of view of the artist to whom every manifestation of human energy was a thrilling spectacle, and who felt for ever the desire to resolve his experience of life into a literary form. On this matter of the passion for form – the attempt at perfection, the quest for which was to his mind the real search for the holy grail, he said the most interesting, the most inspiring things. He mixed with them a thousand illustrations from his own life, from other lives that he had known, from history and fiction, and, above all, from the annals of the time that was dear to him beyond all periods – the Italian *cinque-cento*. I saw that in his books he had only said half of his thought, and what he had kept back – from motives that I deplored when I learned them later – was the richer part. It was his fortune to shock a great many people, but there was not a grain of bravado in his pages (I have always maintained it, though often contradicted), and at bottom the poor fellow, an artist to his finger-tips, and regarding a failure of completeness as a crime, had an extreme dread of scandal. There are people who regret that having gone so far he did not go further; but I regret nothing (putting aside two or three of the motives I just mentioned), for he arrived at perfection, and I don't see how you can go beyond that. The hours I spent in his study – this first one and the few that followed it; they were not, after all, so numerous – seem to glow, as I look back on them, with a tone which is partly that of the brown old room, rich, under the shaded candlelight where we sat and smoked, with the dusky, delicate bindings of valuable books; partly that of his voice, of which I still catch the echo, charged with the images that came at his command. When we went back to the drawing-room we found Miss Ambient alone in possession of it; and she informed us that her sister-in-law had a quarter of an hour before been called by the nurse to see Dolcino, who appeared to be a little feverish.

'Feverish! how in the world does he come to be feverish?' Ambient asked. 'He was perfectly well this afternoon.'

'Beatrice says you walked him about too much – you almost killed him.'

'Beatrice must be very happy – she has an opportunity to triumph!' Mark Ambient said, with a laugh of which the bitterness was just perceptible.

'Surely not if the child is ill,' I ventured to remark, by way of pleading for Mrs Ambient.

'My dear fellow, you are not married – you don't know the nature of wives!' my host exclaimed.

'Possibly not; but I know the nature of mothers.'

'Beatrice is perfect as a mother,' said Miss Ambient, with a tremendous sigh and her fingers interlaced on her embroidered knees.

'I shall go up and see the child,' her brother went on. 'Do you suppose he's asleep?'

'Beatrice won't let you see him, Mark,' said the young lady, looking at me, though she addressed our companion.

'Do you call that being perfect as a mother?' Ambient inquired.

'Yes, from her point of view.'

'Damn her point of view!' cried the author of *Beltraffio*. And he left the room; after which we heard him ascend the stairs.

I sat there for some ten minutes with Miss Ambient, and we, naturally, had some conversation, which was begun, I think, by my asking her what the point of view of her sister-in-law could be.

'Oh, it's so very odd,' she said. 'But we are so very odd, altogether. Don't you find us so? We have lived so much abroad. Have you people like us in America?'

'You are not all alike, surely; so that I don't think I understand your question. We have no one like your brother – I may go so far as that.'

'You have probably more persons like his wife,' said Miss Ambient, smiling.

'I can tell you that better when you have told me about her point of view.'

'Oh yes – oh yes. Well, she doesn't like his ideas. She doesn't like them for the little boy. She thinks them undesirable.'

Being quite fresh from the contemplation of some of Mark Ambient's *arcana*, I was particularly in a position to appreciate this announcement. But the effect of it was to make me (after staring a moment) burst into laughter, which I instantly checked when I remembered that there was a sick child above.

'What has that infant to do with ideas?' I asked. 'Surely, he can't tell one from another. Has he read his father's novels?'

'He's very precocious and very sensitive, and his mother thinks she can't begin to guard him too early.' Miss Ambient's head drooped a little to one side, and her eyes fixed themselves on futurity. Then, suddenly, there was a strange alteration in her face; she gave a smile that was more joyless than her gravity – a conscious, insincere smile, and added, 'When one has children, it's a great responsibility – what one writes.'

'Children are terrible critics,' I answered. 'I am rather glad I haven't got any.'

'Do you also write then? And in the same style as my brother? And do you like that style? And do people appreciate it in America? I don't write, but I think I feel.' To these and various other inquiries and remarks the young lady treated me, till we heard her brother's step in the hall again and Mark Ambient reappeared. He looked flushed and serious, and I supposed that he had seen something to alarm him in the condition of his child. His sister apparently had another idea; she gazed at him a moment as if he were a burning ship on the horizon, and simply murmured – 'Poor old Mark!'

'I hope you are not anxious,' I said.

'No, but I am disappointed. She won't let me in. She has locked the door, and I'm afraid to make a noise.' I suppose there might have been something ridiculous in a confession of this kind, but I liked my new friend so much that for me it didn't detract from his dignity. 'She tells me – from behind the door – that she will let me know if he is worse.'

'It's very good of her,' said Miss Ambient.

I had exchanged a glance with Mark in which it is possible that he read that my pity for him was untinged with contempt – though I know not why he should have cared; and as, presently, his sister got up and took her bedroom candlestick, he proposed that we should go back to his study. We sat there till after midnight; he put himself into his slippers, into an old velvet jacket, lighted an ancient pipe and talked considerably less than he had done before. There were longish pauses in our communion, but they only made me feel that we had advanced in intimacy. They helped me, too, to understand my friend's personal situation, and to perceive that it was by no means the happiest possible. When his face was quiet, it was vaguely troubled; it seemed to me to show that for him, too, life was a struggle, as it has been for many other men of genius. At last I prepared to leave him, and then, to my ineffable joy, he gave me some of the sheets of his forthcoming book – it was not finished, but he had indulged in the luxury, so dear to writers of deliberation, of having it 'set up', from chapter to chapter, as he advanced – he gave me, I say, the early pages, the *prémices*, as the French have it, of this new fruit of his imagination, to take to my room and look over at my leisure. I was just quitting him when the door of his study was noiselessly pushed open, and Mrs Ambient stood before us. She looked at us a moment with her candle in her hand, and then she said to her husband that as she supposed he had not gone to bed she had come down to tell him that Dolcino was more quiet and would probably be better in the morning. Mark Ambient made no reply; he simply slipped past her, in the doorway, as if he were afraid she would seize him in his passage, and bounded upstairs, to judge for himself of his child's condition. Mrs Ambient looked slightly discomfited, and for a moment I thought she was going to give chase to her husband. But she resigned herself, with a sigh, while her eyes wandered over the lamp-lit room, where various books, at which I had been looking, were pulled out of their places on the shelves, and the fumes of tobacco seemed to hang in mid-air. I bade her good-night, and then, without intention, by a kind of fatality, the perversity which had already made me insist unduly on talking with her about her husband's achievements, I alluded to the precious proof-sheets with which Ambient had entrusted me, and which I was nursing there under my arm. 'It is the opening chapters of his new book,' I said. 'Fancy my satisfaction at being allowed to carry them to my room!'

She turned away, leaving me to take my candlestick from the table in the hall; but before we separated, thinking it apparently a good occasion to let me know once for all – since I was beginning, it would seem, to be quite 'thick' with my host – that there was no fitness in my appealing to her for sympathy in such a case; before we separated, I say, she remarked to me, with her quick, round, well-bred utterance, 'I daresay you attribute to me ideas that I haven't got. I don't take that sort of interest in my husband's proof-sheets. I consider his writings most objectionable!'

II

I HAD SOME curious conversation the next morning with Miss Ambient, whom I found strolling in the garden before breakfast. The whole place looked as fresh and trim, amid the twitter of the birds, as if, an hour before, the housemaids had been turned into it with their dust-pans and feather-brushes. I almost hesitated to light a cigarette, and was doubly startled when, in the act of doing so, I suddenly perceived the sister of my host, who had, in any case, something of the oddity of an apparition, standing before me. She might have been posing for her photograph. Her sad-coloured robe arranged itself in serpentine folds at her feet; her hands locked themselves listlessly together in front; and her chin rested upon a *cinque-cento* ruff. The first thing I did, after bidding her good-morning, was to ask her for news of her little nephew – to express the hope that she had

34

heard he was better. She was able to gratify this hope, and spoke as if we might expect to see him during the day. We walked through the shrubberies together, and she gave me a great deal of information about her brother's *ménage*, which offered me an opportunity to mention to her that his wife had told me, the night before, that she thought his productions objectionable.

'She doesn't usually come out with that so soon!' Miss Ambient exclaimed, in answer to this piece of gossip.

'Poor lady, she saw that I am a fanatic.'

'Yes, she won't like you for that. But you mustn't mind, if the rest of us like you! Beatrice thinks a work of art ought to have a "purpose". But she's a charming woman – don't you think her charming? – she's such a type of the lady.'

'She's very beautiful,' I answered; while I reflected that though it was true, apparently, that Mark Ambient was mismated, it was also perceptible that his sister was perfidious. She told me that her brother and his wife had no other difference but this one, that she thought his writings immoral and his influence pernicious. It was a fixed idea; she was afraid of these things for the child. I answered that it was not a trifle – a woman's regarding her husband's mind as a well of corruption; and she looked quite struck with the novelty of my remark. 'But there hasn't been any of the sort of trouble that there so often is among married people,' she said. 'I suppose you can judge for yourself that Beatrice isn't at all – well, whatever they call it when a woman misbehaves herself. And Mark doesn't make love to other people, either. I assure you he doesn't! All the same, of course, from her point of view, you know, she has a dread of my brother's influence on the child – on the formation of his character, of his principles. It is as if it were a subtle poison, or a contagion, or something that would rub off on Dolcino when his father kisses him or holds him on his knee. If she could, she would prevent Mark from ever touching him. Everyone knows it; visitors see it for themselves; so there is no harm in my telling you. Isn't it excessively odd? It comes from Beatrice's being so religious, and so tremendously moral, and all that. And then, of course, we mustn't forget,' my companion added, unexpectedly, 'that some of Mark's ideas are – well, really – rather queer!'

I reflected, as we went into the house, where we found Ambient unfolding the *Observer* at the breakfast-table, that none of them were probably quite so queer as his sister. Mrs Ambient did not appear at breakfast, being rather tired with her ministrations, during the night, to Dolcino. Her husband mentioned, however, that she was hoping to go to church. I afterwards learned that she did go, but I may as well announce without delay that he and I did not accompany her. It was while the church-bell was murmuring in the distance that the author of *Beltraffio* led me forth for the ramble he had spoken of in his note. I will not attempt to say where we went, or to describe what we saw. We kept to the fields and copses and commons, and breathed the same sweet air as the nibbling donkeys and the browsing sheep, whose woolliness seemed to me, in those early days of my acquaintance with English objects, but a part of the general texture of the small, dense landscape, which looked as if the harvest were gathered by the shears. Everything was full of expression for Mark Ambient's visitor – from the big, bandy-legged geese, whose whiteness was a 'note', amid all the tones of green, as they wandered beside a neat little oval pool, the foreground of a thatched and white-washed inn, with a grassy approach and a pictorial sign – from these humble wayside animals to the crests of high woods which let a gable or a pinnacle peep here and there, and looked, even at a distance, like trees of good company, conscious of an individual profile. I admired the hedgerows, I plucked the faint-hued heather, and I was forever stopping to say how charming I thought the thread-like footpaths across the fields, which wandered, in a diagonal of finer grain, from one smooth stile to another. Mark Ambient was abundantly good-natured, and was as much entertained with my observations as I was with the literary allusions of the landscape. We sat and smoked upon stiles, broaching paradoxes in the decent English air; we took short cuts across a park or two, where the bracken was deep, and my companion nodded to the old woman at the gate; we skirted rank covers, which rustled here and there as we passed, and we stretched ourselves at last on a heathery hillside where, if the sun was not too hot, neither was the earth too cold, and where the country lay beneath us in a rich blue mist. Of course I had already told Ambient what I thought of his new novel, having the previous night read every word of the opening chapters before I went to bed.

'I am not without hope of being able to make it my best,' he said, as I went back to the subject, while we turned up our heels to the sky. 'At least the people who dislike my prose – and there are a great many of them, I believe – will dislike this work most.' This was the first time I had heard him allude to the people who couldn't read him – a class which is supposed always to sit heavy upon the consciousness of the man of letters. A man organized for literature, as Mark Ambient was, must certainly have had the normal proportion of sensitiveness, of irritability; the artistic *ego*, capable in some cases of such monstrous development, must have been, in his composition, sufficiently erect and definite. I will not therefore go so far as to say that he never thought of his detractors, or that he had any illusions with regard to the number of his admirers (he could never so far have deceived himself as to believe he was popular); but I may at least affirm that adverse criticism, as I had occasion to perceive later, ruffled him visibly but little, that he had an air of thinking it quite natural he should be offensive to many minds, and that he very seldom talked about the newspapers – which, by the way, were always very stupid in regard to the author of *Beltraffio*. Of course he may have thought about them – the newspapers – night and day; the only point I wish to make is that he didn't show it; while, at the same time, he didn't strike one as a man who was on his guard. I may add that, as regards his hope of making the work on which he was then engaged the best of his books, it was only partly carried out. That place belongs, incontestably, to *Beltraffio*, in spite of the beauty of certain parts of its successor. I am pretty sure, however, that he had, at the moment of which I speak, no sense of failure; he was in love with his idea, which was indeed magnificent, and though for him, as (I suppose) for every artist, the act of execution had in it as much torment as joy, he saw his work growing a little every day and filling out the largest plan he had yet conceived. 'I want to be truer than I have ever been,' he said, settling himself on his back, with his hands clasped behind his head; 'I want to give an impression of life itself. No, you may say what you will. I have always arranged things too much, always smoothed them down and rounded them off and tucked them in – done everything to them that life doesn't do. I have been a slave to the old superstitions.'

'You a slave, my dear Mark Ambient? You have the freest imagination of our day!'

'All the more shame to me to have done some of the things I have! The reconciliation of the two women in *Ginistrella*, for instance – which could never really have taken place. That sort of thing is ignoble; I blush when I think of it! This new affair must be a golden vessel, filled with the purest distillation of the actual; and oh, how it bothers me, the shaping of the vase – the hammering of the metal! I have to hammer it so fine, so smooth; I don't do more than an inch or two a day. And all the while I have to be so careful not to let a drop of the liquor escape! When I see the kind of things that Life does, I despair of ever catching her peculiar trick. She has an impudence, Life! If one risked a fiftieth part of the effects she risks! It takes ever so long to believe it. You don't know yet, my dear fellow. It isn't till one has been watching Life for forty years that one finds out half of what she's up to! Therefore one's earlier things must inevitably contain a mass of rot. And with what one sees, on one side, with its tongue in its cheek, defying one to be real enough, and on the other the *bonnes gens* rolling up their eyes at one's cynicism, the situation has elements of the ludicrous which the artist himself is doubtless in a position to appreciate better than any one else. Of course one mustn't bother about the *bonnes gens*,' Mark Ambient went on, while my thoughts reverted to his ladylike wife, as interpreted by his remarkable sister.

'To sink your shaft deep, and polish the plate through which people look into it – that's what your work consists of,' I remember remarking.

'Ah, polishing one's plate – that is the torment of execution!' he exclaimed, jerking himself up and sitting forward. 'The effort to arrive at a surface – if you think a surface necessary – some people don't, happily for them! My dear fellow, if you could see the surface I dream of – as compared with the one with which I have to content myself. Life is really too short for art – one hasn't time to make one's shell ideally hard. Firm and bright – firm and bright! – the devilish thing has a way, sometimes, of being bright without being firm. When I rap it with my knuckles it doesn't give the right sound. There are horrible little flabby spots where I have taken the second-best word, because I couldn't for the life of me think of the best. If you knew how stupid I am sometimes! They look to me now like pimples and ulcers on the brow of beauty!'

'That's very bad – very bad,' I said, as gravely as I could.

'Very bad? It's the highest social offence I know; it ought – it absolutely ought – I'm quite serious – to be capital. If I knew I should be hanged else, I should manage to find the best word. The people who couldn't – some of them don't know it when they see it – would shut their inkstands, and we shouldn't be deluged by this flood of rubbish!'

I will not attempt to repeat everything that passed between us or to explain just how it was that, every moment I spent in his company, Mark Ambient revealed to me more and more that he looked at all things from the standpoint of the artist, felt all life as literary material. There are people who will tell me that this is a poor way of feeling it, and I am not concerned to defend my statement – having space merely to remark that there is something to be said for any interest which makes a man feel so much. If Mark Ambient did really, as I suggested above, have imaginative contact with 'all life', I, for my part, envy him his *arrière-pensée*. At any rate it was through the receipt of this impression of him that by the time we returned I had acquired the feeling of intimacy I have noted. Before we got up for the homeward stretch he alluded to his wife's having once – or perhaps more than once – asked him whether he should like Dolcino to read *Beltraffio*. I think he was unconscious at the moment of all that this conveyed to me – as well, doubtless, of my extreme curiosity to hear what he had replied. He had said that he hoped very much Dolcino would read all his works – when he was twenty; he should like him to know what his father had done. Before twenty it would be useless – he wouldn't understand them.

'And meanwhile do you propose to hide them – to lock them up in a drawer?' Mrs Ambient had inquired.

'Oh no; we must simply tell him that they are not intended for small boys. If you bring him up properly, after that he won't touch them.'

To this Mrs Ambient had made answer that it would be very awkward when he was about fifteen, and I asked her husband if it was his opinion in general, then, that young people should not read novels.

'Good ones – certainly not!' said my companion. I suppose I had had other views, for I remember saying that, for myself, I was not sure it was bad for them – if the novels were 'good' enough. 'Bad for *them*, I don't say so much!' Ambient exclaimed. 'But very bad, I am afraid, for the novel.' That oblique, accidental allusion to his wife's attitude was followed by a franker style of reference as we walked home. 'The difference between us is simply the opposition between two distinct ways of looking at the world, which have never succeeded in getting on together, or making any kind of common *ménage*, since the beginning of time. They have borne all sorts of names, and my wife would tell you it's the difference between Christian and Pagan. I may be a pagan, but I don't like the name – it sounds sectarian. She thinks me, at any rate, no better than an ancient Greek. It's the difference between making the most of life and making the least – so that you'll get another better one in some other time and place. Will it be a sin to make the most of that one too, I wonder? and shall we have to be bribed off in the future state, as well as in the present? Perhaps I care too much for beauty – I don't know; I delight in it, I adore it, I think of it continually, I try to produce it, to reproduce it. My wife holds that we shouldn't think too much about it. She's always afraid of that – always on her guard. I don't know what she has got on her back! And she's so pretty, too, herself! Don't you think she's lovely? She was, at any rate, when I married her. At that time I wasn't aware of that difference I speak of – I thought it all came to the same thing: in the end, as they say. Well, perhaps it will in the end. I don't know what the end will be. Moreover, I care for seeing things as they are; that's the way I try to show them in my novels. But you mustn't talk to Mrs Ambient about things as they are. She has a mortal dread of things as they are.'

'She's afraid of them for Dolcino,' I said: surprised a moment afterwards at being in a position – thanks to Miss Ambient – to be so explanatory; and surprised even now that Mark shouldn't have shown visibly that he wondered what the deuce I knew about it. But he didn't; he simply exclaimed, with a tenderness that touched me: 'Ah, nothing shall ever hurt *him*!'

He told me more about his wife before we arrived at the gate of his house, and if it be thought that he was querulous, I am afraid I must admit that he had some of the foibles as well as the gifts of the artistic temperament; adding, however, instantly, that hitherto, to the best of my belief, he had very rarely complained. 'She thinks me immoral – that's the long and short of it,' he said, as we paused outside a moment, and his hand rested on one of the bars of his gate; while his conscious, expressive, perceptive eyes – the eyes of a foreigner, I had begun to account them, much more than of the usual Englishman – viewing me now evidently as quite a familiar friend, took part in the declaration. 'It's very strange, when one thinks it all over, and there's a grand comicality in it which I should like to bring out. She is a very nice woman, extraordinarily well behaved, upright, and clever, and with a tremendous lot of good sense about a good many matters. Yet her conception of a novel – she has explained it to me once or twice, and she doesn't do it badly, as exposition – is a thing so false that it makes me blush. It is a thing so hollow, so dishonest, so lying, in which life is so blinked and blinded, so dodged and disfigured, that it makes my ears burn. It's two different ways of looking at the whole affair,' he repeated, pushing open the gate. 'And they are irreconcilable!' he added with a sigh. We went forward to the house, but on the walk, half-way to the door, he stopped, and said to me, 'If you are going into this kind of thing, there's a fact you should know beforehand; it may save you some disappointment. There's a hatred of art – there's a hatred of literature!' I looked up at the charming house, with its genial colour and crookedness, and I answered with a smile that those evil passions might exist, but that I should never have expected to find them there. 'Oh, it doesn't matter, after all,' he said, laughing; which I was glad to hear, for I was reproaching myself with having excited him.

If I had, his excitement soon passed off, for at lunch he was delightful; strangely delightful, considering that the difference between himself and his wife was, as he had said, irreconcilable. He had the art, by his manner, by his smile, by his natural kindliness, of reducing the importance of it in the common concerns of life, and Mrs Ambient, I must add, lent herself to this transaction with a very good grace. I watched her, at table, for further illustrations of that fixed idea of which Miss Ambient had spoken to me; for in the light of the united revelations of her sister-in-law and her husband, she had come to seem to me a very singular personage. I am obliged to say that the signs of a fanatical temperament were not more striking in my hostess than before; it was only after a while that her air of incorruptible conformity, her tapering, monosyllabic correctness, began to appear to be themselves a cold, thin flame. Certainly, at first, she looked like a woman with as few passions as possible; but if she had a passion at all, it would be that of Philistinism. She might have been, for there are guardian-spirits, I suppose, of all great principles – the angel of propriety. Mark Ambient, apparently, ten years before, had simply perceived that she was an angel, without asking himself of what. He had been quite right in calling my attention to her beauty. In looking for the reason why he should have married her, I saw, more than before, that she was, physically speaking, a wonderfully cultivated human plant – that she must have given him many ideas and images. It was impossible to be more pencilled, more garden-like, more delicately tinted and petalled.

If I had had it in my heart to think Ambient a little of a hypocrite for appearing to forget at table everything he had said to me during our walk, I should instantly have cancelled such a judgement on reflecting that the good news his wife was able to give him about their little boy was reason enough for his sudden air of happiness. It may have come partly, too, from a certain remorse at having complained to me of the fair lady who sat there – a desire to show me that he was after all not so miserable. Dolcino continued to be much better, and he had been promised he should come downstairs after he had had his dinner. As soon as we had risen from our own meal Ambient slipped away, evidently for the purpose of going to his child; and no sooner had I observed this than I became aware that his wife had simultaneously vanished. It happened that Miss Ambient and I, both at the same moment, saw the tail of her dress whisk out of a doorway – which led the young lady to smile at me, as if I now knew all the secrets of the place. I passed with her into the garden, and we sat down on a dear old bench which rested against the west wall of the house. It was a perfect spot for the middle period of a Sunday in June, and its felicity seemed to come partly from an antique sun-dial which, rising in front of us and forming the centre of a small, intricate parterre, measured the moments ever so slowly, and made them safe for leisure and talk. The garden bloomed in the suffused afternoon, the tall beeches stood still for an example, and, behind and above us, a rose-tree of many seasons, clinging to the faded grain of the brick, expressed the whole character of the scene in a familiar, exquisite smell. It seemed to me a place for genius to have every sanction, and not to encounter challenges and checks. Miss

Ambient asked me if I had enjoyed my walk with her brother, and whether we had talked of many things.

'Well, of most things,' I said, smiling, though I remembered that we had not talked of Miss Ambient.

'And don't you think some of his theories are very peculiar?'

'Oh, I guess I agree with them all.' I was very particular, for Miss Ambient's entertainment, to guess.

'Do you think art is everything?' she inquired in a moment.

'In art, of course I do!'

'And do you think beauty is everything?'

'I don't know about its being everything. But it's very delightful.'

'Of course it is difficult for a woman to know how far to go,' said my companion. 'I adore everything that gives a charm to life. I am intensely sensitive to form. But sometimes I draw back – don't you see what I mean? – I don't quite see where I shall be landed. I only want to be quiet, after all,' Miss Ambient continued, in a tone of stifled yearning which seemed to indicate that she had not yet arrived at her desire. 'And one must be good, at any rate, must not one?' she inquired, with a cadence apparently intended for an assurance that my answer would settle this recondite question for her. It was difficult for me to make it very original, and I am afraid I repaid her confidence with an unblushing platitude. I remember, moreover, appending to it an inquiry, equally destitute of freshness, and still more wanting perhaps in tact, as to whether she did not mean to go to church, as that was an obvious way of being good. She replied that she had performed this duty in the morning, and that for her, on Sunday afternoon, supreme virtue consisted in answering the week's letters. Then suddenly, without transition, she said to me, 'It's quite a mistake about Dolcino being better. I have seen him, and he's not at all right.'

'Surely his mother would know, wouldn't she?' I suggested.

She appeared for a moment to be counting the leaves on one of the great beeches. 'As regards most matters, one can easily say what, in a given situation, my sister-in-law would do. But as regards this one, there are strange elements at work.'

'Strange elements? Do you mean in the constitution of the child?'

'No, I mean in my sister-in-law's feelings.'

'Elements of affection, of course; elements of anxiety. Why do you call them strange?'

She repeated my words. 'Elements of affection, elements of anxiety. She is very anxious.'

Miss Ambient made me vaguely uneasy – she almost frightened me, and I wished she would go and write her letters. 'His father will have seen him now,' I said, 'and if he is not satisfied he will send for the doctor.'

'The doctor ought to have been here this morning. He lives only two miles away.'

I reflected that all this was very possibly only a part of the general tragedy of Miss Ambient's view of things; but I asked her why she hadn't urged such a necessity upon her sister-in-law. She answered me with a smile of extraordinary significance, and told me that I must have very little idea of what her relations with Beatrice were; but I must do her the justice to add that she went on to make herself a little more comprehensible by saying that it was quite reason enough for her sister not to be alarmed that Mark would be sure to be. He was always nervous about the child, and as they were predestined by nature to take opposite views, the only thing for Beatrice was to cultivate a false optimism. If Mark were not there, she would not be at all easy. I remembered what he had said to me about their dealings with Dolcino – that between them they would put an end to him; but I did not repeat this to Miss Ambient: the less so that just then her brother emerged from the house, carrying his child in his arms. Close behind him moved his wife, grave and pale; the boy's face was turned over Ambient's shoulder, towards his mother. We got up to receive the group, and as they came near us Dolcino turned round. I caught, on his enchanting little countenance, a smile of recognition, and for the moment would have been quite content with it. Miss Ambient, however, received another impression, and I make haste to say that her quick sensibility, in which there was something maternal, argues that in spite of her affectations there was a strain of kindness in her. 'It won't do at all – it won't do at all,' she said to me under her breath. 'I shall speak to Mark about the doctor.'

The child was rather white, but the main difference I saw in him was that he was even more beautiful than the day before. He had been dressed in his festal garments – a velvet suit and a crimson sash – and he looked like a little invalid prince, too young to know condescension, and smiling familiarly on his subjects.

'Put him down, Mark, he's not comfortable,' Mrs Ambient said.

'Should you like to stand on your feet, my boy?' his father asked.

'Oh yes; I'm remarkably well,' said the child.

Mark placed him on the ground; he had shining, pointed slippers, with enormous bows. 'Are you happy now, Mr Ambient?'

'Oh yes, I am particularly happy,' Dolcino replied. The words were scarcely out of his mouth when his mother caught him up, and in a moment; holding him on her knees, she took her place on the bench where Miss Ambient and I had been sitting. This young lady said something to her brother, in consequence of which the two wandered away into the garden together. I remained with Mrs Ambient; but as a servant had brought out a couple of chairs I was not obliged to seat myself beside her. Our conversation was not animated, and I, for my part, felt there would be a kind of hypocrisy in my trying to make myself agreeable to Mrs Ambient. I didn't dislike her – I rather admired her; but I was aware that I differed from her inexpressibly. Then I suspected, what I afterwards definitely knew and have already intimated, that the poor lady had taken a dislike to me; and this of course was not encouraging. She thought me an obtrusive and even depraved young man, whom a perverse Providence had dropped upon their quiet lawn to flatter her husband's worst tendencies. She did me the honour to say to Miss Ambient, who repeated the speech, that she didn't know when she had seen her husband take such a fancy to a visitor; and she measured, apparently, my evil influence by Mark's appreciation of my society. I had a consciousness, not yet acute, but quite sufficient, of all this; but I must say that if it chilled my flow of small-talk, it didn't prevent me from thinking that the beautiful mother and beautiful child, interlaced there against their background of roses, made a picture such as I perhaps should not soon see again. I was free, I supposed, to go into the house and write letters, to sit in the drawing-room, to repair to my own apartment and take a nap; but the only use I made of my freedom was to linger still in my chair and say to myself that the light hand of Sir Joshua might have painted Mark Ambient's wife and son. I found myself looking perpetually at Dolcino, and Dolcino looked back at me, and that was enough to detain me. When he looked at me he smiled, and I felt it was an absolute impossibility to abandon a child who was smiling at one like that. His eyes never wandered; they attached themselves to mine, as if among all the small incipient things of his nature there was a desire to say something to me. If I could have taken him upon my own knee he perhaps would have managed to say it; but it would have been far too delicate a matter to ask his mother to give him up, and it has remained a constant regret for me that on that Sunday afternoon I did not, even for a moment, hold Dolcino in my arms. He had said that he felt remarkably well, and that he was especially happy; but though he may have been happy, with his charming head pillowed on his mother's breast and his little crimson silk legs depending from her lap, I did not think he looked well. He made no attempt to walk about; he was content to swing his legs softly and strike one as languid and angelic.

Mark came back to us with his sister; and Miss Ambient, making some remark about having to attend to her correspondence, passed into the house. Mark came and stood in front of his wife, looking down at the child, who immediately took hold of his hand, keeping it while he remained. 'I think Allingham ought to see him,' Ambient said; 'I think I will walk over and fetch him.'

'That's Gwendolen's idea, I suppose,' Mrs Ambient replied, very sweetly.

'It's not such an out-of-the-way idea, when one's child is ill.'

'I'm not ill, papa; I'm much better now,' Dolcino remarked.

'Is that the truth, or are you only saying it to be agreeable? You have a great idea of being agreeable, you know.'

The boy seemed to meditate on this distinction, this imputation, for a moment; then his exaggerated eyes, which had wandered, caught my own as I watched him. 'Do *you* think me agreeable?' he inquired, with the candour of his age and with a smile that made his father turn round to me, laughing, and ask, mutely, with a glance, 'Isn't he adorable?'

'Then why don't you hop about, if you feel so lusty?' Ambient went on, while the boy swung his hand.

'Because mamma is holding me close!'

'Oh yes; I know how mamma holds you when I come near!' Ambient exclaimed, looking at his wife.

She turned her charming eyes up to him, without deprecation or concession, and after a moment she said, 'You can go for
Allingham if you like. I think myself it would be better. You
ought to drive.'

'She says that to get me away,' Ambient remarked to me,
laughing; after which he started for the doctor's.

I remained there with Mrs Ambient, though our conversation had more pauses than speeches. The boy's little fixed white
face seemed, as before, to plead with me to stay, and after a
while it produced still another effect, a very curious one, which
I shall find it difficult to express. Of course I expose myself to
the charge of attempting to give fantastic reasons for an act
which may have been simply the fruit of a native want of
discretion; and indeed the traceable consequences of that
perversity were too lamentable to leave me any desire to trifle
with the question. All I can say is that I acted in perfect good
faith, and that Dolcino's friendly little gaze gradually kindled
the spark of my inspiration. What helped it to glow were the
other influences – the silent, suggestive garden-nook, the
perfect opportunity (if it was not an opportunity for that, it was
an opportunity for nothing), and the plea that I speak of, which
issued from the child's eyes and seemed to make him say, 'The
mother that bore me and that presses me here to her bosom –
sympathetic little organism that I am – has really the kind of
sensibility which she has been represented to you as lacking; if
you only look for it patiently and respectfully. How is it possible that she shouldn't have it? how is it possible that *I* should

have so much of it (for I am quite full of it, dear strange gentleman), if it were not also in some degree in her? I am my father's child, but I am also my mother's, and I am sorry for the difference between them!' So it shaped itself before me, the vision of reconciling Mrs Ambient with her husband, of putting an end to their great disagreement. The project was absurd, of course, for had I not had his word for it – spoken with all the bitterness of experience – that the gulf that divided them was well-nigh bottomless? Nevertheless, a quarter of an hour after Mark had left us, I said to his wife that I couldn't get over what she told me the night before about her thinking her husband's writings 'objectionable'. I had been so very sorry to hear it, had thought of it constantly, and wondered whether it were not possible to make her change her mind. Mrs Ambient gave me rather a cold stare – she seemed to be recommending me to mind my own business. I wish I had taken this mute counsel, but I did not. I went on to remark that it seemed an immense pity so much that was beautiful should be lost upon her.

'Nothing is lost upon me,' said Mrs Ambient. 'I know they are very beautiful.'

'Don't you like papa's books?' Dolcino asked, addressing his mother, but still looking at me. Then he added to me, 'Won't you read them to me, American gentleman?'

'I would rather tell you some stories of my own,' I said. 'I know some that are very interesting.'

'When will you tell them – tomorrow?'

'Tomorrow, with pleasure, if that suits you.'

Mrs Ambient was silent at this. Her husband, during our walk, had asked me to remain another day; my promise to her son was an implication that I had consented; and it is not probable that the prospect was agreeable to her. This ought, doubtless, to have made me more careful as to what I said next; but all I can say is that it didn't. I presently observed that just after leaving her, the evening before, and after hearing her apply to her husband's writings the epithet I had already quoted, I had, on going up to my room, sat down to the perusal of those sheets of his new book which he had been so good as to lend me. I had sat entranced till nearly three in the morning – I had read them twice over. 'You say you haven't looked at them. I think it's such a pity you shouldn't. Do let me beg you to take them up. They are so very remarkable. I'm sure they will convert you. They place him in – really – such a dazzling light. All that is best in him is there. I have no doubt it's a great liberty, my saying all this; but excuse me, and *do* read them!'

'Do read them, mamma!' Dolcino repeated. 'Do read them!'

She bent her head and closed his lips with a kiss. 'Of course I know he has worked immensely over them,' she said; and after this she made no remark, but sat there looking thoughtful, with her eyes on the ground. The tone of these last words was such as to leave me no spirit for further aggression, and after expressing a fear that her husband had not found the doctor at home, I got up and took a turn about the grounds. When I came back ten minutes later, she was still in her place, watching her boy, who had fallen asleep in her lap. As I drew near she put her finger to her lips, and a moment afterwards she rose, holding the child, and murmured something about its being better that he should go up stairs. I offered to carry him, and held out my hands to take him; but she thanked me and turned away, with the child seated on her arm, his head on her shoulder. 'I am very strong,' she said, as she passed into the house, and her slim, flexible figure bent backwards with the filial weight. So I never touched Dolcino.

I betook myself to Ambient's study, delighted to have a quiet hour to look over his books by myself. The windows were open into the garden, the sunny stillness, the mild light of the English summer, filled the room, without quite chasing away the rich, dusky air which was a part of its charm, and which abode in the serried shelves where old morocco exhaled the fragrance of curious learning, and in the brighter intervals where medals and prints and miniatures were suspended upon a surface of faded stuff. The place had both colour and quiet; I thought it a perfect room for work, and went so far as to say to myself that if it were mine, to sit and scribble in, there was no knowing but that I might learn to write as well as the author of *Beltraffio*. This distinguished man did not turn up, and I rummaged freely among his treasures. At last I took down a book that detained me a while, and seated myself in a fine old leather chair, by the window, to turn it over. I had been occupied in this way for half an hour – a good part of the afternoon had waned – when I become conscious of another presence in the room, and, looking up from my quarto, saw that Mrs Ambient, having pushed open the door in the same noiseless way that marked – or disguised – her entrance the night before, had advanced across the threshold. On seeing me she stopped; she had not, I think, expected to find me. But her hesitation was only of a moment; she came straight to her husband's writing-table, as if she were looking for something. I got up and asked her if I could help her. She glanced about an instant, and then put her hand upon a roll of papers which I recognized, as I had placed it in that spot in the morning, on coming down from my room.

'Is this the new book?' she asked, holding it up.

'The very sheets, with precious annotations.'

'I mean to take your advice.' And she tucked the little bundle under her arm. I congratulated her cordially, and ventured to make of my triumph, as I presumed to call it, a subject of pleasantry. But she was perfectly grave, and turned away from me, as she had presented herself, without a smile; after which I settled down to my quarto again, with the reflection that Mrs Ambient was a queer woman. My triumph, too, suddenly seemed to me rather vain. A woman who couldn't smile in the right place would never understand Mark Ambient. He came in at last in person, having brought the doctor back with him. 'He was away from home,' Mark said, 'and I went after him – to where he was supposed to be. He had left the place, and I followed him to two or three others, which accounts for my delay.' He was now with Mrs Ambient, looking at the child, and was to see Mark again before leaving the house. My host noticed, at the end of ten minutes, that the proof-sheets of his new book had been removed from the table, and when I told him, in reply to his question as to what I knew about them, that Mrs Ambient had carried them off to read, he turned almost pale for an instant with surprise. 'What has suddenly made her so curious?' he exclaimed; and I was obliged to tell him that I was at the bottom of the mystery. I had had it on my conscience to assure her that she really ought to know of what her husband was capable. 'Of what I am capable? *Elle ne s'en doute que trop!*' said Ambient, with a laugh; but he took my meddling very good-naturedly, and contented himself with adding that he was very much afraid she would burn up the sheets, with his emendations, of which he had no duplicate. The doctor paid a long visit in the nursery, and before he came down I retired to my own quarters, where I remained till dinner-time. On entering the drawing-room at this hour I found Miss Ambient in possession, as she had been the evening before.

'I was right about Dolcino,' she said as soon as she saw me, with a strange little air of triumph. 'He is really very ill.'

'Very ill! Why, when I last saw him, at four o'clock, he was in fairly good form.'

'There has been a change for the worse – very sudden and rapid – and when the doctor got here he found diphtheritic symptoms. He ought to have been called, as I knew, in the morning, and the child oughtn't to have been brought into the garden.'

'My dear lady, he was very happy there,' I answered, much appalled.

'He would be happy anywhere. I have no doubt he is happy now, with his poor little throat in a state—' She dropped her voice as her brother came in, and Mark let us know that, as a matter of course, Mrs Ambient would not appear. It was true that Dolcino had developed diphtheritic symptoms, but he was quiet for the present, and his mother was earnestly watching him. She was a perfect nurse, Mark said, and the doctor was coming back at ten o'clock. Our dinner was not very gay; Ambient was anxious and alarmed, and his sister irritated me by her constant tacit assumption, conveyed in the very way she nibbled her bread and sipped her wine, of having 'told me so'. I had had no disposition to deny anything she told me, and I could not see that her satisfaction in being justified by the event made poor Dolcino's throat any better. The truth is that, as the sequel proved, Miss Ambient had some of the qualities of the sibyl, and had therefore, perhaps, a right to the sibylline contortions. Her brother was so preoccupied that I felt my presence to be an indiscretion, and was sorry I had promised to remain over the morrow. I said to Mark that, evidently, I had better leave them in the morning; to which he replied that, on the contrary, if he was to pass the next days in the fidgets my company would be an extreme relief to him. The fidgets had already begun for him, poor fellow, and as we sat in his study with our cigars, after dinner, he wandered to the door whenever he heard the sound of the doctor's wheels. Miss Ambient, who shared this apartment with us, gave me at such moments significant glances; she had gone up stairs before rejoining us, to ask after the child. His mother and his nurse gave a tolerable account of him; but Miss Ambient found his fever high and his symptoms very grave. The doctor came at ten o'clock, and I went to bed after hearing from Mark that he saw no present cause for alarm. He had made every provision for the night, and was to return early in the morning.

I quitted my room at eight o'clock the next day, and as I came downstairs saw, through the open door of the house, Mrs Ambient standing at the front gate of the grounds, in colloquy with the physician. She wore a white dressing-gown, but her shining hair was carefully tucked away in its net, and in the freshness of the morning, after a night of watching, she looked as much 'the type of the lady' as her sister-in-law had described her. Her appearance, I suppose, ought to have reassured me; but I was still nervous and uneasy, so that I shrank from meeting her with the necessary question about Dolcino. None the less, however, was I impatient to learn how the morning found him; and as Mrs Ambient had not seen me, I passed into the grounds by a roundabout way, and, stopping at a further gate, hailed the doctor just as he was driving away. Mrs Ambient had returned to the house before he got into his gig.

'Excuse me – but, as a friend of the family, I should like very much to hear about the little boy.'

The doctor, who was a stout, sharp man, looked at me from head to foot, and then he said, 'I'm sorry to say I haven't seen him.'

'Haven't seen him?'

'Mrs Ambient came down to meet me as I alighted, and told me that he was sleeping so soundly, after a restless night, that she didn't wish him disturbed. I assured her I wouldn't disturb him, but she said he was quite safe now and she could look after him herself.'

'Thank you very much. Are you coming back?'

'No, sir; I'll be hanged if I come back!' exclaimed Dr Allingham, who was evidently very angry. And he started his horse again with the whip.

I wandered back into the garden, and five minutes later Miss Ambient came forth from the house to greet me. She explained that breakfast would not be served for some time, and that she wished to catch the doctor before he went away. I informed her that this functionary had come and departed, and I repeated to her what he had told me about his dismissal. This made Miss Ambient very serious – very serious indeed – and she sank into a bench, with dilated eyes, hugging her elbows with crossed arms. She indulged in many ejaculations, she confessed that she was infinitely perplexed, and she finally told me what her own last news of her nephew had been. She had sat up very late – after me, after Mark – and before going to bed had knocked at the door of the child's room, which was opened to her by the nurse. This good woman had admitted her, and she had found Dolcino quiet, but flushed and 'unnatural', with his mother sitting beside his bed. 'She held his hand in one of hers,' said Miss Ambient, 'and in the other – what do you think? – the proof-sheets of Mark's new book! She was reading them there, intently: did you ever hear of anything so extraordinary? Such a very odd time to be reading an author whom she never could abide!' In her agitation Miss Ambient was guilty of this vulgarism of speech, and I was so impressed by her narrative that it was only in recalling her words later that I noticed the lapse. Mrs Ambient had looked up from her reading with her finger on her lips – I recognized the gesture she had addressed to me in the afternoon – and, though the nurse was about to go to rest, had not encouraged her sister-in-law to relieve her of any part of her vigil. But certainly, then, Dolcino's condition was far from reassuring – his poor little breathing was most painful; and what change could have taken place in him in those few hours that would justify Beatrice in denying the physician access to him? This was the moral of Miss Ambient's anecdote – the moral for herself at least. The moral for me, rather, was that it *was* a very singular time for Mrs Ambient to be going into a novelist she had never appreciated and who had simply happened to be recommended to her by a young American she disliked. I thought of her sitting there in the sick-chamber in the still hours of the night, after the nurse had left her, turning over those pages of genius and wrestling with their magical influence.

I must relate very briefly the circumstances of the rest of my visit to Mark Ambient – it lasted but a few hours longer – and devote but three words to my later acquaintance with him. That lasted five years – till his death – and was full of interest, of satisfaction, and, I may add, of sadness. The main thing to be said with regard to it is, that I had a secret from him. I believe he never suspected it, though of this I am not absolutely sure. If he did, the line he had taken, the line of absolute negation of the matter to himself, shows an immense effort of the will. I may tell my secret now, giving it for what it is worth, now that Mark Ambient has gone, that he has begun to be alluded to as one of the famous early dead, and that his wife does not survive him; now, too, that Miss Ambient, whom I also saw at intervals during the years that followed, has, with her embroideries and her attitudes, her necromantic glances and strange intuitions, retired to a Sisterhood, where, as I am told, she is deeply immured and quite lost to the world.

Mark came into breakfast after his sister and I had for some time been seated there. He shook hands with me in silence, kissed his sister, opened his letters and newspapers, and pretended to drink his coffee. But I could see that these movements were mechanical, and I was little surprised when, suddenly he pushed away everything that was before him, and with his head in his hands and his elbows on the table, sat staring strangely at the cloth.

'What is the matter, *fratello mio*?' Miss Ambient inquired, peeping from behind the urn.

He answered nothing, but got up with a certain violence and strode to the window. We rose to our feet, his sister and I, by a common impulse, exchanging a glance of some alarm, while he stared for a moment into the garden. 'In Heaven's name, what has got possession of Beatrice?' he cried at last, turning round with an almost haggard face. And he looked from one of us to the other; the appeal was addressed to me as well as to his sister.

Miss Ambient gave a shrug. 'My poor Mark, Beatrice is always – Beatrice!'

'She has locked herself up with the boy – bolted and barred the door – she refuses to let me come near him!' Ambient went on.

'She refused to let the doctor see him an hour ago!' Miss Ambient remarked, with intention, as they say on the stage.

'Refused to let the doctor see him? By Heaven, I'll smash in the door!' And Mark brought his fist down upon the table, so that all the breakfast-service rang.

I begged Miss Ambient to go up and try to have speech of her sister-in-law, and I drew Mark out into the garden. 'You're exceedingly nervous, and Mrs Ambient is probably right,' I said to him. 'Women know – women should be supreme in such a situation. Trust a mother – a devoted mother, my dear friend!' With such words as these I tried to soothe and comfort him, and, marvellous to relate, I succeeded, with the help of many cigarettes, in making him walk about the garden and talk, or listen at least to my own ingenuous chatter, for nearly an hour. At the end of this time Miss Ambient returned to us, with a very rapid step, holding her hand to her heart.

'Go for the doctor, Mark; go for the doctor this moment!'

'Is he dying – has she killed him?' poor Ambient cried, flinging away his cigarette.

'I don't know what she has done! But she's frightened, and now she wants the doctor.'

'He told me he would be hanged if he came back,' I felt myself obliged to announce.

'Precisely – therefore Mark himself must go for him, and not a messenger. You must see him and tell him it's to save your child. The trap has been ordered – it's ready.'

'To save him? I'll save him, please God!' Ambient cried, bounding with his great strides across the lawn.

As soon as he had gone I felt that I ought to have volunteered in his place, and I said as much to Miss Ambient; but she checked me by grasping my arm quickly, while we heard the wheels of the dog-cart rattle away from the gate. 'He's off – he's off – and now I can think! To get him away – while I think – while I think!'

'While you think of what, Miss Ambient?'

'Of the unspeakable thing that has happened under this roof!'

Her manner was habitually that of such a prophetess of ill that my first impulse was to believe I must allow here for a great exaggeration. But in a moment I saw that her emotion was real. 'Dolcino *is* dying then – he is dead?'

'It's too late to save him. His mother has let him die! I tell you that, because you are sympathetic, because you have imagination,' Miss Ambient was good enough to add, interrupting my expression of horror. 'That's why you had the idea of making her read Mark's new book!'

'What has that to do with it? I don't understand you – your accusation is monstrous.'

'I see it all – I'm not stupid,' Miss Ambient went on, heedless of the harshness of my tone. 'It was the book that finished her – it was that decided her!'

'Decided her? Do you mean she has murdered her child?' I demanded, trembling at my own words.

'She sacrificed him – she determined to do nothing to make him live. Why else did she lock herself up – why else did she turn away the doctor? The book gave her a horror, she determined to rescue him – to prevent him from ever being touched. He had a crisis at two o'clock in the morning. I know this from the nurse, who had left her then, but whom, for a short time, she called back. Dolcino got much worse, but she insisted on the nurse's going back to bed, and after that she was alone with him for hours.'

'Do you pretend that she has no pity – that she's insane?'

'She held him in her arms – she pressed him to her breast, not to see him; but she gave him no remedies – she did nothing the doctor ordered. Everything is there, untouched. She has had the honesty not even to throw the drugs away!'

I dropped upon the nearest bench, overcome with wonder and agitation: quite as much at Miss Ambient's terrible lucidity as at the charge she made against her sister-in-law. There was an amazing coherency in her story, and it was dreadful to me to see myself figuring in it as so proximate a cause. 'You are a very strange woman, and you say strange things.'

'You think it necessary to protest – but you are quite ready to believe me. You have received an impression of my sister-in-law, you have guessed of what she is capable.'

I do not feel bound to say what concession on this point I made to Miss Ambient, who went on to relate to me that within the last half-hour Beatrice had had a revulsion; that she was tremendously frightened at what she had done; that her fright itself betrayed her; and that she would now give heaven and earth to save the child. 'Let us hope she will!' I said, looking at my watch and trying to time poor Ambient; whereupon my companion repeated, in a singular tone, 'Let us hope so!' When I asked her if she herself could do nothing, and whether she ought not to be with her sister-in-law, she replied, 'You had better go and judge; she is like a wounded tigress!' I never saw Mrs Ambient till six months after this, and therefore cannot pretend to have verified the comparison. At the latter period she was again the type of the lady. 'She'll be nicer to him after this,' I remember Miss Ambient saying, in response to some quick outburst (on my part) of compassion for her brother. Although I had been in the house but thirty-six hours this young lady had treated me with extraordinary confidence, and there was therefore a certain demand which, as an intimate, I might make of her. I extracted from her a pledge that she would never say to her brother what she had just said to me; she would leave him to form his own theory of his wife's conduct. She agreed with me that there was misery enough in the house without her contributing a new anguish, and that Mrs Ambient's proceedings might be explained, to her husband's mind, by the extravagance of a jealous devotion. Poor Mark came back with the doctor much sooner than we could have hoped, but we knew, five minutes afterward, that they arrived too late. Poor little Dolcino was more exquisitely beautiful in death than he had been in life. Mrs Ambient's grief was frantic; she lost her head and said strange things. As for Mark's – but I will not speak of that. *Basta*, as he used to say. Miss Ambient kept her secret – I have already had occasion to say that she had her good points – but it rankled in her conscience like a guilty participation, and, I imagine, had something to do with her retiring ultimately to a Sisterhood. And, *à propos* of consciences, the reader is now in a position to judge of my compunction for my effort to convert Mrs Ambient. I ought to mention that the death of her child in some degree converted her. When the new book came out – it was long delayed – she read it over as a whole, and her husband told me that a few months before her death – she failed rapidly after losing her son, sank into a consumption, and faded away at Mentone – during those few supreme weeks she even dipped into *Beltraffio*.

Sir Edmund Orme

T HE STATEMENT appears to have been written, though the fragment is undated, long after the death of his wife, whom I take to have been one of the persons referred to. There is, however, nothing in the strange story to establish this point, which is, perhaps, not of importance. When I took possession of his effects I found these pages, in a locked drawer, among papers relating to the unfortunate lady's too brief career (she died in childbirth a year after her marriage), letters, memoranda, accounts, faded photographs, cards of invitation. That is the only connection I can point to, and you may easily and will probably say that the tale is too extravagant to have had a demonstrable origin. I cannot, I admit, vouch for his having intended it as a report of real occurrence – I can only vouch for his general veracity. In any case it was written for himself, not for others. I offer it to others – having full option – precisely because it is so singular. Let them, in respect to the form of the thing, bear in mind that it was written quite for himself. I have altered nothing but the names.

* * *

If there's a story in the matter I recognize the exact moment at which it began. This was on a soft, still Sunday noon in November, just after church, on the sunny Parade. Brighton was full of people; it was the height of the season, and the day was even more respectable than lovely – which helped to account for the multitude of walkers. The blue sea itself was decorous; it seemed to doze, with a gentle snore (if that *be* decorum), as if nature were preaching a sermon. After writing letters all the morning I had come out to take a look at it before luncheon. I was leaning over the rail which separates the King's Road from the beach, and I think I was smoking a cigarette, when I became conscious of an intended joke in the shape of a light walking-stick laid across my shoulders. The idea, I found, had been thrown off by Teddy Bostwick, of the Rifles, and was intended as a contribution to talk. Our talk came off as we strolled together – he always took your arm to show you he forgave your obtuseness about his humour – and looked at the people, and bowed to some of them, and wondered who others were, and differed in opinion as to the prettiness of the girls. About Charlotte Marden we agreed, however, as we saw her coming toward us with her mother; and there surely could have been no one who wouldn't have agreed with us. The Brighton air, of old, used to make plain girls pretty and pretty girls prettier still – I don't know whether it works the spell now. The place, at any rate, was rare for complexions, and Miss Marden's was one that made people turn round. It made *us* stop, Heaven knows

— at least, it was one of the things, for we already knew the ladies.

We turned with them, we joined them, we went where they were going. They were only going to the end and back — they had just come out of church. It was another manifestation of Teddy's humour that he got immediate possession of Charlotte, leaving me to walk with her mother. However, I was not unhappy; the girl was before me and I had her to talk about. We prolonged our walk, Mrs Marden kept me, and presently she said she was tired and must sit down. We found a place on a sheltered bench — we gossiped as the people passed. It had already struck me, in this pair, that the resemblance between the mother and the daughter was wonderful even among such resemblances — the more so that it took so little account of a difference of nature. One often hears mature mothers spoken of as warnings — signposts, more or less discouraging, of the way daughters may go. But there was nothing deterrent in the idea that Charlotte, at fifty-five, should be as beautiful, even though it were conditioned on her being as pale and preoccupied, as Mrs Marden. At twenty-two she had a kind of rosy blankness and she was admirably handsome. Her head had the charming shape of her mother's, and her features the same fine order. Then there were looks and movements and tones (moments when you could scarcely say whether it were aspect or sound), which, between the two personalities, were a reflection, a recall.

These ladies had a small fortune and a cheerful little house at Brighton, full of portraits and tokens and trophies (stuffed animals on the top of bookcases, and sallow, varnished fish under glass), to which Mrs Marden professed herself attached by pious memories. Her husband had been 'ordered' there in ill-health, to spend the last years of his life, and she had already mentioned to me that it was a place in which she felt herself still under the protection of his goodness. His goodness appeared to have been great, and she sometimes had the air of defending it against mysterious imputations. Some sense of protection, of an influence invoked and cherished, was evidently necessary to her; she had a dim wistfulness, a longing for security. She wanted friends and she had a good many. She was kind to me on our first meeting, and I never suspected her of the vulgar purpose of 'making up' to me – a suspicion, of course, unduly frequent in conceited young men. It never struck me that she wanted me for her daughter, nor yet, like some unnatural mammas, for herself. It was as if they had had a common deep, shy need and had been ready to say: 'Oh, be friendly to us and be trustful! Don't be afraid, you won't be expected to marry us.' 'Of course there's something about mamma; that's really what makes her such a dear!' Charlotte said to me, confidentially, at an early stage of our acquaintance. She worshipped her mother's appearance. It was the only thing she was vain of; she accepted the raised eyebrows as a charming ultimate fact. 'She looks as if she were waiting for the doctor, dear mamma,' she said on another occasion. 'Perhaps *you're* the doctor; do you think you are?' It appeared in the event that I had some healing power. At any rate when I learned, for she once dropped the remark, that Mrs Marden also thought there was something 'awfully strange' about Charlotte, the relation between the two ladies became extremely interesting. It was happy enough, at bottom; each had the other so much on her mind.

On the Parade the stream of strollers held its course, and Charlotte presently went by with Teddy Bostwick. She smiled and nodded and continued, but when she came back she stopped and spoke to us. Captain Bostwick positively declined to go in, he said the occasion was too jolly: might they therefore take another turn? Her mother dropped a 'Do as you like,' and the girl gave me an impertinent smile over her shoulder as they quitted us. Teddy looked at me with his glass in one eye; but I didn't mind that; it was only of Miss Marden I was thinking as I observed to my companion, laughing:

'She's a bit of a coquette, you know.'

'Don't say that – don't say that!' Mrs Marden murmured.

'The nicest girls always are – just a little,' I was magnanimous enough to plead.

'Then why are they always punished?'

The intensity of the question startled me – it had come out in such a vivid flash. Therefore I had to think a moment before I inquired: 'What do you know about it?'

'I was a bad girl myself.'

'And were you punished?'

'I carry it through life,' said Mrs Marden, looking away from me. 'Ah!' she suddenly panted, in the next breath, rising to her feet and staring at her daughter, who had reappeared again with

Captain Bostwick. She stood a few seconds, with the queerest expression in her face; then she sank upon the seat again and I saw that she had blushed crimson. Charlotte, who had observed her movement, came straight up to her and, taking her hand with quick tenderness, seated herself on the other side of her. The girl had turned pale – she gave her mother a fixed, frightened look. Mrs Marden, who had had some shock which escaped our detection, recovered herself; that is she sat quiet and inexpressive, gazing at the indifferent crowd, the sunny air, the slumbering sea. My eye happened to fall, however, on the interlocked hands of the two ladies, and I quickly guessed that the grasp of the elder one was violent. Bostwick stood before them, wondering what was the matter and asking me from his little vacant disc if *I* knew; which led Charlotte to say to him after a moment, with a certain irritation:

'Don't stand there that way, Captain Bostwick; go away – *please* go away.'

I got up at this, hoping that Mrs Marden wasn't ill; but she immediately begged that we would *not* go away, that we would particularly stay and that we would presently come home to lunch. She drew me down beside her and for a moment I felt her hand pressing my arm in a way that might have been an involuntary betrayal of distress and might have been a private signal. What she might have wished to point out to me I couldn't divine: perhaps she had seen somebody or something abnormal in the crowd. She explained to us in a few minutes that she was all right; that she was only liable to palpitations – they came as quickly as they went. It was time to move, and we moved. The incident was felt to be closed. Bostwick and I lunched with our sociable friends, and when I walked away with him he declared that he had never seen such dear kind creatures.

Mrs Marden had made us promise to come back the next day to tea, and had exhorted us in general to come as often as we could. Yet the next day, when at five o'clock I knocked at the door of the pretty house, it was to learn that the ladies had gone up to town. They had left a message for us with the butler: he was to say that they had suddenly been called – were very sorry. They would be absent a few days. This was all I could extract from the dumb domestic. I went again three days later, but they were still away; and it was not till the end of a week that I got a note from Mrs Marden, saying 'We are back; do come and forgive us.' It was on this occasion, I remember (the occasion of my going just after getting the note), that she told me she had intuitions. I don't know how many people there were in England at that time in that predicament, but there were very few who would have mentioned it; so that the announcement struck me as original, especially as her point was that some of these uncanny promptings were connected with me. There were other people present – idle Brighton folk, old women with frightened eyes and irrelevant interjections – and I had but a few minutes' talk with Charlotte; but the day after this I met them both at dinner and had the satisfaction of sitting next to Miss Marden. I recall that hour as the hour on which it first completely came over me that she was a beautiful, liberal creature. I had seen her personality in patches and gleams, like a song sung in snatches, but now it was before me in a large rosy glow, as if it had been a full volume of sound – I heard the whole of the air. It was sweet, fresh music – I was often to hum it over.

After dinner I had a few words with Mrs Marden; it was at the moment, late in the evening, when tea was handed about. A servant passed near us with a tray, I asked her if she would have a cup, and, on her assenting, took one and handed it to her. She put out her hand for it and I gave it to her, safely as I supposed; but as she was in the act of receiving it she started and faltered, so that the cup and saucer dropped with a crash of porcelain and without, on the part of my interlocutress, the usual woman's movement to save her dress. I stooped to pick up the fragments and when I raised myself Mrs Marden was looking across the room at her daughter, who looked back at her smiling, but with an anxious light in her eyes. 'Dear mamma, what on earth *is* the matter with you?' the silent question seemed to say. Mrs Marden coloured, just as she had done after her strange movement on the Parade the other week, and I was therefore surprised when she said to me with unexpected assurance: 'You should really have a steadier hand!' I had begun to stammer a defence of my hand when I became aware that she had fixed her eyes upon me with an intense appeal. It was ambiguous at first and only added to my confusion; then suddenly I understood, as plainly as if she had murmured 'Make believe it was you – make believe it was you.' The servant came back to take the morsels of the cup and wipe up the spilt tea, and while I was in the midst of making believe Mrs Marden abruptly brushed away from me and from her daughter's attention and went into another room. I noticed that she gave no heed to the state of her dress.

I saw nothing more of either of them that evening, but the next morning, in the King's Road, I met Miss Marden with a roll of music in her muff. She told me she had been a little way alone, to practise duets with a friend, and I asked her if she would go a little way further in company. She gave me leave to attend her to her door, and as we stood before it I inquired if I might go in. 'No, not today – I don't want you,' she said, candidly, though not roughly; while the words caused me to direct a wistful, disconcerted gaze at one of the windows of the house. It fell upon the white face of Mrs Marden, who was looking out at us from the drawing-room. She stood there long enough for me to see that it *was* she and not an apparition, as I had thought for a second, and then she vanished before her daughter had observed her. The girl, during our walk, had said nothing about her. As I had been told they didn't want me I left them alone a little, after which circumstances supervened that kept us still longer apart. I finally went up to London, and while there I received a pressing invitation to come immediately down to Tranton, a pretty old place in Sussex belonging to a couple whose acquaintance I had lately made.

I went to Tranton from town, and on arriving found the Mardens, with a dozen other people, in the house. The first thing Mrs Marden said was: 'Will you forgive me?' and when I asked what I had to forgive she answered: 'My throwing my tea over you.' I replied that it had gone over herself; whereupon she said: 'At any rate I was very rude; but some day I think you'll understand, and then you'll make allowances for me.' The first day I was there she dropped two or three of these references (she had already indulged in more than one), to the mystic initiation that was in store for me; so that I began, as the phrase is, to chaff her about it, to say I would rather it were less wonderful and take it out at once. She answered that when it should come to me I would have to take it out – there would be little enough option. That it *would* come was privately clear to her, a deep presentiment, which was the only reason she had ever mentioned the matter. Didn't I remember she had told me she had intuitions? From the first time of her seeing me she had been sure there were things I should not escape knowing. Meanwhile there was nothing to do but wait and keep cool, not to be precipitate. She particularly wished not to be any more nervous than she was. And I was above all not to be nervous myself – one got used to everything. I declared that though I couldn't make out what she was talking about I was terribly frightened; the absence of a clue gave such a range to one's imagination. I exaggerated on purpose; for if Mrs Marden was mystifying I can scarcely say she was alarming. I couldn't imagine what she meant, but I wondered more than I shuddered. I might have said to myself that she was a little wrong in the upper storey; but that never occurred to me. She struck me as hopelessly right.

There were other girls in the house, but Charlotte Marden was the most charming; which was so generally felt to be the case that she really interfered with the slaughter of ground game. There were two or three men, and I was of the number, who actually preferred her to the society of the beaters. In short she was recognized as a form of sport superior and exquisite. She was kind to all of us – she made us go out late and come in early. I don't know whether she flirted, but several other members of the party thought *they* did. Indeed, as regards himself, Teddy Bostwick, who had come over from Brighton, was visibly sure.

The third day I was at Tranton was a Sunday, and there was a very pretty walk to morning service over the fields. It was grey, windless weather, and the bell of the little old church that nestled in the hollow of the Sussex down sounded near and domestic. We were a straggling procession, in the mild damp air (which, as always at that season, gave one the feeling that after the trees were bare there was more of it – a larger sky), and I managed to fall a good way behind with Miss Marden. I remember entertaining, as we moved together over the turf, a strong impulse to say something intensely personal, something violent and important – important for *me*, such as that I had never seen her so lovely, or that that particular moment was the sweetest of my life. But always, in youth, such words have been on the lips many times before they are spoken; and I had the sense, not that I didn't know her well enough (I cared little for that), but that she didn't know *me* well enough. In the church, where there were old Tranton tombs and brasses, the big Tranton pew was full. Several of us were scattered, and I found a seat for Miss

Marden, and another for myself beside it, at a distance from her mother and from most of our friends. There were two or three decent rustics on the bench, who moved in further to make room for us, and I took my place first, to cut off my companion from our neighbours. After she was seated there was still a space left, which remained empty till service was about half over.

This at least was the moment at which I became aware that another person had entered and had taken the seat. When I noticed him he had apparently been for some minutes in the pew, for he had settled himself and put down his hat beside him, and, with his hands crossed on the nob of his cane, was gazing before him at the altar. He was a pale young man in black, with the air of a gentleman. I was slightly startled on perceiving him, for Miss Marden had not attracted my attention to his entrance by moving to make room for him. After a few minutes, observing that he had no prayer-book, I reached across my neighbour and placed mine before him, on the ledge of the pew; a manoeuvre the motive of which was not unconnected with the possibility that, in my own destitution, Miss Marden would give me one side of *her* velvet volume to hold. The pretext, however, was destined to fail, for at the moment I offered him the book the intruder – whose intrusion I had so condoned – rose from his place without thanking me, stepped noiselessly out of the pew (it had no door), and, so discreetly as to attract no attention, passed down the centre of the church. A few minutes had sufficed for his devotions. His behaviour was unbecoming, his early departure even more than his late arrival; but he managed so quietly that we were not incommoded, and I perceived, on turning a little to glance after him, that nobody was disturbed by his withdrawal. I only noticed, and with surprise, that Mrs Marden had been so affected by it as to rise, involuntarily, an instant, in her place. She stared at him as he passed, but he passed very quickly, and she as quickly dropped down again, though not too soon to catch my eye across the church. Five minutes later I asked Miss Marden, in a low voice, if she would kindly pass me back my prayer-book – I had waited to see if she would spontaneously perform the act. She restored this aid to devotion, but had been so far from troubling herself about it that she could say to me as she did so: 'Why on earth did you put it there?' I was on the point of answering her when she dropped on her knees, and I held my tongue. I had only been going to say: 'To be decently civil.'

After the benediction, as we were leaving our places, I was slightly surprised, again, to see that Mrs Marden, instead of going out with her companions, had come up the aisle to join us, having apparently something to say to her daughter. She said it, but in an instant I observed that it was only a pretext – her real business was with me. She pushed Charlotte forward and suddenly murmured to me: 'Did you see him?'

'The gentleman who sat down here? How could I help seeing him?'

'Hush!' she said, with the intensest excitement; 'don't *speak* to her – don't tell her!' She slipped her hand into my arm, to keep me near her, to keep me, it seemed, away from her daughter. The precaution was unnecessary, for Teddy Bostwick had already taken possession of Miss Marden, and as they passed out of church in front of me I saw one of the other men close up on her other hand. It appeared to be considered that I had had my turn. Mrs Marden withdrew her hand from my arm as soon as we got out, but not before I felt that she had really needed the support. 'Don't speak to anyone – don't tell anyone!' she went on.

'I don't understand. Tell them what?'

'Why, that you saw him.'

'Surely they saw him for themselves.'

'Not one of them, not one of them.' She spoke in a tone of such passionate decision that I glanced at her – she was staring straight before her. But she felt the challenge of my eyes and she stopped short, in the old brown timber porch of the church, with the others well in advance of us, and said, looking at me now and in a quite extraordinary manner: 'You're the only person, the only person in the world.'

'But *you*, dear madam?'

'Oh me – of course. That's my curse!' And with this she moved rapidly away from me to join the body of the party. I hovered on its outskirts on the way home, for I had food for rumination. Whom had I seen and why was the apparition – it rose before my mind's eye very vividly again – invisible to the others? If an exception had been made for Mrs Marden, why did it constitute a curse, and why was I to share so questionable an advantage? This inquiry, carried on in my own locked breast,

kept me doubtless silent enough during luncheon. After luncheon I went out on the old terrace to smoke a cigarette, but I had
only taken a couple of turns when I perceived Mrs Marden's
moulded mask at the window of one of the rooms which opened
on the crooked flags. It reminded me of the same flitting presence at the window at Brighton the day I met Charlotte and
walked home with her. But this time my ambiguous friend didn't
vanish; she tapped on the pane and motioned me to come in. She
was in a queer little apartment, one of the many reception-
rooms of which the ground-floor at Tranton consisted; it was
known as the Indian room and had a decoration vaguely
Oriental – bamboo lounges, lacquered screens, lanterns with
long fringes and strange idols in cabinets, objects not held to
conduce to sociability. The place was little used, and when I
went round to her we had it to ourselves. As soon as I entered
she said to me: 'Please tell me this; are you in love with my
daughter?'

I hesitated a moment. 'Before I answer your question will
you kindly tell me what gives you the idea? I don't consider that
I have been very forward.'

Mrs Marden, contradicting me with her beautiful anxious
eyes, gave me no satisfaction on the point I mentioned; she only
went on strenuously:

'Did you say nothing to her on the way to church?'

'What makes you think I said anything?'

'The fact that you saw him.'

'Saw whom, dear Mrs Marden?'

'Oh, you know,' she answered, gravely, even a little reproach-fully, as if I were trying to humiliate her by making her phrase the unphraseable.

'Do you mean the gentleman who formed the subject of your strange statement in church – the one who came into the pew?'

'You saw him, you saw him!' Mrs Marden panted, with a strange mixture of dismay and relief.

'Of course I saw him; and so did you.'

'It didn't follow. Did you feel it to be inevitable?'

I was puzzled again. 'Inevitable?'

'That you *should* see him?'

'Certainly, since I'm not blind.'

'You might have been; everyone else is.' I was wonderfully at sea, and I frankly confessed it to my interlocutress; but the case was not made clearer by her presently exclaiming: 'I knew you would, from the moment you should be really in love with her! I knew it would be the test – what do I mean? – the proof.'

'Are there such strange bewilderments attached to that high state?' I asked, smiling.

'You perceive there are. You see him, you see him!' Mrs Marden announced, with tremendous exaltation. 'You'll see him again.'

'I've no objection; but I shall take more interest in him if you'll kindly tell me who he is.'

She hesitated, looking down a moment; then she said, raising her eyes: 'I'll tell you if you'll tell me first what you said to her on the way to church.'

'Has she told you I said anything?'

'Do I need that?' smiled Mrs Marden.

'Oh yes, I remember – your intuitions! But I'm sorry to see they're at fault this time; because I really said nothing to your daughter that was the least out of the way.'

'Are you very sure?'

'On my honour, Mrs Marden.'

'Then you consider that you're not in love with her?'

'That's another affair!' I laughed.

'You are – you *are*! You wouldn't have seen him if you hadn't been.'

'Who the deuce *is* he, then, madam?' I inquired with some irritation.

She would still only answer me with another question. 'Didn't you at least *want* to say something to her – didn't you come very near it?'

The question was much to the point; it justified the famous intuitions. 'Very near it – it was the turn of a hair. I don't know what kept me quiet.'

'That was quite enough,' said Mrs Marden. 'It isn't what you say that determines it; it's what you feel. *That's* what he goes by.'

I was annoyed, at last, by her reiterated reference to an identity yet to be established, and I clasped my hands with an air of supplication which covered much real impatience, a sharper curiosity and even the first short throbs of a certain sacred dread. 'I entreat you to tell me whom you're talking about.'

She threw up her arms, looking away from me, as if to shake off both reserve and responsibility. 'Sir Edmund Orme.'

'And who is Sir Edmund Orme?'

At the moment I spoke she gave a start. 'Hush, here they come.' Then as, following the direction of her eyes, I saw Charlotte Marden on the terrace, at the window, she added, with an intensity of warning: 'Don't notice him – *never*!'

Charlotte, who had had her hands beside her eyes, peering into the room and smiling, made a sign that she was to be admitted, on which I went and opened the long window. Her mother turned away, and the girl came in with a laughing challenge: 'What plot in the world are you two hatching here?' Some plan – I forget what – was in prospect for the afternoon, as to which Mrs Marden's participation or consent was solicited – *my* adhesion was taken for granted – and she had been half over the place in her quest. I was flurried, because I saw that Mrs Marden was flurried (when she turned round to meet her daughter she covered it by a kind of extravagance, throwing herself on the girl's neck and embracing her), and to pass it off I said, fancifully, to Charlotte:

'I've been asking your mother for your hand.'

'Oh, indeed, and has she given it?' Miss Marden answered, gaily.

'She was just going to when you appeared there.'

'Well, it's only for a moment – I'll leave you free.'

'Do you like him, Charlotte?' Mrs Marden asked, with a candour I scarcely expected.

'It's difficult to say it *before* him isn't it?' the girl replied, entering into the humour of the thing, but looking at me as if she didn't like me.

She would have had to say it before another person as well, for at that moment there stepped into the room from the terrace (the window had been left open) a gentleman who had come into sight, at least into mine, only within the instant. Mrs Marden had said 'Here *they* come,' but he appeared to have followed her daughter at a certain distance. I immediately recognized him as the personage who had sat beside us in church. This time I saw him better, saw that his face and his whole air were strange. I speak of him as a personage, because one felt, indescribably, as if a reigning prince had come into the room. He held himself with a kind of habitual majesty, as if he were different from us. Yet he looked fixedly and gravely at me, till I wondered what he expected of me. Did he consider that I should bend my knee or kiss his hand? He turned his eyes in the same way on Mrs Marden, but she knew what to do. After the first agitation produced by his approach she took no notice of him whatever; it made me remember her passionate adjuration to me. I had to achieve a great effort to imitate her, for though I knew nothing about him but that he was Sir Edmund Orme I felt his presence as a strong appeal, almost as an oppression. He stood there without speaking – young, pale, handsome, clean-shaven, decorous, with extraordinary light blue eyes and something old-fashioned, like a portrait of years ago, in his head, his manner of wearing his hair. He was in complete mourning (one immediately felt that he was very well dressed), and he carried his hat in his hand. He looked again strangely hard at me, harder than anyone in the world had ever looked before; and I remember feeling rather cold and wishing he would say something. No silence had ever seemed to me so soundless. All this was of course an impression intensely rapid; but that it had consumed some instants was proved to me suddenly by the aspect of Charlotte Marden, who stared from her mother to me and back again (he never looked at her, and she had no appearance of looking at him), and then broke out with: 'What on earth is the matter with you? You've such odd faces!' I felt the colour come back to mine, and when she went on in the same tone: 'One would think you had seen a ghost!' I was conscious that I had turned very red. Sir Edmund Orme never blushed, and I could see that he had no capacity for embarrassment. One had met people of that sort, but never anyone with such a grand indifference.

'Don't be impertinent; and go and tell them all that I'll join them,' said Mrs Marden with much dignity, but with a quaver in her voice.

'And will you come – *you*?' the girl asked, turning away. I made no answer, taking the question, somehow, as meant for her companion. But he was more silent than I, and when she reached the door (she was going out that way), she stopped, with her hand on the knob, and looked at me, repeating it. I assented, springing forward to open the door for her, and as she passed out she exclaimed to me mockingly: 'You haven't got your wits about you – you shan't have my hand!'

I closed the door and turned round to find that Sir Edmund Orme had during the moment my back was presented to him retired by the window. Mrs Marden stood there and we looked at each other long. It had only then – as the girl flitted away – come home to me that her daughter was unconscious of what had happened. It was *that*, oddly enough, that gave me a sudden, sharp shake, and not my own perception of our visitor, which appeared perfectly natural. It made the fact vivid to me that she had been equally unaware of him in church, and the two facts together – now that they were over – set my heart more sensibly beating. I wiped my forehead, and Mrs Marden broke out with a low distressful wail: 'Now you know my life – now you know my life!'

'In God's name who is he – *what* is he?'

'He's a man I wronged.'

'How did you wrong him?'

'Oh, awfully – years ago.'

'Years ago? Why, he's very young.'

'Young – young?' cried Mrs Marden. 'He was born before *I* was!'

'Then why does he look so?'

She came nearer to me, she laid her hand on my arm, and there was something in her face that made me shrink a little. 'Don't you understand – don't you *feel*?' she murmured, reproachfully.

'I feel very queer!' I laughed; and I was conscious that my laugh betrayed it.

'He's dead!' said Mrs Marden, from her white face.

'Dead?' I panted. 'Then that gentleman was——?' I couldn't even say the word.

'Call him what you like – there are twenty vulgar names. He's a perfect presence.'

'He's a splendid presence!' I cried. 'The place is haunted – *haunted*!' I exulted in the word as if it represented the fulfilment of my dearest dream.

'It isn't the place – more's the pity! That has nothing to do with it!'

'Then it's you, dear lady?' I said, as if this were still better.

'No, nor me either – I wish it were!'

'Perhaps it's me,' I suggested with a sickly smile.

'It's nobody but my child – my innocent, innocent child!' And with this Mrs Marden broke down – she dropped into a chair and burst into tears. I stammered some question – I pressed on her some bewildered appeal, but she waved me off, unexpectedly and passionately. I persisted – couldn't I help her, couldn't I intervene? 'You *have* intervened,' she sobbed; 'you're *in* it, you're *in* it.'

'I'm very glad to be in anything so curious,' I boldly declared.

'Glad or not, you can't get out of it.'

'I don't want to get out of it – it's too interesting.'

'I'm glad you like it. Go away.'

'But I want to know more about it.'

'You'll see all you want – go away!'

'But I want to understand what I see.'

'How can you – when I don't understand myself?'

'We'll do so together – we'll make it out.'

At this she got up, doing what she could to obliterate her tears. 'Yes, it will be better together – that's why I've liked you.'

'Oh, we'll see it through!' I declared.

'Then you must control yourself better.'

'I will, I will – with practice.'

'You'll get used to it,' said Mrs Marden, in a tone I never forgot. 'But go and join them – I'll come in a moment.'

I passed out to the terrace and I felt that I had a part to play. So far from dreading another encounter with the 'perfect presence', as Mrs Marden called it, I was filled with an excitement that was positively joyous. I desired a renewal of the sensation – I opened myself wide to the impression, I went round the house as quickly as if I expected to overtake Sir Edmund Orme. I didn't overtake him just then, but the day was not to close without my recognizing that, as Mrs Marden had said, I should see all I wanted of him.

We took, or most of us took, the collective sociable walk which, in the English country-house, is the consecrated pastime on Sunday afternoons. We were restricted to such a regulated ramble as the ladies were good for; the afternoons, moreover, were short, and by five o'clock we were restored to the fireside in the hall, with a sense, on my part at least, that we might have done a little more for our tea. Mrs Marden had said she would join us, but she had not appeared; her daughter, who had seen her again before we went out, only explained that she was tired. She remained invisible all the afternoon, but this was a detail to which I gave as little heed as I had given to the circumstance of my not having Miss Marden to myself during all our walk. I was too much taken up with another emotion to care; I felt beneath my feet the threshold of the strange door, in my life, which had suddenly been thrown open and out of which unspeakable vibrations played up through me like a fountain. I had heard all my days of apparitions, but it was a different thing to have seen one and to know that I should in all probability see it familiarly, as it were, again. I was on the look-out for it, as a pilot for the flash of a revolving light, and I was ready to generalize on the sinister subject, to declare that ghosts were much less alarming and much more amusing than was commonly supposed. There is no doubt that I was extremely nervous. I couldn't get over the distinction conferred upon me – the exception (in the way of mystic enlargement of vision), made in my favour. At the same time I think I did justice to Mrs Marden's absence; it was a commentary on what she had said to me – 'Now you know my life.' She had probably been seeing Sir Edmund Orme for years, and, not having my firm fibre, she had broken down under him. Her nerve was gone, though she had also been able to attest that, in a degree, one got used to him. She had got used to breaking down.

Afternoon tea, when the dusk fell early, was a friendly hour at Tranton; the firelight played into the wide, white last-century hall; sympathies almost confessed themselves, lingering together, before dressing, on deep sofas, in muddy boots, for last words, after walks; and even solitary absorption in the third volume of a novel that was wanted by someone else seemed a form of geniality. I watched my moment and went over to Charlotte Marden when I saw she was about to withdraw. The ladies had left the place one by one, and after I had addressed myself particularly to Miss Marden the three men who were near her gradually dispersed. We had a little vague talk – she appeared preoccupied, and Heaven knows *I* was – after which she said she must go: she should be late for dinner. I proved to her by book that she had plenty of time, and she objected that she must at any rate go up to see her mother: she was afraid she was unwell.

'On the contrary, she's better than she has been for a long time – I'll guarantee that,' I said. 'She has found out that she can have confidence in me, and that has done her good.' Miss Marden had dropped into her chair again. I was standing before her, and she looked up at me without a smile – with a dim distress in her beautiful eyes; not exactly as if I were hurting her, but as if she were no longer disposed to treat as a joke what had passed (whatever it was, it was at the same time difficult to be serious about it) between her mother and myself. But I could answer her inquiry in all kindness and candour, for I was really conscious that the poor lady had put off a part of her burden on me and was proportionately relieved and eased. 'I'm sure she has slept all the afternoon as she hasn't slept for years,' I went on. 'You have only to ask her.'

Charlotte got up again. 'You make yourself out very useful.'

'You've a good quarter of an hour,' I said. 'Haven't I a right to talk to you a little this way, alone, when your mother has given me your hand?'

'And is it *your* mother who has given me yours? I'm much obliged to her, but I don't want it. I think our hands are not our mothers' – they happen to be our own!' laughed the girl.

'Sit down, sit down and let me tell you!' I pleaded.

I still stood before her, urgently, to see if she wouldn't oblige me. She hesitated a moment, looking vaguely this way and that, as if under a compulsion that was slightly painful. The empty hall was quiet – we heard the loud ticking of the great clock. Then she slowly sank down and I drew a chair close to her. This made me face round to the fire again, and with the movement I perceived, disconcertedly, that we were not alone. The next instant, more strangely than I can say, my discomposure, instead of increasing, dropped, for the person before the fire was Sir Edmund Orme. He stood there as I had seen him in the Indian room, looking at me with the expressionless attention which borrowed its sternness from his sombre distinction. I knew so much more about him now that I had to check a movement of recognition, an acknowledgement of his presence. When once I was aware of it, and that it lasted, the sense that we had company, Charlotte and I, quitted me; it was impressed on me on the contrary that I was more intensely alone with Miss Marden. She evidently saw nothing to look at, and I made a tremendous and very nearly successful effort to conceal from her that my own situation was different. I say 'very nearly', because she watched me an instant – while my words were arrested – in a way that made me fear she was going to say again, as she had said in the Indian room: 'What on earth is the matter with you?'

What the matter with me was I quickly told her, for the full knowledge of it rolled over me with the touching spectacle of her unconsciousness. It was touching that she became, in the presence of this extraordinary portent. What was portended, danger or sorrow, bliss or bane, was a minor question; all I saw, as she sat there, was that, innocent and charming, she was close to a horror, as she might have thought it, that happened to be veiled from her but that might at any moment be disclosed. I didn't mind it now, as I found, but nothing was more possible than she should, and if it wasn't curious and interesting it might easily be very dreadful. If I didn't mind it for myself, as I afterwards saw, this was largely because I was so taken up with the idea of protecting *her*. My heart beat high with this idea, on the spot; I determined to do everything I could to keep her sense sealed. What I could do might have been very obscure to me if I had not, in all this, become more aware than of anything else that I loved her. The way to save her was to love her, and the way to love her was to tell her, now and here, that I did so. Sir Edmund Orme didn't prevent me, especially as after a moment he turned his back to us and stood looking discreetly at the fire. At the end of another moment he leaned his head on his arm, against the chimney-piece, with an air of gradual dejection, like a spirit still more weary than discreet.

Charlotte Marden was startled by what I said to her, and she jumped up to escape it; but she took no offence – my tenderness was too real. She only moved about the room with a deprecating murmur, and I was so busy following up any little advantage that I might have obtained that I didn't notice in what manner Sir Edmund Orme disappeared. I only observed presently that he had gone. This made no difference – he had been so small a hindrance; I only remember being struck, suddenly, with something inexorable in the slow, sweet, sad head-shake that Miss Marden gave me.

'I don't ask for an answer now,' I said; 'I only want you to be sure – to know how much depends on it.'

'Oh, I don't want to give it to you, now or ever!' she replied. 'I hate the subject, please – I wish one could be let alone.' And then, as if I might have found something harsh in this irrepressible, artless cry of beauty beset, she added quickly, vaguely, kindly, as she left the room: 'Thank you, thank you – thank you so much!'

At dinner I could be generous enough to be glad, for her, that I was placed on the same side of the table with her, where she couldn't see me. Her mother was nearly opposite to me, and just after we had sat down Mrs Marden gave me one long, deep look, in which all our strange communion was expressed. It meant of course 'She has told me,' but it meant other things beside. At any rate I know what my answering look to her conveyed: 'I've seen him again – I've seen him again!' This didn't prevent Mrs Marden from treating her neighbours with her usual scrupulous blandness. After dinner, when, in the drawing-room, the men joined the ladies and I went straight up to her to tell her how I wished we could have some private conversation, she said immediately, in a low tone, looking down at her fan while she opened and shut it:

'He's here – he's here.'

'Here?' I looked round the room, but I was disappointed.

'Look where *she* is,' said Mrs Marden, with just the faintest asperity. Charlotte was in fact not in the main saloon, but in an apartment into which it opened and which was known as the morning-room. I took a few steps and saw her, through a doorway, upright in the middle of the room, talking with three gentlemen whose backs were practically turned to me. For a moment my quest seemed vain; then I recognized that one of the gentlemen – the middle one – was Sir Edmund Orme. This time it *was* surprising that the others didn't see him. Charlotte seemed to be looking straight at him, addressing her conversation to him. She saw me after an instant, however, and immediately turned her eyes away. I went back to her mother with an annoyed sense that the girl would think I was watching *her*, which would be unjust. Mrs Marden had found a small sofa – a little apart – and I sat down beside her. There were some questions I had so wanted to go into that I wished we were once more in the Indian room. I presently gathered, however, that our privacy was all-sufficient. We communicated so closely and completely now, and with such silent reciprocities, that it would in every circumstance be adequate.

'Oh, yes, he's there,' I said; 'and at about a quarter-past seven he was in the hall.'

'I knew it at the time, and I was so glad!'

'So glad?'

'That it was your affair, this time, and not mine. It's a rest for me.'

'Did you sleep all the afternoon?' I asked.

'As I haven't done for months. But how did you know that?'

'As *you* knew, I take it, that Sir Edmund was in the hall. We shall evidently each of us know things now – where the other is concerned.'

'Where *he* is concerned,' Mrs Marden amended. 'It's a blessing, the way you take it,' she added, with a long, mild sigh.

'I take it as a man who's in love with your daughter.'

'Of course – of course.' Intense as I now felt my desire for the girl to be, I couldn't help laughing a little at the tone of these words; and it led my companion immediately to say: 'Otherwise you wouldn't have seen him.'

'But everyone doesn't see him who's in love with her, or there would be dozens.'

'They're not in love with her as you are.'

'I can, of course, only speak for myself; and I found a moment, before dinner, to do so.'

'She told me immediately.'

'And have I any hope – any chance?'

'That's what *I* long for, what I pray for.'

'Ah, how can I thank you enough?' I murmured.

'I believe it will all pass – if she loves you,' Mrs Marden continued.

'It will all pass?'

'We shall never see him again.'

'Oh, if she loves me I don't care how often I see him!'

'Ah, you take it better than I could,' said my companion. 'You have the happiness not to know – not to understand.'

'I don't indeed. What on earth does he want?'

'He wants to make me suffer.' She turned her wan face upon me with this, and I saw now for the first time, fully, how perfectly, if this had been Sir Edmund Orme's purpose, he had succeeded. 'For what I did to him,' Mrs Marden explained.

'And what did you do to him?'

She looked at me a moment. 'I killed him.' As I had seen him fifty yards away only five minutes before the words gave me a start. 'Yes, I make you jump; be careful. He's there still, but he killed himself. I broke his heart – he thought me awfully bad. We were to have been married, but I broke it off – just at the last. I saw someone I liked better; I had no reason but that. It wasn't for interest, or money, or position, or anything of that sort. All *those* things were his. It was simply that I fell in love with Captain Marden. When I saw him I felt that I couldn't marry anyone else. I wasn't in love with Edmund Orme – my mother, my elder sister had brought it about. But he did love me. I told him I didn't care – that I couldn't, that I *wouldn't*. I threw him over, and he took something, some abominable drug or draught that proved fatal. It was dreadful, it was horrible, he was found that way – he died in agony. I married Captain Marden, but not for five years. I was happy, perfectly happy; time obliterates. But when my husband died I began to see him.'

I had listened intently, but I wondered. 'To see your husband?'

'Never, never *that* way, thank God! To see *him*, with Chartie – always with Chartie. The first time it nearly killed me – about seven years ago, when she first came out. Never when I'm by myself – only with her. Sometimes not for months, then every day for a week. I've tried everything to break the spell – doctors and *régimes* and climates; I've prayed to God on my knees. That day at Brighton, on the Parade with you, when you thought I was ill, that was the first for an age. And then, in the evening, when I knocked my tea over you, and the day you were at the door with Charlotte and I saw you from the window – each time he was there.'

'I see, I see.' I was more thrilled than I could say. 'It's an apparition like another.'

'Like another? Have you ever seen another?'

'No, I mean the sort of thing one has heard of. It's tremendously interesting to encounter a case.'

'Do you call me a "case"?' Mrs Marden asked, with exquisite resentment.

'I mean myself.'

'Oh, you're the right one!' she exclaimed. 'I was right when I trusted you.'

'I'm devoutly grateful you did; but what made you do it?'

'I had thought the whole thing out – I had had time to in those dreadful years, while he was punishing me in my daughter.'

'Hardly that,' I objected, 'if she never knew.'

'That has been my terror, that she *will*, from one occasion to another. I've an unspeakable dread of the effect on her.'

'She shan't, she shan't!' I declared, so loud that several people looked round. Mrs Marden made me get up, and I had no more talk with her that evening. The next day I told her I must take my departure from Tranton – it was neither comfortable nor considerate to remain as a rejected suitor. She was disconcerted, but she accepted my reasons, only saying to me out of her mournful eyes: 'You'll leave me alone then with my burden?' It was of course understood between us that for many weeks to come there would be no discretion in 'worrying poor Charlotte': such were the terms in which, with odd feminine and maternal inconsistency, she alluded to an attitude on my part that she favoured. I was prepared to be heroically considerate, but it seemed to me that even this delicacy permitted me to say a word to Miss Marden before I went. I begged her, after breakfast, to take a turn with me on the terrace, and as she hesitated, looking at me distantly, I informed her that it was only to ask her a question and to say good-bye – I was leaving Tranton for *her*.

She came out with me, and we passed slowly round the house three or four times. Nothing is finer than this great airy platform, from which every look is a sweep of the country, with the sea on the furthest edge. It might have been that as we passed the windows we were conspicuous to our friends in the house, who would divine, sarcastically, why I was so significantly bolting. But I didn't care; I only wondered whether they wouldn't really this time make out Sir Edmund Orme, who joined us on one of our turns and strolled slowly on the other side of my companion. Of what transcendent essence he was composed I knew not; I have no theory about him (leaving that to others), any more than I have one about such or such another of my fellow-mortals whom I have elbowed in life. He was as positive, as individual, as ultimate a fact as any of these. Above all he was as respectable, as sensitive a fact; so that I should no more have thought of taking a liberty, of practising an experiment with him, of touching him, for instance, or speaking to him, since he set the example of silence, than I should have thought of committing any other social grossness. He had always, as I saw more fully later, the perfect propriety of his position – had always the appearance of being dressed and, in attitude and aspect, of comporting himself, as the occasion demanded. He looked strange, incontestably, but somehow he always looked *right*. I very soon came to attach an idea of beauty to his unmentionable presence, the beauty of an old story of love and pain. What I ended by feeling was that he was on my side, that he was watching over my interest, that he was looking to it that my heart shouldn't be broken. Oh, he had taken it seriously, his own catastrophe – he had certainly proved that in his day. If poor Mrs Marden, as she told me, had thought it out, I also subjected the case to the finest analysis of which my intellect was capable. It was a case of retributive justice. The mother was to pay, in

suffering, for the suffering she had inflicted, and as the disposition to jilt a lover might have been transmitted to the daughter,
the daughter was to be watched, so that *she* might be made to
suffer should she do an equal wrong. She might reproduce her
mother in character as vividly as she did in face. On the day she
should transgress, in other words, her eyes would be opened
suddenly and unpitiedly to the 'perfect presence', which she
would have to work as she could into her conception of a young
lady's universe. I had no great fear for her, because I didn't
believe she was, in any cruel degree, a coquette. We should have
a good deal of ground to get over before I, at least, should be in
a position to be sacrificed by her. She couldn't throw me over
before she had made a little more of me.

The question I asked her on the terrace that morning was
whether I might continue, during the winter, to come to Mrs
Marden's house. I promised not to come too often and not to
speak to her for three months of the question I had raised the
day before. She replied that I might do as I liked, and on this
we parted.

I carried out the vow I had made her; I held my tongue for
my three months. Unexpectedly to myself there were moments
of this time when she struck me as capable of playing with a
man. I wanted so to make her like me that I became subtle and
ingenious, wonderfully alert, patiently diplomatic. Sometimes I
thought I had earned my reward, brought her to the point of
saying: 'Well, well, you're the best of them all – you may speak
to me now.' Then there was a greater blankness than ever in her

beauty, and on certain days a mocking light in her eyes, of which the meaning seemed to be: 'If you don't take care, I *will* accept you, to have done with you the more effectually.' Mrs Marden was a great help to me simply by believing in me, and I valued her faith all the more that it continued even though there was a sudden intermission of the miracle that had been wrought for me. After our visit to Tranton Sir Edmund Orme gave us a holiday, and I confess it was at first a disappointment to me. I felt less designated, less connected with Charlotte. 'Oh, don't cry till you're out of the wood,' her mother said; 'he has let me off sometimes for six months. He'll break out again when you least expect it – he knows what he's about.' For her these weeks were happy, and she was wise enough not to talk about me to the girl. She was so good as to assure me that I was taking the right way, that I looked as if I felt secure and that in the long run women give way to that. She had known them do it even when the man was a fool for looking so – or was a fool on any terms. For herself she felt it to be a good time, a sort of St Martin's summer of the soul. She was better than she had been for years, and she had me to thank for it. The sense of visitation was light upon her – she wasn't in anguish every time she looked round. Charlotte contradicted me very often, but she contradicted herself still more. That winter was a wonder of mildness, and we often sat out in the sun. I walked up and down with Charlotte, and Mrs Marden, sometimes on a bench, sometimes in a bath-chair, waited for us and smiled at us as we passed. I always looked out for a sign in her face – 'He's with you, he's with you' (she would see him before I should), but nothing came; the season had brought us also a sort of spiritual softness. Toward the end of April the air was so like June that, meeting my two friends one night at some Brighton sociability – an evening party with amateur music – I drew Miss Marden unresistingly out upon a balcony to which a window in one of the rooms stood open. The night was close and thick, the stars were dim, and below us, under the cliff, we heard the regular rumble of the sea. We listened to it a little and we heard mixed with it, from within the house, the sound of a violin accompanied by a piano – a performance which had been our pretext for passing out.

'Do you like me a little better?' I asked, abruptly, after a minute. 'Could you listen to me again?'

I had no sooner spoken than she laid her hand quickly, with a certain force, on my arm. 'Hush! – isn't there someone there?' She was looking into the gloom of the far end of the balcony. This balcony ran the whole width of the house, a width very great in the best of the old houses at Brighton. We were lighted a little by the open window behind us, but the other windows, curtained within, left the darkness undiminished, so that I made out but dimly the figure of a gentleman standing there and look-ing at us. He was in evening dress, like a guest – I saw the vague shine of his white shirt and the pale oval of his face – and he might perfectly have been a guest who had stepped out in advance of us to take the air. Miss Marden took him for one at first – then evidently, even in a few seconds, she saw that the intensity of his gaze was unconventional. What else she saw I couldn't determine; I was too taken up with my own impression to do more than feel the quick contact of her uneasiness. My own impression was in fact the strongest of sensations, a sensation of horror; for what could the thing mean but that the girl at last *saw?* I heard her give a sudden, gasping 'Ah!' and move quickly into the house. It was only afterwards that I knew that I myself had had a totally new emotion – my horror passing into anger, and my anger into a stride along the balcony with a gesture of reprobation. The case was simplified to the vision of a frightened girl whom I loved. I advanced to vindicate her security, but I found nothing there to meet me. It was either all a mistake or Sir Edmund Orme had vanished.

I followed Miss Marden immediately, but there were symptoms of confusion in the drawing-room when I passed in. A lady had fainted, the music had stopped; there was a shuffling of chairs and a pressing forward. The lady was not Charlotte, as I feared, but Mrs Marden, who had suddenly been taken ill. I remember the relief with which I learned this, for to see Charlotte stricken would have been anguish, and her mother's condition gave a channel to her agitation. It was of course all a matter for the people of the house and for the ladies, and I could have no share in attending to my friends or in conducting them to their carriage. Mrs Marden revived and insisted on going home, after which I uneasily withdrew.

I called the next morning to ask about her and was informed that she was better, but when I asked if Miss Marden would see me the message sent down was that it was impossible.

There was nothing for me to do all day but to roam about with a beating heart. But toward evening I received a line in pencil, brought by hand – 'Please come; mother wishes you.' Five minutes afterward I was at the door again and ushered into the drawing-room. Mrs Marden lay upon the sofa, and as soon as I looked at her I saw the shadow of death in her face. But the first thing she said was that she was better, ever so much better; her poor old heart had been behaving queerly again, but now it was quiet. She gave me her hand and I bent over her with my eyes in hers, and in this way I was able to read what she didn't speak – 'I'm really very ill, but appear to take what I say exactly as I say it.' Charlotte stood there beside her, looking not frightened now, but intensely grave, and not meeting my eyes. 'She has told me – she has told me!' her mother went on.

'She has told you?' I stared from one of them to the other, wondering if Mrs Marden meant that the girl had spoken to her of the circumstances on the balcony.

'That you spoke to her again – that you're admirably faithful.'

I felt a thrill of joy at this; it showed me that that memory had been uppermost, and also that Charlotte had wished to say the thing that would soothe her mother most, not the thing that would alarm her. Yet I now knew, myself, as well as if Mrs Marden had told me, that she knew and had known at the moment what her daughter had seen. 'I spoke – I spoke, but she gave me no answer,' I said.

'She will now, won't you, Chartie? I want it so, I want it!' the poor lady murmured, with ineffable wistfulness.

'You're very good to me,' Charlotte said to me, seriously and sweetly, looking fixedly on the carpet. There was something different in her, different from all the past. She had recognized something, she felt a coercion. I could see that she was trembling.

'Ah, if you would let me show you *how* good I can be!' I exclaimed, holding out my hands to her. As I uttered the words I was touched with the knowledge that something had happened. A form had constituted itself on the other side of the bed, and the form leaned over Mrs Marden. My whole being went forth into a mute prayer that Charlotte shouldn't see it and that I should be able to betray nothing. The impulse to glance toward Mrs Marden was even stronger than the involuntary movement of taking in Sir Edmund Orme; but I could resist even that, and Mrs Marden was perfectly still. Charlotte got up to give me her hand, and with the definite act she saw. She gave, with a shriek, one stare of dismay, and another sound, like a wail of one of the lost, fell at the same instant on my ear. But I had already sprung toward the girl to cover her, to veil her face. She had already thrown herself into my arms. I held her there a moment – bending over her, given up to her, feeling each of her throbs with my own and not knowing which was which; then, all of a sudden, coldly, I gathered that we were alone. She released herself. The figure beside the sofa had vanished; but Mrs Marden lay in her place with closed eyes, with something in her stillness that gave us both another terror. Charlotte expressed it in the cry of 'Mother, mother!' with which she flung herself down. I fell on my knees beside her. Mrs Marden had passed away.

Was the sound I heard when Chartie shrieked – the other and still more tragic sound I mean – the despairing cry of the poor lady's death-shock or the articulate sob (it was like a waft from a great tempest), of the exorcized and pacified spirit? Possibly the latter, for that was, mercifully, the last of Sir Edmund Orme.

Brooksmith

WE ARE SCATTERED now, the friends of the late Mr Oliver Offord; but whenever we chance to meet I think we are conscious of a certain esoteric respect for each other. 'Yes, you too have been in Arcadia,' we seem not too grumpily to allow. When I pass the house in Mansfield Street I remember that Arcadia was there. I don't know who has it now, and don't want to know; it's enough to be so sure that if I should ring the bell there would be no such luck for me as that Brooksmith should open the door. Mr Offord, the most agreeable, the most attaching of bachelors, was a retired diplomatist, living on his pension and on something of his own over and above; a good deal confined, by his infirmities, to his fireside and delighted to be found there any afternoon in the year, from five o'clock on, by such visitors as Brooksmith allowed to come up. Brooksmith was his butler and his most intimate friend, to whom we all stood, or I should say sat, in the same relation in which the subject of the sovereign finds himself to the prime minister. By having been for years, in foreign lands, the most delightful

Englishman anyone had ever known, Mr Offord had in my opinion rendered signal service to his country. But I suppose he had been too much liked – liked even by those who didn't like *it* – so that as people of that sort never get titles or dotations for the horrid things they've *not* done, his principal reward was simply that we went to see him.

Oh, we went perpetually, and it was not our fault if he was not overwhelmed with this particular honour. Any visitor who came once came again; to come merely once was a slight nobody, I'm sure, had ever put upon him. His circle therefore was essentially composed of *habitués*, who were *habitués* for each other as well as for him, as those of a happy *salon* should be. I remember vividly every element of the place, down to the intensely Londonish look of the grey opposite houses, in the gap of the white curtains of the high windows, and the exact spot where, on a particular afternoon, I put down my tea-cup for Brooksmith, lingering an instant, to gather it up as if he were plucking a flower. Mr Offord's drawing-room was indeed Brooksmith's garden, his pruned and tended human *parterre*, and if we all flourished there and grew well in our places it was largely owing to his supervision.

Many persons have heard much, though most have doubtless seen little, of the famous institution of the *salon*, and many are born to the depression of knowing that this finest flower of social life refuses to bloom where the English tongue is spoken. The explanation is usually that our women have not the skill to cultivate it – the art to direct through a smiling land, between suggestive shores, a sinuous stream of talk. My affectionate, my pious memory of Mr Offord contradicts this induction only, I fear, more insidiously to confirm it. The sallow and slightly smoked drawing-room in which he spent so large a portion of the last years of his life certainly deserved the distinguished name; but on the other hand it couldn't be said at all to owe its stamp to any intervention throwing into relief the fact that there was no Mrs Offord. The dear man had indeed, at the most, been capable of one of those sacrifices to which women are deemed peculiarly apt: he had recognized – under the influence, in some degree, it is true, of physical infirmity – that if you wish people to find you at home you must manage not to be out. He had in short accepted the truth which many dabblers in the social art are slow to learn, that you must really, as they say, take a line, and that the only way as yet discovered of being at home is to stay at home. Finally his own fireside had become a summary of his habits. Why should he ever have left it? – since this would have been leaving what was notoriously pleasantest in London, the compact charmed cluster (thinning away indeed into casual couples) round the fine old last-century chimney-piece which, with the exception of the remarkable collection of miniatures, was the best thing the place contained. Mr Offord wasn't rich; he had nothing but his pension and the use for life of the some-what superannuated house.

When I'm reminded by some opposed discomfort of the present hour how perfectly we were all handled there, I ask myself once more what had been the secret of such perfection.

One had taken it for granted at the time, for anything that is supremely good produces more acceptance than surprise. I felt we were all happy, but I didn't consider how our happiness was managed. And yet there were questions to be asked, questions that strike me as singularly obvious now that there's nobody to answer them. Mr Offord had solved the insoluble; he had, without feminine help – save in the sense that ladies were dying to come to him and that he saved the lives of several – established a *salon*; but I might have guessed that there was a method in his madness, a law in his success. He hadn't hit it off by a mere fluke. There was an art in it all, and how was the art so hidden? Who indeed if it came to that was the occult artist? Launching this inquiry the other day I had already got hold of the tail of my reply. I was helped by the very wonder of some of the conditions that came back to me – those that used to seem as natural as sunshine in a fine climate.

How was it for instance that we never were a crowd, never either too many or too few, always the right people *with* the right people – there must really have been no wrong people at all – always coming and going, never sticking fast nor overstaying, yet never popping in or out with an indecorous familiarity? How was it that we all sat where we wanted and moved when we wanted and met whom we wanted and escaped whom we wanted; joining, according to the accident of inclination, the general circle or falling in with a single talker on a convenient sofa? Why were all the sofas so convenient, the accidents so happy, the talkers so ready, the listeners so willing, the subjects presented to you in a rotation as quickly fore-ordained as the courses at dinner? A dearth of topics would have been as unheard of as a lapse in the service. These speculations couldn't fail to lead me to the fundamental truth that Brooksmith had been somehow at the bottom of the mystery. If he hadn't established the *salon* at least he had carried it on. Brooksmith in short was the artist!

We felt this covertly at the time, without formulating it, and were conscious, as an ordered and prosperous community, of his even-handed justice, all untainted with flunkeyism. He had none of that vulgarity – his touch was infinitely fine. The delicacy of it was clear to me on the first occasion my eyes rested, as they were so often to rest again, on the domestic revealed, in the turbid light of the street, by the opening of the house-door. I saw on the spot that though he had plenty of school he carried it without arrogance – he had remained articulate and human. *L'École Anglaise* Mr Offord used laughingly to call him when, later on, it happened more than once that we had some conversation about him. But I remember accusing Mr Offord of not doing him quite ideal justice. That he wasn't one of the giants of the school, however, was admitted by my old friend, who really understood him perfectly and was devoted to him, as I shall show; which doubtless poor Brooksmith had himself felt, to his cost, when his value in the market was originally determined. The utility of his class in general is estimated by the foot and the inch, and poor Brooksmith had only about five feet three to put into circulation. He acknowledged the inadequacy of this provision, and I'm sure was penetrated with the everlasting fitness of the relation between service and stature. If *he* had been Mr Offord he certainly would have found Brooksmith wanting, and indeed the laxity of his employer on this score was one of many things he had had to condone and to which he had at last indulgently adapted himself.

I remember the old man's saying to me: 'Oh my servants, if they can live with me a fortnight they can live with me for ever. But it's the first fortnight that tries 'em.' It was in the first fortnight for instance that Brooksmith had had to learn that he was exposed to being addressed as 'my dear fellow' and 'my poor child'. Strange and deep must such a probation have been to him, and he doubtless emerged from it tempered and purified. This was written to a certain extent in his appearance; in his spare, brisk little person, in his cloistered white face and extraordinarily polished hair, which told of responsibility, looked as if it were kept up to the same high standard as the plate; in his small, clear, anxious eyes, even in the permitted, though not exactly encouraged, tuft on his chin. 'He thinks me rather mad, but I've broken him in, and now he likes the place, he likes the company,' said the old man. I embraced this fully after I had become aware that Brooksmith's main characteristic was a deep and shy refinement, though I remember I was rather puzzled when, on another occasion, Mr Offord remarked: 'What he likes is the talk — mingling in the conversation.' I was conscious I had never seen Brooksmith permit himself this freedom, but I guessed in a moment that what Mr Offord alluded to was a participation more intense than any speech could have represented – that of being perpetually present on a hundred legitimate pretexts, errands, necessities, and breathing the very atmosphere of criticism, the famous criticism of life. 'Quite an education, sir, isn't it, sir?' he said to me one day at the foot of the stairs when he was letting me out; and I've always remembered the words and the tone as the first sign of the quickening drama of poor Brooksmith's fate. It was indeed an education, but to what was this sensitive young man of thirty-five, of the servile class, being educated?

Practically and inevitably, for the time, to companionship, to the perpetual, the even exaggerated reference and appeal of a person brought to dependence by his time of life and his infirmities and always addicted moreover – this was the exaggeration – to the art of giving you pleasure by letting you do things for him. There were certain things Mr Offord was capable of pretending he liked you to do even when he didn't – this, I mean, if he thought *you* liked them. If it happened that you didn't either – which was rare, yet might be – of course there were cross-purposes; but Brooksmith was there to prevent their going very far. This was precisely the way he acted as moderator; he averted misunderstandings or cleared them up. He had been capable, strange as it may appear, of acquiring for this purpose an insight into the French tongue, which was often used at Mr Offord's; for besides being habitual to most of the foreigners, and they were many, who haunted the place or arrived with letters – letters often requiring a little worried consideration, of which Brooksmith always had cognizance – it had really become the primary language of the master of the house. I don't know if all the *malentendus* were in French, but almost all the explanations were, and this didn't a bit prevent Brooksmith's following them. I know Mr Offord used to read passages to him from Montaigne and Saint-Simon, for he read perpetually when alone – when *they* were alone, that is – and Brooksmith was always about. Perhaps you'll say no wonder Mr Offord's butler regarded him as 'rather mad'. However, if I'm not sure what he thought about Montaigne I'm convinced he admired Saint-Simon. A certain feeling for letters must have rubbed off on him from the mere handling of his master's books, which he was always carrying to and fro and putting back in their places.

I often noticed that if an anecdote or a quotation, much more a lively discussion, was going forward, he would, if busy with the fire or the curtains, the lamp or the tea, find a pretext for remaining in the room till the point should be reached. If his purpose was to catch it you weren't discreet, you were in fact scarce human, to call him off, and I shall never forget a look, a hard, stony stare – I caught it in its passage – which, one day when there were a good many people in the room, he fastened upon the footman who was helping him in the service and who, in an undertone, had asked him some irrelevant question. It was the only manifestation of harshness I ever observed on Brooksmith's part, and I at first wondered what was the matter. Then I became conscious that Mr Offord was relating a very curious anecdote, never before perhaps made so public, and imparted to the narrator by an eye-witness of the fact, bearing on Lord Byron's life in Italy. Nothing would induce me to reproduce it here, but Brooksmith had been in danger of losing it. If I ever should venture to reproduce it I shall feel how much I lose in not having my fellow auditor to refer to.

The first day Mr Offord's door was closed was therefore a dark date in contemporary history. It was raining hard and my umbrella was wet, but Brooksmith received it from me exactly as if this were a preliminary for going upstairs. I observed however that instead of putting it away he held it poised and trickling over the rug, and I then became aware that he was looking at me with deep, acknowledging eyes – his air of universal responsibility. I immediately understood – there was scarce need of question and answer as they passed between us. When I took in that our good friend had given up as never before, though only for the occasion, I exclaimed dolefully: 'What a difference it will make – and to how many people!'

'I shall be one of them, sir!' said Brooksmith; and that was the beginning of the end.

Mr Offord came down again, but the spell was broken, the great sign being that the conversation was for the first time not directed. It wandered and stumbled, a little frightened, like a lost child – it had let go the nurse's hand. 'The worst of it is that now we shall talk about my health – *c'est la fin de tout*,' Mr Offord said when he reappeared; and then I recognized what a note of change that would be – for he had never tolerated anything so provincial. We 'ran' to each other's health as little as to the daily weather. The talk became ours, in a word – not his; and as ours, even when *he* talked, it could only be inferior. In this form it was a distress to Brooksmith, whose attention now wandered from it altogether: he had so much closer a vision of his master's intimate conditions than our superficialities represented. There were better hours, and he was more in and out of the room, but I could see he was conscious of the decline, almost of the collapse, of our great institution. He seemed to wish to take counsel with me about it, to feel responsible for its going on in some form or other. When for the second period – the first had lasted several days – he had to tell me that his employer didn't receive, I half expected to hear him say after a moment: 'Do you think I ought to, sir, in his place?' – as he might have asked me, with the return of autumn, if I thought he had better light the drawing-room fire.

He had a resigned philosophic sense of what his guests – our guests, as I came to regard them in our colloquies – would expect. His feeling was that he wouldn't absolutely have approved of himself as a substitute for Mr Offord; but he was so saturated with the religion of habit that he would have made, for our friends, the necessary sacrifice to the divinity. He would take them on a little further, till they could look about them. I think I saw him also mentally confronted with the opportunity to deal – for once in his life – with some of his own dumb preferences, his limitations of sympathy, *weeding* a little in prospect and returning to a purer tradition. It was not unknown to me that he considered that toward the end of our host's career a certain laxity of selection had crept in.

At last it came to be the case that we all found the closed door more often than the open one; but even when it was closed Brooksmith managed a crack for me to squeeze through; so that practically I never turned away without having paid a visit. The difference simply came to be that the visit was to Brooksmith. It took place in the hall, at the familiar foot of the stairs, and we didn't sit down, at least Brooksmith didn't; moreover it was devoted wholly to one topic and always had the air of being already over – beginning, so to say, at the end. But it was always interesting – it always gave me something to think about. It's true that the subject of my meditation was ever the same – ever 'It's all very well, but what *will* become of Brooksmith?' Even my private answer to this question left me still unsatisfied. No doubt Mr Offord would provide for him, but *what* would he provide? – that was the great point. He couldn't provide society; and society had become a necessity of Brooksmith's nature. I must add that he never showed a symptom of what I may call sordid solicitude – anxiety on his own account. He was rather livid and intensely grave, as befitted a man before whose eyes the 'shade of that which once was great' was passing away. He had the solemnity of a person winding up, under depressing circumstances, a long-established and celebrated business; he was a kind of social executor or liquidator. But his manner seemed to testify exclusively to the uncertainty of *our* future. I couldn't in those days have afforded it – I lived in two rooms in Jermyn Street and didn't 'keep a man'; but even if my income had permitted I shouldn't have ventured to say to Brooksmith (emulating Mr Offord), 'My dear fellow, I'll take you on.' The whole tone of our intercourse was so much more an implication that it was I who should now want a lift. Indeed there was a tacit assurance in Brooksmith's whole attitude that he should have me on his mind.

One of the most assiduous members of our circle had been Lady Kenyon, and I remember his telling me one day that her ladyship had in spite of her own infirmities, lately much aggravated, been in person to inquire. In answer to this I remarked that she would feel it more than anyone. Brooksmith had a pause before saying in a certain tone – there's no reproducing some of his tones – 'I'll go and see her.' I went to see her myself and learned he had waited on her; but when I said to her, in the form of a joke but with a core of earnest, that when all was over some of us ought to combine, to club together, and set Brooksmith up on his own account, she replied a trifle disappointingly: 'Do you mean in a public-house?' I looked at her in a way that I think Brooksmith himself would have approved, and then I answered: 'Yes, the Offord Arms.' What I had meant of course was that for the love of art itself we ought to look to it that such a peculiar faculty and so much acquired experience shouldn't be wasted. I really think that if we had caused a few black-edged cards to be struck off and circulated – 'Mr Brooksmith will continue to receive on the old premises from four to seven; business carried on as usual during the alterations' – the greater number of us would have rallied.

Several times he took me upstairs — always by his own proposal — and our dear old friend, in bed (in a curious flowered and brocaded *casaque* which made him, especially as his head was tied up in a handkerchief to match, look, to my imagination, like the dying Voltaire) held for ten minutes a sadly shrunken little *salon*. I felt indeed each time as if I were attending the last *coucher* of some social sovereign. He was royally whimsical about his sufferings and not at all concerned — quite as if the Constitution provided for the case — about his successor. He glided over *our* sufferings charmingly, and none of his jokes — it was a gallant abstention, some of them would have been so easy — were at our expense. Now and again, I confess, there was one at Brooksmith's, but so pathetically sociable as to make the excellent man look at me in a way that seemed to say: 'Do exchange a glance with me, or I shan't be able to stand it.' What he wasn't able to stand was not what Mr Offord said about him, but what he wasn't able to say in return. His idea of conversation for himself was giving you the convenience of speaking to him; and when he went to 'see' Lady Kenyon, for instance, it was to carry her the tribute of his receptive silence. Where would the speech of his betters have been if proper service had been a manifestation of sound? In that case the fundamental difference would have had to be shown by *their* dumbness, and many of them, poor things, were dumb enough without that provision. Brooksmith took an unfailing interest in the preservation of the fundamental difference; it was the thing he had most on his conscience.

What had become of it, however, when Mr Offord passed away like any inferior person – was relegated to eternal stillness after the manner of a butler above-stairs? His aspect on the event – for the several successive days – may be imagined, and the multiplication by funereal observance of the things he didn't say. When everything was over – it was late the same day – I knocked at the door of the house of mourning as I so often had done before. I could never call on Mr Offord again, but I had come literally to call on Brooksmith. I wanted to ask him if there was anything I could do for him, tainted with vagueness as this inquiry could only be. My presumptuous dream of taking him into my own service had died away: my service wasn't worth his being taken into. My offer could only be to help him to find another place, and yet there was an indelicacy, as it were, in taking for granted that his thoughts would immediately be fixed on another. I had a hope that he would be able to give his life a different form – though certainly not the form, the frequent result of such bereavements, of his setting up a little shop. That would have been dreadful; for I should have wished to forward any enterprise he might embark in, yet how could I have brought myself to go and pay him shillings and take back coppers, over a counter? My visit then was simply an intended compliment. He took it as such, gratefully and with all the tact in the world. He knew I really couldn't help him and that I knew he knew I couldn't; but we discussed the situation – with a good deal of elegant generality – at the foot of the stairs, in the hall already dismantled, where I had so often discussed other situations with him. The executors were in possession, as was still more apparent when he made me pass for a few minutes into the dining-room, where various objects were muffled up for removal.

Two definite facts, however, he had to communicate; one being that he was to leave the house for ever that night (servants, for some mysterious reason, seem always to depart by night), and the other – he mentioned it only at the last and with hesitation – that he was already aware his late master had left him a legacy of eighty pounds. 'I'm very glad,' I said, and Brooksmith was of the same mind: 'It was so like him to think of me.' This was all that passed between us on the subject, and I know nothing of his judgement of Mr Offord's memento. Eighty pounds are always eighty pounds, and no one has ever left *me* an equal sum; but, all the same, for Brooksmith, I was disappointed. I don't know what I had expected, but it was almost a shock. Eighty pounds might stock a small shop – a *very* small shop; but, I repeat, I couldn't bear to think of that. I asked my friend if he had been able to save a little, and he replied: 'No, sir; I've had to do things.' I didn't inquire what things they might have been; they were his own affair, and I took his word for them as assentingly as if he had had the greatness of an ancient house to keep up; especially as there was something in his manner that seemed to convey a prospect of further sacrifice.

'I shall have to turn round a bit, sir – I shall have to look about me,' he said; and then he added indulgently, magnanimously: 'If you should happen to hear of anything for me—'

I couldn't let him finish; this was, in its essence, too much in the really grand manner. It would be a help to my getting him off my mind to be able to pretend I *could* find the right place, and that help he wished to give me, for it was doubtless painful to him to see me in so false a position. I interposed with a few words to the effect of how well aware I was that wherever he should go, whatever he should do, he would miss our old friend terribly – miss him even more than I should, having been with him so much more. This led him to make the speech that has remained with me as the very text of the whole episode.

'Oh sir, it's sad for *you*, very sad indeed, and for a great many gentlemen and ladies; that it is, sir. But for me, sir, it is, if I may say so, still graver even than that: it's just the loss of something that was everything. For me, sir,' he went on with rising tears, 'he was just *all*, if you know what I mean, sir. You have others, sir, I daresay – not that I would have you understand me to speak of them as in any way tantamount. But you have the pleasures of society, sir; if it's only in talking about him, sir, as I daresay you do freely – for all his blest memory has to fear from it – with gentlemen and ladies who have had the same honour. That's not for me, sir, and I've to keep my associations to myself. Mr Offord was *my* society, and now, you see, I just haven't any. You go back to conversation, sir, after all, and I go back to my place,' Brooksmith stammered, without exaggerated irony or dramatic bitterness, but with a flat unstudied veracity and his hand on the knob of the street-door. He turned it to let me out and then he added: 'I just go downstairs, sir, again, and I stay there.'

'My poor child,' I replied in my emotion, quite as Mr Offord used to speak, 'my dear fellow, leave it to me: *we'll* look after you, we'll all do something for you.'

'Ah, if you could give me someone *like* him! But there ain't two such in the world,' Brooksmith said as we parted.

He had given me his address – the place where he would be to be heard of. For a long time I had no occasion to make use of the information: he proved on trial so very difficult a case. The people who knew him and had known Mr Offord didn't want to take him, and yet I couldn't bear to try to thrust him among strangers – strangers to his past when not to his present. I spoke to many of our old friends about him and found them all governed by the odd mixture of feelings of which I myself was conscious – as well as disposed, further, to entertain a suspicion that he was 'spoiled', with which I then would have nothing to do. In plain terms a certain embarrassment, a sensible awkwardness when they thought of it, attached to the idea of using him as a menial: they had met him so often in society. Many of them would have asked him, and did ask him, or rather did ask me to ask him, to come and see them, but a mere visiting-list was not what I wanted for him. He was too short for people who were very particular; nevertheless I heard of an opening in a diplomatic household which led me to write him a note, though I was looking much less for something grand than for something human. Five days later I heard from him. The secretary's wife had decided, after keeping him waiting till then, that she couldn't take a servant out of a house in which there hadn't been a lady. The note had a P.S.: 'It's a good job there wasn't, sir, such a lady as some.'

A week later he came to see me and told me he was 'suited', committed to some highly respectable people – they were something quite immense in the City – who lived on the Bayswater side of the Park. 'I daresay it will be rather poor, sir,' he admitted; 'but I've seen the fireworks, haven't I, sir? – it can't be fireworks *every* night. After Mansfield Street there ain't much choice.' There was a certain amount, however, it seemed; for the following year, calling one day on a country cousin, a lady of a certain age who was spending a fortnight in town with some friends of her own, a family unknown to me and resident in Chester Square, the door of the house was opened, to my surprise and gratification, by Brooksmith in person. When I came out I had some conversation with him, from which I gathered that he had found the large City people too dull for endurance, and I guessed, though he didn't say it, that he had found them vulgar as well. I don't know what judgement he would have passed on his actual patrons if my relative hadn't been their friend; but in view of that connection he abstained from comment.

None was necessary, however, for before the lady in question brought her visit to a close they honoured me with an invitation to dinner, which I accepted. There was a largeish party on the occasion, but I confess I thought of Brooksmith rather more than of the seated company. They required no depth of attention – they were all referable to usual irredeemable inevitable types. It was the world of cheerful commonplace and conscious gentility and prosperous density, a full-fed, material, insular world, a world of hideous florid plate and ponderous order and thin conversation. There wasn't a word said about Byron, or even about a minor bard then much in view. Nothing would have induced me to look at Brooksmith in the course of the repast, and I felt sure that not even my overturning the wine would have induced him to meet my eye. We were in intellectual sympathy – we felt, as regards each other, a degree of social responsibility. In short we had been in Arcadia together, and we had both come to *this*! No wonder we were ashamed to be confronted. When he had helped on my overcoat, as I was going away, we parted, for the first time since the earliest days of Mansfield Street, in silence. I thought he looked lean and wasted, and I guessed that his new place wasn't more 'human' than his previous one. There was plenty of beef and beer, but there was no reciprocity. The question for him to have asked before accepting the position wouldn't have been 'How many footmen are kept?' but 'How much imagination?'

The next time I went to the house – I confess it wasn't very soon – I encountered his successor, a personage who evidently enjoyed the good fortune of never having quitted his natural level. Could any be higher? he seemed to ask – over the heads of three footmen and even of some visitors. He made me feel as if Brooksmith were dead; but I didn't dare to inquire – I couldn't have borne his 'I haven't the least idea, sir.' I despatched a note to the address that worthy had given me after Mr Offord's death, but I received no answer. Six months later however I was favoured with a visit from an elderly, dreary, dingy person who introduced herself to me as Mr Brooksmith's aunt and from whom I learned that he was out of place and out of health and had allowed her to come and say to me that if I could spare half an hour to look in at him he would take it as a rare honour.

I went the next day – his messenger had given me a new address – and found my friend lodged in a short sordid street in Marylebone, one of those corners of London that wear the last expression of sickly meanness. The room into which I was shown was above the small establishment of a dyer and cleaner who had inflated kid gloves and discoloured shawls in his shop-front. There was a great deal of grimy infant life up and down the place, and there was a hot moist smell within, as of the 'boiling' of dirty linen. Brooksmith sat with a blanket over his legs at a clean little window where, from behind stiff bluish-white curtains, he could look across at a huckster's and a tinsmith's and a small greasy public-house. He had passed through an illness and was convalescent, and his mother, as well as his aunt, was in attendance on him. I liked the nearer relative, who was bland and intensely humble, but I had my doubts of the remoter, whom I connected perhaps unjustly with the opposite public-house – she seemed somehow greasy with the same grease – and whose furtive eye followed every movement of my hand as to see if it weren't going into my pocket. It didn't take this direction – I couldn't, unsolicited, put myself at that sort of ease with Brooksmith. Several times the door of the room opened and mysterious old women peeped in and shuffled back again. I don't know who they were; poor Brooksmith seemed encompassed with vague, prying, beery females.

He was vague himself, and evidently weak, and much embarrassed, and not an allusion was made between us to Mansfield Street. The vision of the *salon* of which he had been an ornament hovered before me, however, by contrast, sufficiently. He assured me he was really getting better, and his mother remarked that he would come round if he could only get his spirits up. The aunt echoed this opinion, and I became more sure that in her own case she knew where to go for such a purpose. I'm afraid I was rather weak with my old friend, for I neglected the opportunity, so exceptionally good, to rebuke the levity which had led him to throw up honourable positions – fine, stiff, steady berths in Bayswater and Belgravia, with morning prayers, as I knew, attached to one of them. Very likely his reasons had been profane and sentimental; he didn't want morning prayers, he wanted to be somebody's dear fellow; but I couldn't be the person to rebuke him. He shuffled these episodes out of sight – I saw he had no wish to discuss them. I noted further, strangely enough, that it would probably be a questionable pleasure for him to see me again: he doubted now even of my power to condone his aberrations. He didn't wish to have to explain; and his behaviour was likely in future to need explanation. When I bade him farewell he looked at me a moment with eyes that said everything: 'How can I talk about those exquisite years in this place, before these people, with the old women poking their heads in? It was very good of you to come to see me; it wasn't my idea – *she* brought you. We've said everything; it's over; you'll lose all patience with me, and I'd rather you shouldn't see the rest.' I sent him some money in a letter the next day, but I saw the rest only in the light of a barren sequel.

A whole year after my visit to him I became aware once, in dining out, that Brooksmith was one of the several servants who hovered behind our chairs. He hadn't opened the door of the house to me, nor had I recognized him in the array of retainers in the hall. This time I tried to catch his eye, but he never gave me a chance, and when he handed me a dish I could only be careful to thank him audibly. Indeed I partook of two *entrées* of which I had my doubts, subsequently converted into certainties, in order not to snub him. He looked well enough in health, but much older, and wore in an exceptionally marked degree the glazed and expressionless mask of the British domestic *de race*. I saw with dismay that if I hadn't known him I should have taken him, on the showing of his countenance, for an extravagant illustration of irresponsive servile gloom. I said to myself that he had become a reactionary, gone over to the Philistines, thrown himself into religion, the religion of his 'place', like a foreign lady *sur le retour*. I divined moreover that he was only engaged for the evening – he had become a mere waiter, had joined the band of the white-waistcoated who 'go out'. There was something pathetic in this fact – it was a terrible vulgarization of Brooksmith. It was the mercenary prose of butlerhood; he had given up the struggle for the poetry. If reciprocity was what he had missed, where was the reciprocity now? Only in the bottoms of the wineglasses and the five shillings – or whatever they get – clapped into his hand by the permanent man. However, I supposed he had taken up a precarious branch of his profession because it after all sent him less downstairs. His relations with London society were more superficial, but they were of course more various. As I went away on this occasion I looked out for him eagerly among the four or five attendants whose perpendicular persons, fluting the walls of London passages, are supposed to lubricate the process of departure; but he was not on duty. I asked one of the others if he were not in the house, and received the prompt answer: 'Just left, sir. Anything I can do for you, sir?' I wanted to say 'Please give him my kind regards'; but I abstained – I didn't want to compromise him; and I never came across him again.

Often and often, in dining out, I looked for him, sometimes accepting invitations on purpose to multiply the chances of my meeting him. But always in vain; so that as I met many other members of the casual class over and over again I at last adopted the theory that he always procured a list of expected guests beforehand and kept away from the banquets which he thus learned I was to grace. At last I gave up hope, and one day at the end of three years I received another visit from his aunt. She was drearier and dingier, almost squalid, and she was in great tribulation and want. Her sister, Mrs Brooksmith, had been dead a year, and three months later her nephew had disappeared. He had always looked after her a bit – since her troubles; I never knew what her troubles had been – and now she hadn't so much as a petticoat to pawn. She had also a niece, to whom she had been everything before her troubles, but the niece had treated her most shameful. These were details; the great and romantic fact was Brooksmith's final evasion of his fate. He had gone out to wait one evening as usual, in a white waistcoat she had done up for him with her own hands – being due at a large party up Kensington way. But he had never come home again, and had never arrived at the large party, nor at any party that anyone could make out. No trace of him had come to light – no gleam of the white waistcoat had pierced the obscurity of his doom. This news was a sharp shock to me, for I had my ideas about his real destination. His aged relative had promptly, as she said, guessed the worst. Somehow and somewhere he had got out of the way altogether, and now I trust that, with characteristic deliberation, he is changing the plates of the immortal gods. As my depressing visitant also said, he never *had* got his spirits up. I was fortunately able to dismiss her with her own somewhat improved. But the dim ghost of poor Brooksmith is one of those that I see. He had indeed been spoiled.

Owen Wingrave

I

'UPON MY HONOUR you must be off your head!' cried Spencer Coyle, as the young man, with a white face, stood there panting a little and repeating 'Really, I've quite decided,' and 'I assure you I've thought it all out.' They were both pale, but Owen Wingrave smiled in a manner exasperating to his interlocutor, who however still discriminated sufficiently to see that his grimace (it was like an irrelevant leer) was the result of extreme and conceivable nervousness.

'It was certainly a mistake to have gone so far; but that is exactly why I feel I mustn't go further,' poor Owen said, waiting mechanically, almost humbly (he wished not to swagger, and indeed he had nothing to swagger about) and carrying through the window to the stupid opposite houses the dry glitter of his eyes.

'I'm unspeakably disgusted. You've made me dreadfully ill,' Mr Coyle went on, looking thoroughly upset.

'I'm very sorry. It was the fear of the effect on you that kept me from speaking sooner.'

'You should have spoken three months ago. Don't you know your mind from one day to the other?'

The young man for a moment said nothing. Then he replied with a little tremor: 'You're very angry with me, and I expected it. I'm awfully obliged to you for all you've done for me. I'll do anything else for you in return, but I can't do that. Everyone else will let me have it, of course. I'm prepared for it – I'm prepared for everything. That's what has taken the time: to be sure I was prepared. I think it's your displeasure I feel most and regret most. But little by little you'll get over it.'

'*You'll* get over it rather faster, I suppose!' Spencer Coyle satirically exclaimed. He was quite as agitated as his young friend, and they were evidently in no condition to prolong an encounter in which they each drew blood. Mr Coyle was a professional 'coach'; he prepared young men for the army, taking only three or four at a time, to whom he applied the irresistible stimulus of which the possession was both his secret and his fortune. He had not a great establishment; he would have said himself that it was not a wholesale business. Neither his system, his health nor his temper could have accommodated itself to numbers; so he weighed and measured his pupils and turned away more applicants than he passed. He was an artist in his line, caring only for picked subjects and capable of sacrifices almost passionate for the individual. He liked ardent young men (there were kinds of capacity to which he was indifferent) and he had taken a particular fancy to Owen Wingrave. This young man's facility really fascinated him. His candidates usually did wonders, and he might have sent up a multitude. He was a person of exactly the stature of the great Napoleon, with a certain flicker of genius in his light blue eye: it had been said of him that he looked like a pianist. The tone of his favourite pupil now expressed, without intention indeed, a superior wisdom which irritated him. He had not especially suffered before from Wingrave's high opinion of himself, which had seemed justified by remarkable parts; but today it struck him as intolerable. He cut short the discussion, declining absolutely to regard their relations as terminated, and remarked to his pupil that he had better go off somewhere (down to Eastbourne, say; the sea would bring him round) and take a few days to find his feet and come to his senses. He could afford the time, he was so well up: when Spencer Coyle remembered how well up he was he could have boxed his ears. The tall, athletic young man was not physically a subject for simplified reasoning; but there was a troubled gentleness in his handsome face, the index of compunction mixed with pertinacity, which signified that if it could have done any good he would have turned both cheeks. He evidently didn't pretend that his wisdom was superior; he only presented it as his own. It was his own career after all that was in question. He couldn't refuse to go through the form of trying Eastbourne or at least of holding his tongue, though there was that in his manner which implied that if he should do so it would be really to give Mr Coyle a chance to recuperate. He didn't feel a bit overworked, but there was nothing more natural than that with their tremendous pressure Mr Coyle should be. Mr Coyle's own intellect would derive an advantage from his pupil's holiday. Mr Coyle saw what he meant, but he controlled himself; he only demanded, as his right, a truce of three days. Owen Wingrave granted it, though as fostering sad illusions this went visibly against his conscience; but before they separated the famous crammer remarked:

'All the same I feel as if I ought to see someone. I think you mentioned to me that your aunt had come to town?'

'Oh yes; she's in Baker Street. Do go and see her,' the boy said comfortingly.

Mr Coyle looked at him an instant. 'Have you broached this folly to her?'

'Not yet – to no one. I thought it right to speak to you first.'

'Oh, what you "think right"!' cried Spencer Coyle, outraged by his young friend's standards. He added that he would probably call on Miss Wingrave; after which the recreant youth got out of the house.

Owen Wingrave didn't however start punctually for Eastbourne; he only directed his steps to Kensington Gardens, from which Mr Coyle's desirable residence (he was terribly expensive and had a big house) was not far removed. The famous coach 'put up' his pupils, and Owen had mentioned to the butler that he would be back to dinner. The spring day was warm to his young blood, and he had a book in his pocket which, when he had passed into the gardens and, after a short stroll, dropped into a chair, he took out with the slow, soft sigh that finally ushers in a pleasure postponed. He stretched his long legs and began to read it; it was a volume of Goethe's poems. He had been for days in a state of the highest tension, and now that the cord had snapped the relief was proportionate; only it was characteristic of him that this deliverance should take the form of an intellectual pleasure. If he had thrown up the probability of a magnificent career it was not to dawdle along Bond Street nor parade his indifference in the window of a club. At any rate he had in a few moments forgotten everything – the tremendous pressure, Mr Coyle's disappointment, and even his formidable aunt in Baker Street. If these watchers had overtaken him there would surely have been some excuse for their exasperation. There was no doubt he was perverse, for his very choice of a pastime only showed how he had got up his German.

'What the devil's the matter with him, do *you* know?' Spencer Coyle asked that afternoon of young Lechmere, who had never before observed the head of the establishment to set a fellow such an example of bad language. Young Lechmere was not only Wingrave's fellow-pupil, he was supposed to be his intimate, indeed quite his best friend, and had unconsciously performed for Mr Coyle the office of making the promise of his great gifts more vivid by contrast. He was short and sturdy and as a general thing uninspired, and Mr Coyle, who found no amusement in believing in him, had never thought him less exciting than as he stared now out of a face from which you could never guess whether he had caught an idea. Young Lechmere concealed such achievements as if they had been youthful indiscretions. At any rate he could evidently conceive no reason why it should be thought there was anything more than usual the matter with the companion of his studies; so Mr Coyle had to continue:

'He declines to go up. He chucks the whole thing!'

The first thing that struck young Lechmere in the case was the freshness it had imparted to the governor's vocabulary.

'He doesn't want to go to Sandhurst?'

'He doesn't want to go anywhere. He gives up the army altogether. He objects,' said Mr Coyle, in a tone that made young Lechmere almost hold his breath, 'to the military profession.'

'Why, it has been the profession of all his family!'

'Their profession? It has been their religion! Do you know Miss Wingrave?'

'Oh, yes. Isn't she awful?' young Lechmere candidly ejaculated.

His instructor demurred.

'She's formidable, if you mean that, and it's right she should be; because somehow in her very person, good maiden lady as she is, she represents the might, she represents the traditions and the exploits of the British army. She represents the expansive property of the English name. I think his family can be trusted to come down on him, but every influence should be set in motion. I want to know what yours is. Can *you* do anything in the matter?'

'I can try a couple of rounds with him,' said young Lechmere reflectively. 'But he knows a fearful lot. He has the most extraordinary ideas.'

'Then he has told you some of them – he has taken you into his confidence?'

'I've heard him jaw by the yard,' smiled the honest youth. 'He has told me he despises it.'

'What *is* it he despises? I can't make out.'

The most consecutive of Mr Coyle's nurslings considered a moment, as if he were conscious of a responsibility.

'Why, I think, military glory. He says we take the wrong view of it.'

'He oughtn't to talk to *you* that way. It's corrupting the youth of Athens. It's sowing sedition.'

'Oh, I'm all right!' said young Lechmere. 'And he never told me he meant to chuck it. I always thought he meant to see it through, simply because he had to. He'll argue on any side you like. It's a tremendous pity – I'm sure he'd have a big career.'

'Tell him so, then; plead with him; struggle with him – for God's sake.'

'I'll do what I can – I'll tell him it's a regular shame.'

'Yes, strike *that* note – insist on the disgrace of it.'

The young man gave Mr Coyle a more perceptive glance. 'I'm sure he wouldn't do anything dishonourable.'

'Well – it won't look right. He must be made to feel *that* – work it up. Give him a comrade's point of view – that of a brother-in-arms.'

'That's what I thought we were going to be!' young Lechmere mused romantically, much uplifted by the nature of the mission imposed on him. 'He's an awfully good sort.'

'No one will think so if he backs out!' said Spencer Coyle.

'They mustn't say it to *me*!' his pupil rejoined with a flush.

Mr Coyle hesitated a moment, noting his tone and aware that in the perversity of things, though this young man was a born soldier, no excitement would ever attach to *his* alternatives save perhaps on the part of the nice girl to whom at an early day he was sure to be placidly united. 'Do you like him very much – do you believe in him?'

Young Lechmere's life in these days was spent in answering terrible questions; but he had never been subjected to so queer an interrogation as this. 'Believe in him? Rather!'

'Then *save* him!'

The poor boy was puzzled, as if it were forced upon him by this intensity that there was more in such an appeal than could appear on the surface; and he doubtless felt that he was only entering into a complex situation when after another moment, with his hands in his pockets, he replied hopefully but not pompously: 'I daresay I can bring him round!'

II

BEFORE SEEING young Lechmere Mr Coyle had determined to telegraph an inquiry to Miss Wingrave. He had prepaid the answer, which, being promptly put into his hand, brought the interview we have just related to a close. He immediately drove off to Baker Street, where the lady had said she awaited him, and five minutes after he got there, as he sat with Owen Wingrave's remarkable aunt, he repeated over several times, in his angry sadness and with the infallibility of his experience: 'He's so intelligent – he's so intelligent!' He had declared it had been a luxury to put such a fellow through.

'Of course he's intelligent, what else could he be? We've never, that I know of, had but *one* idiot in the family!' said Jane Wingrave. This was an allusion that Mr Coyle could understand, and it brought home to him another of the reasons for the disappointment, the humiliation as it were, of the good people at Paramore, at the same time that it gave an example of the conscientious coarseness he had on former occasions observed in his interlocutress. Poor Philip Wingrave, her late brother's eldest son, was literally imbecile and banished from view; deformed, unsocial, irretrievable, he had been relegated to a private asylum and had become among the friends of the family only a little hushed lugubrious legend. All the hopes of the house, picturesque Paramore, now unintermittently old Sir Philip's rather melancholy home (his infirmities would keep him there to the last) were therefore collected on the second boy's head, which nature, as if in compunction for her previous botch, had, in addition to making it strikingly handsome, filled with marked originalities and talents. These two had been the only children of the old man's only son, who, like so many of his ancestors, had given up a gallant young life to the service of his country. Owen Wingrave the elder had received his death-cut, in close-quarters, from an Afghan sabre; the blow had come crashing across his skull. His wife, at that time in India, was about to give birth to her third child; and when the event took place, in darkness and anguish, the baby came lifeless into the world and the mother sank under the multiplication of her woes. The second of the little boys in England, who was at Paramore with his grandfather, became the peculiar charge of his aunt, the only unmarried one, and during the interesting Sunday that, by urgent invitation, Spencer Coyle, busy as he was, had, after consenting to put Owen through, spent under that roof, the celebrated crammer received a vivid impression of the influence exerted at least in intention by Miss Wingrave. Indeed the picture of this short visit remained with the observant little man a curious one – the vision of an impoverished Jacobean house, shabby and remarkably 'creepy', but full of character still and full of felicity as a setting for the distinguished figure of the peaceful old soldier. Sir Philip Wingrave, a relic rather than a celebrity, was a small, brown, erect octogenarian, with smouldering eyes and a studied courtesy. He liked to do the diminished honours of his house, but even when with a shaky hand he lighted a bedroom candle for a deprecating guest it was impossible not to feel that beneath the surface he was a merciless old warrior. The eye of the imagination could glance back into his crowded Eastern past – back at episodes in which his scrupulous forms would only have made him more terrible.

Mr Coyle remembered also two other figures – a faded inoffensive Mrs Julian, domesticated there by a system of frequent visits as the widow of an officer and a particular friend of Miss Wingrave, and a remarkably clever little girl of eighteen, who was this lady's daughter and who struck the speculative visitor as already formed for other relations. She was very impertinent to Owen, and in the course of a long walk that he had taken with the young man and the effect of which, in much talk, had been to clinch his high opinion of him, he had learned (for Owen chattered confidentially) that Mrs Julian was the sister of a very gallant gentleman, Captain Hume-Walker, of the Artillery, who had fallen in the Indian Mutiny and between whom and Miss Wingrave (it had been that lady's one known concession) a passage of some delicacy, taking a tragic turn, was believed to have been enacted. They had been engaged to be married, but she had given way to the jealousy of her nature – had broken with him and sent him off to his fate, which had been horrible. A passionate sense of having wronged him, a hard eternal remorse had thereupon taken possession of her, and when his poor sister, linked also to a soldier, had by a still heavier blow been left almost without resources, she had devoted herself charitably to a long expiation. She had sought comfort in taking

Mrs Julian to live much of the time at Paramore, where she became an unremunerated though not uncriticized housekeeper, and Spencer Coyle suspected that it was a part of this comfort that she could at her leisure trample on her. The impression of Jane Wingrave was not the faintest he had gathered on that intensifying Sunday – an occasion singularly tinged for him with the sense of bereavement and mourning and memory, of names never mentioned, of the far-away plaint of widows and the echoes of battles and bad news. It was all military indeed, and Mr Coyle was made to shudder a little at the profession of which he helped to open the door to harmless young men. Miss Wingrave moreover might have made such a bad conscience worse – so cold and clear a good one looked at him out of her hard, fine eyes and trumpeted in her sonorous voice.

She was a high, distinguished person; angular but not awkward, with a large forehead and abundant black hair, arranged like that of a woman conceiving perhaps excusably of her head as 'noble', and irregularly streaked today with white. If however she represented for Spencer Coyle the genius of a military race it was not that she had the step of a grenadier or the vocabulary of a camp-follower; it was only that such sympathies were vividly implied in the general fact to which her very presence and each of her actions and glances and tones were a constant and direct allusion – the paramount valour of her family. If she was military it was because she sprang from a military house and because she wouldn't for the world have been anything but what the Wingraves had been.

She was almost vulgar about her ancestors, and if one had been tempted to quarrel with her one would have found a fair pretext in her defective sense of proportion. This temptation however said nothing to Spencer Coyle, for whom as a strong character revealing itself in colour and sound she was a spectacle and who was glad to regard her as a force exerted on his own side. He wished her nephew had more of her narrowness instead of being almost cursed with the tendency to look at things in their relations. He wondered why when she came up to town she always resorted to Baker Street for lodgings. He had never known nor heard of Baker Street as a residence – he associated it only with bazaars and photographers. He divined in her a rigid indifference to everything that was not the passion of her life. Nothing really mattered to her but that, and she would have occupied apartments in Whitechapel if they had been a feature in her tactics. She had received her visitor in a large cold, faded room, furnished with slippery seats and decorated with alabaster vases and wax-flowers. The only little personal comfort for which she appeared to have looked out was a fat catalogue of the Army and Navy Stores, which reposed on a vast, desolate table-cover of false blue. Her clear forehead – it was like a porcelain slate, a receptacle for addresses and sums – had flushed when her nephew's crammer told her the extraordinary news; but he saw she was fortunately more angry than frightened. She had essentially, she would always have, too little imagination for fear, and the healthy habit moreover of facing everything had taught her that the occasion usually found her a quantity to reckon with. Mr Coyle saw that her only fear at present could have been that of not being able to prevent her nephew from being absurd and that to such an apprehension as this she was in fact inaccessible. Practically too she was not troubled by surprise; she recognized none of the futile, none of the subtle sentiments. If Philip had for an hour made a fool of himself she was angry; disconcerted as she would have been on learning that he had confessed to debts or fallen in love with a low girl. But there remained in any annoyance the saving fact that no one could make a fool of *her*.

'I don't know when I've taken such an interest in a young man – I think I never have, since I began to handle them,' Mr Coyle said. 'I like him, I believe in him – it's been a delight to see how he was going.'

'Oh, I know how they go!' Miss Wingrave threw back her head with a familiar briskness, as if a rapid procession of the generations had flashed before her, rattling their scabbards and spurs. Spencer Coyle recognized the intimation that she had nothing to learn from anybody about the natural carriage of a Wingrave, and he even felt convicted by her next words of being, in her eyes, with the troubled story of his check, his weak complaint of his pupil, rather a poor creature. 'If you like him,' she exclaimed, 'for mercy's sake keep him quiet!'

Mr Coyle began to explain to her that this was less easy than she appeared to imagine; but he perceived that she understood very little of what he said. The more he insisted that the boy had a kind of intellectual independence, the more this struck her as a conclusive proof that her nephew was a Wingrave and a soldier. It was not till he mentioned to her that Owen had spoken of the profession of arms as of something that would be 'beneath' him, it was not till her attention was arrested by this intenser light on the complexity of the problem that Miss Wingrave broke out after a moment's stupefied reflection: 'Send him to see me immediately!'

'That's exactly what I wanted to ask your leave to do. But I've wanted also to prepare you for the worst, to make you understand that he strikes me as really obstinate and to suggest to you that the most powerful arguments at your command – especially if you should be able to put your hand on some intensely practical one – will be none too effective.'

'I think I've got a powerful argument.' Miss Wingrave looked very hard at her visitor. He didn't know in the least what it was, but he begged her to put it forward without delay. He promised that their young man should come to Baker Street that evening, mentioning however that he had already urged him to spend without delay a couple of days at Eastbourne. This led Jane Wingrave to inquire with surprise what virtue there might be in *that* expensive remedy, and to reply with decision when Mr Coyle had said 'The virtue of a little rest, a little change, a little relief to overwrought nerves,' 'Ah, don't coddle him – he's costing us a great deal of money! I'll talk to him and I'll take him down to Paramore; then I'll send him back to you straightened out.'

Spencer Coyle hailed this pledge superficially with satisfaction, but before he quitted Miss Wingrave he became conscious that he had really taken on a new anxiety – a restlessness that made him say to himself, groaning inwardly: 'Oh, she *is* a grenadier at bottom, and she'll have no tact. I don't know what her powerful argument is; I'm only afraid she'll be stupid and make him worse. The old man's better – *he's* capable of tact, though he's not quite an extinct volcano. Owen will probably put him in a rage. In short the difficulty is that the boy's the best of them.'

Spencer Coyle felt afresh that evening at dinner that the boy was the best of them. Young Wingrave (who, he was pleased to observe, had not yet proceeded to the seaside) appeared at the repast as usual, looking inevitably a little self-conscious, but not too original for Bayswater. He talked very naturally to Mrs Coyle, who had thought him from the first the most beautiful young man they had ever received; so that the person most ill at ease was poor Lechmere, who took great trouble, as if from the deepest delicacy, not to meet the eye of his misguided mate. Spencer Coyle however paid the penalty of his own profundity in feeling more and more worried; he could so easily see that there were all sorts of things in his young friend that the people of Paramore wouldn't understand. He began even already to react against the notion of his being harassed – to reflect that after all he had a right to his ideas – to remember that he was of a substance too fine to be in fairness roughly used. It was in this way that the ardent little crammer, with his whimsical perceptions and complicated sympathies, was generally condemned not to settle down comfortably either into his displeasures or into his enthusiasms. His love of the real truth never gave him a chance to enjoy them. He mentioned to Wingrave after dinner the propriety of an immediate visit to Baker Street, and the young man, looking 'queer', as he thought – that is smiling again with the exaggerated glory he had shown in their recent interview – went off to face the ordeal. Spencer Coyle noted that he was scared – he was afraid of his aunt; but somehow this didn't strike him as a sign of pusillanimity. *He* should have been scared, he was well aware, in the poor boy's place, and the sight of his pupil marching up to the battery in spite of his terrors was a positive suggestion of the temperament of the soldier. Many a plucky youth would have shirked this particular peril.

'He *has* got ideas!' young Lechmere broke out to his instructor after his comrade had quitted the house. He was evidently bewildered and agitated – he had an emotion to work off. He had before dinner gone straight at his friend, as Mr Coyle had requested, and had elicited from him that his scruples were founded on an overwhelming conviction of the stupidity – the 'crass barbarism' he called it – of war. His great complaint was that people hadn't invented anything cleverer, and he was determined to show, the only way he could, that *he* wasn't such an ass.

'And he thinks all the great generals ought to have been shot, and that Napoleon Bonaparte in particular, the greatest, was a criminal, a monster for whom language has no adequate name!' Mr Coyle rejoined, completing young Lechmere's picture. 'He favoured you, I see, with exactly the same pearls of wisdom that he produced for me. But I want to know what *you* said.'

'I said they were awful rot!' Young Lechmere spoke with emphasis, and he was slightly surprised to hear Mr Coyle laugh incongruously at this just declaration and then after a moment continue:

'It's all very curious – I daresay there's something in it. But it's a pity!'

'He told me when it was that the question began to strike him in that light. Four or five years ago, when he did a lot of reading about all the great swells and their campaigns – Hannibal and Julius Caesar, Marlborough and Frederick and Bonaparte. He *has* done a lot of reading, and he says it opened his eyes. He says that a wave of disgust rolled over him. He talked about the "immeasurable misery" of wars, and asked me why nations don't tear to pieces the governments, the rulers that go in for them. He hates poor old Bonaparte worst of all.'

'Well, poor old Bonaparte *was* a brute. He was a frightful ruffian,' Mr Coyle unexpectedly declared. 'But I suppose you didn't admit that.'

'Oh, I daresay he was objectionable, and I'm very glad we laid him on his back. But the point I made to Wingrave was that his own behaviour would excite no end of remark.' Young Lechmere hesitated an instant, then he added: 'I told him he must be prepared for the worst.'

'Of course he asked you what you meant by the "worst",' said Spencer Coyle.

'Yes, he asked me that, and do you know what I said? I said people would say that his conscientious scruples and his wave of disgust are only a pretext. Then he asked, "A pretext for what?"'

'Ah, he rather had you there!' Mr Coyle exclaimed with a little laugh that was mystifying to his pupil.

'Not a bit – for I told him.'

'What did you tell him?'

Once more, for a few seconds, with his conscious eyes in his instructor's, the young man hung fire.

'Why, what we spoke of a few hours ago. The appearance he'd present of not having—' The honest youth faltered a moment, then brought it out: 'The military temperament, don't you know? But do you know what he said to that?' young Lechmere went on.

'Damn the military temperament!' the crammer promptly replied.

Young Lechmere stared. Mr Coyle's tone left him uncertain if he were attributing the phrase to Wingrave or uttering his own opinion, but he exclaimed:

'Those were exactly his words!'

'He doesn't care,' said Mr Coyle.

'Perhaps not. But it isn't fair for him to abuse *us* fellows. I told him it's the finest temperament in the world, and that there's nothing so splendid as pluck and heroism.'

'Ah! there you had *him*.'

'I told him it was unworthy of him to abuse a gallant, a magnificent profession. I told him there's no type so fine as that of the soldier doing his duty.'

'That's essentially *your* type, my dear boy.' Young Lechmere blushed; he couldn't make out (and the danger was naturally unexpected to him) whether at that moment he didn't exist mainly for the recreation of his friend. But he was partly re-assured by the genial way this friend continued, laying a hand on his shoulder. 'Keep *at* him that way! we may do something. I'm extremely obliged to you.' Another doubt however remained unassuaged – a doubt which led him to exclaim to Mr Coyle before they dropped the painful subject:

'He *doesn't* care! But it's awfully odd he shouldn't!'

'So it is, but remember what you said this afternoon – I mean about your not advising people to make insinuations to *you*.'

'I believe I should knock a fellow down!' said young Lechmere. Mr Coyle had got up; the conversation had taken place while they sat together after Mrs Coyle's withdrawal from the dinner-table and the head of the establishment administered to his disciple, on principles that were a part of his thorough-ness, a glass of excellent claret. The disciple, also on his feet, lingered an instant, not for another 'go', as he would have called it, at the decanter, but to wipe his microscopic moustache with prolonged and unusual care. His companion saw he had some-thing to bring out which required a final effort, and waited for him an instant with a hand on the knob of the door. Then as young Lechmere approached him Spencer Coyle grew conscious of an unwonted intensity in the round and ingenuous face. The boy was nervous, but he tried to behave like a man of the world. 'Of course, it's between ourselves,' he stammered, 'and I wouldn't breathe such a word to anyone who wasn't interested in poor Wingrave as you are. But do you think he funks it?'

Mr Coyle looked at him so hard for an instant that he was visibly frightened at what he had said.

'Funks it! Funks what?'

'Why, what we're talking about – the service.' Young Lechmere gave a little gulp and added with a *naïveté* almost pathetic to Spencer Coyle: 'The dangers, you know!'

'Do you mean he's thinking of his skin?'

Young Lechmere's eyes expanded appealingly, and what his instructor saw in his pink face – he even thought he saw a tear – was the dread of a disappointment shocking in the degree in which the loyalty of admiration had been great.

'Is he – is he *afraid*?' repeated the honest lad, with a quaver of suspense.

'Dear no!' said Spencer Coyle, turning his back.

Young Lechmere felt a little snubbed and even a little ashamed; but he felt still more relieved.

III

LESS THAN A week after this Spencer Coyle received a note from Miss Wingrave, who had immediately quitted London with her nephew. She proposed that he should come down to Paramore for the following Sunday – Owen was really so tiresome. On the spot, in that house of examples and memories and in combination with her poor dear father, who was 'dreadfully annoyed', it might be worth their while to make a last stand. Mr Coyle read between the lines of this letter that the party at Paramore had got over a good deal of ground since Miss Wingrave, in Baker Street, had treated his despair as superficial. She was not an insinuating woman, but she went so far as to put the question on the ground of his conferring a particular favour on an afflicted family; and she expressed the pleasure it would give them if he should be accompanied by Mrs Coyle, for whom she enclosed a separate invitation. She mentioned that she was also writing, subject to Mr Coyle's approval, to young Lechmere. She thought such a nice manly boy might do her wretched nephew some good. The celebrated crammer determined to embrace this opportunity; and now it was the case not so much that he was angry as that he was anxious. As he directed his answer to Miss Wingrave's letter he caught himself smiling at the thought that at bottom he was going to defend his young friend rather than to attack him. He said to his wife, who was a fair, fresh, slow woman – a person of much more presence than himself

– that she had better take Miss Wingrave at her word: it was such an extraordinary, such a fascinating specimen of an old English home. This last allusion was amicably sarcastic – he had already accused the good lady more than once of being in love with Owen Wingrave. She admitted that she was, she even gloried in her passion; which shows that the subject, between them, was treated in a liberal spirit. She carried out the joke by accepting the invitation with eagerness. Young Lechmere was delighted to do the same; his instructor had good-naturedly taken the view that the little break would freshen him up for his last spurt.

It was the fact that the occupants of Paramore did indeed take their trouble hard that struck Spencer Coyle after he had been an hour or two in that fine old house. This very short second visit, beginning on the Saturday evening, was to constitute the strangest episode of his life. As soon as he found himself in private with his wife – they had retired to dress for dinner – they called each other's attention with effusion and almost with alarm to the sinister gloom that was stamped on the place. The house was admirable with its old grey front which came forward in wings so as to form three sides of a square, but Mrs Coyle made no scruple to declare that if she had known in advance the sort of impression she was going to receive she would never have put her foot in it. She characterized it as 'uncanny', she accused her husband of not having warned her properly. He had mentioned to her in advance certain facts, but while she almost feverishly dressed she had innumerable questions to ask. He

hadn't told her about the girl, the extraordinary girl, Miss Julian
— that is, he hadn't told her that this young lady, who in plain
terms was a mere dependant, would be in effect, and as a consequence of the way she carried herself, the most important person
in the house. Mrs Coyle was already prepared to announce that
she hated Miss Julian's affectations. Her husband above all
hadn't told her that they should find their young charge looking
five years older.

'I couldn't imagine that,' said Mr Coyle, 'nor that the character of the crisis here would be quite so perceptible. But I
suggested to Miss Wingrave the other day that they should press
her nephew in real earnest, and she has taken me at my word.
They've cut off his supplies — they're trying to starve him out.
That's not what I meant — but indeed I don't quite *know* today
what I meant. Owen feels the pressure, but he won't yield.' The
strange thing was that, now that he was there, the versatile little
coach felt still more that his own spirit had been caught up by a
wave of reaction. If he was there it was because he was on poor
Owen's side. His whole impression, his whole apprehension,
had on the spot become much deeper. There was something in
the dear boy's very resistance that began to charm him. When
his wife, in the intimacy of the conference I have mentioned,
threw off the mask and commended even with extravagance the
stand his pupil had taken (he was too good to be a horrid soldier
and it was noble of him to suffer for his convictions — wasn't he
as upright as a young hero, even though as pale as a Christian
martyr?) the good lady only expressed the sympathy which,

under cover of regarding his young friend as a rare exception, he had already recognized in his own soul.

For, half an hour ago, after they had had superficial tea in the brown old hall of the house, his young friend had proposed to him, before going to dress, to take a turn outside, and had even, on the terrace, as they walked together to one of the far ends of it, passed his hand entreatingly into his companion's arm, permitting himself thus a familiarity unusual between pupil and master and calculated to show that he had guessed whom he could most depend on to be kind to him. Spencer Coyle on his own side had guessed something, so that he was not surprised at the boy's having a particular confidence to make. He had felt on arriving that each member of the party had wished to get hold of him first, and he knew that at that moment Jane Wingrave was peering through the ancient blur of one of the windows (the house had been modernized so little that the thick dim panes were three centuries old) to see if her nephew looked as if he were poisoning the visitor's mind. Mr Coyle lost no time therefore in reminding the youth (and he took care to laugh as he did so) that he had not come down to Paramore to be corrupted. He had come down to make, face to face, a last appeal to him – he hoped it wouldn't be utterly vain. Owen smiled sadly as they went, asking him if he thought he had the general air of a fellow who was going to knock under.

'I think you look strange – I think you look ill,' Spencer Coyle said very honestly. They had paused at the end of the terrace.

'I've had to exercise a great power of resistance, and it rather takes it out of one.'

'Ah, my dear boy, I wish your great power – for you evidently possess it – were exerted in a better cause!'

Owen Wingrave smiled down at his small instructor. 'I don't believe that!' Then he added, to explain why: 'Isn't what you want, if you're so good as to think well of my character, to see me exert *most* power, in whatever direction? Well, *this* is the way I exert most.' Owen Wingrave went on to relate that he had had some terrible hours with his grandfather, who had denounced him in a way to make one's hair stand up on one's head. He had expected them not to like it, not a bit, but he had had no idea they would make such a row. His aunt was different, but she was equally insulting. Oh, they had made him feel they were ashamed of him; they accused him of putting a public dishonour on their name. He was the only one who had ever backed out – he was the first for three hundred years. Everyone had known he was to go up, and now everyone would know he was a young hypocrite who suddenly pretended to have scruples. They talked of his scruples as you wouldn't talk of a cannibal's god. His grandfather had called him outrageous names. 'He called me – he called me—' Here the young man faltered, his voice failed him. He looked as haggard as was possible to a young man in such magnificent health.

'I probably know!' said Spencer Coyle, with a nervous laugh.

Owen Wingrave's clouded eyes, as if they were following the far-off consequences of things, rested for an instant on a distant object. Then they met his companion's and for another moment sounded them deeply. 'It isn't true. No, it isn't. It's not *that*!'

'I don't suppose it is! But what *do* you propose instead of it?'

'Instead of what?'

'Instead of the stupid solution of war. If you take that away you should suggest at least a substitute.'

'That's for the people in charge, for governments and cabinets,' said Owen Wingrave. '*They'll* arrive soon enough at a substitute, in the particular case, if they're made to understand that they'll be hung if they don't find one. Make it a capital crime – that'll quicken the wits of ministers!' His eyes brightened as he spoke, and he looked assured and exalted. Mr Coyle gave a sigh of perplexed resignation – it was a monomania. He fancied after this for a moment that Owen was going to ask him if he too thought he was a coward; but he was relieved to observe that he either didn't suspect him of it or shrank uncomfortably from putting the question to the test. Spencer Coyle wished to show confidence, but somehow a direct assurance that he didn't doubt of his courage appeared too gross a compliment – it would be like saying he didn't doubt of his honesty. The difficulty was presently averted by Owen's continuing: 'My grandfather can't break the entail, but I shall have nothing but this place, which, as you know, is small and, with the way rents are going, has quite ceased to yield an income. He has some money – not much, but such as it is he cuts me off. My aunt does the same – she has let me know her intentions. She was to have left me her six hundred a year. It was all settled; but now what's settled is that I don't get a penny of it if I give up the army. I must add in fairness that I have from my mother three hundred a year of my own. And I tell you the simple truth when I say that I don't care a rap for the loss of the money.' The young man drew a long, slow breath, like a creature in pain; then he subjoined: '*That's* not what worries me!'

'What are you going to do?' asked Spencer Coyle.

'I don't know; perhaps nothing. Nothing great, at all events. Only something peaceful!'

Owen gave a weary smile, as if, worried as he was, he could yet appreciate the humorous effect of such a declaration from a Wingrave; but what it suggested to his companion, who looked up at him with a sense that he was after all not a Wingrave for nothing and had a military steadiness under fire, was the exasperation that such a programme, uttered in such a way and striking them as the last word of the inglorious, might well have engendered on the part of his grandfather and his aunt. 'Perhaps nothing' – when he might carry on the great tradition! Yes, he wasn't weak, and he was interesting; but there *was* a point of view from which he was provoking. 'What *is* it then that worries you?' Mr Coyle demanded.

'Oh, the house – the very air and feeling of it. There are strange voices in it that seem to mutter at me – to say dreadful things as I pass. I mean the general consciousness and responsibility of what I'm doing. Of course it hasn't been easy for me – not a bit. I assure you I don't enjoy it.' With a light in them that was like a longing for justice Owen again bent his eyes on those of the little coach; then he pursued: 'I've started up all the old ghosts. The very portraits glower at me on the walls. There's one of my great-great-grandfather (the one the extraordinary story you know is about – the old fellow who hangs on the second landing of the big staircase) that fairly stirs on the canvas – just heaves a little – when I come near it. I have to go up and downstairs – it's rather awkward! It's what my aunt calls the family circle. It's all constituted here, it's a kind of indestructible presence, it stretches away into the past, and when I came back with her the other day Miss Wingrave told me I wouldn't have the impudence to stand in the midst of it and say such things. I *had* to say them to my grandfather; but now that I've said them it seems to me that the question's ended. I want to go away – I don't care if I never come back again.'

'Oh, you *are* a soldier; you must fight it out!' Mr Coyle laughed.

The young man seemed discouraged at his levity, but as they turned round, strolling back in the direction from which they had come, he himself smiled faintly after an instant and replied:

'Ah, we're tainted – all!'

They walked in silence part of the way to the old portico; then Spencer Coyle, stopping short after having assured himself that he was at a sufficient distance from the house not to be heard, suddenly put the question: 'What does Miss Julian say?'

'Miss Julian?' Owen had perceptibly coloured.

'I'm sure *she* hasn't concealed her opinion.'

'Oh, it's the opinion of the family circle, for she's a member of it of course. And then she has her own as well.'

'Her own opinion?'

'Her own family circle.'

'Do you mean her mother – that patient lady?'

'I mean more particularly her father, who fell in battle. And her grandfather, and *his* father, and her uncles and great-uncles – they all fell in battle.'

'Hasn't the sacrifice of so many lives been sufficient? Why should she sacrifice *you*?'

'Oh, she *hates* me!' Owen declared, as they resumed their walk.

'Ah, the hatred of pretty girls for fine young men!' exclaimed Spencer Coyle.

He didn't believe in it, but his wife did, it appeared perfectly, when he mentioned this conversation while, in the fashion that has been described, the visitors dressed for dinner. Mrs Coyle had already discovered that nothing could have been nastier than Miss Julian's manner to the disgraced youth during the half-hour the party had spent in the hall; and it was this lady's judgement that one must have had no eyes in one's head not to see that she was already trying outrageously to flirt with young Lechmere. It was a pity they had brought that silly boy: he was down in the hall with her at that moment. Spencer Coyle's version was different; he thought there were finer elements involved. The girl's footing in the house was inexplicable on any ground save that of her being predestined to Miss Wingrave's nephew. As the niece of Miss Wingrave's own unhappy intended she had been dedicated early by this lady to the office of healing by a union with Owen the tragic breach that had separated their elders; and if in reply to this it was to be said that a girl of spirit couldn't enjoy in such a matter having her duty cut out for her, Owen's enlightened friend was ready with the argument that a young person in Miss Julian's position would never be such a fool as really to quarrel with a capital chance. She was familiar at Paramore and she felt safe; therefore she might trust herself to the amusement of pretending that she had her option. But it was all innocent coquetry. She had a curious charm, and it was vain to pretend that the heir of that house wouldn't seem good enough to a girl, clever as she might be, of eighteen. Mrs Coyle reminded her husband that the poor young man was precisely now *not* of that house: this problem was among the questions that exercised their wits after the two men had taken the turn on the terrace. Spencer Coyle told his wife that Owen was afraid of the portrait of his great-great-grandfather. He would show it to her, since she hadn't noticed it, on their way downstairs.

'Why of his great-great-grandfather more than of any of the others?'

'Oh, because he's the most formidable. He's the one who's sometimes seen.'

'Seen where?' Mrs Coyle had turned round with a jerk.

'In the room he was found dead in – the White Room they've always called it.'

'Do you mean to say the house has a *ghost*?' Mrs Coyle almost shrieked. 'You brought me here without telling me?'

'Didn't I mention it after my other visit?'

'Not a word. You only talked about Miss Wingrave.'

'Oh, I was full of the story – you have simply forgotten.'

'Then you should have reminded me!'

'If I had thought of it I would have held my peace, for you wouldn't have come.'

'I wish, indeed, I hadn't!' cried Mrs Coyle. 'What *is* the story?'

'Oh, a deed of violence that took place here ages ago. I think it was in George the First's time. Colonel Wingrave, one of their ancestors, struck in a fit of passion one of his children, a lad just growing up, a blow on the head of which the unhappy child died. The matter was hushed up for the hour – some other explanation was put about. The poor boy was laid out in one of those rooms on the other side of the house, and amid strange smothered rumours the funeral was hurried on. The next morning, when the household assembled, Colonel Wingrave was missing; he was looked for vainly, and at last it occurred to someone that he might perhaps be in the room from which his child had been carried to burial. The seeker knocked without an answer – then opened the door. Colonel Wingrave lay dead on the floor, in his clothes, as if he had reeled and fallen back, without a wound, without a mark, without anything in his appearance to indicate that he had either struggled or suffered. He was a strong, sound man – there was nothing to account for such a catastrophe. He is supposed to have gone to the room during the night, just before going to bed, in some fit of compunction or some fascination of dread. It was only after this that the truth about the boy came out. But no one ever sleeps in the room.'

Mrs Coyle had fairly turned pale. 'I hope not! Thank Heaven they haven't put *us* there!'

'We're at a comfortable distance; but I've seen the gruesome chamber.'

'Do you mean you've been *in* it?'

'For a few moments. They're rather proud of it and my young friend showed it to me when I was here before.'

Mrs Coyle stared. 'And what is it like?'

'Simply like an empty, dull, old-fashioned bedroom, rather big, with the things of the "period" in it. It's panelled from floor to ceiling, and the panels evidently, years and years ago, were painted white. But the paint has darkened with time and there are three or four quaint little ancient "samplers", framed and glazed, hung on the walls.'

Mrs Coyle looked round with a shudder. 'I'm glad there are no samplers here! I never heard anything so jumpy! Come down to dinner.'

On the staircase as they went down her husband showed her the portrait of Colonel Wingrave – rather a vigorous representation, for the place and period, of a gentleman with a hard, handsome face, in a red coat and a peruke. Mrs Coyle declared that his descendant Sir Philip was wonderfully like him; and her husband could fancy, though he kept it to himself, that if one should have the courage to walk about the old corridors of Paramore at night one might meet a figure that resembled him roaming, with the restlessness of a ghost, hand in hand with the figure of a tall boy. As he proceeded to the drawing-room with his wife he found himself suddenly wishing that he had made more of a point of his pupil's going to Eastbourne. The evening however seemed to have taken upon itself to dissipate any such whimsical forebodings, for the grimness of the family circle, as Spencer Coyle had preconceived its composition, was mitigated by an infusion of the 'neighbourhood'. The company at dinner was recruited by two cheerful couples – one of them the vicar and his wife, and by a silent young man who had come down to fish. This was a relief to Mr Coyle, who had begun to wonder what was after all expected of him and why he had been such a fool as to come, and who now felt that for the first hours at least the situation would not have directly to be dealt with. Indeed he found, as he had found before, sufficient occupation for his ingenuity in reading the various symptoms of which the picture before him was an expression. He should probably have an irritating day on the morrow: he foresaw the difficulty of the long decorous Sunday and how dry Jane Wingrave's ideas, elicited in a strenuous conference, would taste. She and her father would make him feel that they depended upon him for the impossible, and if they should try to associate him with a merely stupid policy he might end by telling them what he thought of it – an accident not required to make his visit a sensible mistake. The old man's actual design was evidently to let their friends see in it a positive mark of their being all right. The presence of the great London coach was tantamount to a profession of faith in the results of the impending examination. It had clearly been obtained from Owen, rather to Spencer Coyle's surprise, that he would do nothing to interfere with the apparent harmony. He let the allusions to his hard work pass and, holding his tongue about his affairs, talked to the ladies as amicably as if he had not been 'cut off'. When Spencer Coyle looked at him once or twice across the table, catching his eye, which showed an indefinable passion, he saw a puzzling pathos in his laughing face: one couldn't resist a pang for a young lamb so visibly marked for sacrifice. 'Hang him – what a pity he's such a fighter!' he privately sighed, with a want of logic that was only superficial.

This idea however would have absorbed him more if so much of his attention had not been given to Kate Julian, who, now that he had her well before him, struck him as a remarkable and even as a possibly fascinating young woman. The fascination resided not in any extraordinary prettiness, for if she was handsome, with her long Eastern eyes, her magnificent hair and her general unabashed originality, he had seen complexions rosier and features that pleased him more: it resided in a strange impression that she gave of being exactly the sort of person whom, in her position, common considerations, those of prudence and perhaps even a little those of decorum, would have enjoined on her not to be. She was what was vulgarly termed a dependant

— penniless, patronized, tolerated; but something in her aspect and manner signified that if her situation was inferior, her spirit, to make up for it, was above precautions or submissions. It was not in the least that she was aggressive, she was too indifferent for that; it was only as if, having nothing either to gain or to lose, she could afford to do as she liked. It occurred to Spencer Coyle that she might really have had more at stake than her imagination appeared to take account of; whatever it was, at any rate, he had never seen a young woman at less pains to be on the safe side. He wondered inevitably how the peace was kept between Jane Wingrave and such an inmate as this; but those questions of course were unfathomable deeps. Perhaps Kate Julian lorded it even over her protectress. The other time he was at Paramore he had received an impression that, with Sir Philip beside her, the girl could fight with her back to the wall. She amused Sir Philip, she charmed him, and he liked people who weren't afraid; between him and his daughter, moreover, there was no doubt which was the higher in command. Miss Wingrave took many things for granted, and most of all the rigour of discipline and the fate of the vanquished and the captive.

But between their clever boy and so original a companion of his childhood what odd relation would have grown up? It couldn't be indifference, and yet on the part of happy, handsome, youthful creatures it was still less likely to be aversion. They weren't Paul and Virginia, but they must have had their common summer and their idyll: no nice girl could have disliked such a nice fellow for anything but not liking *her*, and no nice fellow could have resisted such propinquity. Mr Coyle remembered indeed that Mrs Julian had spoken to him as if the propinquity had been by no means constant, owing to her daughter's absences at school, to say nothing of Owen's; her visits to a few friends who were so kind as to 'take her' from time to time; her sojourns in London — so difficult to manage, but still managed by God's help — for 'advantages', for drawing and singing, especially drawing or rather painting, in oils, in which she had had immense success. But the good lady had also mentioned that the young people were quite brother and sister, which *was* a little, after all, like Paul and Virginia. Mrs Coyle had been right, and it was apparent that Virginia was doing her best to make the time pass agreeably for young Lechmere. There was no such whirl of conversation as to render it an effort for Mr Coyle to reflect on these things, for the tone of the occasion, thanks principally to the other guests, was not disposed to stray — it tended to the repetition of anecdote and the discussion of rents, topics that huddled together like uneasy animals. He could judge how intensely his hosts wished the evening to pass off as if nothing had happened; and this gave him the measure of their private resentment. Before dinner was over he found himself fidgety about his second pupil. Young Lechmere, since he began to cram, had done all that might have been expected of him; but this couldn't blind his instructor to a present perception of his being in moments of relaxation as innocent as a babe. Mr Coyle had considered that the amusements of Paramore would probably give him a fillip, and the poor fellow's manner testified to the soundness of the forecast. The fillip had been unmistakably administered; it had come in the form of a revelation. The light on young Lechmere's brow announced with a candour that was almost an appeal for compassion, or at least a deprecation of ridicule, that he had never seen anything like Miss Julian.

IV

IN THE DRAWING-ROOM after dinner the girl found an occasion to approach Spencer Coyle. She stood before him a moment, smiling while she opened and shut her fan, and then she said abruptly, raising her strange eyes: 'I know what you've come for, but it isn't any use.'

'I've come to look after *you* a little. Isn't *that* any use?'

'It's very kind. But I'm not the question of the hour. You won't do anything with Owen.'

Spencer Coyle hesitated a moment. 'What will *you* do with his young friend?'

She stared, looked round her.

'Mr Lechmere? Oh, poor little lad! We've been talking about Owen. He admires him so.'

'So do I. I should tell you that.'

'So do we all. That's why we're in such despair.'

'Personally then you'd *like* him to be a soldier?' Spencer Coyle inquired.

'I've quite set my heart on it. I adore the army and I'm awfully fond of my old playmate,' said Miss Julian.

Her interlocutor remembered the young man's own different version of her attitude; but he judged it loyal not to challenge the girl.

'It's not conceivable that your old playmate shouldn't be fond of you. He must therefore wish to please you; and I don't see why – between you – you don't set the matter right.'

'Wish to please me!' Miss Julian exclaimed. 'I'm sorry to say he shows no such desire. He thinks me an impudent wretch. I've told him what I think of *him*, and he simply hates me.'

'But you think so highly! You just told me you admire him.'

'His talents, his possibilities, yes; even his appearance, if I may allude to such a matter. But I don't admire his present behaviour.'

'Have you had the question out with him?' Spencer Coyle asked.

'Oh, yes, I've ventured to be frank – the occasion seemed to excuse it. He couldn't like what I said.'

'What did you say?'

Miss Julian, thinking a moment, opened and shut her fan again.

'Why, that such conduct isn't that of a gentleman!'

After she had spoken her eyes met Spencer Coyle's, who looked into their charming depths.

'Do you want then so much to send him off to be killed?'

'How odd for *you* to ask that — in such a way!' she replied with a laugh. 'I don't understand your position: I thought your line was to *make* soldiers!'

'You should take my little joke. But, as regards Owen Wingrave, there's no "making" needed,' Mr Coyle added. 'To my sense —' the little crammer paused a moment, as if with a consciousness of responsibility for his paradox — 'to my sense he *is*, in a high sense of the term, a fighting man.'

'Ah, let him prove it!' the girl exclaimed, turning away.

Spencer Coyle let her go; there was something in her tone that annoyed and even a little shocked him. There had evidently been a violent passage between these young people, and the reflection that such a matter was after all none of his business only made him more sore. It was indeed a military house, and she was at any rate a person who placed her ideal of manhood (young persons doubtless always had their ideals of manhood) in the type of the belted warrior. It was a taste like another; but, even a quarter of an hour later, finding himself near young Lechmere, in whom this type was embodied, Spencer Coyle was still so ruffled that he addressed the innocent lad with a certain magisterial dryness. 'You're not to sit up late, you know. That's not what I brought you down for.' The dinner-guests were taking leave and the bedroom candles twinkled in a monitory row. Young Lechmere however was too agreeably agitated to be accessible to a snub: he had a happy preoccupation which almost engendered a grin.

'I'm only too eager for bedtime. Do you know there's an awfully jolly room?'

'Surely they haven't put you there?'

'No indeed: no one has passed a night in it for ages. But that's exactly what I want to do – it would be tremendous fun.'

'And have you been trying to get Miss Julian's permission?'

'Oh, *she* can't give leave, she says. But she believes in it, and she maintains that no man dare.'

No man *shall*! A man in your critical position in particular must have a quiet night,' said Spencer Coyle.

Young Lechmere gave a disappointed but reasonable sigh.

'Oh, all right. But mayn't I sit up for a little go at Wingrave? I haven't had any yet.'

Mr Coyle looked at his watch.

'You may smoke *one* cigarette.'

He felt a hand on his shoulder, and he turned round to see his wife tilting candle-grease upon his coat. The ladies were going to bed and it was Sir Philip's inveterate hour; but Mrs Coyle confided to her husband that after the dreadful things he had told her she positively declined to be left alone, for no matter how short an interval, in any part of the house. He promised to follow her within three minutes, and after the orthodox hand-shakes the ladies rustled away. The forms were kept up at Paramore as bravely as if the old house had no present heartache. The only one of which Spencer Coyle noticed the omission was some salutation to himself from Kate Julian. She gave him neither a word nor a glance, but he saw her look hard at Owen Wingrave. Her mother, timid and pitying, was apparently the only person from whom this young man caught an inclination of the head. Miss Wingrave marshalled the three ladies – her little procession of twinkling tapers – up the wide oaken stairs and past the watching portrait of her ill-fated ancestor. Sir Philip's servant appeared and offered his arm to the old man, who turned a perpendicular back on poor Owen when the boy made a vague movement to anticipate this office. Spencer Coyle learned afterwards that before Owen had forfeited favour it had always, when he was at home, been his privilege at bedtime to conduct his grand-father ceremoniously to rest. Sir Philip's habits were contemp-tuously different now. His apartments were on the lower floor and he shuffled stiffly off to them with his valet's help, after fixing for a moment significantly on the most responsible of his visitors the thick red ray, like the glow of stirred embers, that always made his eyes conflict oddly with his mild manners. They seemed to say to Spencer Coyle, 'We'll let the young scoundrel have it tomorrow!' One might have gathered from them that the young scoundrel, who had now strolled to the other end of the hall, had at least forged a cheque. Mr Coyle watched him an instant, saw him drop nervously into a chair and then with a restless movement get up. The same movement brought him back to where his late instructor stood addressing a last injunction to young Lechmere.

'I'm going to bed and I should like you particularly to conform to what I said to you a short time ago. Smoke a single cigarette with your friend here and then go to your room. You'll have me down on you if I hear of your having, during the night, tried any preposterous games.' Young Lechmere, looking down with his hands in his pockets, said nothing – he only poked at the corner of a rug with his toe; so that Spencer Coyle, dissatisfied with so tacit a pledge, presently went on, to Owen: 'I must request you, Wingrave, not to keep this sensitive subject sitting up – and indeed to put him to bed and turn his key in the door.' As Owen stared an instant, apparently not understanding the motive of so much solicitude, he added: 'Lechmere has a morbid curiosity about one of your legends – of your historic rooms. Nip it in the bud.'

'Oh, the legend's rather good, but I'm afraid the room's an awful sell!' Owen laughed.

'You know you don't *believe* that, my boy!' young Lechmere exclaimed.

'I don't think he does,' said Mr Coyle, noticing Owen's mottled flush.

'He wouldn't try a night there himself!' young Lechmere pursued.

'I know who told you that,' rejoined Owen, lighting a cigarette in an embarrassed way at the candle, without offering one to either of his companions.

'Well, what if she did?' asked the younger of these gentlemen, rather red. 'Do you want them *all* yourself?' he continued facetiously, fumbling in the cigarette-box.

Owen Wingrave only smoked quietly; then he exclaimed:

'Yes – what if she did? But she doesn't know,' he added.

'She doesn't know what?'

'She doesn't know anything! – I'll tuck him in!' Owen went on gaily to Mr Coyle, who saw that his presence, now that a certain note had been struck, made the young men uncomfortable. He was curious, but there was a kind of discretion, with his pupils, that he had always pretended to practise; a discretion that however didn't prevent him as he took his way upstairs from recommending them not to be donkeys.

At the top of the staircase, to his surprise, he met Miss Julian, who was apparently going down again. She had not begun to undress, nor was she perceptibly disconcerted at seeing him. She nevertheless, in a manner slightly at variance with the rigour with which she had overlooked him ten minutes before, dropped the words: 'I'm going down to look for something. I've lost a jewel.'

'A jewel?'

'A rather good turquoise, out of my locket. As it's the only ornament I have the honour to possess—!' And she passed down.

'Shall I go with you and help you?' asked Spencer Coyle.

The girl paused a few steps below him, looking back with her Oriental eyes.

'Don't I hear voices in the hall?'

'Those remarkable young men are there.'

'*They'll* help me.' And Kate Julian descended.

Spencer Coyle was tempted to follow her, but remembering his standard of tact he rejoined his wife in their apartment. He delayed however to go to bed, and though he went into his dressing-room he couldn't bring himself even to take off his coat. He pretended for half an hour to read a novel; after which, quietly, or perhaps I should say agitatedly, he passed from the dressing-room into the corridor. He followed this passage to the door of the room which he knew to have been assigned to young Lechmere and was comforted to see that it was closed. Half an hour earlier he had seen it standing open; therefore he could take for granted that the bewildered boy had come to bed. It was of this he had wished to assure himself, and having done so he was on the point of retreating. But at the same instant he heard a sound in the room – the occupant was doing, at the window, something which showed him that he might knock without the reproach of waking his pupil up. Young Lechmere came in fact to the door in his shirt and trousers. He admitted his visitor in some surprise, and when the door was closed again Spencer Coyle said:

'I don't want to make your life a burden to you, but I had it on my conscience to see for myself that you're not exposed to undue excitement.'

'Oh, there's plenty of that!' said the ingenuous youth. 'Miss Julian came down again.'

'To look for a turquoise?'

'So she said.'

'Did she find it?'

'I don't know. I came up. I left her with poor Wingrave.'

'Quite the right thing,' said Spencer Coyle.

'I don't know,' young Lechmere repeated uneasily. 'I left them quarrelling.'

'What about?'

'I don't understand. They're a quaint pair!'

Spencer Coyle hesitated. He had, fundamentally, principles and scruples, but what he had in particular just now was a curiosity, or rather, to recognize it for what it was, a sympathy, which brushed them away.

'Does it strike you that *she's* down on him?' he permitted himself to inquire.

'Rather! – when she tells him he lies!'

'What do you mean?'

'Why, before *me*. It made me leave them; it was getting too hot. I stupidly brought up the question of the haunted room again, and said how sorry I was that I had had to promise you not to try my luck with it.'

'You can't pry about in that gross way in other people's houses – you can't take such liberties, you know!' Mr Coyle interjected.

'I'm all right – see how good I am. I don't want to go *near* the place!' said young Lechmere, confidingly. 'Miss Julian said to me, "Oh, I daresay *you'd* risk it, but –" and she turned and laughed at poor Owen – "that's more than we can expect of a gentleman who has taken *his* extraordinary line." I could see that something had already passed between them on the subject – some teasing or challenging of hers. It may have been only chaff, but his chucking the profession had evidently brought up the question of his pluck.'

'And what did Owen say?'

'Nothing at first; but presently he brought out very quietly: "I spent all last night in the confounded place." We both stared and cried out at this and I asked him what he had seen there. He said he had seen nothing, and Miss Julian replied that he ought to tell his story better than that – he ought to make something good of it. "It's not a story – it's a simple fact," said he; on which she jeered at him and wanted to know why, if he had done it, he hadn't told her in the morning, since he knew what she thought of him. "I know, but I don't care," said Wingrave. This made her angry, and she asked him quite seriously whether he would care if he should know she believed him to be trying to deceive us.'

'Ah, what a brute!' cried Spencer Coyle.

'She's a most extraordinary girl – I don't know what she's up to.'

'Extraordinary indeed – to be romping and bandying words at that hour of the night with fast young men!'

Young Lechmere reflected a moment. 'I mean because I think she likes him.'

Spencer Coyle was so struck with this unwonted symptom of subtlety that he flashed out: 'And do you think he likes *her*?'

But his interlocutor only replied with a puzzled sigh and a plaintive 'I don't know – I give it up! – I'm sure he *did* see something or hear something,' young Lechmere added.

'In that ridiculous place? What makes you sure?'

'I don't know – he looks as if he had. He behaves as if he had.'

'Why then shouldn't he mention it?'

Young Lechmere thought a moment. 'Perhaps it's too gruesome!'

Spencer Coyle gave a laugh. 'Aren't you glad then *you're* not in it?'

'Uncommonly!'

'Go to bed, you goose,' said Spencer Coyle, with another laugh. 'But before you go tell me what he said when she told him he was trying to deceive you.'

'"Take me there yourself, then, and lock me in!"'

'And *did* she take him?'

'I don't know – I came up.'

Spencer Coyle exchanged a long look with his pupil.

'I don't think they're in the hall now. Where's Owen's own room?'

'I haven't the least idea.'

Mr Coyle was perplexed; he was in equal ignorance, and he couldn't go about trying doors. He bade young Lechmere sink to slumber, and came out into the passage. He asked himself if he should be able to find his way to the room Owen had formerly shown him, remembering that in common with many of the others it had its ancient name painted upon it. But the corridors of Paramore were intricate; moreover, some of the servants would still be up, and he didn't wish to have the appearance of roaming over the house. He went back to his own quarters, where Mrs Coyle soon perceived that his inability to rest had not subsided. As she confessed for her own part, in the dreadful place, to an increased sense of 'creepiness', they spent the early part of the night in conversation, so that a portion of their vigil was inevitably beguiled by her husband's account of his colloquy with little Lechmere and by their exchange of opinions upon it. Toward two o'clock Mrs Coyle became so nervous about their persecuted young friend, and so possessed by the fear that that wicked girl had availed herself of his invitation to put him to an abominable test, that she begged her husband to go and look into the matter at whatever cost to his own equilibrium. But Spencer Coyle, perversely, had ended, as the perfect stillness of the night settled upon them, by charming himself into a tremulous acquiescence in Owen's readiness to face a formidable ordeal – an ordeal the more formidable to an excited imagination as the poor boy now knew from the experience of the previous night how resolute an effort he should have to make. 'I hope he *is* there,' he said to his wife: 'it puts them all so in the wrong!' At any rate he couldn't take upon himself to explore a house he knew so little. He was inconsequent – he didn't prepare for bed. He sat in the dressing-room with his light and his novel, waiting to find himself nodding. At last, however, Mrs Coyle turned over and ceased to talk, and at last too he fell asleep in his chair. How long he slept he only knew afterwards by computation; what he knew to begin with was that he had started up, in confusion, with the sense of a sudden appalling sound. His sense cleared itself quickly, helped doubtless by a confirmatory cry of horror from his wife's room. But he gave no heed to his wife; he had already bounded into the passage. There the sound was repeated – it was the 'Help! help!' of a woman in agonized terror. It came from a distant quarter of the house, but the quarter was sufficiently indicated. Spencer Coyle rushed straight before him, with the sound of opening doors and alarmed voices in his ears and the faintness of the early dawn in his eyes. At a turn of one of the passages he came upon the white figure of a girl in a swoon on a bench, and in the vividness of the revelation he read as he went that Kate Julian, stricken in her pride too late with a chill of compunction for what she had mockingly done, had, after coming to release the victim of her derision, reeled away, overwhelmed, from the catastrophe that was her work – the catastrophe that the next moment he found himself aghast at on the threshold of an open door. Owen Wingrave, dressed as he had last seen him, lay dead on the spot on which his ancestor had been found. He looked like a young soldier on a battlefield.

The Visits

THE OTHER DAY, after her death, when they were discussing her, someone said in reference to the great number of years she had lived, the people she had seen and the stories she knew: 'What a pity no one ever took any notes of her talk!' For a London epitaph that was almost exhaustive, and the subject presently changed. One of the listeners had taken many notes, but he didn't confess it on the spot. The following story is a specimen of my exactitude – I took it down, *verbatim*, having that faculty, the day after I heard it. I choose it, at hazard, among those of her reminiscences that I have preserved; it's not worse than the others. I will give you some of the others too – when occasion offers – so that you may judge.

I met in town that year a dear woman whom I had scarcely seen since I was a girl; she had dropped out of the world; she came up but once in five years. We had been together as very young creatures, and then we had married and gone our ways. It was arranged between us that after I should have paid a certain visit

in August in the west of England I would take her – it would be
very convenient, she was just over the Cornish border – on the
way to my other engagements: I would work her in, as you say
nowadays. She wanted immensely to show me her home, and
she wanted still more to show me her girl, who had not come
up to London, choosing instead, after much deliberation, to go
abroad for a month with her brother and her brother's coach –
he had been cramming for something – and Mrs Coach of
course. All that Mrs Chantry had been able to show me in town
was her husband, one of those country gentlemen with a
moderate property and an old place who are a part of the
essence in their own neighbourhood and not a part of anything
anywhere else.

A couple of days before my visit to Chantry Court the people
to whom I had gone from town took me over to see some friends
of theirs who lived, ten miles away, in a place that was supposed
to be fine. As it was a long drive we stayed to luncheon; and then
as there were gardens and other things that were more or less on
show we struggled along to tea, so as to get home just in time for
dinner. There were a good many other people present, and
before luncheon a very pretty girl came into the drawing-room,
a real maiden in her flower, less than twenty, fresh and fair and
charming, with the expression of someone I knew. I asked who
she was, and was told she was Miss Chantry, so that in a moment
I spoke to her, mentioning that I was an old friend of her
mother's and that I was coming to pay them a visit. She looked
rather frightened and blank, was apparently unable to say that

she had ever heard of me, and hinted at no pleasure in the idea that she was to hear of me again. But this didn't prevent my perceiving that she was lovely, for I was wise enough even then not to think it necessary to measure people by the impression that one makes on them. I saw that any I should make on Louisa Chantry would be much too clumsy a test. She had been staying at the house at which I was calling; she had come alone, as the people were old friends and to a certain extent neighbours, and was going home in a few days. It was a daughterless house, but there was inevitable young life: a couple of girls from the vicarage, a married son and his wife, a young man who had 'ridden over' and another young man who was staying.

Louisa Chantry sat opposite to me at luncheon, but too far for conversation, and before we got up I had discovered that if her manner to me had been odd it was not because she was inanimate. She was on the contrary in a state of intense though carefully muffled vibration. There was some fever in her blood, but no one perceived it, no one, that is, with an exception – an exception which was just a part of the very circumstance. This single suspicion was lodged in the breast of the young man whom I have alluded to as staying in the house. He was on the same side of the table as myself and diagonally facing the girl; therefore what I learned about him was for the moment mainly what she told me; meaning by 'she' her face, her eyes, her movements, her whole perverted personality. She was extremely on her guard, and I should never have guessed her secret but for an accident. The accident was that the only time she dropped her eyes upon him during the repast I happened to notice it. It might not have been much to notice, but it led to my seeing that there was a little drama going on and that the young man would naturally be the hero. It was equally natural that in this capacity he should be the cause of my asking my left-hand neighbour, who happened to be my host, for some account of him. But 'Oh, that fellow? he's my nephew,' was a description which, to appear copious, required that I should know more about the uncle.

We had coffee on the terrace of the house; a terrace laid out in one quarter, oddly and charmingly, in grass where the servants who waited upon us seemed to tread, processionally, on soundless velvet. There I had a good look at my host's nephew and a longer talk with my friend's daughter, in regard to whom I had become conscious of a faint, formless anxiety. I remember saying to her, gropingly, instinctively: 'My dear child, can I do anything for you? I shall perhaps see your mother before you do. Can I for instance say anything to her *from* you?' This only made her blush and turn away; and it was not till too many days had passed that I guessed that what had looked out at me unwittingly in her little gazing trepidation was something like 'Oh, just take me away in spite of myself!' Superficially, conspicuously, there was nothing in the young man to take her away from. He was a person of the middle condition, and save that he didn't look at all humble might have passed for a poor relation. I mean that he had rather a seedy, shabby air, as if he were wearing out old clothes (he had on faded things that didn't match); and I formed vaguely the theory that he was a specimen of the numerous youthful class that goes to seek its fortune in the colonies, keeps strange company there and comes home without a penny. He had a brown, smooth, handsome face, a slightly swaggering, self-conscious ease, and was probably objected to in the house. He hung about, smoking cigarettes on the terrace, and nobody seemed to have much to say to him – a circumstance which, as he managed somehow to convey, left him absolutely indifferent. Louisa Chantry strolled away with one of the girls from the vicarage; the party on the terrace broke up and the nephew disappeared.

It was settled that my friends and I should take leave at half-past five, and I begged to be abandoned in the interval to my devices. I turned into the library and, mounted on ladders, I handled old books and old prints and soiled my gloves. Most of the others had gone to look at the church, and I was left in possession. I wandered into the rooms in which I knew there were pictures; and if the pictures were not good there was some interesting china which I followed from corner to corner and from cabinet to cabinet. At last I found myself on the threshold of a small room which appeared to terminate the series and in which, between the curtains draping the doorways, there appeared to be rows of rare old plates on velvet screens. I was on the point of going in when I became aware that there was something else beside, something which threw me back. Two persons were standing side by side at the window, looking out together with their backs to me – two persons as to whom I immediately felt that they believed themselves to be alone and unwatched. One of them was Louisa Chantry, the other was the young man whom my host had described as his nephew. They were so placed as not to see me, and when I recognized them I checked myself instinctively. I hesitated a moment; then I turned away altogether. I can't tell you why, except that if I had gone in I should have had somehow the air of discovering them. There was no visible reason why they should have been embarrassed by discovery, inasmuch as, so far as I could see, they were doing no harm, were only standing more or less together, without touching, and for the moment apparently saying nothing. Were they watching something out of the window? I don't know; all I know is that the observation I had made at luncheon gave me a sense of responsibility. I might have taken my responsibility the other way and broken up their communion; but I didn't feel this to be sufficiently my business. Later on I wished I had.

I passed through the rooms again, and then out of the house. The gardens were ingenious, but they made me think (I have always that conceited habit) how much cleverer *I* should have been about them. Presently I met several of the rest of the party coming back from the church; on which my hostess took possession of me, declaring there was a point of view I must absolutely be treated to. I saw she was a walking woman and that this meant half a mile in the park. But I was good for that, and we wandered off together while the others returned to the house. It was present to me that I ought to ask my companion, for Helen Chantry's sake, a question about Louisa – whether for instance she had happened to notice the way the girl seemed to be going.

But it was difficult to say anything without saying too much; so that to begin with I merely risked the observation that our young friend was remarkably pretty. As the point admitted of no discussion this didn't take us very far; nor was the subject much enlarged by our unanimity as to the fact that she was also remarkably nice. I observed that I had had very little chance to talk with her, for which I was sorry, having known her mother for years. My hostess, at this, looked vaguely round, as if she had missed her for the first time. 'Sure enough, she has not been about. I daresay she's been writing to her mother – she's always writing to her mother.' 'Not always,' I mentally reflected; but I waited discreetly, admiring everything and rising to the occasion and the views, before I inquired casually who the young man might be who had sat two or three below me at luncheon – the rather good-looking young man, with the regular features and the brownish clothes – not the one with the moustache.

'Oh, poor Jack Brandon,' said my companion, in a tone calculated to make him seem no one in particular.

'Is he very poor?' I asked, with a laugh.

'Oh dear, yes. There are nine of them – fancy! – all boys; and there's nothing for anyone but the eldest. He's my husband's nephew – his poor mother's my sister-in-law. He sometimes turns up here when he has nothing better to do; but I don't think he likes us much.' l saw she meant that they didn't like *him*; and I exposed myself to suspicion by asking if he had been with them long. But my friend was not very plastic, and she simplified my whole theory of the case by replying after she had thought a moment that she wasn't clear about it – she thought he had come only the morning before. It seemed to me I could safely feel a little further, so I inquired if he were likely to stay many days. 'Oh dear, no; he'll go tomorrow!' said my hostess. There was nothing whatever to show that she saw a connection between my odd interest in Mr Brandon and the subject of our former reference; there was only a quick lucidity on the subject of the young man's departure. It reassured me, for no great complications would have arisen in forty-eight hours.

In retracing our steps we passed again through a part of the gardens. Just after we had entered them my hostess, begging me to excuse her, called at a man who was raking leaves to ask him a question about his wife. I heard him reply 'Oh, she's very bad, my lady,' and I followed my course. Presently my lady turned round with him, as if to go to see his wife, who apparently was ill and on the place. I continued to look about me – there were such charming things; and at the end of five minutes I missed my way – I had not taken the direction of the house. Suddenly at the turn of a walk, the angle of a great clipped hedge, I found myself face to face with Jack Brandon. He was moving rapidly, looking down, with his hands in his pockets, and he started and stared at me a moment. I said, 'Oh, how d'ye do?' and I was on the point of adding, 'Won't you kindly show me the right way?' But with a summary salute and a queer expression of face he had already passed me. I looked after him an instant and I all but stopped him; then one of the faintest voices of the air told me that Louisa Chantry would not be far off, that in fact if I were to go on a few steps I should find her. I continued and I passed through an arched aperture of the hedge, a kind of door in the partition. This corner of the place was like an old French garden, a little enclosed apartment, with statues set into the niches of the high walls of verdure. I paused in admiration; then just opposite to me I saw poor Louisa. She was on a bench, with her hands clasped in her lap, her head bent, her eyes staring down before her. I advanced on the grass, attracting her attention; and I was close to her before she looked at me, before she sprang up and showed me a face convulsed with nameless pain. She was so pale that I thought she was ill – I had a vision of her companion's having rushed off for help. She stood gazing at me with expanded eyes and parted lips, and what I was mainly conscious of was that she had become ten years older. Whatever troubled her it was something pitiful – something that prompted me to hold out my two hands to her and exclaim tenderly, 'My poor child, my poor child!' She wavered a moment, as if she wanted to escape me but couldn't trust herself to run; she looked away from me, turning her head this way and that. Then as I went close to her she covered her face with her two hands, she let me lay mine upon her and draw her to my breast. As she dropped her head upon it she burst into tears, sobbing soundlessly and tragically. I asked her no question, I only held her so long as she would, letting her pour out the passion which I felt at the same time she made a tremendous effort to smother. She couldn't smother it, but she could break away violently; and this she quickly did, hurrying out of the nook where our little scene

– and some other greater scene, I judged, just before it – had taken place, and leaving me infinitely mystified. I sat down on the bench a moment and thought it over; then I succeeded in discovering a path to the house.

The carriage was at the door for our drive home, but my companions, who had had tea, were waiting for our hostess, of whom they wished to take leave and who had not yet come in. I reported her as engaged with the wife of one of the gardeners, but we lingered a little in the hall, a largeish group, to give her time to arrive. Two other persons were absent, one of whom was Louisa Chantry and the other the young man whom I had just seen quitting her in the garden. While I sat there, a trifle abstracted, still somewhat agitated by the sequel to that incident and at the same time impatient of our last vague dawdle, one of the footmen presented me with a little folded note. I turned away to open it, and at the very moment our hostess fortunately came in. This diverted the attention of the others from the action of the footman, whom, after I had looked at the note, I immediately followed into the drawing-room. He led me through it and through two or three others to the door of the little retreat in which, nearly an hour before, I had come upon Louisa Chantry and Mr Brandon. The note was from Louisa, it contained the simple words 'Would you very kindly speak to me an instant before you go?' She was waiting for me in the most sequestered spot she had been able to select, and there the footman left us. The girl came straight at me and in an instant she had grasped my hands. I became aware that her condition had changed; her tears were gone, she had a concentrated purpose. I could scarcely see her beautiful young face – it was pressed, beseechingly, so close to mine. I only felt, as her dry, shining eyes almost dazzled me, that a strong light had been waved back and forth before me. Her words at first seemed to me incoherent; then I understood that she was asking me for a pledge.

'Excuse me, forgive me for bringing you here – to say something I can't say before all those people. *Do* forgive me – it was so awfully kind of you to come. I couldn't think of any other way – just for two seconds. I want you to swear to me,' she went on, with her hands now raised and intensely clasped.

'To swear, dearest child?'

'I'm not your dearest child – I'm not anyone's! But *don't* tell mamma. Promise me – promise me,' she insisted.

'Tell her what? – I don't understand.'

'Oh, you do – you do!' she kept on; 'and if you're going to Chantry you'll see her, you'll be with her, you may see her before I do. On my knees I ask you for a vow!'

She seemed on the point of throwing herself at my feet, but I stopped her, I kept her erect. 'When shall *you* see your mother?'

'As soon as I can. I want to get home – I want to get home!' With this I thought she was going to cry again, but she controlled herself and only pressed me with feverish eyes.

'You have some great trouble – for heaven's sake tell me what it is.'

'It isn't anything – it will pass. Only don't breathe it to mamma!'

'How can I breathe it if I don't know what it is?'

'You do know – you know what I mean.' Then after an instant's pause she added: 'What I did in the garden.'

'*What* did you do in the garden?'

'I threw myself on your neck and I sobbed – I behaved like a maniac.'

'Is that all you mean?'

'It's what I don't want mamma to know – it's what I beseech you to keep silent about. If you don't I'll never, never go home. Have *mercy* on me!' the poor child quavered.

'Dear girl, I only want to be tender to you – to be perfect. But tell me first: has anyone acted wrongly to you?'

'No one – *no* one. I speak the truth.'

She looked into my eyes, and I looked far into hers. They were wild with pain and yet they were so pure that they made me confusedly believe her. I hesitated a moment; then I risked the question: 'Isn't Mr Brandon responsible for anything?'

'For nothing – for nothing! Don't blame *him*!' the girl passionately cried.

'He hasn't made love to you?'

'Not a word – before God! Oh, it was too awful!' And with this she broke away from me, flung herself on her knees before a sofa, burying her face in it and in her arms. 'Promise me, promise me, promise me!' she continued to wail.

I was horribly puzzled but I was immeasurably touched. I stood looking a moment at her extravagant prostration; then I said: 'I'm dreadfully in the dark, but I promise.'

This brought her to her feet again, and again she seized my hands. 'Solemnly, sacredly?' she panted.

'Solemnly, sacredly.'

'Not a syllable – not a hint?'

'Dear Louisa,' I said kindly, 'when I promise I perform.'

'You see I don't know you. And when do you go to Chantry?'

'Day after tomorrow. And when do you?'

'Tomorrow if I can.'

'Then you'll see your mother first – it will be all right,' I said smiling.

'All right, all right!' she repeated, with her woeful eyes. 'Go, go!' she added, hearing a step in the adjoining room.

The footman had come back to announce that my friends were seated in the carriage, and I was careful to say before him in a different tone: 'Then there's nothing more I can do for you?'

'Nothing – good-bye,' said Louisa, tearing herself away too abruptly to take my kiss, which, to follow the servant again, I left unbestowed. I felt awkward and guilty as I took leave of the company, murmuring something to my entertainers about having had an arrangement to make with Miss Chantry. Most of the people bade us good-bye from the steps, but I didn't see Jack Brandon. On our drive home in the waning afternoon my other friends doubtless found me silent and stupid.

I went to Chantry two days later, and was disappointed to find that the daughter of the house had not returned, though indeed after parting with her I had been definitely of the opinion that she was much more likely to go to bed and be ill. Her mother however had not heard that she was ill, and my inquiry about the young lady was of course full of circumspection. It was a little difficult, for I had to talk about her, Helen being particularly delighted that we had already made acquaintance. No day had been fixed for her return, but it came over my friend that she oughtn't to be absent during too much of my visit. She was the best thing they had to show — she was the flower and the charm of the place. It had other charms as well — it was a sleepy, silvery old home, exquisitely grey and exquisitely green; a house where you could have confidence in your leisure: it would be as genuine as the butter and the claret. The very look of the pleasant, prosaic drawing-room suggested long mornings of fancy work, of Berlin wool and premeditated patterns, new stitches and mild pauses. My good Helen was always in the middle of something eternal, of which the past and the future were rolled up in oilcloth and tissue paper, and the intensest moments of conversation were when it was spread out for pensive opinions. These used to drop sometimes even from Christopher Chantry when he straddled vaguely in with muddy leggings and the raw materials of a joke. He had a mind like a large, full milk-pan, and his wit was as thick as cream.

One evening I came down to dinner a little early and, to my surprise, found my troubled maiden in possession of the drawing-room. She was evidently troubled still, and had been waiting there in the hope of seeing me alone. We were too quickly interrupted by her parents, however, and I had no conversation with her till I sat down to the piano after dinner and beckoned to her to come and stand by it. Her father had gone off to smoke; her mother dozed by one of the crackling little fires of the summer's end.

'Why didn't you come home the day you told me you meant to?'

She fixed her eyes on my hands. 'I couldn't, I couldn't!'

'You look to me as if you were very ill.'

'I am,' the girl said simply.

'You ought to see someone. Something ought to be done.'

She shook her head with quiet despair. 'It would be no use – no one would know.'

'What do you mean – would know?'

'No one would understand.'

'You ought to make them!'

'Never – never!' she repeated. 'Never!'

'I confess *I* don't,' I replied, with a kind of angry renunciation. I played louder, with the passion of my uneasiness and the aggravation of my responsibility.

'No, you don't indeed,' said Louisa Chantry.

I had only to accept this disadvantage, and after a moment I went on: 'What became of Mr Brandon?'

'I don't know.'

'Did he go away?'

'That same evening.'

'Which same evening?'

'The day you were there. I never saw him again.'

I was silent a minute, then I risked: 'And you never will, eh?'

'Never – never.'

'Then why shouldn't you get better?'

She also hesitated, after which she answered: 'Because I'm going to die.'

My music ceased, in spite of me, and we sat looking at each other. Helen Chantry woke up with a little start and asked what was the matter. I rose from the piano and I couldn't help saying 'Dear Helen, I haven't the least idea.' Louisa sprang up, pressing her hand to her left side, and the next instant I cried aloud 'She's faint – she's ill – do come to her!' Mrs Chantry bustled over to us, and immediately afterwards the girl had thrown herself on her mother's breast, as she had thrown herself days before on mine; only this time without tears, without cries, in the strangest, most tragic silence. She was not faint, she was only in despair – that at least is the way I really saw her. There was something in her contact that scared poor Helen, that operated a sudden revelation: I can see at this hour the queer frightened look she gave me over Louisa's shoulder. The girl however in a moment disengaged herself, declaring that she was not ill, only tired, very tired, and wanted to go to bed. 'Take her, take her – go with her,' I said to her mother; and I pushed them, got them out of the room, partly to conceal my own trepidation. A few moments after they had gone Christopher Chantry came in, having finished his cigar, and I had to mention to him – to explain their absence – that his daughter was so fatigued that she had withdrawn under her mother's superintendence. 'Didn't she seem done up, awfully done up? What on earth, at that confounded place, did she go in for?' the dear man asked with his pointless kindness. I couldn't tell him this was just what I myself wanted to know; and while I pretended to read I wondered inextinguishably what indeed she had 'gone in' for. It had become still more difficult to keep my vow than I had expected; it was also very difficult that evening to converse with Christopher Chantry. His wife's continued absence rendered some conversation necessary; yet it had the advantage of making him remark, after it had lasted an hour, that he must go to see what was the matter. He left me, and soon afterwards I betook myself to my room; bedtime was elastic in the early sense at Chantry. I knew I should only have to wait awhile for Helen to come to me, and in fact by eleven o'clock she arrived.

'She's in a very strange state – something happened there.'

'And *what* happened, pray?'

'I can't make out; she won't tell me.'

'Then what makes you suppose so?'

'She has broken down utterly; she says there was something.'

'Then she does tell you?'

'Not a bit. She only begins and then stops short – she says it's too dreadful.'

'Too dreadful?'

'She says it's *horrible*,' my poor friend murmured, with tears in her eyes and tragic speculation in her mild maternal face.

'But in what way? Does she give you no facts, no clue?'

'It was something she did.'

We looked at each other a moment. 'Did?' I echoed. 'Did to whom?'

'She won't tell me – she says she *can't*. She tries to bring it out, but it sticks in her throat.'

'Nonsense. She did nothing,' I said.

'What *could* she do?' Helen asked, gazing at me.

'She's ill, she's in a fever, her mind's wandering.'

'So I say to her father.'

'And what does *she* say to him?'

'Nothing – she won't speak to him. He's with her now, but she only lies there letting him hold her hand, with her face turned away from him and her eyes closed.'

'You must send for the doctor immediately.'

'I've already sent for him.'

'Should you like me to sit up with her?'

'Oh, I'll do that!' Helen said. Then she asked: 'But if you were there the other day, what did *you* see?'

'Nothing whatever,' I resolutely answered.

'*Really* nothing?'

'Really, my dear child.'

'But was there nobody there who could have made up to her?'

I hesitated a moment. 'My poor Helen, you should have seen them!'

'She wouldn't look at anybody that wasn't remarkably nice,' Helen mused.

'Well – I don't want to abuse your friends – but nobody was remarkably nice. Believe me, she hasn't looked at anybody, and nothing whatever has occurred. She's ill, and it's a mere morbid fancy.'

'It's a mere morbid fancy—!' Mrs Chantry gobbled down this formula. I felt that I was giving her another still more acceptable, and which she as promptly adopted, when I added that Louisa would soon get over it.

I may as well say at once that Louisa never got over it. There followed an extraordinary week, which I look back upon as one of the most uncomfortable of my life. The doctor had something to say about the action of his patient's heart – it was weak and slightly irregular, and he was anxious to learn whether she had lately been exposed to any violent shock or emotion – but he could give no name to the disorder under the influence of which she had begun unmistakably to sink. She lay on the sofa in her room – she refused to go to bed, and in the absence of complications it was not insisted on – utterly white, weak and abstracted, shaking her head at all suggestion, waving away all nourishment save the infinitesimally little that enabled her to stretch out her hand from time to time (at intervals of very unequal length) and begin 'Mother, mother!' as if she were mustering courage for a supreme confession. The courage never came; she was haunted by a strange impulse to speak, which in turn was checked on her lips by some deeper horror or some stranger fear. She seemed to seek relief spasmodically from some unforgettable consciousness and then to find the greatest relief of all in impenetrable silence. I knew these things only from her mother, for before me (I went gently in and out of her room two or three times a day) she gave no sign whatever. The little local doctor, after the first day, acknowledged himself at sea and expressed a desire to consult with a colleague at Exeter. The colleague journeyed down to us and shuffled and stammered: he recommended an appeal to a high authority in London. The high authority was summoned by telegraph and paid us a flying visit. He enunciated the valuable opinion that it was a very curious case and dropped the striking remark that in so charming a home a young lady ought to bloom like a flower. The young lady's late hostess came over, but she could throw no light on anything: all that she had ever noticed was that Louisa had seemed 'rather blue' for a day or two before she brought her visit to a close. Our days were dismal enough and our nights were dreadful, for I took turns with Helen in sitting up with the girl. Chantry Court itself seemed conscious of the riddle that made its chambers ache; it bowed its grey old head over the fate of its daughter. The people who had been coming were put off; dinner became a ceremony enacted mainly by the servants. I sat alone with Christopher Chantry, whose honest hair, in his mystification, stuck out as if he had been overhauling accounts. My hours with Louisa were even more intensely silent, for she almost never looked at me. In the watches of the night however I at last saw more clearly into what she was thinking of. Once when I caught her wan eyes resting upon me I took advantage of it to kneel down by her bed and speak to her with the utmost tenderness.

'If you can't say it to your mother, can you say it perhaps to *me*?'

She gazed at me for some time. 'What does it matter now – if I'm dying?'

I shook my head and smiled. 'You won't die if you get it off your mind.'

'You'd be cruel to him,' she said. 'He's innocent – he's innocent.'

'Do you mean *you're* guilty? What trifle are you magnifying?'

'Do you call it a trifle—?' She faltered and paused.

'Certainly I do, my dear.' Then I risked a great stroke. 'I've often done it myself!'

'*You?* Never, never! I was cruel to him,' she added.

This puzzled me; I couldn't work it into my conception. 'How were you cruel?'

'In the garden. I changed suddenly, I drove him away, I told him he filled me with horror.'

'Why did you do that?'

'Because my shame came over me.'

'Your shame?'

'What I had done in the house.'

'And what had you done?'

She lay a few moments with her eyes closed, as if she were living it over. 'I broke out to him, I told him,' she began at last. But she couldn't continue, she was powerless to utter it.

'Yes, I know what you told him. Millions of girls have told young men that before.'

'They've been asked, they've been asked! They didn't speak *first*! I didn't even know him, he didn't care for me, I had seen him for the first time the day before. I said strange things to him, and he behaved like a gentleman.'

'Well he might!'

'Then before he could turn round, when we had simply walked out of the house together and strolled in the garden – it was as if I were borne along in the air by the wonder of what I had said – it rolled over me that I was lost.'

'Lost?'

'That I had been horrible – that I had been mad. Nothing could never unsay it. I frightened him – I almost struck him.'

'Poor fellow!' I smiled.

'Yes – pity him. He was kind. But he'll see me that way – always!'

I hesitated as to the answer it was best to make to this; then I produced: 'Don't think he'll remember you – he'll see other girls.'

'Ah, he'll *forget* me!' she softly and miserably wailed; and I saw that I had said the wrong thing. I bent over her more closely, to kiss her, and when I raised my head her mother was on the other side of the bed. She fell on her knees there for the same purpose, and when Louisa felt her lips she stretched out her arms to embrace her. She had the strength to draw her close, and I heard her begin again, for the hundredth time, 'Mother, mother—'

'Yes, my own darling.'

Then for the hundredth time I heard her stop. There was an intensity in her silence. It made me wildly nervous; I got up and turned away.'

'Mother, mother,' the girl repeated, and poor Helen replied with a sound of passionate solicitation. But her daughter only exhaled in the waiting hush, while I stood at the window where the dawn was faint, the most miserable moan in the world. 'I'm dying,' she said, articulately; and she died that night, after an hour, unconscious. The doctor arrived almost at the moment; this time he was sure it must have been the heart. The poor parents were in stupefaction, and I gave up half my visits and stayed with them a month. But in spite of their stupefaction I kept my vow.

Collaboration

I DON'T KNOW HOW much people care for my work, but they like my studio (of which indeed I am exceedingly fond myself), as they show by their inclination to congregate there at dusky hours on winter afternoons, or on long dim evenings when the place looks well with its rich combinations and low-burning lamps and the bad pictures (my own) are not particularly visible. I won't go into the question of how many of these are purchased, but I rejoice in the distinction that my invitations are never declined. Some of my visitors have been good enough to say that on Sunday evenings in particular there is no pleasanter place in Paris – where so many places are pleasant – none friendlier to easy talk and repeated cigarettes, to the exchange of points of view and the comparison of accents. The air is as international as only Parisian air can be; women, I surmise, think they look well in it; they come also because they fancy they are doing something Bohemian, just as many of the men come because they suppose they are doing something correct. The old heraldic cushions on the divans, embossed with rusty gold, are favourable both to expansion and to contraction – that, of course, of contracting parties – and the Italian brocade on the walls appeals to one's highest feelings. Music makes its home there – though I confess I am not quite the master of *that* house, and when it is going on in a truly receptive hush I enjoy the way my company leans back and gazes through the thin smoke of cigarettes up at the distant Tiepolo in the almost palatial ceiling. I make sure the piano, the tobacco and the tea are all of the best.

For the conversation, I leave that mostly to take care of itself. There are discussions, of course, and differences – sometimes even a violent circulation of sense and sound; but I have a consciousness that beauty flourishes and that harmonies prevail in the end. I have occasionally known a visitor to be rude to me because he disliked another visitor's opinions – I had seen an old habitué slip away without bidding me good-night on the arrival of some confident specimen of *les jeunes*; but as a general thing we have it out together on the spot – the place is really a chamber of justice, a temple of reconciliation: we understand each other if we only sit up late enough. Art protects her children in the long run – she only asks them to trust her. She is like the Catholic Church – she guarantees paradise to the faithful. Music, moreover, is a universal solvent; though I've not an infallible ear I've a sufficient sense of the matter for that. Ah, the wounds I've known it to heal – the bridges I've known it to build – the ghosts I've known it to lay! Though I've seen people stalk out I've never observed them not to steal back. My studio in short is the theatre of a cosmopolite drama, a comedy essentially 'of character'.

One of the liveliest scenes of the performance was the evening, last winter, on which I became aware that one of my compatriots – an American, my good friend Alfred Bonus – was engaged in a controversy somewhat acrimonious, on a literary subject, with Herman Heidenmauer, the young composer who had been playing to us divinely a short time before and whom I thought of neither as a disputant nor as an Englishman. I perceived in a moment that something had happened to present him in this combined character to poor Bonus, who was so ardent a patriot that he lived in Paris rather than in London, who had met his interlocutor for the first time on this occasion, and who apparently had been misled by the perfection with which Heidenmauer spoke English – he spoke it really better than Alfred Bonus. The young musician, a born Bavarian, had spent a few years in England, where he had a commercial stepbrother planted and more or less prosperous – a helpful man who had watched over his difficult first steps, given him a temporary home, found him publishers and pupils, smoothed the way to a stupefied hearing for his first productions. He knew his London and might at a first glance have been taken for one of its products; but he had, in addition to a genius of the sort that London fosters but doesn't beget, a very German soul. He brought me a note from an old friend on the other side of the Channel, and I liked him as soon as I looked at him; so much indeed that I could forgive him for making me feel thin and empirical, conscious that *he* was one of the higher kind whom the future has looked in the face. He had met through his gold spectacles her deep eyes, and some mutual communication had occurred. This had given him a confidence which passed for conceit only with those who didn't know the reason.

I guessed the reason early, and, as may be imagined, he didn't grudge me the knowledge. He was happy and various – as little as possible the mere long-haired music-monger. His hair was short – it was only his legs and his laughter that were long. He was fair and rosy, and his gold spectacles glittered as if in response to the example set them by his beautiful young golden beard. You would have been sure he was an artist without going so far as to decide upon his particular passion; for you would have been conscious that whatever this passion might be it was acquainted with many of the others and mixed with them to its profit. Yet these discoveries had not been fully made by Alfred Bonus, whose occupation was to write letters to the American journals about the way the 'boys' were coming on in Paris; for in such a case he probably would not have expected such nebulous greatness to condense at a moment's notice. Bonus is clever and critical, and a sort of self-appointed emissary or agent of the great republic. He has it at heart to prove that the Americans in Europe *do* get on – taking for granted on the part of the Americans at home an interest in this subject greater, as I often assure him, than any really felt. 'Come, now, do *I* get on?' I often ask him; and I sometimes push the inquiry so far as to stammer: 'And you, my dear Bonus, do *you* get on?' He is apt to look a little injured on such occasions, as if he would like to say in reply: 'Don't you call it success to have Sunday evenings at which I'm a regular attendant? And can you question for a moment the figure I make at them?' It has even occurred to me that he suspects me of painting badly on purpose to spite him — that is to interfere with his favourite dogma. Therefore to spite me in return he's in the heroic predicament of refusing to admit that I'm a failure. He takes a great interest in the plastic arts, but his intensest sympathy is for literature. This sentiment is somewhat starved, as in that school the boys languish as yet on a back seat. To show what they are doing Bonus has to retreat upon the studios, but there is nothing he enjoys so much as having, when the rare chance offers, a good literary talk. He follows the French movement closely and explains it profusely to our compatriots, whom he mystifies, but who guess he's rather loose.

I forget how his conversation with Heidenmauer began — it was, I think, some difference of opinion about one of the English poets that set them afloat. Heidenmauer knows the English poets, and the French, and the Italian, and the Spanish, and the Russian — he is a wonderful representative of that Germanism which consists in the negation of intellectual frontiers. It is the English poets that, if I'm not mistaken, he loves best, and probably the harm was done by his having happened to say so. At any rate Alfred Bonus let him have it, without due notice perhaps, which is rather Alfred's way, on the question (a favourite one with my compatriot) of the backward state of literature

in England, for which after all Heidenmauer was not responsible. Bonus believes in responsibility – the responsibility of
others, an attitude which tends to make some of his friends
extremely secretive, though perhaps it would have been justified
– as to this I'm not sure – had Heidenmauer been, under the
circumstances, technically British. Before he had had time to
explain that he was not, the other persons present had become
aware that a kind of challenge had passed – that nation, in a
sudden startled flurry, somehow found itself pitted against
nation. There was much vagueness at first as to which of the
nations were engaged and as to what their quarrel was about,
the question coming presently to appear less simple than the
spectacle (so easily conceivable) of a German's finding it hot for
him in a French house, a house French enough at any rate to
give countenance to the idea of his quick defeat.

How could the right cause fail of protection in any house of
which Madame de Brindes and her charming daughter were so
good as to be assiduous frequenters? I recollect perfectly the
pale gleam of joy in the mother's handsome face when she
gathered that what had happened was that a detested German
was on his defence. She wears her eternal mourning (I admit
it's immensely becoming) for a triple woe, for multiplied griefs
and wrongs, all springing from the crash of the Empire, from
the battlefields of 1870. Her husband fell at Sedan, her father
and her brother on still darker days; both her own family and
that of M. de Brindes, their general situation in life, were, as
may be said, creations of the Empire, so that from one hour to

the other she found herself sinking with the wreck. You won't recognize her under the name I give her, but you may none the less have admired, between their pretty lemon-coloured covers, the touching tales of Claude Lorrain. She plies an ingenious, pathetic pen and has reconciled herself to effort and privation for the sake of her daughter. I say privation, because these distinguished women are poor, receive with great modesty and have broken with a hundred of those social sanctities than are dearer to French souls than to any others. They have gone down into the market-place, and Paule de Brindes, who is three-and-twenty today and has a happy turn for keeping a water-colour liquid, earns a hundred francs here and there. She is not so handsome as her mother, but she has magnificent hair and what the French call a look of race, and is, or at least was till the other day, a frank and charming young woman. There is something exquisite in the way these ladies are earnestly, conscientiously modern. From the moment they accept necessities they accept them all, and poor Madame de Brindes flatters herself that she has made her dowerless daughter one of us others. The girl goes out alone, talks with young men and, although she only paints landscape, takes a free view of the *convenances*. Nothing can please either of them more than to tell them they have thrown over their superstitions. They haven't, thank Heaven; and when I want to be reminded of some of the prettiest in the world – of a thousand fine scruples and pleasant forms, and of what grace can do for the sake of grace – I know where to go for it.

It was a part of this pious heresy – much more august in the way they presented it than some of the aspects of the old faith – that Paule should have become 'engaged', quite like a *jeune mees*, to my brilliant friend Félix Vendemer. He is such a votary of the modern that he was inevitably interested in the girl of the future and had matched one reform with another, being ready to marry without a penny, as the clearest way of expressing his appreciation, this favourable specimen of the type. He simply fell in love with Mademoiselle de Brindes and behaved, on his side, equally like one of us others, except that he begged me to ask her mother for her hand. I was inspired to do so with eloquence, and my friends were not insensible of such an opportunity to show that they now lived in the world of realities. Vendemer's sole fortune is his genius, and he and Paule, who confessed to an answering flame, plighted their troth like a pair of young rustics or (what comes for French people to the same thing) young Anglo-Saxons. Madame de Brindes thinks such doings at bottom very vulgar; but vulgar is what she tries hard to be, she is so convinced it is the only way to make a living. Vendemer had had at that time only the first of his successes, which was not, as you will remember – and unfortunately for Madame de Brindes – of this remunerative kind. Only a few people recognized the perfection of his little volume of verse: my acquaintance with him originated in my having been one of the few. A volume of verse was a scanty provision to marry on, so that, still like a pair of us others, the luckless lovers had to bide their time. Presently, however, came the success (again a success only with those who care for quality, not with the rough and ready public) of his comedy in verse at the Français. This charming work had just been taken off (it had been found not to make money), when the various parties to my little drama met Heidenmauer at my studio.

Vendemer, who has, as indeed the others have, a passion for music, was tremendously affected by hearing him play two or three of his compositions, and I immediately saw that the immitigable German quality was a morsel much less bitter for him than for the two uncompromising ladies. He went so far as to speak to Heidenmauer frankly, to thank him with effusion, an effort of which neither of the quivering women would have been capable. Vendemer was in the room the night Alfred Bonus raised his little breeze; I saw him lean on the piano and listen with a queer face looking however rather wonderingly at Heidenmauer. Before this I had noticed the instant paleness (her face was admirably expressive) with which Madame de Brindes saw her prospective son-in-law make up, as it were, to the original Teuton, whose national character was intensified to her aching mind, as it would have been to that of most Frenchwomen in her place, by his wash of English colour. A German was bad enough – but a German with English aggravations! Her senses were too fine to give her the excuse of not feeling that his compositions were interesting, and she was capable, magnanimously, of listening to them with dropped eyes; but (much as it ever cost her not to be perfectly courteous), she couldn't have made even the most superficial speech to him about them. Marie de Brindes could never have spoken to Herman Heidenmauer. It was a narrowness if you will, but a narrowness that to my vision was enveloped in a dense atmosphere – a kind of sunset bloom – of enriching and fortifying things. Herman Heidenmauer himself, like the man of imagination and the lover of life that he was, would have entered into it delightedly, been charmed with it as a fine case of bigotry. This was conspicuous in Marie de Brindes: her loyalty to the national idea was that of a *dévote* to a form of worship. She never spoke of France, but she always made me think of it, and with an authority which the women of her race seem to me to have in the question much more than the men. I daresay I'm rather in love with her, though, being considerably younger, I've never told her so – as if she would in the least mind that! I have indeed been a little checked by a spirit of allegiance to Vendemer; suspecting always (excuse my sophistication) that in the last analysis it is the mother's charm that he feels – or originally felt – in the daughter's. He spoke of the elder lady to me in those days with the insistence with which only a Frenchman can speak of the objects of his affection. At any rate there was always something symbolic and slightly ceremonial to me in her delicate cameo-face and her general black-robed presence: she made me think of a priestess or a mourner, of revolutions and sieges, detested treaties and ugly public things. I pitied her, too, for the strife of the elements in her – for the way she must have felt a noble enjoyment mutilated. She was too good for that, and yet she was too rigid for anything else; and the sight of such dismal perversions made me hate more than ever the stupid terms on which nations have organized their intercourse.

When she gathered that one of my guests was simply cramming it down the throat of another that the English literary mind was not even literary, she turned away with a vague shrug and a pitiful look at her daughter for the taste of people who took their pleasure so poorly: the truth in question would be so obvious that it was not worth making a scene about. Madame de Brindes evidently looked at any scene between the English and the Americans as a quarrel proceeding vaguely from below stairs – a squabble sordidly domestic. Her almost immediate departure with her daughter operated as a lucky interruption, and I caught for the first time in the straight, spare girl, as she followed her mother, a little of the air that Vendemer had told me he found in her, the still exaltation, the brown uplifted head that we attribute, or that at any rate he made it visible to me that he attributed, to the dedicated Maid. He considered that his intended bore a striking resemblance to Jeanne d'Arc, and he marched after her on this occasion like a square-shouldered armour-bearer. He reappeared, however, after he had put the ladies into a cab, and half an hour later the rest of my friends, with the sole exception of Bonus, having dispersed, he was sitting up with me in the empty studio for another *bout de causerie*. At first perhaps I was too occupied with reprimanding my compatriot to give much attention to what Vendemer might have to say; I remember at any rate that I had asked Bonus what had induced him to make so grave a blunder. He was not even yet, it appeared, aware of his blunder, so that I had to inquire by what odd chance he had taken Heidenmauer for a bigoted Briton.

'If I spoke to him as one he answered as one; that's bigoted enough,' said Alfred Bonus.

'He was confused and amused at your onslaught: he wondered what fly had stung you.'

'The fly of patriotism,' Vendemer suggested.

'Do *you* like him – a beast of a German?' Bonus demanded.

'If he's an Englishman he isn't a German – *il faut opter*. We can hang him for the one or for the other, we can't hang him for both. I was immensely struck with those things he played.'

'They had no charm for me, or doubtless I too should have been demoralized,' Alfred said.

'He seemed to know nothing about Miss Brownrigg. Now Miss Brownrigg's great.'

'I like the things and even the people you quarrel about, you big babies of the same breast. *C'est à se tordre!*' Vendemer declared.

'I may be very abject, but I *do* take an interest in the American novel,' Alfred rejoined.

'I hate such expressions: there's no such thing as the American novel.'

'Is there by chance any such thing as the French?'

'*Pas d'avantage* – for the artist himself; how can you ask? I don't know what is meant by French art and English art and American art: those seem to me mere cataloguers' and reviewers' and tradesmen's names, representing preoccupations utterly foreign to the artist. Art is art in every country, and the novel (since Bonus mentions that) is the novel in every tongue, and hard enough work they have to live up to that privilege, without our adding another muddle to the problem. The reader, the consumer may call things as he likes, but we leave him to his little amusements.' I suggested that we were all readers and consumers; which only made Vendemer continue: 'Yes, and only a small handful of us have the ghost of a palate. But you and I and Bonus are of the handful.'

'What do you mean by the handful?' Bonus inquired.

Vendemer hesitated a moment. 'I mean the few intelligent people, and even the few people who are not—' He paused again an instant, long enough for me to request him not to say what they were 'not', and then went on: 'People in a word who have the honour to live in the only country worth living in.'

'And pray what country is that?'

'The land of dreams – the country of art.'

'Oh, the land of dreams! I live in the land of realities!' Bonus exclaimed. 'What do you all mean then by chattering so about *le roman russe*?'

'It's a convenience – to identify the work of three or four, *là-bas*, because we're so far from it. But do you see them *writing* "le roman russe"?'

'I happen to know that that's exactly what they want to do, some of them,' said Bonus. 'Some of the idiots, then! There are plenty of those everywhere. Anything born under that silly star is sure not to count.'

'Thank God I'm not an artist!' said Bonus.

'Dear Alfred's a critic,' I explained.

'And I'm not ashamed of my country,' he subjoined.

'Even a critic perhaps may be an artist,' Vendemer mused.

'Then as the great American critic Bonus may be the great American artist,' I went on.

'Is that what you're supposed to give us – "American" criticism?' Vendemer asked, with dismay in his expressive, ironic face. 'Take care, take care, or it will be more American than critical, and then where will *you* be? However,' he continued, laughing and with a change of tone, 'I may see the matter in too lurid a light, for I've just been favoured with a judgement conceived in the purest spirit of our own national genius.' He looked at me a moment and then he remarked, 'That dear Madame de Brindes doesn't approve of my attitude.'

'Your attitude?'

'Toward your German friend. She let me know it when I went downstairs with her – told me I was much too cordial, that I must observe myself.'

'And what did you reply to that?'

'I answered that the things he had played were extraordinarily beautiful.'

'And how did she meet that?'

'By saying that he's an enemy of our country.'

'She had you there,' I rejoined.

Yes, I could only reply, "*Chère madame, voyons!*"'

'That was meagre.'

'Evidently, for it did no more for me than to give her a chance to declare that he can't possibly be here for any good and that he belongs to a race it's my sacred duty to loathe.'

'I see what she means.'

'I don't then – where artists are concerned. I said to her, "*Ah, madame, vous savez que pour moi il n'y a que l'art!*"'

'It's very exciting!' I laughed. 'How could she parry that?'

'"I know it, my dear child – but for *him*?" That's the way she parried it. "Very well, for him?" I asked. "For him there's the insolence of the victor and a secret scorn for our incurable illusions!"'

'Heidenmauer has no insolence and no secret scorn.'

Vendemer was silent a moment. 'Are you very sure of that?'

'Oh, I like him! He's out of all that, and far above it. But what did Mademoiselle Paule say?' I inquired.

'She said nothing – she only looked at me.'

'Happy man!'

'Not a bit. She looked at me with strange eyes, in which I could read "Go straight, my friend – go straight!" *Oh, les femmes, les femmes!*'

'What's the matter with them now?'

'They've a mortal hatred of art!'

'It's a true, deep instinct,' said Alfred Bonus.

'But what passed further with Madame de Brindes?' I went on.

'She only got into her cab, pushing her daughter first; on which I slammed the door rather hard and came up here. *Cela m'a porté sur les nerfs.*'

'I'm afraid I haven't soothed them,' Bonus said, looking for his hat. When he had found it he added: 'When the English have beaten us and pocketed our *milliards* I'll forgive them; but not till then!' And with this he went off, made a little uncomfortable, I think, by Vendemer's sharper alternatives, while the young Frenchman called after him: 'My dear fellow, at night all cats are grey!'

Vendemer, when we were left alone together, mooned about the empty studio awhile and asked me three or four questions about Heidenmauer. I satisfied his curiosity as well as I could, but I demanded the reason of it. The reason he gave was that one of the young German's compositions had already begun to haunt his memory; but that was a reason which, to my sense, still left something unexplained. I didn't, however, challenge him, before he quitted me, further than to warn him against being deliberately perverse.

'What do you mean by being deliberately perverse?' He fixed me so with his intensely living French eye that I became almost blushingly conscious of a certain insincerity and, instead of telling him what I meant, tried to get off with the deplorable remark that the prejudices of Mesdames de Brindes were after all respectable. 'That's exactly what makes them so odious!' cried Vendemer.

A few days after this, late in the afternoon, Herman Heidenmauer came in to see me and found the young Frenchman seated at my piano – trying to win back from the keys some echo of a passage in the *Abendlied* we had listened to on the

Sunday evening. They met, naturally, as good friends, and Heidenmauer sat down with instant readiness and gave him again the page he was trying to recover. He asked him for his address, that he might send him the composition, and at Vendemer's request, as we sat in the firelight, played half a dozen other things. Vendemer listened in silence but to my surprise took leave of me before the lamp was brought in. I asked him to stay to dinner (I had already appealed to Heidenmauer to stay), but he explained that he was engaged to dine with Madame de Brindes – *à la maison*, as he always called it. When he had gone Heidenmauer, with whom on departing he had shaken hands without a word, put to me the same questions about him that Vendemer had asked on the Sunday evening about the young German, and I replied that my visitor would find in a small volume of remarkable verse published by Lemerre, which I placed in his hands, much of the information he desired. This volume, which had just appeared, contained, beside a reprint of Vendemer's earlier productions, many of them admirable lyrics, the drama that had lately been played at the Français, and Heidenmauer took it with him when he left me. But he left me late, and before this occurred, all the evening, we had much talk about the French nation. In the foreign colony of Paris the exchange of opinions on this subject is one of the most inevitable and by no means the least interesting of distractions; it furnishes occupation to people rather conscious of the burden of leisure. Heidenmauer had been little in Paris, but he was all the more open to impressions; they evidently poured in upon him and he gave them a generous hospitality. In the diffused white light of his fine German intelligence old colours took on new tints to me, and while we spun fancies about the wonderful race around us I added to my little stock of notions about his own. I saw that his admiration for our neighbours was a very high tide, and I was struck with something bland and unconscious (noble and serene in its absence of precautions) in the way he let his doors stand open to it. It would have been exasperating to many Frenchmen; he looked at them through his clear spectacles with such an absence of suspicion that they might have anything to forgive him, such a thin metaphysical view of instincts and passions. He had the air of not allowing for recollections and nerves, and would doubtless give them occasion to make afresh some of their reflections on the tact of *ces gens-là*.

A couple of days after I had given him Vendemer's book he came back to tell me that he found great beauty in it. 'It speaks to me – it speaks to me,' he said with his air of happy proof. 'I liked the songs – I liked the songs. Besides,' he added, 'I like the little romantic play – it has given me wonderful ideas; more ideas than anything has done for a long time. Yes – yes.'

'What kind of ideas?'

'Well, this kind.' And he sat down to the piano and struck the keys. I listened without more questions, and after a while I began to understand. Suddenly he said: 'Do you know the words of *that*?' and before I could answer he was rolling out one of the lyrics of the little volume. The poem was strange and obscure, yet irresistibly beautiful, and he had translated it into music still more tantalizing than itself. He sounded the words with his German accent, barely perceptible in English but strongly marked in French. He dropped them and took them up again; he was playing with them, feeling his way. '*This* is my idea!' he broke out; he had caught it, in one of its mystic mazes, and he rendered it with a kind of solemn freshness. There was a phrase he repeated, trying it again and again, and while he did so he chanted the words of the song as if they were an illuminating flame, an inspiration. I was rather glad on the whole that Vendemer didn't hear what his pronunciation made of them, but as I was in the very act of rejoicing I became aware that the author of the verses had opened the door. He had pushed it gently, hearing the music; then hearing also his own poetry he had paused and stood looking at Heidenmauer. The young German nodded and laughed and, irreflectively, spontaneously, greeted him with a friendly '*Was sagen Sie dazu?*' I saw Vendemer change colour; he blushed red and, for an instant, as he stood wavering, I thought he was going to retreat. But I beckoned him in and, on the divan beside me, patted a place for him to sit.

He came in but didn't take this place; he went and stood before the fire to warm his feet, turning his back to us. Heidenmauer played and played, and after a little Vendemer turned round; he looked about him for a seat, dropped into it and sat with his elbows on his knees and his head in his hands. Presently Heidenmauer called out, in French, above the music: 'I like your songs — I like them immensely!' but the young

Frenchman neither spoke nor moved. When, however, five minutes later Heidenmauer stopped he sprang up with an entreaty to him to go on, to go on for the love of God. '*Foilà-foilà!*' cried the musician, and with hands for an instant suspended he wandered off into mysterious worlds. He played Wagner and then Wagner again – a great deal of Wagner; in the midst of which, abruptly, he addressed himself again to Vendemer, who had gone still further from the piano, launching to me, however from his corner a '*Dieu, que c'est beau!*' which I saw that Heidenmauer caught. 'I've a conception for an opera, you know – I'd give anything if you'd do the libretto!' Our German friend laughed out, after this, with clear good nature, and the rich appeal brought Vendemer slowly to his feet again, staring at the musician across the room and turning this time perceptibly pale.

I felt there was a drama in the air, and it made me a little nervous; to conceal which I said to Heidenmauer: 'What's your conception? What's your subject?'

'My conception would be realized in the subject of M. Vendemer's play – if he'll do that for me in a great lyric manner!' And with this the young German, who had stopped playing to answer me, quitted the piano and Vendemer got up to meet him. 'The subject is splendid – it has taken possession of me. Will you do it with me? Will you work with me? We shall make something great!'

'Ah, you don't know what you ask!' Vendemer answered, with his pale smile.

'I do – I do: I've thought of it. It will be bad for me in my country; I shall suffer for it. They won't like it – they'll abuse me for it – they'll say of me *pis que pendre*.' Heidenmauer pronounced it *bis que bendre*.

'They'll hate my libretto so?' Vendemer asked.

'Yes, your libretto – they'll say it's immoral and horrible. And they'll say *I'm* immoral and horrible for having worked with you,' the young composer went on, with his pleasant healthy lucidity. 'You'll injure my career. Oh yes, I shall suffer!' he joyously, exultingly cried.

'*Et moi donc!*' Vendemer exclaimed.

'Public opinion, yes. I shall also make *you* suffer – I shall nip your prosperity in the bud. All that's *des bêtises – tes pétisses*,' said poor Heidenmauer. 'In art there are no countries.'

'Yes, art is terrible, art is monstrous,' Vendemer replied, looking at the fire.

'I love your songs – they have extraordinary beauty.'

'And Vendemer has an equal taste for your compositions,' I said to Heidenmauer.

'Tempter!' Vendemer murmured to me, with a strange look.

'*C'est juste!* I mustn't meddle – which will be all the easier as I'm dining out and must go and dress. You two make yourselves at home and fight it out here.'

'Do you *leave* me?' asked Vendemer, still with his strange look.

'My dear fellow, I've only just time.'

'We will dine together – he and I – at one of those characteristic places, and we will look at the matter in its different relations,' said Heidenmauer. 'Then we will come back here to finish – your studio is so good for music.'

'There are some things it *isn't* good for,' Vendemer remarked, looking at our companion.

'It's good for poetry – it's good for truth,' smiled the composer.

'You'll stay *here* and dine together,' I said; 'my servant can manage that.'

'No, no – we'll go out and we'll walk together. We'll talk a great deal,' Heidenmauer went on. 'The subject is so comprehensive,' he said to Vendemer, as he lighted another cigar.

'The subject?'

'Of your drama. It's so universal.'

'Ah, the universe – *il n'y a que ça!*' I laughed, to Vendemer, partly with a really amused sense of the exaggerated woe that looked out of his poetic eyes and that seemed an appeal to me not to forsake him, to throw myself into the scale of the associations he would have to stifle, and partly to encourage him, to express my conviction that two such fine minds couldn't in the long run be the worse for coming to an agreement. I might have been a more mocking Mephistopheles handing over his pure spirit to my literally German Faust.

When I came home at eleven o'clock I found him alone in my studio, where, evidently, for some time, he had been moving up and down in agitated thought. The air was thick with Bavarian fumes, with the reverberation of mighty music and great ideas, with the echoes of that 'universe' to which I had so mercilessly consigned him. But I judged in a moment that Vendemer was in a very different phase of his evolution from the one in which I had left him. I had never seen his handsome, sensitive face so intensely illuminated.

'*Ça y est – ça y est!*' he exclaimed, standing there with his hands in his pockets and looking at me.

'You've really agreed to do something together?'

'We've sworn a tremendous oath – we've taken a sacred engagement.'

'My dear fellow, you're a hero.'

'Wait and see! *C'est un très-grand esprit.*'

'So much the better!'

'*C'est un bien beau génie.* Ah, we've risen – we soar; *nous sommes dans les grandes espaces!*' my friend continued with his dilated eyes.

'It's very interesting – because it will cost you something.'

'It will cost me everything!' said Félix Vendemer in a tone I seem to hear at this hour. 'That's just the beauty of it. It's the chance of chances to testify for art – to affirm an indispensable truth.'

'An indispensable truth?' I repeated, feeling myself soar too, but into the splendid vague.

'Do you know the greatest crime that can be perpetrated against it?'

'Against it?' I asked, still soaring.

'Against the religion of art – against the love for beauty – against the search for the Holy Grail?' The transfigured look with which he named these things, the way his warm voice filled the rich room, was a revelation of the wonderful talk that had taken place.

'Do you know – for one of *us* – the really damnable, the only unpardonable, sin?'

'Tell me, so that I may keep clear of it!'

'To profane *our* golden air with the hideous invention of patriotism.'

'It was a clever invention in its time!' I laughed.

'I'm not talking about its time – I'm talking about its place. It was never anything but a fifth-rate impertinence here. In art there are no countries – no idiotic nationalities, no frontiers, nor *douanes*, nor still more idiotic fortresses and bayonets. It has the unspeakable beauty of being the region in which those abominations cease, the medium in which such vulgarities simply can't live. What therefore are we to say of the brutes who wish to drag them all in – to crush to death with them all the flowers of such a garden, to shut out all the light of such a sky?' I was far from desiring to defend the 'brutes' in question, though there rose before me even at that moment a sufficiently vivid picture of the way, later on, poor Vendemer would have to face them. I quickly perceived indeed that the picture was, to his own eyes, a still more crowded canvas. Félix Vendemer, in the centre of it, was an admirable, a really sublime figure. If there had been wonderful talk after I quitted the two poets the wonder was not over yet – it went on far into the night for my benefit. We looked at the prospect in many lights, turned the subject about almost every way it would go; but I am bound to say there was one relation in which we tacitly agreed to forbear to consider it. We neither of us uttered the name of Paule de Brindes – the outlook in that direction would be too serious. And yet if Félix Vendemer, exquisite and incorruptible artist that he was, had fallen in love with the idea of 'testifying', it was from that direction that the finest part of his opportunity to do so would proceed.

I was only too conscious of this when, within the week, I received a hurried note from Madame de Brindes, begging me as a particular favour to come and see her without delay. I had not seen Vendemer again, but I had had a characteristic call from Heidenmauer, who, though I could imagine him perfectly in a Prussian helmet, with a needle-gun, perfectly, on definite occasion, a sturdy, formidable soldier, gave me a renewed impression of inhabiting, in the expansion of his genius and the exercise of his intelligence, no land of red tape, no province smaller nor more pedantically administered than the totality of things. I was reminded afresh too that *he* foresaw no striking salon-picture, no *chic* of execution nor romance of martyrdom, or at any rate devoted very little time to the consideration of such objects. He doubtless did scant justice to poor Vendemer's attitude, though he said to me of him, by the way, with his rosy deliberation: 'He has good ideas – he has good ideas. The French mind has – for me – the taste of a very delightful *bon-bon*!' He only measured the angle of convergence, as he called it, of their two projections. He was in short not preoccupied with the personal gallantry of their experiment; he was preoccupied with its 'aesthetic and harmonic basis'.

It was without her daughter that Madame de Brindes received me, when I obeyed her summons, in her scrap of a *quatrième* in the Rue de Miromesnil.

'Ah, *cher monsieur*, how could you have permitted such a horror – how could you have given it the countenance of your roof, of your influence?' There were tears in her eyes, and I don't think that for the moment I have ever been more touched by a reproach. But I pulled myself together sufficiently to affirm my faith as well as to disengage my responsibility. I explained that there was no horror to me in the matter, that if I was not a German neither was I a Frenchman, and that all I had before me was two young men inflamed by a great idea and nobly determined to work together to give it a great form.

A great idea – to go over to *ces gens-là*?'

'To go over to them?'

'To put yourself on their side – to throw yourself into the arms of those who hate us – to fall into their abominable trap!'

'What do you call their abominable trap?'

'Their false *bonhomie*, the very impudence of their intrigues, their profound, scientific deceit, and their determination to get the advantage of us by exploiting our generosity.'

'You attribute to such a man as Heidenmauer too many motives and too many calculations. He's quite ideally superior!'

'Oh, German idealism – we know what that means! We've no use for their superiority; let them carry it elsewhere – let them leave us alone. Why do they thrust themselves in upon us and set old wounds throbbing by their detested presence? We don't go near *them*, or ever wish to hear their ugly names or behold their *visages de bois*; therefore the most rudimentary good taste, the tact one would expect even from naked savages, might suggest to them to seek their amusements elsewhere. But *their* taste, *their* tact – I can scarcely trust myself to speak!'

Madame de Brindes did speak however at considerable further length and with a sincerity of passion which left one quite without arguments. There was no argument to meet the fact that Vendemer's attitude wounded her, wounded her daughter, *jusqu'au fond de l'âme*, that it represented for them abysses of shame and suffering and that for himself it meant a whole future compromised, a whole public alienated. It was vain doubtless to talk of such things; if people didn't *feel* them, if they hadn't the fibre of loyalty, the high imagination of honour, all explanations, all supplications were but a waste of noble emotion. M. Vendemer's perversity was monstrous – she had had a sickening discussion with him. What she desired of me was to make one last appeal to him, to put the solemn truth before him, to try to bring him back to sanity. It was as if he had temporarily lost his reason. It was to be made clear to him, *par exemple*, that unless he should recover it Mademoiselle de Brindes would unhesitatingly withdraw from her engagement.

'Does she *really* feel as you do?' I asked.

'Do you think I put words into her mouth? She feels as a *fille de France* is obliged to feel!'

'Doesn't she love him then?'

'She adores him. But she won't take him without his honour.'

'I don't understand such refinements!' I said.

'Oh, *vous autres*!' cried Madame de Brindes. Then with eyes glowing through her tears she demanded: 'Don't you know she knows how her father died?' I was on the point of saying 'What has that to do with it?' but I withheld the question, for after all I could conceive that it might have something. There was no disputing about tastes, and I could only express my sincere conviction that Vendemer was profoundly attached to Mademoiselle Paule. 'Then let him prove it by making her a sacrifice!' my strenuous hostess replied; to which I rejoined that I would repeat our conversation to him and put the matter before him as strongly as I could. I delayed a little to take leave, wondering if the girl would not come in – I should have been so much more content to receive her strange recantation from her own lips. I couldn't say this to Madame de Brindes; but she guessed I meant it, and before we separated we exchanged a look in which our mutual mistrust was written – the suspicion on her side that I should not be a very passionate intercessor and the conjecture on mine that she might be misrepresenting her daughter. This slight tension, l must add, was only momentary, for I have had a chance of observing Paule de Brindes since then, and the two ladies were soon satisfied that I pitied them enough to have been eloquent.

My eloquence has been of no avail, and I have learned (it has been one of the most interesting lessons of my life) of what transcendent stuff the artist may sometimes be made. Herman Heidenmauer and Félix Vendemer are, at the hour I write, immersed in their monstrous collaboration. There were postponements and difficulties at first, and there will be more serious ones in the future, when it is a question of giving the finished work to the world. The world of Paris will stop its ears in horror, the German Empire will turn its mighty back, and the authors of what I foresee (oh, I've been treated to specimens!) as a perhaps really epoch-making musical revelation (is Heidenmauer's style rubbing off on me?) will perhaps have to beg for a hearing in communities fatally unintelligent. It may very well be that they will not obtain any hearing at all for years. I like at any rate to think that time works for them. At present they work for themselves and for each other, amid drawbacks of several kinds. Separating after the episode in Paris, they have met again on alien soil, at a little place on the Genoese Riviera where sunshine is cheap and tobacco bad, and they live (the two together) for five francs a day, which is all they can muster between them. It appears that when Heidenmauer's London step-brother was informed of the young composer's unnatural alliance he instantly withdrew his subsidy. The return of it is contingent on the rupture of the unholy union and the destruction by flame of all the manuscript. The pair are very poor and the whole thing depends on their staying power. They are so preoccupied with their opera that they have no time for potboilers. Vendemer is in a feverish hurry, lest perhaps he should find himself chilled. There are still other details which contribute to the interest of the episode and which, for me, help to render it a most refreshing, a really great little case. It rests me, it delights me, there is something in it that makes for civilization. In their way they are working for human happiness. The strange course taken by Vendemer (I mean his renunciation of his engagement) must moreover be judged in the light of the fact that he was really in love. Something had to be sacrificed, and what he clung to most (he's extraordinary, I admit) was the truth he had the opportunity of proclaiming. Men give up their love for advantages every day, but they rarely give it up for such discomforts.

Paule de Brindes was the less in love of the two; I see her often enough to have made up my mind about that. But she's mysterious, she's odd; there was at any rate a sufficient wrench in her life to make her often absent-minded. Does her imagination hover about Félix Vendemer? A month ago, going into their rooms one day when her mother was not at home (the *bonne* had admitted me under a wrong impression) I found her at the piano, playing one of Heidenmauer's compositions – playing it without notes and with infinite expression. How had she got hold of it? How had she learned it? This was her secret – she blushed so that I didn't pry into it. But what is she doing, under the singular circumstances, with a composition of Herman Heidenmauer's? She never met him, she never heard him play, but that once. It will be a pretty complication if it shall appear that the young German genius made on that occasion more than one intense impression. This needn't appear, however, inasmuch as, being naturally in terror of the discovery by her mother of such an anomaly, she may count on me absolutely not to betray her. I hadn't fully perceived how deeply susceptible she is to music. She must have a strange confusion of feelings – a dim, haunting trouble, with a kind of ache of impatience for the wonderful opera somewhere in the depths of it. Don't we live fast, after all, and doesn't the old order change? Don't say art isn't mighty! I shall give you some more illustrations of it yet.

Nona Vincent

I

'I WONDERED WHETHER you wouldn't read it to me,' said Mrs Alsager, as they lingered a little near the fire before he took leave. She looked down at the fire sideways, drawing her dress away from it and making her proposal with a shy sincerity that added to her charm. Her charm was always great for Allan Wayworth, and the whole air of her house, which was simply a sort of distillation of herself, so soothing, so beguiling that he always made several false starts before departure. He had spent some such good hours there, had forgotten, in her warm, golden drawing-room, so much of the loneliness and so many of the worries of his life, that it had come to be the immediate answer to his longings, the cure for his aches, the harbour of refuge from his storms. His tribulations were not unprecedented, and some of his advantages, if of a usual kind, were marked in degree, inasmuch as he was very clever for one so young, and very independent for one so poor. He was eight-and-twenty, but he had lived a good deal and was full of ambitions and curiosities and disappointments. The opportunity to talk of some of these in Grosvenor Place corrected perceptibly the immense inconvenience of London. This inconvenience took for him principally the line of insensibility to Allan Wayworth's literary form. He had a literary form, or he thought he had, and her intelligent recognition of the circumstance was the sweetest consolation Mrs Alsager could have administered. She was even more literary and more artistic than he, inasmuch as he could often work off his overflow (this was his occupation, his profession), while the generous woman, abounding in happy thoughts, but unedited and unpublished, stood there in the rising tide like the nymph of a fountain in the plash of the marble basin.

The year before, in a big newspapery house, he had found himself next her at dinner, and they had converted the intensely material hour into a feast of reason. There was no motive for her asking him to come to see her but that she liked him, which it was the more agreeable to him to perceive as he perceived at the same time that she was exquisite. She was enviably free to act upon her likings, and it made Wayworth feel less unsuccessful to infer that for the moment he happened to be one of them. He kept the revelation to himself, and indeed there was nothing to turn his head in the kindness of a kind woman. Mrs Alsager occupied so completely the ground of possession that she would have been condemned to inaction had it not been for the principle of giving. Her husband, who was twenty years her senior, a massive personality in the City and a heavy one at home (wherever he stood, or even sat, he was monumental), owned half a big newspaper and the whole of a great many other things. He admired his wife, though she bore no children, and liked her to have other tastes than his, as that seemed to give a greater acreage to their life. His own appetites went so far he could scarcely see the boundary, and his theory was to trust her to push the limits of hers, so that between them the pair should astound by their consumption. His ideas were prodigiously vulgar, but some of them had the good fortune to be carried out by a person of perfect delicacy. Her delicacy made her play strange tricks with them, but he never found this out. She attenuated him without his knowing it, for what he mainly thought was that he had aggrandized *her*. Without her he really would have been bigger still, and society, breathing more freely, was practically under an obligation to her which, to do it justice, it acknowledged by an attitude of mystified respect. She felt a tremulous need to throw her liberty and her leisure into the things of the soul – the most beautiful things she knew. She found them, when she gave time to seeking, in a hundred places, and particularly in a dim and sacred region – the region of active pity – over her entrance into which she dropped curtains so thick that it would have been an impertinence to lift them. But she cultivated other beneficent passions, and if she cherished the dream of something fine the moments at which it most seemed to her to come true were when she saw beauty plucked flower-like in the garden of art. She loved the perfect work – she had the artistic chord. This chord could vibrate only to the touch of another, so that appreciation, in her spirit, had the added intensity of regret. She could understand the joy of creation, and she thought it scarcely enough to be told that she herself created happiness. She would have liked, at any rate, to choose her way; but it was just here that her liberty failed her. She had not the voice – she had only the vision. The only envy she was capable of was directed to those who, as she said, could do something.

As everything in her, however, turned to gentleness, she was admirably hospitable to such people as a class. She believed Allan Wayworth could do something, and she liked to hear him talk of the ways in which he meant to show it. He talked of them almost to no one else – she spoiled him for other listeners. With her fair bloom and her quiet grace she was indeed an ideal public, and if she had ever confided to him that she would have liked to scribble (she had in fact not mentioned it to a creature), he would have been in a perfect position for asking her why a woman whose face had so much expression should not have felt that she achieved. How in the world could she express better? There was less than that in Shakespeare and Beethoven. She had never been more generous than when, in compliance with her invitation, which I have recorded, he brought his play to read to her. He had spoken of it to her before, and one dark November afternoon, when her red fireside was more than ever an escape from the place and the season, he had broken out as he came in – 'I've done it, I've done it!' She made him tell her all about it – she took an interest really minute and asked questions delightfully apt. She had spoken from the first as if he were on the point of being acted, making him jump, with her participation, all sorts of dreary intervals. She liked the theatre as she liked all the arts of expression, and he had known her to go all the way to Paris for a particular performance. Once he had gone with her – the time she took that stupid Mrs Mostyn. She had been struck, when he sketched it, with the subject of his drama, and had spoken words that helped him to believe in it. As soon as he had rung down his curtain on the last act he rushed off to see her, but after that he kept the thing for repeated last touches. Finally, on Christmas day, by arrangement, she sat there and listened to it. It was in three acts and in prose, but rather of the romantic order, though dealing with contemporary English life, and he fondly believed that it showed the hand if not of the master, at least of the prize pupil.

Allan Wayworth had returned to England, at two-and-twenty, after a miscellaneous continental education; his father, the correspondent, for years, in several foreign countries successively, of a conspicuous London journal, had died just after this, leaving his mother and her two other children, portionless girls, to subsist on a very small income in a very dull German town. The young man's beginnings in London were difficult, and he had aggravated them by his dislike of journalism. His father's connection with it would have helped him, but he was (insanely, most of his friends judged – the great exception was always Mrs Alsager) *intraitable* on the question of form. Form – in his sense – was not demanded by English newspapers, and he couldn't give it to them in *their* sense. The demand for it was not great anywhere, and Wayworth spent costly weeks in polishing little compositions for magazines that didn't pay for style. The only person who paid for it was really Mrs Alsager: she had an infallible instinct for the perfect. She paid in her own way, and if Allan Wayworth had been a wage-earning person it would have made him feel that if he didn't receive his legal dues his palm was at least occasionally conscious of a gratuity. He had his limitations, his perversities, but the finest parts of him were the most alive, and he was restless and sincere. It is however the impression he produced on Mrs Alsager that most concerns us: she thought him not only remarkably good-looking but altogether original. There were some usual bad things he would never do – too many prohibitive puddles for him in the short cut to success.

For himself, he had never been so happy as since he had seen his way, as he fondly believed, to some sort of mastery of the scenic idea, which struck him as a very different matter now that he looked at it from within. He had had his early days of contempt for it, when it seemed to him a jewel, dim at the best, hidden in a dunghill, a taper burning low in an air thick with vulgarity. It was hedged about with sordid approaches, it was not worth sacrifice and suffering. The man of letters, in dealing with it, would have to put off all literature, which was like asking the bearer of a noble name to forego his immemorial heritage. Aspects change, however, with the point of view: Wayworth had waked up one morning in a different bed altogether. It is needless here to trace this accident to its source; it would have been much more interesting to a spectator of the young man's life to follow some of the consequences. He had been made (as he felt) the subject of a special revelation, and he wore his hat like a man in love. An angel had taken him by the hand and guided him to the shabby door which opens, it appears, into an interior both splendid and austere. The scenic idea was magnificent when once you had embraced it — the dramatic form had a purity which made some others look ingloriously rough. It had the high dignity of the exact sciences, it was mathematical and architectural. It was full of the refreshment of calculation and construction, the incorruptibility of line and law. It was bare, but it was erect, it was poor, but it was noble; it reminded him of some sovereign famed for justice who should have lived in a palace despoiled. There was a fearful amount of concession in it, but what you kept had a rare intensity. You were perpetually throwing over the cargo to save the ship, but what a motion you gave her when you made her ride the waves — a motion as rhythmic as the dance of a goddess! Wayworth took long London walks and thought of these things — London poured into his ears the mighty hum of its suggestion. His imagination glowed and melted down material, his intentions multiplied and made the air a golden haze. He saw not only the thing he should do, but the next and the next and the next; the future opened before him and he seemed to walk on marble slabs. The more he tried the dramatic form the more he loved it, the more he looked at it the more he perceived in it. What he perceived in it indeed he now perceived everywhere; if he stopped, in the London dusk, before some flaring shop-window, the place immediately constituted itself behind footlights, became a framed stage for his figures. He hammered at these figures in his lonely lodging, he shaped them and he shaped their tabernacle; he was like a goldsmith chiselling a casket, bent over with the passion for perfection. When he was neither roaming the streets with his vision nor worrying his problem at his table, he was exchanging ideas on the general question with Mrs Alsager, to whom he promised details that would amuse her in later and still happier hours. Her eyes were full of tears when he read her the last words of the finished work, and she murmured, divinely:

'And now – to get it done, to get it done!'

'Yes, indeed – to get it done!' Wayworth stared at the fire, slowly rolling up his type-copy. 'But that's a totally different part of the business, and altogether secondary.'

'But of course you want to be acted?'

'Of course I do – but it's a sudden descent. I want to intensely, but I'm sorry I want to.'

'It's there indeed that the difficulties begin,' said Mrs Alsager, a little off her guard.

'How can you say that? It's there that they end!'

'Ah, wait to see where they end!'

'I mean they'll now be of a totally different order,' Wayworth explained. 'It seems to me there can be nothing in the world more difficult than to write a play that will stand an all-round test, and that in comparison with them the complications that spring up at this point are of an altogether smaller kind.'

'Yes, they're not inspiring,' said Mrs Alsager; 'they're discouraging, because they're vulgar. The other problem, the working out of the thing itself, is pure art.'

'How well you understand everything!' The young man had got up, nervously, and was leaning against the chimney-piece with his back to the fire and his arms folded. The roll of his copy, in his fist, was squeezed into the hollow of one of them. He looked down at Mrs Alsager, smiling gratefully, and she answered him with a smile from eyes still charmed and suffused. 'Yes, the vulgarity will begin now,' he presently added.

'You'll suffer dreadfully.'

'I shall suffer in a good cause.'

'Yes, giving *that* to the world! You must leave it with me, I must read it over and over,' Mrs Alsager pleaded, rising to come nearer and draw the copy, in its cover of greenish-grey paper, which had a generic identity now to him, out of his grasp. 'Who in the world will do it? – who in the world *can*?' she went on, close to him, turning over the leaves. Before he could answer she had stopped at one of the pages; she turned the book round to him, pointing out a speech. 'That's the most beautiful place – those lines are a perfection.' He glanced at the spot she indicated, and she begged him to read them again – he had read them admirably before. He knew them by heart, and, closing the book while she held the other end of it, he murmured them over to her – they had indeed a cadence that pleased him – watching, with a facetious complacency which he hoped was pardonable, the applause in her face. 'Ah, who can utter such lines as *that*?' Mrs Alsager broke out; 'whom can you find to do *her*?'

'We'll find people to do them all!'

'But not people who are worthy.'

'They'll be worthy enough if they're willing enough. I'll work with them – I'll grind it into them.' He spoke as if he had produced twenty plays.

'Oh, it will be interesting!' she echoed.

'But I shall have to find my theatre first. I shall have to get a manager to believe in me.'

'Yes – they're so stupid!'

'But fancy the patience I shall want, and how I shall have to watch and wait,' said Allan Wayworth. 'Do you see me hawking it about London?'

'Indeed I don't – it would be sickening.'

'It's what I shall have to do. I shall be old before it's produced.'

'I shall be old very soon if it isn't!' Mrs Alsager cried. 'I know one or two of them,' she mused.

'Do you mean you would speak to them?'

'The thing is to get them to read it. I could do that.'

'That's the utmost I ask. But it's even for that I shall have to wait.'

She looked at him with kind sisterly eyes. 'You shan't wait.'

'Ah, you dear lady!' Wayworth murmured.

'That is *you* may, but *I* won't! Will you leave me your copy?' she went on, turning the pages again.

'Certainly; I have another.' Standing near him she read to herself a passage here and there; then, in her sweet voice, she read some of them out. 'Oh, if *you* were only an actress!' the young man exclaimed.

'That's the last thing I am. There's no comedy in *me*!'

She had never appeared to Wayworth so much his good genius. 'Is there any tragedy?' he asked, with the levity of complete confidence.

She turned away from him, at this, with a strange and charming laugh and a 'Perhaps that will be for you to determine!' But before he could disclaim such a responsibility she had faced him again and was talking about Nona Vincent as if she had been the most interesting of their friends and her situation at that moment an irresistible appeal to their sympathy. Nona Vincent was the heroine of the play, and Mrs Alsager had taken a tremendous fancy to her. 'I can't *tell* you how I like that woman!' she exclaimed in a pensive rapture of credulity which could only be balm to the artistic spirit.

'I'm awfully glad she lives a bit. What I feel about her is that she's a good deal like *you*,' Wayworth observed.

Mrs Alsager stared an instant and turned faintly red. This was evidently a view that failed to strike her; she didn't, however, treat it as a joke. 'I'm not impressed with the resemblance. I don't see myself doing what she does.'

'It isn't so much what she *does*,' the young man argued, drawing out his moustache.

'But what she does is the whole point. She simply tells her love – I should never do that.'

'If you repudiate such a proceeding with such energy, why do you like her for it?'

'It isn't what I like her for.'

'What else, then? That's intensely characteristic.'

Mrs Alsager reflected, looking down at the fire; she had the air of having half a dozen reasons to choose from. But the one she produced was unexpectedly simple; it might even have been prompted by despair at not finding others. 'I like her because *you* made her!' she exclaimed with a laugh, moving again away from her companion.

Wayworth laughed still louder. 'You made her a little yourself. I've thought of her as looking like you.'

'She ought to look much better,' said Mrs Alsager. 'No, certainly, I shouldn't do what *she* does.'

'Not even in the same circumstances?'

'I should never find myself in such circumstances. They're exactly your play, and have nothing in common with such a life as mine. However,' Mrs Alsager went on, 'her behaviour was natural for *her*, and not only natural, but, it seems to me, thoroughly beautiful and noble. I can't sufficiently admire the talent and tact with which you make one accept it, and I tell you frankly that it's evident to me there must be a brilliant future before a young man who, at the start, has been capable of such a stroke as that. Thank Heaven I can admire Nona Vincent as intensely as I feel that I don't resemble her!'

'Don't exaggerate that,' said Allan Wayworth.

'My admiration?'

'Your dissimilarity. She has your face, your air, your voice, your motion; she has many elements of your being.'

'Then she'll damn your play!' Mrs Alsager replied. They joked a little over this, though it was not in the tone of pleasantry that Wayworth's hostess soon remarked: 'You've got your remedy, however: have her done by the right woman.'

'Oh, have her "done" – have her "done"!' the young man gently wailed.

'I see what you mean, my poor friend. What a pity, when it's such a magnificent part – such a chance for a clever serious girl! Nona Vincent is practically your play – it will be open to her to carry it far or to drop it at the first corner.'

'It's a charming prospect,' said Allan Wayworth, with sudden scepticism. They looked at each other with eyes that, for a lurid moment, saw the worst of the worst; but before they parted they had exchanged vows and confidences that were dedicated wholly to the ideal. It is not to be supposed, however, that the knowledge that Mrs Alsager would help him made Wayworth less eager to help himself. He did what he could and felt that she, on her side, was doing no less; but at the end of a year he was obliged to recognize that their united effort had mainly produced the fine flower of discouragement. At the end of a year the lustre had, to his own eyes, quite faded from his unappreciated masterpiece, and he found himself writing for a biographical dictionary little lives of celebrities he had never heard of. To be printed, anywhere and anyhow, was a form of glory for a man so unable to be acted, and to be paid, even at encyclopaedic rates, had the consequence of making one resigned and verbose. He couldn't smuggle style into a dictionary, but he could at least reflect that he had done his best to learn from the drama that it is a gross impertinence almost anywhere. He had knocked at the door of every theatre in London, and, at a ruinous expense, had multiplied type-copies of *Nona Vincent* to replace the neat transcripts that had descended into the managerial abyss. His play was not even declined – no such flattering intimation was given him that it had been read. What the managers would do for Mrs Alsager concerned him little today; the thing that was relevant was that they would do nothing for *him*. That charming woman felt humbled to the earth, so little response had she had from the powers on which she counted. The two never talked about the play now, but he tried to show her a still finer friendship, that she might not think he felt she had failed him. He still walked about London with his dreams, but as months succeeded months and he left the year behind him they were dreams not so much of success as of revenge. Success seemed a colourless name for the reward of his patience; something fiercely florid, something sanguinolent was more to the point. His best consolation however was still in the scenic idea; it was not till now that he discovered how incurably he was in love with it. By the time a vain second year had chafed itself away he cherished his fruitless faculty the more for the obloquy it seemed to suffer. He lived, in his best hours, in a world of subjects and situations; he wrote another play and made it as different from its predecessor as such a very good thing could be. It might be a very good thing, but when he had committed it to the theatrical limbo indiscriminating fate took no account of the difference. He was at last able to leave England for three or four months; he went to Germany to pay a visit long deferred to his mother and sisters.

Shortly before the time he had fixed for his return he received from Mrs Alsager a telegram consisting of the words: 'Loder wishes see you – putting *Nona* instant rehearsal.' He spent the few hours before his departure in kissing his mother and sisters, who knew enough about Mrs Alsager to judge it lucky this respectable married lady was not there – a relief, however, accompanied with speculative glances at London and the morrow. Loder, as our young man was aware, meant the new 'Renaissance', but though he reached home in the evening it was not to this convenient modern theatre that Wayworth first proceeded. He spent a late hour with Mrs Alsager, an hour that throbbed with calculation. She told him that Mr Loder was charming, he had simply taken up the play in its turn; he had hopes of it, moreover, that on the part of a professional pessimist might almost be qualified as ecstatic. It had been cast, with a margin for objections, and Violet Grey was to do the heroine. She had been capable, while he was away, of a good piece of work at that foggy old playhouse the 'Legitimate'; the piece was a clumsy *réchauffé*, but she at least had been fresh. Wayworth remembered Violet Grey – hadn't he, for two years, on a fond policy of 'looking out', kept dipping into the London theatres to pick up prospective interpreters? He had not picked up many as yet, and this young lady at all events had never wriggled in his net. She was pretty and she was odd, but he had never prefigured her as Nona Vincent, nor indeed found himself attracted by what he already felt sufficiently launched in the profession to speak of as her artistic personality. Mrs Alsager was different – she declared that she had been struck not a little by some of her tones. The girl was interesting in the thing at the 'Legitimate', and Mr Loder, who had his eye on her, described her as ambitious and intelligent. She wanted awfully to get on – and some of those ladies were so lazy! Wayworth was sceptical – he had seen Miss Violet Grey, who was terribly itinerant, in a dozen theatres but only in one aspect. Nona Vincent had a dozen aspects, but only one theatre; yet with what a feverish curiosity the young man promised himself to watch the actress on the morrow! Talking the matter over with Mrs Alsager now seemed the very stuff that rehearsal was made of. The near prospect of being acted laid a finger even on the lip of inquiry; he wanted to go on tiptoe till the first night, to make no condition but that they should speak his lines, and he felt that he wouldn't so much as raise an eyebrow at the scene-painter if he should give him an old oak chamber.

He became conscious, the next day, that his danger would be other than this, and yet he couldn't have expressed to himself what it would be. Danger was there, doubtless – danger was everywhere, in the world of art, and still more in the world of commerce; but what he really seemed to catch, for the hour, was the beating of the wings of victory. Nothing could undermine that, since it was victory simply to be acted. It would be victory even to be acted badly; a reflection that didn't prevent him, however, from banishing, in his politic optimism, the word 'bad' from his vocabulary. It had no application, in the compromise of practice; it didn't apply even to his play, which he was conscious he had already outlived and as to which he foresaw that, in the coming weeks, frequent alarm would alternate, in his spirit, with frequent esteem. When he went down to the dusky daylit theatre (it arched over him like the temple of fame) Mr Loder, who was as charming as Mrs Alsager had announced, struck him as the genius of hospitality. The manager began to explain why, for so long, he had given no sign; but that was the last thing that interested Wayworth now, and he could never remember afterwards what reasons Mr Loder had enumerated. He liked, in the whole business of discussion and preparation, even the things he had thought he should probably dislike, and he revelled in those he had thought he should like. He watched Miss Violet Grey that evening with eyes that sought to penetrate her possibilities. She certainly had a few; they were qualities of voice and face, qualities perhaps even of intelligence; he sat there at any rate with a fostering, coaxing attention, repeating over to himself as convincingly as he could that she was not common – a circumstance all the more creditable as the part she was playing seemed to him desperately so. He perceived that this was why it pleased the audience; he divined that it was the part they enjoyed rather than the actress. He had a private panic, wondering how, if they liked *that* form, they could possibly like his. His form had now become quite an ultimate idea to him. By the time the evening was over some of Miss Violet Grey's features, several of the turns of her head, a certain vibration of her voice, had taken their place in the same category. She *was* interesting, she was distinguished; at any rate he had accepted her: it came to the same thing. But he left the theatre that night without speaking to her – moved (a little even to his own mystification) by an odd procrastinating impulse. On the morrow he was to read his three acts to the company, and then he should have a good deal to say; what he felt for the moment was a vague indisposition to commit himself. Moreover he found a slight confusion of annoyance in the fact that though he had been trying all the evening to look at Nona Vincent in Violet Grey's person, what subsisted in his vision was simply Violet Grey in Nona's. He didn't wish to see the actress so directly, or even so simply as that; and it had been very fatiguing, the effort to focus Nona both through the performer and through the 'Legitimate'. Before he went to bed that night he posted three words to Mrs Alsager – 'She's not a bit like it, but I daresay I can make her do.'

He was pleased with the way the actress listened, the next day, at the reading; he was pleased indeed with many things, at the reading, and most of all with the reading itself. The whole affair loomed large to him and he magnified it and mapped it out. He enjoyed his occupation of the big, dim, hollow theatre, full of the echoes of 'effect' and of a queer smell of gas and success – it all seemed such a passive canvas for his picture. For the first time in his life he was in command of resources; he was acquainted with the phrase, but had never thought he should know the feeling. He was surprised at what Loder appeared ready to do, though he reminded himself that he must never show it. He foresaw that there would be two distinct concomitants to the artistic effort of producing a play, one consisting of a great deal of anguish and the other of a great deal of amusement. He looked back upon the reading, afterwards, as the best hour in the business, because it was then that the piece had most struck him as represented. What came later was the doing of others; but this, with its imperfections and failures, was all his own. The drama lived, at any rate, for that hour, with an intensity that it was promptly to lose in the poverty and patchiness of rehearsal; he could see its life reflected, in a way that was sweet to him, in the stillness of the little semi-circle of attentive and inscrutable, of water-proofed and muddy-booted, actors. Miss Violet Grey was the auditor he had most to say to, and he tried on the spot, across the shabby stage, to let her have the soul of her part. Her attitude was graceful, but though she appeared to listen with all her faculties her face remained perfectly blank; a fact, however, not discouraging to Wayworth, who liked her better for not being premature. Her companions gave discernible signs of recognizing the passages of comedy; yet Wayworth forgave her even then for being inexpressive. She evidently wished before everything else to be simply sure of what it was all about.

He was more surprised even than at the revelation of the scale on which Mr Loder was ready to proceed by the discovery that some of the actors didn't like their parts, and his heart sank as he asked himself what he could possibly do with them if they were going to be so stupid. This was the first of his disappointments; somehow he had expected every individual to become instantly and gratefully conscious of a rare opportunity, and from the moment such a calculation failed he was at sea, or mindful at any rate that more disappointments would come. It was impossible to make out what the manager liked or disliked; no judgement, no comment escaped him; his acceptance of the play and his views about the way it should be mounted had apparently converted him into a veiled and shrouded figure. Wayworth was able to grasp the idea that they would all move now in a higher and sharper air than that of compliment and confidence. When he talked with Violet Grey after the reading he gathered that she was really rather crude: what better proof of it could there be than her failure to break out instantly with an expression of delight about her great chance? This reserve, however, had evidently nothing to do with high pretensions; she had no wish to make him feel that a person of her eminence was superior to easy raptures. He guessed, after a little, that she was puzzled and even somewhat frightened – to a certain extent she had not understood. Nothing could appeal to him more than the opportunity to clear up her difficulties, in the course of the examination of which he quickly discovered that, so far as she *had* understood, she had understood wrong. If she was crude it was only a reason the more for talking to her; he kept saying to her 'Ask me – ask me: ask me everything you can think of.'

She asked him, she was perpetually asking him, and at the
first rehearsals, which were without form and void to a degree
that made them strike him much more as the death of an experiment than as the dawn of a success, they threshed things out
immensely in a corner of the stage, with the effect of his coming
to feel that at any rate she was in earnest. He felt more and more
that his heroine was the keystone of his arch, for which indeed
the actress was very ready to take her. But when he reminded
this young lady of the way the whole thing practically depended
on her she was alarmed and even slightly scandalized: she spoke
more than once as if that could scarcely be the right way to
construct a play – make it stand or fall by one poor nervous girl.
She was almost morbidly conscientious, and in theory he liked
her for this, though he lost patience three or four times with the
things she couldn't do and the things she could. At such times
the tears came to her eyes; but they were produced by her own
stupidity, she hastened to assure him, not by the way he spoke,
which was awfully kind under the circumstances. Her sincerity
made her beautiful, and he wished to heaven (and made a point
of telling her so) that she could sprinkle a little of it over Nona.
Once, however, she was so touched and troubled that the sight
of it brought the tears for an instant to his own eyes; and it so
happened that, turning at this moment, he found himself face to
face with Mr Loder. The manager stared, glanced at the actress,
who turned in the other direction, and then smiling at Wayworth,
exclaimed, with the humour of a man who heard the gallery
laugh every night:

'I say – I say!'

'What's the matter?' Wayworth asked.

'I'm glad to see Miss Grey is taking such pains with you.'

'Oh, yes – she'll turn me out!' said the young man, gaily. He was quite aware that it was apparent he was not superficial about Nona, and abundantly determined, into the bargain, that the rehearsal of the piece should not sacrifice a shade of thoroughness to any extrinsic consideration.

Mrs Alsager, whom, late in the afternoon, he used often to go and ask for a cup of tea, thanking her in advance for the rest she gave him and telling her how he found that rehearsal (as *they* were doing it – it was a caution!) took it out of one – Mrs Alsager, more and more his good genius and, as he repeatedly assured her, his ministering angel, confirmed him in this superior policy and urged him on to every form of artistic devotion. She had, naturally, never been more interested than now in his work; she wanted to hear everything about everything. She treated him as heroically fatigued, plied him with luxurious restoratives, made him stretch himself on cushions and rose-leaves. They gossiped more than ever, by her fire, about the artistic life; he confided to her, for instance, all his hopes and fears, all his experiments and anxieties, on the subject of the representative of Nona. She was immensely interested in this young lady and showed it by taking a box again and again (she had seen her half a dozen times already), to study her capacity through the veil of her present part. Like Allan Wayworth she found her encouraging only by fits, for she had fine flashes of badness. She was intelligent, but she cried aloud for training, and the training was so absent that the intelligence had only a fraction of its effect. She was like a knife without an edge – good steel that had never been sharpened; she hacked away at her hard dramatic loaf, she couldn't cut it smooth.

II

'CERTAINLY MY leading lady won't make Nona much like *you*!' Wayworth one day gloomily remarked to Mrs Alsager. There were days when the prospect seemed to him awful.

'So much the better. There's no necessity for that.'

'I wish you'd train her a little – you could so easily,' the young man went on; in response to which Mrs Alsager requested him not to make such cruel fun of her. But she was curious about the girl, wanted to hear of her character, her private situation, how she lived and where, seemed indeed desirous to befriend her. Wayworth might not have known much about the private situation of Miss Violet Grey, but, as it happened, he was able, by the time his play had been three weeks in rehearsal, to supply information on such points. She was a charming, exemplary person, educated, cultivated, with highly modern tastes, an excellent musician. She had lost her parents and was very much alone in the world, her only two relations being a sister, who was married to a civil servant (in a highly responsible post) in

India, and a dear little old-fashioned aunt (really a great-aunt) with whom she lived at Notting Hill, who wrote children's books and who, it appeared, had once written a Christmas pantomime. It was quite an artistic home – not on the scale of Mrs Alsager's (to compare the smallest things with the greatest!) but intensely refined and honourable. Wayworth went so far as to hint that it would be rather nice and human on Mrs Alsager's part to go there – they would take it so kindly if she should call on them. She had acted so often on his hints that he had formed a pleasant habit of expecting it: it made him feel so wisely responsible about giving them. But this one appeared to fall to the ground, so that he let the subject drop. Mrs Alsager, however, went yet once more to the 'Legitimate', as he found by her saying to him abruptly, on the morrow: 'Oh, she'll be very good – she'll be very good.' When they said 'she', in these days, they always meant Violet Grey, though they pretended, for the most part, that they meant Nona Vincent.

'Oh yes,' Wayworth assented, 'she wants so to!'

Mrs Alsager was silent a moment; then she asked, a little inconsequently, as if she had come back from a reverie: 'Does she want to *very* much?'

'Tremendously – and it appears she has been fascinated by the part from the first.'

'Why then didn't she say so?'

'Oh, because she's so funny.'

'She *is* funny,' said Mrs Alsager, musingly; and presently she added: 'She's in love with you.'

Wayworth stared, blushed very red, then laughed out. 'What is there funny in that?' he demanded; but before his interlocutress could satisfy him on this point he inquired, further, how she knew anything about it. After a little graceful evasion she explained that the night before, at the 'Legitimate', Mrs Beaumont, the wife of the actor-manager, had paid her a visit in her box; which had happened, in the course of their brief gossip, to lead to her remarking that she had never been 'behind'. Mrs Beaumont offered on the spot to take her round, and the fancy had seized her to accept the invitation. She had been amused for the moment, and in this way it befell that her conductress, at her request, had introduced her to Miss Violet Grey, who was waiting in the wing for one of her scenes. Mrs Beaumont had been called away for three minutes, and during this scrap of time, face to face with the actress, she had discovered the poor girl's secret. Wayworth qualified it as a senseless thing, but wished to know what had led to the discovery. She characterized this inquiry as superficial for a painter of the ways of women; and he doubtless didn't improve it by remarking profanely that a cat might look at a king and that such things were convenient to know. Even on this ground, however, he was threatened by Mrs Alsager, who contended that it might not be a joking matter to the poor girl. To this Wayworth, who now professed to hate talking about the passions he might have inspired, could only reply that he meant it couldn't make a difference to Mrs Alsager.

'How in the world do you know what makes a difference to *me*?' this lady asked, with incongruous coldness, with a haughtiness indeed remarkable in so gentle a spirit.

He saw Violet Grey that night at the theatre, and it was she who spoke first of her having lately met a friend of his.

'She's in love with you,' the actress said, after he had made a show of ignorance; 'doesn't that tell you anything?'

He blushed redder still than Mrs Alsager had made him blush, but replied, quickly enough and very adequately, that hundreds of women were naturally dying for him.

'Oh, I don't care, for you're not in love with *her*!' the girl continued.

'Did she tell you that too?' Wayworth asked; but she had at that moment to go on.

Standing where he could see her he thought that on this occasion she threw into her scene, which was the best she had in the play, a brighter art than ever before, a talent that could play with its problem. She was perpetually doing things out of rehearsal (she did two or three tonight, in the other man's piece), that he as often wished to heaven Nona Vincent might have the benefit of. She appeared to be able to do them for everyone but him — that is for everyone but Nona. He was conscious, in these days, of an odd new feeling, which mixed (this was a part of its oddity) with a very natural and comparatively old one and which in its most definite form was a dull ache of regret that this young lady's unlucky star should have placed her on the stage. He wished in his worst uneasiness that, without going further, she would give it up; and yet it soothed that uneasiness to remind himself that he saw grounds to hope she would go far enough to make a marked success of Nona. There were strange and painful moments when, as the interpretress of Nona, he almost hated her; after which, however, he always assured himself that he exaggerated, inasmuch as what made this aversion seem great, when he was nervous, was simply its contrast with the growing sense that there *were* grounds – totally different – on which she pleased him. She pleased him as a charming creature – by her sincerities and her perversities, by the varieties and surprises of her character and by certain happy facts of her person. In private her eyes were sad to him and her voice was rare. He detested the idea that she should have a disappointment or an humiliation, and he wanted to rescue her altogether, to save and transplant her. One way to save her was to see to it, to the best of his ability, that the production of his play should be a triumph; and the other way – it was really too queer to express – was almost to wish that it shouldn't be. Then, for the future, there would be safety and peace, and not the peace of death – the peace of a different life. It is to be added that our young man clung to the former of these ways in proportion as the latter perversely tempted him. He was nervous at the best, increasingly and intolerably nervous; but the immediate remedy was to rehearse harder and harder, and above all to work it out with Violet Grey. Some of her comrades reproached him with working it out only with her, as if she were the whole affair; to which he replied that they could afford to be neglected, they were all so tremendously good. She was the only person concerned whom he didn't flatter. The author and the actress stuck so to the business in hand that she had very little time to speak to him again of Mrs Alsager, of whom indeed her imagination appeared adequately to have disposed. Wayworth once remarked to her that Nona Vincent was supposed to be a good deal like his charming friend; but she gave a blank 'Supposed by whom?' in consequence of which he never returned to the subject. He confided his nervousness as freely as usual to Mrs Alsager, who easily understood that he had a peculiar complication of anxieties. His suspense varied in degree from hour to hour, but any relief there might have been in this was made up for by its being of several different kinds. One afternoon, as the first performance drew near, Mrs Alsager said to him, in giving him his cup of tea and on his having mentioned that he had not closed his eyes the night before:

'You must indeed be in a dreadful state. Anxiety for another is still worse than anxiety for one's self.'

'For another?' Wayworth repeated, looking at her over the rim of his cup.

'My poor friend, you're nervous about Nona Vincent, but you're infinitely more nervous about Violet Grey.'

'She *is* Nona Vincent!'

'No, she isn't – not a bit!' said Mrs Alsager, abruptly.

'Do you really think so?' Wayworth cried, spilling his tea in his alarm.

'What I think doesn't signify – I mean what I think about that. What I meant to say was that great as is your suspense about your play, your suspense about your actress is greater still.'

'I can only repeat that my actress *is* my play.'

Mrs Alsager looked thoughtfully into the teapot.

'Your actress is your—'

'My what?' the young man asked, with a little tremor in his voice, as his hostess paused.

'Your very dear friend. You're in love with her – at present.' And with a sharp click Mrs Alsager dropped the lid on the fragrant receptacle.

'Not yet – not yet!' laughed her visitor.

'You will be if she pulls you through.'

'You declare that she *won't* pull me through.'

Mrs Alsager was silent a moment, after which she softly murmured: 'I'll pray for her.'

'You're the most generous of women!' Wayworth cried; then coloured as if the words had not been happy. They would have done indeed little honour to a man of tact.

The next morning he received five hurried lines from Mrs Alsager. She had suddenly been called to Torquay, to see a relation who was seriously ill; she should be detained there several days, but she had an earnest hope of being able to return in time for his first night. In any event he had her unrestricted good wishes. He missed her extremely, for these last days were a great strain and there was little comfort to be derived from Violet Grey. She was even more nervous than himself, and so pale and altered that he was afraid she would be too ill to act. It was settled between them that they made each other worse and that he had now much better leave her alone. They had pulled Nona so to pieces that nothing seemed left of her — she must at least have time to grow together again. He left Violet Grey alone, to the best of his ability, but she carried out imperfectly her own side of the bargain. She came to him with new questions — she waited for him with old doubts, and half an hour before the last dress-rehearsal, on the eve of production, she proposed to him a totally fresh rendering of his heroine. This incident gave him such a sense of insecurity that he turned his back on her without a word, bolted out of the theatre, dashed along the Strand and walked as far as the Bank. Then he jumped into a hansom and came westward, and when he reached the theatre again the business was nearly over. It appeared, almost to his disappointment, not bad enough to give him the consolation of the old playhouse adage that the worst dress-rehearsals make the best first nights.

The morrow, which was a Wednesday, was the dreadful day; the theatre had been closed on the Monday and the Tuesday. Everyone, on the Wednesday, did his best to let everyone else alone, and everyone signally failed in the attempt. The day, till seven o'clock, was understood to be consecrated to rest, but everyone except Violet Grey turned up at the theatre. Wayworth looked at Mr Loder, and Mr Loder looked in another direction, which was as near as they came to conversation. Wayworth was in a fidget, unable to eat or sleep or sit still, at times almost in terror. He kept quiet by keeping, as usual, in motion; he tried to walk away from his nervousness. He walked in the afternoon toward Notting Hill, but he succeeded in not breaking the vow he had taken not to meddle with his actress. She was like an acrobat poised on a slippery ball – if he should touch her she would topple over. He passed her door three times and he thought of her three hundred. This was the hour at which he most regretted that Mrs Alsager had not come back – for he had called at her house only to learn that she was still at Torquay. This was probably queer, and it was probably queerer still that she hadn't written to him; but even of these things he wasn't sure, for in losing, as he had now completely lost, his judgement of his play, he seemed to himself to have lost his judgement of everything. When he went home, however, he found a telegram from the lady of Grosvenor Place – 'Shall be able to come – reach town by seven.' At half-past eight o'clock, through a little aperture in the curtain of the 'Renaissance', he saw her in her box with a cluster of friends – completely beautiful and benefi-cent. The house was magnificent – too good for his play, he felt; too good for any play. Everything now seemed too good – the scenery, the furniture, the dresses, the very programmes. He seized upon the idea that this was probably what was the matter with the representative of Nona – she was only too good. He had completely arranged with this young lady the plan of their relations during the evening; and though they had altered everything else that they had arranged they had promised each other not to alter this. It was wonderful the number of things they had promised each other. He would start her, he would see her off – then he would quit the theatre and stay away till just before the end. She besought him to stay away – it would make her infinitely easier. He saw that she was exquisitely dressed – she had made one or two changes for the better since the night before, and that seemed something definite to turn over and over in his mind as he rumbled foggily home in the four-wheeler in which, a few steps from the stage-door, he had taken refuge as soon as he knew that the curtain was up. He lived a couple of miles off, and he had chosen a four-wheeler to drag out the time.

When he got home his fire was out, his room was cold, and he lay down on his sofa in his overcoat. He had sent his landlady to the dress-circle, on purpose; she would overflow with words and mistakes. The house seemed a black void, just as the streets had done – everyone was, formidably, at his play. He was quieter at last than he had been for a fortnight, and he felt too weak even to wonder how the thing was going. He believed afterwards that he had slept an hour; but even if he had he felt it to be still too early to return to the theatre. He sat down by his lamp and tried to read – to read a little compendious life of a great English statesman, out of a 'series'. It struck him as brilliantly clever, and he asked himself whether that perhaps were not rather the sort of thing he ought to have taken up: not the statesmanship, but the art of brief biography. Suddenly he became aware that he must hurry if he was to reach the theatre at all – it was a quarter to eleven o'clock. He scrambled out and, this time, found a hansom – he had lately spent enough money in cabs to add to his hope that the profits of his new profession would be great. His anxiety, his suspense flamed up again, and as he rattled eastward – he went fast now – he was almost sick with alternations. As he passed into the theatre the first man – some underling – who met him, cried to him, breathlessly: 'You're wanted, sir – you're wanted!' He thought his tone very ominous – he devoured the man's eyes with his own, for a betrayal: did he mean that he was wanted for execution? Someone else pressed him, almost pushed him, forward; he was already on the stage. Then he became conscious of a sound more or less continuous, but seemingly faint and far, which he took at first for the voice of the actors heard through their canvas walls, the beautiful built-in room of the last act. But the actors were in the wing, they surrounded him; the curtain was down and they were coming off from before it. They had been called, and *he* was called – they all greeted him with 'Go on – go on!' He was terrified – he couldn't go on – he didn't believe in the applause, which seemed to him only audible enough to sound half-hearted.

'Has it gone? – *has* it gone?' he gasped to the people round him; and he heard them say 'Rather – rather!' perfunctorily, mendaciously too, as it struck him, and even with mocking laughter, the laughter of defeat and despair. Suddenly, though all this must have taken but a moment, Loder burst upon him from somewhere with a 'For God's sake don't keep them, or they'll *stop*!' 'But I can't go on for *that*!' Wayworth cried, in anguish; the sound seemed to him already to have ceased. Loder had hold of him and was shoving him; he resisted and looked round frantically for Violet Grey, who perhaps would tell him the truth. There was by this time a crowd in the wing, all with strange grimacing painted faces, but Violet was not among them and her very absence frightened him. He uttered her name with an accent that he afterwards regretted – it gave them, as he thought, both away; and while Loder hustled him before the curtain he heard someone say 'She took her call and disappeared.' She had had a call, then – this was what was most present to the young man as he stood for an instant in the glare of the footlights, looking blindly at the great vaguely peopled horseshoe and greeted with plaudits which now seemed to him at once louder than he deserved and feebler than he desired. They sank to rest quickly, but he felt it to be long before he could back away, before he could, in his turn, seize the manager by the arm and cry huskily – 'Has it really gone – *really*?'

Mr Loder looked at him hard and replied after an instant: 'The play's all right!'

Wayworth hung upon his lips. 'Then what's all wrong?'

'We must do something to Miss Grey.'

'What's the matter with her?'

'She isn't *in* it!'

'Do you mean she has failed?'

'Yes, damn it – she has failed.'

Wayworth stared. 'Then how can the play be all right?'

'Oh, we'll save it – we'll save it.'

'Where's Miss Grey – where *is* she?' the young man asked.

Loder caught his arm as he was turning away again to look for his heroine. 'Never mind her now – she knows it!'

Wayworth was approached at the same moment by a gentleman he knew as one of Mrs Alsager's friends – he had perceived him in that lady's box. Mrs Alsager was waiting there for the successful author; she desired very earnestly that he would come round and speak to her. Wayworth assured himself first that Violet had left the theatre – one of the actresses could tell him that she had seen her throw on a cloak, without changing her dress, and had learned afterwards that she had, the next moment, flung herself, after flinging her aunt, into a cab. He had wished to invite half a dozen persons, of whom Miss Grey and her elderly relative were two, to come home to supper with him; but she had refused to make any engagement beforehand (it would be so dreadful to have to keep it if she shouldn't have made a hit), and this attitude had blighted the pleasant plan, which fell to the ground. He had called her morbid, but she was immovable. Mrs Alsager's messenger let him know that he was expected to supper in Grosvenor Place, and half an hour afterwards he was seated there among complimentary people and flowers and popping corks, eating the first orderly meal he had partaken of for a week. Mrs Alsager had carried him off in her brougham – the other people who were coming got into things of their own. He stopped her short as soon as she began to tell him how tremendously everyone had been struck by the piece; he nailed her down to the question of Violet Grey. Had she spoilt the play, had she jeopardized or compromised it – had she been utterly bad, had she been good in any degree?

'Certainly the performance would have seemed better if *she* had been better,' Mrs Alsager confessed.

'And the play would have seemed better if the performance had been better,' Wayworth said, gloomily, from the corner of the brougham.

'She does what she can, and she has talent, and she looked lovely. But she doesn't *see* Nona Vincent. She doesn't see the type – she doesn't see the individual – she doesn't see the woman you meant. She's out of it – she gives you a different person.'

'Oh, the woman I meant!' the young man exclaimed, looking at the London lamps as he rolled by them. 'I wish to God she had known *you*!' he added, as the carriage stopped. After they had passed into the house he said to his companion:

'You see she *won't* pull me through.'

'Forgive her – be kind to her!' Mrs Alsager pleaded.

'I shall only thank her. The play may go to the dogs.'

'If it does – if it does,' Mrs Alsager began, with her pure eyes on him.

'Well, what if it does?'

She couldn't tell him, for the rest of her guests came in together; she only had time to say: 'It *shan't* go to the dogs!'

He came away before the others, restless with the desire to go to Notting Hill even that night, late as it was, haunted with the sense that Violet Grey had measured her fall. When he got into the street, however, he allowed second thoughts to counsel another course; the effect of knocking her up at two o'clock in the morning would hardly be to soothe her. He looked at six newspapers the next day and found in them never a good word for her. They were well enough about the piece, but they were unanimous as to the disappointment caused by the young actress whose former efforts had excited such hopes and on whom, on this occasion, such pressing responsibilities rested. They asked in chorus what was the matter with her, and they declared in chorus that the play, which was not without promise, was handicapped (they all used the same word) by the odd want of correspondence between the heroine and her interpreter. Wayworth drove early to Notting Hill, but he didn't take the newspapers with him; Violet Grey could be trusted to have sent out for them by the peep of dawn and to have fed her anguish full. She declined to see him – she only sent down word by her aunt that she was extremely unwell and should be unable to act that night unless she were suffered to spend the day unmolested and in bed. Wayworth sat for an hour with the old lady, who understood everything and to whom he could speak frankly. She gave him a touching picture of her niece's condition, which was all the more vivid for the simple words in which it was expressed: 'She feels she isn't right, you know – she feels she isn't right!'

'Tell her it doesn't matter – it doesn't matter a straw!' said Wayworth.

'And she's so proud – you know how proud she is!' the old lady went on.

'Tell her I'm more than satisfied, that I accept her gratefully as she is.'

'She says she injures your play, that she ruins it,' said his interlocutress.

'She'll improve, immensely – she'll grow into the part,' the young man continued.

'She'd improve if she knew how – but she says she doesn't. She has given all she has got, and she doesn't know what's wanted.'

'What's wanted is simply that she should go straight on and trust me.'

'How can she trust you when she feels she's losing you?'

'Losing me?' Wayworth cried.

'You'll never forgive her if your play is taken off!'

'It will run six months,' said the author of the piece.

The old lady laid her hand on his arm. 'What will you do for her if it does?'

He looked at Violet Grey's aunt a moment. 'Do you say your niece is very proud?'

'Too proud for her dreadful profession.'

'Then she wouldn't wish you to ask me that,' Wayworth answered, getting up.

When he reached home he was very tired, and for a person to whom it was open to consider that he had scored a success he spent a remarkably dismal day. All his restlessness had gone, and fatigue and depression possessed him. He sank into his old chair by the fire and sat there for hours with his eyes closed. His landlady came in to bring his luncheon and mend the fire, but he feigned to be asleep, so as not to be spoken to. It is to be supposed that sleep at last overtook him, for about the hour that dusk began to gather he had an extraordinary impression, a visit that, it would seem, could have belonged to no waking consciousness. Nona Vincent, in face and form, the living heroine of his play, rose before him in his little silent room, sat down with him at his dingy fireside. She was not Violet Grey, she was not Mrs Alsager, she was not any woman he had seen upon earth, nor was it any masquerade of friendship or of penitence. Yet she was more familiar to him than the women he had known best, and she was ineffably beautiful and consoling. She filled the poor room with her presence, the effect of which was as soothing as some odour of incense. She was as quiet as an affectionate sister, and there was no surprise in her being there. Nothing more real had ever befallen him, and nothing, somehow, more reassuring. He felt her hand rest upon his own, and all his senses seemed to open to her message. She struck him, in the strangest way, both as his creation and as his inspirer, and she gave him the happiest consciousness of success. If she was so charming, in the red firelight, in her vague, clear-coloured garments, it was because he had made her so, and yet if the weight seemed lifted from his spirit it was because she drew it away. When she bent her deep eyes upon him they seemed to speak of safety and freedom and to make a green garden of the future. From time to time she smiled and said: 'I live – I live – I live.' How long she stayed he couldn't have told, but when his landlady blundered in with the lamp Nona Vincent was no longer there. He rubbed his eyes, but no dream had ever been so intense; and as he slowly got out of his chair it was with a deep still joy – the joy of the artist – in the thought of how right he had been, how exactly like herself he had made her. She had come to show him that. At the end of five minutes, however, he felt sufficiently mystified to call his landlady back – he wanted to ask her a question. When the good woman reappeared the question hung fire an instant; then it shaped itself as the inquiry:

'Has any lady been here?'

'No, sir – no lady at all.'

The woman seemed slightly scandalized. 'Not Miss Vincent?'

'Miss Vincent, sir?'

'The young lady of my play, don't you know?'

'Oh, sir, you mean Miss Violet Grey!'

'No I don't, at all. I think I mean Mrs Alsager.'

'There has been no Mrs Alsager, sir.'

'Nor anybody at all like her?'

The woman looked at him as if she wondered what had suddenly taken him. Then she asked in an injured tone: 'Why shouldn't I have told you if you'd 'ad callers, sir?'

'I thought you might have thought I was asleep.'

'Indeed you were, sir, when I came in with the lamp – and well you'd earned it, Mr Wayworth!'

The landlady came back an hour later to bring him a telegram; it was just as he had begun to dress to dine at his club and go down to the theatre.

'See me tonight in front, and don't come near me till it's over.'

It was in these words that Violet communicated her wishes for the evening. He obeyed them to the letter; he watched her from the depths of a box. He was in no position to say how she might have struck him the night before, but what he saw during these charmed hours filled him with admiration and gratitude. She *was* in it, this time; she had pulled herself together, she had taken possession, she was felicitous at every turn. Fresh from his revelation of Nona he was in a position to judge, and as he judged he exulted. He was thrilled and carried away, and he was moreover intensely curious to know what had happened to her, by what unfathomable art she had managed in a few hours to effect such a change of base. It was as if *she* had had a revelation of Nona, so convincing a clearness had been breathed upon the picture. He kept himself quiet in the *entr'actes* – he would speak to her only at the end; but before the play was half over the manager burst into his box.

'It's prodigious, what she's up to!' cried Mr Loder, almost more bewildered than gratified. 'She has gone in for a new reading – a blessed somersault in the air!'

'Is it quite different?' Wayworth asked, sharing his mystification.

'Different? Hyperion to a satyr! It's devilish good, my boy!'

'It's devilish good,' said Wayworth, 'and it's in a different key altogether from the key of her rehearsal.'

'I'll run you six months!' the manager declared; and he rushed round again to the actress, leaving Wayworth with a sense that she had already pulled him through. She had with the audience an immense personal success.

When he went behind, at the end, he had to wait for her; she only showed herself when she was ready to leave the theatre. Her aunt had been in her dressing-room with her, and the two ladies appeared together. The girl passed him quickly, motioning him to say nothing till they should have got out of the place. He saw that she was immensely excited, lifted altogether above her common artistic level. The old lady said to him: 'You must come home to supper with us: it has been all arranged.' They had a brougham, with a little third seat, and he got into it with them. It was a long time before the actress would speak. She leaned back in her corner, giving no sign but still heaving a little, like a subsiding sea, and with all her triumph in the eyes that shone through the darkness. The old lady was hushed to awe, or at least to discretion, and Wayworth was happy enough to wait. He had really to wait till they had alighted at Notting Hill, where the elder of his companions went to see that supper had been attended to.

'I was better – I was better,' said Violet Grey, throwing off her cloak in the little drawing-room.

'You were perfection. You'll be like that every night, won't you?'

She smiled at him. 'Every night? There can scarcely be a miracle every day.'

'What do you mean by a miracle?'

'I've had a revelation.'

Wayward stared. 'At what hour?'

'The right hour – this afternoon. Just in time to save me – and to save *you*.'

'At five o'clock? Do you mean you had a visit?'

'She came to me – she stayed two hours.'

'Two hours? Nona Vincent?'

'Mrs Alsager.' Violet Grey smiled more deeply. 'It's the same thing.'

'And how did Mrs Alsager save you?'

'By letting me look at her. By letting me hear her speak. By letting me know her.'

'And what did she say to you?'

'Kind things – encouraging, intelligent things.'

'Ah, the dear woman!' Wayworth cried.

'You ought to like her – she likes *you*. She was just what I wanted,' the actress added.

'Do you mean she talked to you about Nona?'

'She said you thought she was like her. She *is* – she's exquisite.'

'She's exquisite,' Wayworth repeated. 'Do you mean she tried to coach you?'

'Oh, no – she only said she would be so glad if it would help me to see her. And I felt it did help me. I don't know what took place – she only sat there, and she held my hand and smiled at me, and she had tact and grace, and she had goodness and beauty, and she soothed my nerves and lighted up my imagination. Somehow she seemed to *give* it all to me. I took it – I took it. I kept her before me, I drank her in. For the first time, in the whole study of the part, I had my model – I could make my copy. All my courage came back to me, and other things came that I hadn't felt before. She was different – she was delightful; as I've said, she was a revelation. She kissed me when she went away – and you may guess if I kissed *her*. We were awfully affectionate, but it's *you* she likes!' said Violet Grey.

Wayworth had never been more interested in his life, and he had rarely been more mystified. 'Did she wear vague, dear-coloured garments?' he asked, after a moment.

Violet Grey stared, laughed, then bade him go in to supper. '*You* know how she dresses!'

He was very well pleased at supper, but he was silent and a little solemn. He said he would go to see Mrs Alsager the next day. He did so, but he was told at her door that she had returned to Torquay. She remained there all winter, all spring, and the next time he saw her his play had run two hundred nights and he had married Violet Grey. His plays sometimes succeed, but his wife is not in them now, nor in any others. At these representations Mrs Alsager continues frequently to be present.

The Real Thing

I

WHEN THE PORTER'S wife (she used to answer the house-bell), announced 'A gentleman – with a lady, sir,' I had, as I often had in those days, for the wish was father to the thought, an immediate vision of sitters. Sitters my visitors in this case proved to be; but not in the sense I should have preferred. However, there was nothing at first to indicate that they might not have come for a portrait. The gentleman, a man of fifty, very high and very straight, with a moustache slightly grizzled and a dark grey walking-coat admirably fitted, both of which I noted professionally – I don't mean as a barber or yet as a tailor – would have struck me as a celebrity if celebrities often were striking. It was a truth of which I had for some time been conscious that a figure with a good deal of frontage was, as one might say, almost never a public institution. A glance at the lady helped to remind me of this paradoxical law: she also looked too distinguished to be a 'personality'. Moreover one would scarcely come across two variations together.

Neither of the pair spoke immediately – they only prolonged the preliminary gaze which suggested that each wished to give the other a chance. They were visibly shy; they stood there letting me take them in – which, as I afterwards perceived, was the most practical thing they could have done. In this way their embarrassment served their cause. I had seen people painfully reluctant to mention that they desired anything so gross as to be represented on canvas; but the scruples of my new friends appeared almost insurmountable. Yet the gentleman might have said 'I should like a portrait of my wife,' and the lady might have said 'I should like a portrait of my husband.' Perhaps they were not husband and wife – this naturally would make the matter more delicate. Perhaps they wished to be done together – in which case they ought to have brought a third person to break the news.

'We come from Mr Rivet,' the lady said at last, with a dim smile which had the effect of a moist sponge passed over a 'sunk' piece of painting, as well as of a vague allusion to vanished beauty. She was as tall and straight, in her degree, as her companion, and with ten years less to carry. She looked as sad as a woman could look whose face was not charged with expression; that is her tinted oval mask showed friction as an exposed surface shows it. The hand of time had played over her freely, but only to simplify. She was slim and stiff, and so well-dressed, in dark blue cloth, with lappets and pockets and buttons, that it was clear she employed the same tailor as her husband. The couple had an indefinable air of prosperous thrift – they evidently got a good deal of luxury for their money. If I was to be one of their luxuries it would behove me to consider my terms.

'Ah, Claude Rivet recommended me?' I inquired; and I added that it was very kind of him, though I could reflect that, as he only painted landscape, this was not a sacrifice.

The lady looked very hard at the gentleman, and the gentleman looked round the room. Then staring at the floor a moment and stroking his moustache, he rested his pleasant eyes on me with the remark: 'He said you were the right one.'

'I try to be, when people want to sit.'

'Yes, we should like to,' said the lady anxiously.

'Do you mean together?'

My visitors exchanged a glance. 'If you could do anything with *me*, I suppose it would be double,' the gentleman stammered.

'Oh yes, there's naturally a higher charge for two figures than for one.'

'We should like to make it pay,' the husband confessed.

'That's very good of you,' I returned, appreciating so unwonted a sympathy – for I supposed he meant pay the artist.

A sense of strangeness seemed to dawn on the lady. 'We mean for the illustrations – Mr Rivet said you might put one in.'

'Put one in – an illustration?' I was equally confused.

'Sketch her off, you know,' said the gentleman, colouring.

It was only then that I understood the service Claude Rivet had rendered me; he had told them that I worked in black and white, for magazines, for story-books, for sketches of contemporary life, and consequently had frequent employment for models. These things were true, but it was not less true (I may confess it now – whether because the aspiration was to lead to everything or to nothing I leave the reader to guess), that I couldn't get the honours, to say nothing of the emoluments, of a great painter of portraits out of my head. My 'illustrations' were my pot-boilers; I looked to a different branch of art (far and away the most interesting, it had always seemed to me) to perpetuate my fame. There was no shame in looking to it also to make my fortune; but that fortune was by so much further from being made from the moment my visitors wished to be 'done' for nothing. I was disappointed; for in the pictorial sense I had immediately *seen* them. I had seized their type – I had already settled what I would do with it. Something that wouldn't absolutely have pleased them, I afterwards reflected.

'Ah, you're – you're – a––?' I began, as soon as I had mastered my surprise. I couldn't bring out the dingy word 'models'; it seemed to fit the case so little.

'We haven't had much practice,' said the lady.

'We've got to *do* something, and we've thought that an artist in your line might perhaps make something of us,' her husband threw off. He further mentioned that they didn't know many artists and that they had gone first, on the off-chance (he painted views of course, but sometimes put in figures – perhaps I remembered), to Mr Rivet, whom they had met a few years before at a place in Norfolk where he was sketching.

'We used to sketch a little ourselves,' the lady hinted.

'It's very awkward, but we absolutely *must* do something,' her husband went on.

'Of course, we're not so *very* young,' she admitted, with a wan smile.

With the remark that I might as well know something more about them, the husband had handed me a card extracted from a neat new pocket-book (their appurtenances were all of the freshest) and inscribed with the words 'Major Monarch'. Impressive as these words were they didn't carry my knowledge much further; but my visitor presently added: 'I've left the army, and we've had the misfortune to lose our money. In fact our means are dreadfully small.'

'It's an awful bore,' said Mrs Monarch.

They evidently wished to be discreet – to take care not to swagger because they were gentlefolks. I perceived they would have been willing to recognize this as something of a drawback, at the same time that I guessed at an underlying sense – their consolation in adversity – that they *had* their points. They certainly had; but these advantages struck me as preponderantly social; such for instance as would help to make a drawing-room look well. However, a drawing-room was always, or ought to be, a picture.

In consequence of his wife's allusion to their age Major Monarch observed: 'Naturally, it's more for the figure that we thought of going in. We can still hold ourselves up.' On the instant I saw that the figure was indeed their strong point. His 'naturally' didn't sound vain, but it lighted up the question. '*She* has got the best,' he continued, nodding at his wife, with a pleasant after-dinner absence of circumlocution. I could only reply, as if we were in fact sitting over our wine, that this didn't prevent his own from being very good; which led him in turn to rejoin: 'We thought that if you ever have to do people like us, we might be something like it. *She*, particularly – for a lady in a book, you know.'

I was so amused by them that, to get more of it, I did my best to take their point of view; and though it was an embarrassment to find myself appraising physically, as if they were animals on hire or useful blacks, a pair whom I should have expected to meet only in one of the relations in which criticism is tacit, I looked at Mrs Monarch judicially enough to be able to exclaim, after a moment, with conviction: 'Oh yes, a lady in a book!' She was singularly like a bad illustration.

'We'll stand up, if you like,' said the Major; and he raised himself before me with a really grand air.

I could take his measure at a glance – he was six feet two and a perfect gentleman. It would have paid any club in process of formation and in want of a stamp to engage him at a salary to stand in the principal window. What struck me immediately was that in coming to me they had rather missed their vocation; they could surely have been turned to better account for advertising purposes. I couldn't of course see the thing in detail, but I could see them make someone's fortune – I don't mean their own. There was something in them for a waistcoat-maker, an hotel-keeper or a soap-vendor. I could imagine 'We always use it' pinned on their bosoms with the greatest effect; I had a vision of the promptitude with which they would launch a *table d'hôte*.

Mrs Monarch sat still, not from pride but from shyness, and presently her husband said to her: 'Get up, my dear, and show how smart you are.' She obeyed, but she had no need to get up to show it. She walked to the end of the studio, and then she came back blushing, with her fluttered eyes on her husband. I was reminded of an incident I had accidentally had a glimpse of in Paris – being with a friend there, a dramatist about to produce a play – when an actress came to him to ask to be entrusted with a part. She went through her paces before him, walked up and down as Mrs Monarch was doing. Mrs Monarch did it quite as well, but I abstained from applauding. It was very odd to see such people apply for such poor pay. She looked as if she had ten thousand a year. Her husband had used the word that described her: she was, in the London current jargon, essentially and typically 'smart'. Her figure was, in the same order of ideas, conspicuously and irreproachably 'good'. For a woman of her age her waist was surprisingly small; her elbow moreover had the orthodox crook. She held her head at the conventional angle; but why did she come to *me*? She ought to have tried on jackets at a big shop. I feared my visitors were not only destitute, but 'artistic' – which would be a great complica-tion. When she sat down again I thanked her, observing that what a draughtsman most valued in his model was the faculty of keeping quiet.

'Oh, *she* can keep quiet,' said Major Monarch. Then he added, jocosely: 'I've always kept her quiet.'

'I'm not a nasty fidget, am I?' Mrs Monarch appealed to her husband.

He addressed his answer to me. 'Perhaps it isn't out of place to mention – because we ought to be quite business-like, oughtn't we? – that when I married her she was known as the Beautiful Statue.'

'Oh dear!' said Mrs Monarch, ruefully.

'Of course I should want a certain amount of expression,' I rejoined.

'Of *course*!' they both exclaimed.

'And then I suppose you know that you'll get awfully tired.'

'Oh, we *never* get tired!' they eagerly cried.

'Have you had any kind of practice?'

They hesitated – they looked at each other. 'We've been photographed, *immensely*,' said Mrs Monarch.

'She means the fellows have asked us,' added the Major.

'I see – because you're so good-looking.'

'I don't know what they thought, but they were always after us.'

'We always got our photographs for nothing,' smiled Mrs Monarch.

'We might have brought some, my dear,' her husband remarked.

'I'm not sure we have any left. We've given quantities away,' she explained to me.

'With our autographs and that sort of thing,' said the Major.

'Are they to be got in the shops?' I inquired, as a harmless pleasantry.

'Oh, yes; *hers* – they used to be.'

'Not now,' said Mrs Monarch, with her eyes on the floor.

II

I COULD FANCY the 'sort of thing' they put on the presentation-copies of their photographs, and I was sure they wrote a beautiful hand. It was odd how quickly I was sure of everything that concerned them. If they were now so poor as to have to earn shillings and pence, they never had had much of a margin. Their good looks had been their capital, and they had good-humouredly made the most of the career that this resource marked out for them. It was in their faces, the blankness, the deep intellectual repose of the twenty years of country-house visiting which had given them pleasant intonations. I could see the sunny drawing-rooms, sprinkled with periodicals she didn't read, in which Mrs Monarch had continuously sat; I could see the wet shrubberies in which she had walked, equipped to admiration for either exercise. I could see the rich covers the Major had helped to shoot and the wonderful garments in which, late at night, he repaired to the smoking-room to talk about them, I could imagine their leggings and waterproofs, their knowing tweeds and rugs, their rolls of sticks and cases of tackle and neat umbrellas; and I could evoke the exact appearance of their servants and the compact variety of their luggage on the platforms of country stations.

They gave small tips, but they were liked; they didn't do anything themselves, but they were welcome. They looked so well everywhere; they gratified the general relish for stature, complexion and 'form'. They knew it without fatuity or vulgarity, and they respected themselves in consequence. They were not superficial; they were thorough and kept themselves up – it had been their line. People with such a taste for activity had to have some line. I could feel how, even in a dull house, they could have been counted upon for cheerfulness. At present something had happened – it didn't matter what, their little income had grown less, it had grown least – and they had to do something for pocket-money. Their friends liked them, but didn't like to support them. There was something about them that represented credit – their clothes, their manners, their type; but if credit is a large empty pocket in which an occasional chink reverberates, the chink at least must be audible. What they wanted of me was to help to make it so. Fortunately they had no children – I soon divined that. They would also perhaps wish our relations to be kept secret: this was why it was 'for the figure' – the reproduction of the face would betray them.

I liked them – they were so simple; and I had no objection to them if they would suit. But, somehow, with all their perfections I didn't easily believe in them. After all they were amateurs, and the ruling passion of my life was the detestation of the amateur. Combined with this was another perversity – an innate preference for the represented subject over the real one: the defect of the real one was so apt to be a lack of representation. I liked things that appeared; then one was sure. Whether they *were* or not was a subordinate and almost always a profitless question. There were other considerations, the first of which was that I already had two or three people in use, notably a young person with big feet, in alpaca, from Kilburn, who for a couple of years had come to me regularly for my illustrations and with whom I was still – perhaps ignobly – satisfied. I frankly explained to my visitors how the case stood; but they had taken more precautions than I supposed. They had reasoned out their opportunity, for Claude Rivet had told them of the projected *édition de luxe* of one of the writers of our day – the rarest of the novelists – who, long neglected by the multitudinous vulgar and dearly prized by the attentive (need I mention Philip Vincent?) had had the happy fortune of seeing, late in life, the dawn and then the full light of a higher criticism – an estimate in which, on the part of the public, there was something really of expiation. The edition in question, planned by a publisher of taste, was practically an act of high reparation; the wood-cuts with which it was to be enriched were the homage of English art to one of the most independent representatives of English letters. Major and

Mrs Monarch confessed to me that they had hoped I might be able to work *them* into my share of the enterprise. They knew I was to do the first of the books, 'Rutland Ramsay', but I had to make clear to them that my participation in the rest of the affair – this first book was to be a test – was to depend on the satisfaction I should give. If this should be limited my employers would drop me without a scruple. It was therefore a crisis for me, and naturally I was making special preparations, looking about for new people, if they should be necessary, and securing the best types. I admitted however that I should like to settle down to two or three good models who would do for everything.

'Should we have often to – a – put on special clothes?' Mrs Monarch timidly demanded.

'Dear, yes – that's half the business.'

'And should we be expected to supply our own costumes?'

'Oh, no; I've got a lot of things. A painter's models put on – or put off – anything he likes!'

'And do you mean – a – the same?'

'The same?'

Mrs Monarch looked at her husband again.

'Oh, she was just wondering,' he explained, 'if the costumes are in *general* use.' I had to confess that they were, and I mentioned further that some of them (I had a lot of genuine, greasy last-century things) had served their time, a hundred years ago, on living, world-stained men and women. 'We'll put on anything that *fits*,' said the Major.

'Oh, I arrange that – they fit in the pictures.'

'I'm afraid I should do better for the modern books. I would come as you like,' said Mrs Monarch.

'She has got a lot of clothes at home: they might do for contemporary life,' her husband continued.

'Oh, I can fancy scenes in which you'd be quite natural.' And indeed I could see the slipshod rearrangements of stale properties – the stories I tried to produce pictures for without the exasperation of reading them – whose sandy tracts the good lady might help to people. But I had to return to the fact that for this sort of work – the daily mechanical grind – I was already equipped; the people I was working with were fully adequate.

'We only thought we might be more like *some* characters,' said Mrs Monarch mildly, getting up.

Her husband also rose; he stood looking at me with a dim wistfulness that was touching in so fine a man. 'Wouldn't it be rather a pull sometimes to have – a – to have—?' He hung fire; he wanted me to help him by phrasing what he meant. But I couldn't – I didn't know. So he brought it out, awkwardly: 'The *real* thing; a gentleman, you know, or a lady.' I was quite ready to give a general assent – I admitted that there was a great deal in that. This encouraged Major Monarch to say, following up his appeal with an unacted gulp: 'It's awfully hard – we've tried everything.' The gulp was communicative; it proved too much for his wife. Before I knew it Mrs Monarch had dropped again upon a divan and burst into tears. Her husband sat down beside her, holding one of her hands; whereupon she quickly dried her eyes with the other, while I felt embarrassed as she looked up at me. 'There isn't a confounded job I haven't applied for – waited for – prayed for. You can fancy we'd be pretty bad first. Secretaryships and that sort of thing? You might as well ask for a peerage. I'd be *anything* – I'm strong; a messenger or a coal-heaver. I'd put on a gold-laced cap and open carriage-doors in front of the haberdasher's; I'd hang about a station, to carry portmanteaus; I'd be a postman. But they won't *look* at you; there are thousands, as good as yourself, already on the ground. *Gentlemen*, poor beggars, who have drunk their wine, who have kept their hunters!'

I was as reassuring as I knew how to be, and my visitors were presently on their feet again while, for the experiment, we agreed on an hour. We were discussing it when the door opened and Miss Churm came in with a wet umbrella. Miss Churm had to take the omnibus to Maida Vale and then walk half a mile. She looked a trifle blowsy and slightly splashed. I scarcely ever saw her come in without thinking afresh how odd it was that, being so little in herself, she should yet be so much in others. She was a meagre little Miss Churm, but she was an ample heroine of romance. She was only a freckled cockney, but she could represent everything, from a fine lady to a shepherdess; she had the faculty, as she might have had a fine voice or long hair. She couldn't spell, and she loved beer, but she had two or three 'points', and practice, and a knack, and mother-wit, and a kind of whimsical sensibility, and a love of the theatre, and seven sisters, and not an ounce of respect, especially for the *h*. The first thing my visitors saw was that her umbrella was wet, and in their spotless perfection they visibly winced at it. The rain had come on since their arrival.

'I'm all in a soak; there *was* a mess of people in the 'bus. I wish you lived near a stytion,' said Miss Churm. I requested her to get ready as quickly as possible, and she passed into the room in which she always changed her dress. But before going out she asked me what she was to get into this time.

'It's the Russian princess, don't you know?' I answered; 'the one with the "golden eyes", in black velvet, for the long thing in the *Cheapside*.'

'Golden eyes? I *say*!' cried Miss Churm, while my companions watched her with intensity as she withdrew. She always arranged herself, when she was late, before I could turn round; and I kept my visitors a little, on purpose, so that they might get an idea, from seeing her, what would be expected of themselves. I mentioned that she was quite my notion of an excellent model – she was really very clever.

'Do you think she looks like a Russian princess?' Major Monarch asked, with lurking alarm.

'When I make her, yes.'

'Oh, if you have to *make* her——!' he reasoned, acutely.

'That's the most you can ask. There are so many that are not makeable.'

'Well now, *here's* a lady –' and with a persuasive smile he passed his arm into his wife's – 'who's already made!'

'Oh, I'm not a Russian princess,' Mrs Monarch protested, a little coldly. I could see that she had known some and didn't like them. There, immediately, was a complication of a kind that I never had to fear with Miss Churm.

This young lady came back in black velvet – the gown was rather rusty and very low on her lean shoulders – and with a Japanese fan in her red hands. I reminded her that in the scene I was doing she had to look over someone's head. 'I forget whose it is; but it doesn't matter. Just look over a head.'

'I'd rather look over a stove,' said Miss Churm; and she took her station near the fire. She fell into position, settled herself into a tall attitude, gave a certain backward inclination to her head and a certain forward droop to her fan, and looked, at least to my prejudiced sense, distinguished and charming, foreign and dangerous. We left her looking so, while I went downstairs with Major and Mrs Monarch.

'I think I could come about as near it as that,' said Mrs Monarch.

'Oh, you think she's shabby, but you must allow for the alchemy of art.'

However, they went off with an evident increase of comfort, founded on their demonstrable advantage in being the real thing. I could fancy them shuddering over Miss Churm. She was very droll about them when I went back, for I told her what they wanted.

'Well, if *she* can sit I'll tyke to bookkeeping,' said my model.

'She's very lady-like,' I replied, as an innocent form of aggravation.

'So much the worse for *you*. That means she can't turn round.'

'She'll do for the fashionable novels.'

'Oh yes, she'll *do* for them!' my model humorously declared. 'Ain't they had enough without her?' I had often sociably denounced them to Miss Churm.

III

IT WAS FOR the elucidation of a mystery in one of these works that I first tried Mrs Monarch. Her husband came with her, to be useful if necessary – it was sufficiently clear that as a general thing he would prefer to come with her. At first I wondered if this were for 'propriety's' sake – if he were going to be jealous and meddling. The idea was too tiresome, and if it had been confirmed it would speedily have brought our acquaintance to a close. But I soon saw there was nothing in it and that if he accompanied Mrs Monarch it was (in addition to the chance of being wanted) simply because he had nothing else to do. When she was away from him his occupation was gone – she never *had* been away from him. I judged, rightly, that in their awkward situation their close union was their main comfort and that this union had no weak spot. It was a real marriage, an encouragement to the hesitating, a nut for pessimists to crack. Their address was humble (I remember afterwards thinking it had been the only thing about them that was really professional), and I could fancy the lamentable lodgings in which the Major

would have been left alone. He could bear them with his wife —
he couldn't bear them without her.

He had too much tact to try and make himself agreeable
when he couldn't be useful; so he simply sat and waited, when
I was too absorbed in my work to talk. But I liked to make him
talk – it made my work, when it didn't interrupt it, less sordid,
less special. To listen to him was to combine the excitement of
going out with the economy of staying at home. There was
only one hindrance: that I seemed not to know any of the
people he and his wife had known. I think he wondered
extremely, during the term of our intercourse, whom the deuce
I *did* know. He hadn't a stray sixpence of an idea to fumble for;
so we didn't spin it very fine – we confined ourselves to questions of leather and even of liquor (saddlers and breeches-
makers and how to get good claret cheap), and matters like
'good trains' and the habits of small game. His lore on these last
subjects was astonishing, he managed to interweave the station-
master with the ornithologist. When he couldn't talk about
greater things he could talk cheerfully about smaller, and since
I couldn't accompany him into reminiscences of the fashionable world he could lower the conversation without a visible
effort to my level.

So earnest a desire to please was touching in a man who could
so easily have knocked one down. He looked after the fire and
had an opinion on the draught of the stove, without my asking
him, and I could see that he thought many of my arrangements
not half clever enough. I remember telling him that if I were

only rich I would offer him a salary to come and teach me how to live. Sometimes he gave a random sigh, of which the essence was: 'Give me even such a bare old barrack as *this*, and I'd do something with it!' When I wanted to use him he came alone; which was an illustration of the superior courage of women. His wife could bear her solitary second floor, and she was in general more discreet; showing by various small reserves that she was alive to the propriety of keeping our relations markedly professional – not letting them slide into sociability. She wished it to remain clear that she and the Major were employed, not cultivated, and if she approved of me as a superior, who could be kept in his place, she never thought me quite good enough for an equal.

She sat with great intensity, giving the whole of her mind to it, and was capable of remaining for an hour almost as motionless as if she were before a photographer's lens. I could see she had been photographed often, but somehow the very habit that made her good for that purpose unfitted her for mine. At first I was extremely pleased with her lady-like air, and it was a satisfaction, on coming to follow her lines, to see how good they were and how far they could lead the pencil. But after a few times I began to find her too insurmountably stiff; do what I would with it my drawing looked like a photograph or a copy of a photograph. Her figure had no variety of expression – she herself had no sense of variety. You may say that this was my business, was only a question of placing her. I placed her in every conceivable position, but she managed to obliterate their differences. She was always a lady certainly, and into the bargain was always the same lady. She was the real thing, but always the same thing. There were moments when I was oppressed by the serenity of her confidence that she *was* the real thing. All her dealings with me and all her husband's were an implication that this was lucky for *me*. Meanwhile I found myself trying to invent types that approached her own, instead of making her own transform itself – in the clever way that was not impossible, for instance, to poor Miss Churm. Arrange as I would and take the precautions I would, she always, in my pictures, came out too tall – landing me in the dilemma of having represented a fascinating woman as seven feet high, which, out of respect perhaps to my own very much scantier inches, was far from my idea of such a personage.

The case was worse with the Major – nothing I could do would keep *him* down, so that he became useful only for the representation of brawny giants. I adored variety and range, I cherished human accidents, the illustrative note; I wanted to characterize closely, and the thing in the world I most hated was the danger of being ridden by a type. I had quarrelled with some of my friends about it – I had parted company with them for maintaining that one *had* to be, and that if the type was beautiful (witness Raphael and Leonardo), the servitude was only a gain. I was neither Leonardo nor Raphael; I might only be a presumptuous young modern searcher, but I held that everything was to be sacrificed sooner than character. When they averred that the haunting type in question could easily *be* character, I retorted, perhaps superficially: 'Whose?' It couldn't be everybody's – it might end in being nobody's.

After I had drawn Mrs Monarch a dozen times I perceived more clearly than before that the value of such a model as Miss Churm resided precisely in the fact that she had no positive stamp, combined of course with the other fact that what she did have was a curious and inexplicable talent for imitation. Her usual appearance was like a curtain which she could draw up at request for a capital performance. This performance was simply suggestive; but it was a word to the wise – it was vivid and pretty. Sometimes, even, I thought it, though she was plain herself, too insipidly pretty; I made it a reproach to her that the figures drawn from her were monotonously (*bêtement*, as we used to say) graceful. Nothing made her more angry: it was so much her pride to feel that she could sit for characters that had nothing in common with each other. She would accuse me at such moments of taking away her 'reputytion'.

It suffered a certain shrinkage, this queer quantity, from the repeated visits of my new friends. Miss Churm was greatly in demand, never in want of employment, so I had no scruple in putting her off occasionally, to try them more at my ease. It was certainly amusing at first to do the real thing – it was amusing to do Major Monarch's trousers. They *were* the real thing, even if he did come out colossal. It was amusing to do his wife's back hair (it was so mathematically neat) and the particular 'smart' tension of her tight stays. She lent herself especially to positions in which the face was somewhat averted or blurred; she abounded in lady-like back views and *profils perdus*. When she stood erect she took naturally one of the attitudes in which court-painters represent queens and princesses; so that I found myself wondering whether, to draw out this accomplishment, I couldn't get the editor of the *Cheapside* to publish a really royal romance, 'A Tale of Buckingham Palace'. Sometimes, however, the real thing and the make-believe came into contact; by which I mean that Miss Churm, keeping an appointment or coming to make one on days when I had much work in hand, encountered her invidious rivals. The encounter was not on their part, for they noticed her no more than if she had been the housemaid; not from intentional loftiness, but simply because, as yet, professionally, they didn't know how to fraternize, as I could guess that they would have liked – or at least that the Major would. They couldn't talk about the omnibus – they always walked; and they didn't know what else to try – she wasn't interested in good trains or cheap claret. Besides, they must have felt – in the air – that she was amused at them, secretly derisive of their ever knowing how. She was not a person to conceal her scepticism if she had had a chance to show it. On the other hand Mrs Monarch didn't think her tidy; for why else did she take pains to say to me (it was going out of the way, for Mrs Monarch) that she didn't like dirty women?

One day when my young lady happened to be present with my other sitters (she even dropped in, when it was convenient, for a chat), I asked her to be so good as to lend a hand in getting tea – a service with which she was familiar and which was one of a class that, living as I did in a small way, with slender domestic resources, I often appealed to my models to render. They liked to lay hands on my property, to break the sitting, and sometimes the china – I made them feel Bohemian. The next time I saw Miss Churm after this incident she surprised me greatly by making a scene about it – she accused me of having wished to humiliate her. She had not resented the outrage at the time, but had seemed obliging and amused, enjoying the comedy of asking Mrs Monarch, who sat vague and silent, whether she would have cream and sugar, and putting an exaggerated simper into the question. She had tried intonations – as if she too wished to pass for the real thing; till I was afraid my other visitors would take offence.

Oh, *they* were determined not to do this; and their touching patience was the measure of their great need. They would sit by the hour, uncomplaining, till I was ready to use them; they would come back on the chance of being wanted and would walk away cheerfully if they were not. I used to go to the door with them to see in what magnificent order they retreated. I tried to find other employment for them – I introduced them to several artists. But they didn't 'take', for reasons I could appreciate, and I became conscious, rather anxiously, that after such disappointments they fell back upon me with a heavier weight. They did me the honour to think that it was I who was most *their* form. They were not picturesque enough for the painters, and in those days there were not so many serious workers in black and white. Besides, they had an eye to the great job I had mentioned to them – they had secretly set their hearts on supplying the right essence for my pictorial vindication of our fine novelist. They knew that for this undertaking I should want no costume-effects, none of the frippery of past ages – that it was a case in which everything would be contemporary and satirical and, presumably, genteel. If I could work them into it their future would be assured, for the labour would of course be long and the occupation steady.

One day Mrs Monarch came without her husband – she explained his absence by his having had to go to the City. While she sat there in her usual anxious stiffness there came, at the door, a knock which I immediately recognized as the subdued appeal of a model out of work. It was followed by the entrance of a young man whom I easily perceived to be a foreigner and who proved in fact an Italian acquainted with no English word but my name, which he uttered in a way that made it seem to include all others. I had not then visited his country, nor was I proficient in his tongue; but as he was not so meanly constituted – what Italian is? – as to depend only on that member for expression he conveyed to me, in familiar but graceful mimicry, that he was in search of exactly the employment in which the lady before me was engaged. I was not struck with him at first, and while I continued to draw I emitted rough sounds of discouragement and dismissal. He stood his ground, however, not importunately, but with a dumb, dog-like fidelity in his eyes which amounted to innocent impudence – the manner of a devoted servant (he might have been in the house for years), unjustly suspected. Suddenly I saw that this very attitude and expression made a picture, whereupon I told him to sit down and wait till I should be free. There was another picture in the way he obeyed me, and I observed as I worked that there were others still in the way he looked wonderingly, with his head thrown back, about the high studio. He might have been crossing himself in St Peter's. Before I finished I said to myself: 'The fellow's a bankrupt orange-monger, but he's a treasure.'

When Mrs Monarch withdrew he passed across the room like a flash to open the door for her, standing there with the rapt, pure gaze of the young Dante spellbound by the young Beatrice. As I never insisted, in such situations, on the blankness of the British domestic, I reflected that he had the making of a servant (and I needed one, but couldn't pay him to be only that), as well as of a model; in short I made up my mind to adopt my bright adventurer if he would agree to officiate in the double capacity. He jumped at my offer, and in the event my rashness (for I had known nothing about him) was not brought home to me. He proved a sympathetic though a desultory ministrant, and had in a wonderful degree the *sentiment de la pose*. It was uncultivated, instinctive; a part of the happy instinct which had guided him to my door and helped him to spell out my name on the card nailed to it. He had had no other introduction to me than a guess, from the shape of my high north window, seen outside, that my place was a studio and that as a studio it would contain an artist. He had wandered to England in search of fortune, like other itinerants, and had embarked, with a partner and a small green hand-cart, on the sale of penny ices. The ices had melted away and the partner had dissolved in their train. My young man wore tight yellow trousers with reddish stripes and his name was Oronte. He was sallow but fair, and when I put him into some old clothes of my own he looked like an Englishman. He was as good as Miss Churm, who could look, when required, like an Italian.

IV

I THOUGHT Mrs Monarch's face slightly convulsed when, on her coming back with her husband, she found Oronte installed. It was strange to have to recognize in a scrap of a *lazzarone* a competitor to her magnificent Major. It was she who scented danger first, for the Major was anecdotically unconscious. But Oronte gave us tea, with a hundred eager confusions (he had never seen such a queer process), and I think she thought better of me for having at last an 'establishment'. They saw a couple of drawings that I had made of the establishment, and Mrs Monarch hinted that it never would have struck her that he had sat for them. 'Now the drawings you make from *us*, they look exactly like us,' she reminded me, smiling in triumph; and I recognized that this was indeed just their defect. When I drew the Monarchs I couldn't, somehow, get away from them – get into the character I wanted to represent; and I had not the least desire my model should be discoverable in my picture. Miss Churm never was, and Mrs Monarch thought I hid her, very properly, because she was vulgar; whereas if she was lost it was only as the dead who go to Heaven are lost – in the gain of an angel the more.

By this time I had got a certain start with 'Rutland Ramsay', the first novel in the great projected series; that is I had produced a dozen drawings, several with the help of the Major and his wife, and I had sent them in for approval. My understanding with the publishers, as I have already hinted, had been that I was to be left to do my work, in this particular case, as I liked, with the whole book committed to me; but my connection with the rest of the series was only contingent. There were moments when, frankly, it *was* a comfort to have the real thing under one's hand; for there were characters in 'Rutland Ramsay' that were very much like it. There were people presumably as straight as the Major and women of as good a fashion as Mrs Monarch. There was a great deal of country-house life – treated, it is true, in a fine, fanciful, ironical, generalized way – and there was a considerable implication of knickerbockers and kilts. There were certain things I had to settle at the outset; such things for instance as the exact appearance of the hero, the particular bloom of the heroine. The author of course gave me a lead, but there was a margin for interpretation. I took the Monarchs into my confidence, I told them frankly what I was about, I mentioned my embarrassments and alternatives. 'Oh, take *him*!' Mrs Monarch murmured sweetly, looking at her husband; and 'What could you want better than my wife?' the

Major inquired, with the comfortable candour that now prevailed between us.

I was not obliged to answer these remarks – I was only obliged to place my sitters. I was not easy in mind, and I postponed, a little timidly perhaps, the solution of the question. The book was a large canvas, the other figures were numerous, and I worked off at first some of the episodes in which the hero and the heroine were not concerned. When once I had set *them* up I should have to stick to them – I couldn't make my young man seven feet high in one place and five feet nine in another. I inclined on the whole to the latter measurement, though the Major more than once reminded me that *he* looked about as young as anyone. It was indeed quite possible to arrange him, for the figure, so that it would have been difficult to detect his age. After the spontaneous Oronte had been with me a month, and after I had given him to understand several different times that his native exuberance would presently constitute an insurmountable barrier to our further intercourse, I waked to a sense of his heroic capacity. He was only five feet seven, but the remaining inches were latent. I tried him almost secretly at first, for I was really rather afraid of the judgement my other models would pass on such a choice. If they regarded Miss Churm as little better than a snare, what would they think of the representation by a person so little the real thing as an Italian street-vendor of a protagonist formed by a public school?

If I went a little in fear of them it was not because they bullied me, because they had got an oppressive foothold, but because in their really pathetic decorum and mysteriously permanent newness they counted on me so intensely. I was therefore very glad when Jack Hawley came home: he was always of such good counsel. He painted badly himself, but there was no one like him for putting his finger on the place. He had been absent from England for a year; he had been somewhere – I don't remember where – to get a fresh eye. I was in a good deal of dread of any such organ, but we were old friends; he had been away for months and a sense of emptiness was creeping into my life. I hadn't dodged a missile for a year.

He came back with a fresh eye, but with the same old black velvet blouse, and the first evening he spent in my studio we smoked cigarettes till the small hours. He had done no work himself, he had only got the eye; so the field was clear for the production of my little things. He wanted to see what I had done for the *Cheapside*, but he was disappointed in the exhibition. That at least seemed the meaning of two or three comprehensive groans which, as he lounged on my big divan, on a folded leg, looking at my latest drawings, issued from his lips with the smoke of the cigarette.

'What's the matter with you?' I asked.

'What's the matter with *you*?'

'Nothing save that I'm mystified.'

'You are indeed. You're quite off the hinge. What's the meaning of this new fad?' And he tossed me, with visible irreverence, a drawing in which I happened to have depicted both my majestic models. I asked if he didn't think it good, and he replied that it struck him as execrable, given the sort of thing I had always represented myself to him as wishing to arrive at; but I let that pass, I was so anxious to see exactly what he meant. The two figures in the picture looked colossal, but I supposed this was *not* what he meant, inasmuch as, for aught he knew to the contrary, I might have been trying for that. I maintained that I was working exactly in the same way as when he last had done me the honour to commend me. 'Well, there's a big hole somewhere,' he answered; 'wait a bit and I'll discover it.' I depended upon him to do so: where else was the fresh eye? But he produced at last nothing more luminous than 'I don't know – I don't like your types.' This was lame, for a critic who had never consented to discuss with me anything but the question of execution, the direction of strokes and the mystery of values.

'In the drawings you've been looking at I think my types are very handsome.'

'Oh, they won't do!'

'I've had a couple of new models.'

'I see you have. *They* won't do.'

'Are you very sure of that?'

'Absolutely – they're stupid.'

'You mean *I* am – for I ought to get round that.'

'You *can't* – with such people. Who are they?'

I told him, as far as was necessary, and he declared, heartlessly: '*Ce sont des gens qu'il faut mettre à la porte.*'

'You've never seen them; they're awfully good,' I compassionately objected.

'Not seen them? Why, all this recent work of yours drops to pieces with them. It's all I want to see of them.'

'No one else has said anything against it – the *Cheapside* people are pleased.'

'Everyone else is an ass, and the *Cheapside* people the biggest asses of all. Come, don't pretend, at this time of day, to have pretty illusions about the public, especially about publishers and editors. It's not for *such* animals you work – it's for those who know, *coloro che sanno*; so keep straight for *me* if you can't keep straight for yourself. There's a certain sort of thing you tried for from the first – and a very good thing it is. But this twaddle isn't *in* it.' When I talked with Hawley later about 'Rutland Ramsay' and its possible successors he declared that I must get back into my boat again or I would go to the bottom. His voice in short was the voice of warning.

I noted the warning, but I didn't turn my friends out of doors. They bored me a good deal; but the very fact that they bored me admonished me not to sacrifice them – if there was anything to be done with them – simply to irritation. As I look back at this phase they seem to me to have pervaded my life not a little. I have a vision of them as most of the time in my studio, seated, against the wall, on an old velvet bench to be out of the way, and looking like a pair of patient courtiers in a royal ante-chamber. I am convinced that during the coldest weeks of the winter they held their ground because it saved them fire. Their newness was losing its gloss, and it was impossible not to feel that they were objects of charity. Whenever Miss Churm arrived they went away, and after I was fairly launched in 'Rutland Ramsay' Miss Churm arrived pretty often. They managed to express to me tacitly that they supposed I wanted her for the low life of the book, and I let them suppose it, since they had attempted to study the work – it was lying about the studio – without discovering that it dealt only with the highest circles. They had dipped into the most brilliant of our novelists without deciphering many passages. I still took an hour from them, now and again, in spite of Jack Hawley's warning: it would be time enough to dismiss them, if dismissal should be necessary, when the rigour of the season was over. Hawley had made their acquaintance – he had met them at my fireside – and thought them a ridiculous pair. Learning that he was a painter they tried to approach him, to show him too that they were the real thing; but he looked at them, across the big room, as if they were miles away: they were a compendium of everything that he most objected to in the social system of his country. Such people as that, all convention and patent-leather, with ejaculations that stopped conversation, had no business in a studio. A studio was a place to learn to see, and how could you see through a pair of feather beds?

The main inconvenience I suffered at their hands was that, at first, I was shy of letting them discover how my artful little servant had begun to sit to me for 'Rutland Ramsay'. They knew that I had been odd enough (they were prepared by this time to allow oddity to artists) to pick a foreign vagabond out of the streets, when I might have had a person with whiskers and credentials; but it was some time before they learned how high I rated his accomplishments. They found him in an attitude more than once, but they never doubted I was doing him as an organ-grinder. There were several things they never guessed, and one of them was that for a striking scene in the novel, in which a footman briefly figured, it occurred to me to make use of Major Monarch as the menial. I kept putting this off, I didn't like to ask him to don the livery – besides the difficulty of finding a livery to fit him. At last, one day late in the winter, when I was at work on the despised Oronte (he caught one's idea in an instant), and was in the glow of feeling that I was going very straight, they came in, the Major and his wife, with their society laugh about nothing (there was less and less to laugh at), like country-callers – they always reminded me of that – who have walked across the park after church and are presently persuaded to stay to luncheon. Luncheon was over, but they could stay to tea – I knew they wanted it. The fit was on me, however, and I couldn't let my ardour cool and my work wait, with the fading daylight, while my model prepared it. So I asked Mrs Monarch if she would mind laying it out – a request which, for an instant, brought all the blood to her face. Her eyes were on her husband's for a second, and some mute telegraphy passed between them. Their folly was over the next instant; his cheerful shrewdness put an end to it. So far from pitying their wounded pride, I must add, I was moved to give it as complete a lesson as I could. They bustled about together and got out the cups and saucers and made the kettle boil. I know they felt as if they were waiting on my servant, and when the tea was prepared I said: 'He'll have a cup, please – he's tired.' Mrs Monarch brought him one where he stood, and he took it from her as if he had been a gentleman at a party, squeezing a crush-hat with an elbow.

Then it came over me that she had made a great effort for me – made it with a kind of nobleness – and that I owed her a compensation. Each time I saw her after this I wondered what the compensation could be. I couldn't go on doing the wrong thing to oblige them. Oh, it *was* the wrong thing, the stamp of the work for which they sat – Hawley was not the only person to say it now. I sent in a large number of the drawings I had made for 'Rutland Ramsay', and I received a warning that was more to the point than Hawley's. The artistic adviser of the house for which I was working was of opinion that many of my illustrations were not what had been looked for. Most of these illustrations were the subjects in which the Monarchs had figured. Without going into the question of what *had* been looked for, I saw at this rate I shouldn't get the other books to do. I hurled myself in despair upon Miss Churm, I put her through all her paces. I not only adopted Oronte publicly as my hero, but one morning when the Major looked in to see if I didn't require him to finish a figure for the *Cheapside*, for which he had begun to sit the week before, I told him that I had changed my mind – I would do the drawing from my man. At this my visitor turned pale and stood looking at me. 'Is *he* your idea of an English gentleman?' he asked.

I was disappointed, I was nervous, I wanted to get on with my work; so I replied with irritation: 'Oh, my dear Major – I can't be ruined for *you*!'

He stood another moment; then, without a word, he quitted the studio. I drew a long breath when he was gone, for I said to myself that I shouldn't see him again. I had not told him definitely that I was in danger of having my work rejected, but I was vexed at his not having felt the catastrophe in the air, read with me the moral of our fruitless collaboration, the lesson that, in the deceptive atmosphere of art, even the highest respectability may fail of being plastic.

I didn't owe my friends money, but I did see them again. They reappeared together, three days later, and under the circumstances there was something tragic in the fact. It was a proof to me that they could find nothing else in life to do. They had threshed the matter out in a dismal conference – they had digested the bad news that they were not in for the series. If they were not useful to me even for the *Cheapside* their function seemed difficult to determine, and I could only judge at first that they had come, forgivingly, decorously, to take a last leave. This made me rejoice in secret that I had little leisure for a scene; for I had placed both my other models in position together and I was pegging away at a drawing from which I hoped to derive glory. It had been suggested by the passage in which Rutland Ramsay, drawing up a chair to Artemisia's piano-stool, says extraordinary things to her while she ostensibly fingers out a difficult piece of music. I had done Miss Churm at the piano before – it was an attitude in which she knew how to take on an absolutely poetic grace. I wished the two figures to 'compose' together, intensely, and my little Italian had entered perfectly into my conception. The pair were vividly before me, the piano had been pulled out; it was a charming picture of blended youth and murmured love, which I had only to catch and keep. My visitors stood and looked at it, and I was friendly to them over my shoulder.

They made no response, but I was used to silent company and went on with my work, only a little disconcerted (even though exhilarated by the sense that *this* was at least the ideal thing) at not having got rid of them after all. Presently I heard Mrs Monarch's sweet voice beside, or rather above me: 'I wish her hair was a little better done.' I looked up and she was staring with a strange fixedness at Miss Churm, whose back was turned to her. 'Do you mind my just touching it?' she went on – a question which made me spring up for an instant, as with the instinctive fear that she might do the young lady a harm. But she quieted me with a glance I shall never forget – I confess I should like to have been able to paint *that* – and went for a moment to my model. She spoke to her softly, laying a hand upon her shoulder and bending over her; and as the girl, understanding, gratefully assented, she disposed her rough curls, with a few quick passes, in such a way as to make Miss Churm's head twice as charming. It was one of the most heroic personal services I have ever seen rendered. Then Mrs Monarch turned away with a low sigh and, looking about her as if for something to do, stooped to the floor with a noble humility and picked up a dirty rag that had dropped out of my paint-box.

The Major meanwhile had also been looking for something to do and, wandering to the other end of the studio, saw before him my breakfast things, neglected, unremoved. 'I say, can't I be useful *here*?' he called out to me with an irrepressible quaver. I assented with a laugh that I fear was awkward and for the next ten minutes, while I worked, I heard the light clatter of china and the tinkle of spoons and glass. Mrs Monarch assisted her husband – they washed up my crockery, they put it away. They wandered off into my little scullery, and I afterwards found that they had cleaned my knives and that my slender stock of plate had an unprecedented surface. When it came over me, the latent eloquence of what they were doing, I confess that my drawing was blurred for a moment – the picture swam. They had accepted their failure, but they couldn't accept their fate. They had bowed their heads in bewilderment to the perverse and cruel law in virtue of which the real thing could be so much less precious than the unreal; but they didn't want to starve. If my servants were my models, my models might be my servants. They would reverse the parts – the others would sit for the ladies and gentlemen, and *they* would do the work. They would still be in the studio – it was an intense dumb appeal to me not to turn them out. 'Take us on,' they wanted to say – 'we'll do *anything*.'

When all this hung before me the *afflatus* vanished – my pencil dropped from my hand. My sitting was spoiled and I got rid of my sitters, who were also evidently rather mystified and awestruck. Then, alone with the Major and his wife, I had a most uncomfortable moment, He put their prayer into a single sentence: 'I say, you know – just let *us* do for you, can't you?' I couldn't – it was dreadful to see them emptying my slops; but I pretended I could, to oblige them, for about a week. Then I gave them a sum of money to go away; and I never saw them again. I obtained the remaining books, but my friend Hawley repeats that Major and Mrs Monarch did me a permanent harm, got me into a second-rate trick. If it be true I am content to have paid the price – for the memory.

The Private Life

WE TALKED OF London, face to face with a great bristling, primeval glacier. The hour and the scene were one of those impressions which make up a little, in Switzerland, for the modern indignity of travel – the promiscuities and vulgarities, the station and the hotel, the gregarious patience, the struggle for a scrappy attention, the reduction to a numbered state. The high valley was pink with the mountain rose, the cool air as fresh as if the world were young. There was a faint flush of afternoon on undiminished snows, and the fraternizing tinkle of the unseen cattle came to us with a cropped and sun-warmed odour. The balconied inn stood on the very neck of the sweetest pass in the Oberland, and for a week we had had company and weather. This was felt to be great luck, for one would have made up for the other had either been bad.

The weather certainly would have made up for the company; but it was not subjected to this tax, for we had by a happy chance the *fleur des pois*: Lord and Lady Mellifont, Clare Vawdrey, the greatest (in the opinion of many) of our literary glories, and Blanche Adney, the greatest (in the opinion of all) of our theatrical. I mention these first, because they were just the people whom in London, at that time, people tried to 'get'. People endeavoured to 'book' them six weeks ahead, yet on this occasion we had come in for them, we had all come in for each other, without the least wire-pulling. A turn of the game had pitched us together, the last of August, and we recognized our luck by remaining so, under protection of the barometer. When the golden days were over – that would come soon enough – we should wind down opposite sides of the pass and disappear over the crest of surrounding heights. We were of the same general communion, we participated in the same miscellaneous publicity. We met, in London, with irregular frequency; we were more or less governed by the laws and the language, the traditions and the shibboleths of the same dense social state. I think all of us, even the ladies, 'did' something, though we pretended we didn't when it was mentioned. Such things are not mentioned indeed in London, but it was our innocent pleasure to be different here. There had to be some way to show the difference, inasmuch as we were under the impression that this was our annual holiday. We felt at any rate that the conditions were more human than in London, or that at least we ourselves were. We were frank about this, we talked about it: it was what we were talking about as we looked at the flushing glacier, just as someone called attention to the prolonged absence of Lord Mellifont and Mrs Adney. We were seated on the terrace of the inn, where there were benches and little tables, and those of us who were most bent on proving that we had returned to nature were, in the queer Germanic fashion, having coffee before meat.

The remark about the absence of our two companions was not taken up, not even by Lady Mellifont, not even by little Adney, the fond composer; for it had been dropped only in the briefest intermission of Clare Vawdrey's talk. (This celebrity was 'Clarence' only on the title-page.) It was just that revelation of our being after all human that was his theme. He asked the company whether, candidly, everyone hadn't been tempted to say to everyone else: 'I had no idea you were really so nice.' I had had, for my part, an idea that *he* was, and even a good deal nicer, but that was too complicated to go into then; besides it is exactly my story. There was a general understanding among us that when Vawdrey talked we should be silent, and not, oddly enough, because he at all expected it. He didn't, for of all abundant talkers he was the most unconscious, the least greedy and professional. It was rather the religion of the host, of the hostess, that prevailed among us: it was their own idea, but they always looked for a listening circle when the great novelist dined with them. On the occasion I allude to there was probably no one present with whom, in London, he had not dined, and we felt the force of this habit. He had dined even with me; and on the evening of that dinner, as on this Alpine afternoon, I had been at no pains to hold my tongue, absorbed as I inveterately was in a study of the question which always rose before me, to such a height, in his fair, square, strong stature.

This question was all the more tormenting that he never suspected himself (I am sure) of imposing it, any more than he had ever observed that every day of his life every one listened to him at dinner. He used to be called 'subjective' in the weekly papers, but in society no distinguished man could have been less so. He never talked about himself; and this was a topic on which, though it would have been tremendously worthy of him, he apparently never even reflected. He had his hours and his habits, his tailor and his hatter, his hygiene and his particular wine, but all these things together never made up an attitude. Yet they constituted the only attitude he ever adopted, and it was easy for him to refer to our being 'nicer' abroad than at home. *He* was exempt from variations, and not a shade either less or more nice in one place than in another. He differed from other people, but never from himself (save in the extraordinary sense which I will presently explain), and struck me as having neither moods nor sensibilities nor preferences. He might have been always in the same company, so far as he recognized any influence from age or condition or sex: he addressed himself to women exactly as he addressed himself to men, and gossiped with all men alike, talking no better to clever folk than to dull. I used to feel a despair at his way of liking one subject – so far as I could tell – precisely as much as another: there were some I hated so myself. I never found him anything but loud and cheerful and copious, and I never heard him utter a paradox or express a shade or play with an idea. That fancy about our being 'human' was, in his conversation, quite an exceptional flight. His opinions were sound and second-rate, and of his perceptions it was too mysti-fying to think. I envied him his magnificent health.

Vawdrey had marched, with his even pace and his perfectly good conscience, into the flat country of anecdote, where stories are visible from afar like windmills and signposts; but I observed after a little that Lady Mellifont's attention wandered. I happened to be sitting next her. I noticed that her eyes rambled a little anxiously over the lower slopes of the mountains. At last, after looking at her watch, she said to me: 'Do you know where they went?'

'Do you mean Mrs Adney and Lord Mellifont?'

'Lord Mellifont and Mrs Adney.' Her ladyship's speech seemed – unconsciously indeed – to correct me, but it didn't occur to me that this was because she was jealous. I imputed to her no such vulgar sentiment: in the first place, because I liked her, and in the second because it would always occur to one quickly that it was right, in any connection, to put Lord Mellifont first. He *was* first – extraordinarily first. I don't say greatest or wisest or most renowned, but essentially at the top of the list and the head of the table. That is a position by itself, and his wife was naturally accustomed to see him in it. My phrase had sounded as if Mrs Adney had taken him; but it was not possible for him to be taken – he only took. No one, in the nature of things, could know this better than Lady Mellifont. I had originally been rather afraid of her, thinking her, with her stiff silences and the extreme blackness of almost everything that made up her person, somewhat hard, even a little saturnine. Her paleness seemed slightly grey, and her glossy black hair metallic, like the brooches and bands and combs with which it was inveterately adorned. She was in perpetual mourning, and wore numberless ornaments of jet and onyx, a thousand clicking chains and bugles and beads. I had heard Mrs Adney call her the queen of night, and the term was descriptive if you understood that the night was cloudy. She had a secret, and if you didn't find it out as you knew her better you at least perceived that she was gentle and unaffected and limited, and also rather submissively sad. She was like a woman with a painless malady. I told her that I had merely seen her husband and his companion stroll down the glen together about an hour before, and suggested that Mr Adney would perhaps know something of their intentions.

Vincent Adney, who, though he was fifty years old, looked like a good little boy on whom it had been impressed that children should not talk before company, acquitted himself with remarkable simplicity and taste of the position of husband of a great exponent of comedy. When all was said about her making it easy for him, one couldn't help admiring the charmed affection with which he took everything for granted. It is difficult for a husband who is not on the stage, or at least in the theatre, to be graceful about a wife who is; but Adney was more than graceful – he was exquisite, he was inspired. He set his beloved to music; and you remember how genuine his music could be – the only English compositions I ever saw a foreigner take an interest in. His wife was in them, somewhere, always; they were like a free, rich translation of the impression she produced. She seemed, as one listened, to pass laughing, with loosened hair, across the scene. He had been only a little fiddler at her theatre, always in his place during the acts; but she had made him something rare and misunderstood. Their superiority had become a kind of partnership, and their happiness was a part of the happiness of their friends. Adney's one discomfort was that he couldn't write a play for his wife, and the only way he meddled with her affairs was by asking impossible people if *they* couldn't.

Lady Mellifont, after looking across at him a moment, remarked to me that she would rather not put any question to him. She added the next minute: 'I had rather people shouldn't see I'm nervous.'

'*Are* you nervous?'

'I always become so if my husband is away from me for any time.'

'Do you imagine something has happened to him?'

'Yes, always. Of course I'm used to it.'

'Do you mean his tumbling over precipices — that sort of thing?'

'I don't know exactly what it is: it's the general sense that he'll never come back.'

She said so much and kept back so much that the only way to treat the condition she referred to seemed the jocular. 'Surely he'll never forsake you!' I laughed.

She looked at the ground a moment. 'Oh, at bottom I'm easy.'

'Nothing can ever happen to a man so accomplished, so infallible, so armed at all points,' I went on, encouragingly.

'Oh, you don't know how he's armed!' she exclaimed, with such an odd quaver that I could account for it only by her being nervous. This idea was confirmed by her moving just afterwards, changing her seat rather pointlessly, not as if to cut our conversation short, but because she was in a fidget. I couldn't know what was the matter with her, but I was presently relieved to see Mrs Adney come toward us. She had in her hand a big bunch of wild flowers, but she was not closely attended by Lord Mellifont. I quickly saw, however, that she had no disaster to announce; yet as I knew there was a question Lady Mellifont would like to hear answered, but did not wish to ask, I expressed to her immediately the hope that his lordship had not remained in a crevasse.

'Oh, no; he left me but three minutes ago. He has gone into the house.' Blanche Adney rested her eyes on mine an instant – a mode of intercourse to which no man, for himself, could ever object. The interest, on this occasion, was quickened by the particular thing the eyes happened to say. What they usually said was only: 'Oh, yes I'm charming, I know, but don't make a fuss about it. I only want a new part – I do, I do!' At present they added, dimly, surreptitiously, and of course sweetly – for that was the way they did everything: 'It's all right, but something did happen. Perhaps I'll tell you later.' She turned to Lady Mellifont, and the transition to simple gaiety suggested her mastery of her profession. 'I've brought him safe. We had a charming walk.'

'I'm so very glad,' returned Lady Mellifont, with her faint smile; continuing vaguely, as she got up: 'He must have gone to dress for dinner. Isn't it rather near?' She moved away, to the hotel, in her leave-taking, simplifying fashion, and the rest of us, at the mention of dinner, looked at each other's watches, as if to shift the responsibility of such grossness. The head-waiter, essentially, like all head-waiters, a man of the world, allowed us hours and places of our own, so that in the evening, apart under the lamp, we formed a compact, an indulged little circle. But it was only the Mellifonts who 'dressed' and as to whom it was recognized that they naturally *would* dress: she in exactly the same manner as on any other evening of her ceremonious exist-ence (she was not a woman whose habits could take account of anything so mutable as fitness); and he, on the other hand, with remarkable adjustment and suitability. He was almost as much a man of the world as the head-waiter, and spoke almost as many languages; but he abstained from courting a comparison of dress-coats and white waistcoats, analysing the occasion in a much finer way – into black velvet and blue velvet and brown velvet, for instance, into delicate harmonies of necktie and subtle informalities of shirt. He had a costume for every func-tion and a moral for every costume; and his functions and costumes and morals were ever a part of the amusement of life – a part at any rate of its beauty and romance – for an immense circle of spectators. For his particular friends indeed these things were more than an amusement; they were a topic, a social support and of course, in addition, a subject of perpetual suspense. If his wife had not been present before dinner they were what the rest of us probably would have been putting our heads together about.

Clare Vawdrey had a fund of anecdote on the whole question: he had known Lord Mellifont almost from the beginning. It was a peculiarity of this nobleman that there could be no conversation about him that didn't instantly take the form of anecdote, and a still further distinction that there could apparently be no anecdote that was not on the whole to his honour. If he had come into a room at any moment, people might have said frankly: 'Of course we were telling stories about you!' As consciences go, in London, the general conscience would have been good. Moreover it would have been impossible to imagine his taking such a tribute otherwise than amiably, for he was always as unperturbed as an actor with the right cue. He had never in his life needed the prompter – his very embarrassments had been rehearsed. For myself, when he was talked about I always had an odd impression that we were speaking of the dead – it was with that peculiar accumulation of relish. His reputation was a kind of gilded obelisk, as if he had been buried beneath it; the body of legend and reminiscence of which he was to be the subject had crystallized in advance.

This ambiguity sprang, I suppose, from the fact that the mere sound of his name and air of his person, the general expectation he created, were, somehow, too exalted to be verified. The experience of his urbanity always came later; the prefigurement, the legend paled before the reality. I remember

that on the evening I refer to the reality was particularly opera-
tive. The handsomest man of his period could never have
looked better, and he sat among us like a bland conductor
controlling by an harmonious play of arm an orchestra still a
little rough. He directed the conversation by gestures as irresistible as they were vague; one felt as if without him it wouldn't
have had anything to call a tone. This was essentially what he
contributed to any occasion – what he contributed above all to
English public life. He pervaded it, he coloured it, he embel-
lished it, and without him it would scarcely have had a vocabulary. Certainly it would not have had a style; for a style was
what it had in having Lord Mellifont. He *was* a style. I was
freshly struck with it as, in the *salle à manger* of the little Swiss
inn, we resigned ourselves to inevitable veal. Confronted with
his form (I must parenthesize that it was not confronted much),
Clare Vawdrey's talk suggested the reporter contrasted with
the bard. It was interesting to watch the shock of characters
from which, of an evening, so much would be expected. There
was however no concussion – it was all muffled and minimized
in Lord Mellifont's tact. It was rudimentary with him to find
the solution of such a problem in playing the host, assuming
responsibilities which carried with them their sacrifice. He had
indeed never been a guest in his life; he was the host, the patron,
the moderator at every board. If there was a defect in his
manner (and I suggest it under my breath), it was that he had a
little more art than any conjunction – even the most complicated – could possibly require. At any rate one made one's

reflections in noticing how the accomplished peer handled the situation and how the sturdy man of letters was unconscious that the situation (and least of all he himself as part of it) was handled. Lord Mellifont poured forth treasures of tact, and Clare Vawdrey never dreamed he was doing it.

Vawdrey had no suspicion of any such precaution even when Blanche Adney asked him if he saw yet their third act — an inquiry into which she introduced a subtlety of her own. She had a theory that he was to write her a play and that the heroine, if he would only do his duty, would be the part for which she had immemorially longed. She was forty years old (this could be no secret to those who had admired her from the first), and she could now reach out her hand and touch her uttermost goal. This gave a kind of tragic passion — perfect actress of comedy as she was — to her desire not to miss the great thing. The years had passed, and still she had missed it; none of the things she had done was the thing she had dreamed of, so that at present there was no more time to lose. This was the canker in the rose, the ache beneath the smile. It made her touching — made her sadness even sweeter than her laughter. She had done the old English and the new French, and had charmed her generation; but she was haunted by the vision of a bigger chance, of something truer to the conditions that lay near her. She was tired of Sheridan and she hated Bowdler; she called for a canvas of a finer grain. The worst of it, to my sense, was that she would never extract her modern comedy from the great mature novelist, who was as incapable of producing it as he was of threading a needle. She coddled him, she talked to him, she made love to him, as she frankly proclaimed; but she dwelt in illusions – she would have to live and die with Bowdler.

It is difficult to be cursory over this charming woman, who was beautiful without beauty and complete with a dozen deficiencies. The perspective of the stage made her over, and in society she was like the model off the pedestal. She was the picture walking about, which to the artless social mind was a perpetual surprise – a miracle. People thought she told them the secrets of the pictorial nature, in return for which they gave her relaxation and tea. She told them nothing and she drank the tea; but they had, all the same, the best of the bargain. Vawdrey was really at work on a play; but if he had begun it because he liked her I think he let it drag for the same reason. He secretly felt the atrocious difficulty – knew that from his hand the finished piece would have received no active life. At the same time nothing could be more agreeable than to have such a question open with Blanche Adney, and from time to time he put something very good into the play. If he deceived Mrs Adney it was only because in her despair she was determined to be deceived. To her question about their third act he replied that, before dinner, he had written a magnificent passage.

'Before dinner?' I said. 'Why, *cher maître*, before dinner you were holding us all spellbound on the terrace.'

My words were a joke, because I thought his had been; but for the first time that I could remember I perceived a certain confusion in his face. He looked at me hard, throwing back his head quickly, the least bit like a horse who has been pulled up short. 'Oh, it was before that,' he replied, naturally enough.

'Before that you were playing billiards with *me*,' Lord Mellifont intimated.

'Then it must have been yesterday,' said Vawdrey.

But he was in a tight place. 'You told me this morning you did nothing yesterday,' the actress objected.

'I don't think I really know when I do things.' Vawdrey looked vaguely, without helping himself, at a dish that was offered him.

'It's enough if *we* know,' smiled Lord Mellifont.

'I don't believe you've written a line,' said Blanche Adney.

'I think I could repeat you the scene.' Vawdrey helped himself to *haricots verts*.

'Oh, do – oh, do!' two or three of us cried.

'After dinner, in the salon; it will be an immense *régal*,' Lord Mellifont declared.

'I'm not sure, but I'll try,' Vawdrey went on.

'Oh, you lovely man!' exclaimed the actress, who was practising Americanisms, being resigned even to an American comedy.

'But there must be this condition,' said Vawdrey: 'you must make your husband play.'

'Play while you're reading? Never!'

'I've too much vanity,' said Adney.

Lord Mellifont distinguished him. 'You must give us the overture, before the curtain rises. That's a peculiarly delightful moment.'

'I shan't read – I shall just speak,' said Vawdrey.

'Better still, let me go and get your manuscript,' the actress suggested.

Vawdrey replied that the manuscript didn't matter; but an hour later, in the salon, we wished he might have had it. We sat expectant, still under the spell of Adney's violin. His wife, in the foreground, on an ottoman, was all impatience and profile, and Lord Mellifont, in the chair – it was always *the* chair, Lord Mellifont's – made our grateful little group feel like a social science congress or a distribution of prizes. Suddenly, instead of beginning, our tame lion began to roar out of tune – he had clean forgotten every word. He was very sorry, but the lines absolutely wouldn't come to him; he was utterly ashamed, but his memory was a blank. He didn't look in the least ashamed – Vawdrey had never looked ashamed in his life; he was only imperturbably and merrily natural. He protested that he had never expected to make such a fool of himself, but we felt that this wouldn't prevent the incident from taking its place among his jolliest reminiscences. It was only *we* who were humiliated, as if he had played us a premeditated trick. This was an occasion, if ever, for Lord Mellifont's tact, which descended on us all like balm: he told us, in his charming artistic way, his way of bridging over arid intervals (he had a *débit* – there was nothing to approach it in England – like the actors of the Comédie

Française), of his own collapse on a momentous occasion, the delivery of an address to a mighty multitude, when, finding he had forgotten his memoranda, he fumbled, on the terrible platform, the cynosure of every eye, fumbled vainly in irreproachable pockets for indispensable notes. But the point of his story was finer than that of Vawdrey's pleasantry; for he sketched with a few light gestures the brilliancy of a performance which had risen superior to embarrassment, had resolved itself, we were left to divine, into an effort recognized at the moment as not absolutely a blot on what the public was so good as to call his reputation.

'Play up – play up!' cried Blanche Adney, tapping her husband and remembering how, on the stage, a *contretemps* is always drowned in music. Adney threw himself upon his fiddle, and I said to Clare Vawdrey that his mistake could easily be corrected by his sending for the manuscript. If he would tell me where it was I would immediately fetch it from his room. To this he replied: 'My dear fellow, I'm afraid there *is* no manuscript.'

'Then you've not written anything?'

'I'll write it tomorrow.'

'Ah, you trifle with us,' I said, in much mystification.

Vawdrey hesitated an instant. 'If there *is* anything, you'll find it on my table.'

At this moment one of the others spoke to him, and Lady Mellifont remarked audibly, as if to correct gently our want of consideration, that Mr Adney was playing something very beautiful. I had noticed before that she appeared extremely fond of music; she always listened to it in a hushed transport. Vawdrey's attention was drawn away, but it didn't seem to me that the words he had just dropped constituted a definite permission to go to his room. Moreover I wanted to speak to Blanche Adney; I had something to ask her. I had to await my chance, however, as we remained silent awhile for her husband, after which the conversation became general. It was our habit to go to bed early, but there was still a little of the evening left. Before it quite waned I found an opportunity to tell the actress that Vawdrey had given me leave to put my hand on his manuscript. She adjured me, by all I held sacred, to bring it immediately, to give it to her; and her insistence was proof against my suggestion that it would now be too late for him to begin to read; besides which the charm was broken – the others wouldn't care. It was not too late for *her* to begin; therefore I was to possess myself, without more delay, of the precious pages. I told her she should be obeyed in a moment, but I wanted her first to satisfy my just curiosity. What had happened before dinner, while she was on the hills with Lord Mellifont?

'How do you know anything happened?'

'I saw it in your face when you came back.'

'And they call me an actress!' cried Mrs Adney.

'What do they call *me*?' I inquired.

'You're a searcher of hearts – that frivolous thing an observer.'

'I wish you'd let an observer write you a play!' I broke out.

'People don't care for what you write: you'd break any run of luck.'

'Well, I see plays all round me,' I declared; 'the air is full of them tonight.'

'The air? Thank you for nothing! I only wish my table-drawers were.'

'Did he make love to you on the glacier?' I went on.

She stared; then broke into the graduated ecstasy of her laugh. 'Lord Mellifont, poor dear? What a funny place! It would indeed be the place for *our* love!'

'Did he fall into a crevasse?' I continued.

Blanche Adney looked at me again as she had done for an instant when she came up, before dinner, with her hands full of flowers. 'I don't know into what he fell. I'll tell you tomorrow.'

'He did come down, then?'

'Perhaps he went up,' she laughed. 'It's really strange.'

'All the more reason you should tell me tonight.'

'I must think it over; I must puzzle it out.'

'Oh, if you want conundrums I'll throw in another,' I said. 'What's the matter with the master?'

'The master of what?'

'Of every form of dissimulation. Vawdrey hasn't written a line.'

'Go and get his papers and we'll see.'

'I don't like to expose him,' I said.

'Why not, if I expose Lord Mellifont?'

'Oh, I'd do anything for that,' I conceded. 'But why should Vawdrey have made a false statement? It's very curious.'

'It's very curious,' Blanche Adney repeated, with a musing air and her eyes on Lord Mellifont. Then, rousing herself, she added: 'Go and look in his room.'

'In Lord Mellifont's?'

She turned to me quickly. '*That* would be a way!'

'A way to what?'

'To find out – to find out!' She spoke gaily and excitedly, but suddenly checked herself. 'We're talking nonsense,' she said.

'We're mixing things up, but I'm struck with your idea. Get Lady Mellifont to let you.'

'Oh, *she* has looked!' Mrs Adney murmured, with the oddest dramatic expression. Then, after a movement of her beautiful uplifted hand, as if to brush away a fantastic vision, she exclaimed imperiously: 'Bring me the scene – bring me the scene!'

'I go for it,' I answered; 'but don't tell me I can't write a play.'

She left me, but my errand was arrested by the approach of a lady who had produced a birthday-book – we had been threatened with it for several evenings – and who did me the honour to solicit my autograph. She had been asking the others, and she couldn't decently leave me out. I could usually remember my name, but it always took me some time to recall my date, and even when I had done so I was never very sure. I hesitated between two days and I remarked to my petitioner that I would sign on both if it would give her any satisfaction. She said that surely I had been born only once; and I replied of course that on the day I made her acquaintance I had been born again. I mention the feeble joke only to show that, with the obligatory inspection of the other autographs, we gave some minutes to this transaction. The lady departed with her book, and then I became aware that the company had dispersed. I was alone in the little salon that had been appropriated to our use. My first impression was one of disappointment: if Vawdrey had gone to bed I didn't wish to disturb him. While I hesitated, however, I recognized that Vawdrey had not gone to bed. A window was open, and the sound of voices outside came in to me: Blanche was on the terrace with her dramatist, and they were talking about the stars. I went to the window for a glimpse – the Alpine night was splendid. My friends had stepped out together; the actress had picked up a cloak; she looked as I had seen her look in the wing of the theatre. They were silent awhile, and I heard the roar of a neighbouring torrent. I turned back into the room, and its quiet lamplight gave me an idea. Our companions had dispersed – it was late for a pastoral country – and we three should have the place to ourselves. Clare Vawdrey had written his scene – it was magnificent; and his reading it to us there, at such an hour, would be an episode intensely memorable. I would bring down his manuscript and meet the two with it as they came in.

I quitted the salon for this purpose; I had been in Vawdrey's room and knew it was on the second floor, the last in a long corridor. A minute later my hand was on the knob of his door, which I naturally pushed open without knocking. It was equally natural that in the absence of its occupant the room should be dark; the more so as, the end of the corridor being at that hour unlighted, the obscurity was not immediately diminished by the opening of the door. I was only aware at first that I had made no mistake and that, the window-curtains not being drawn, I was confronted with a couple of vague starlighted apertures. Their aid, however, was not sufficient to enable me to find what I had come for, and my hand, in my pocket, was already on the little box of matches that I always carried for cigarettes. Suddenly I withdrew it with a start, uttering an ejaculation, an apology. I had entered the wrong room; a glance prolonged for three seconds showed me a figure seated at a table near one of the windows – a figure I had at first taken for a travelling-rug thrown over a chair. I retreated, with a sense of intrusion; but as I did so I became aware, more rapidly than it takes me to express it, in the first place that this was Vawdrey's room and in the second that, most singularly, Vawdrey himself sat before me. Checking myself on the threshold I had a momentary feeling of bewilderment, but before I knew it I had exclaimed: 'Hullo! is that you, Vawdrey?'

He neither turned nor answered me, but my question received an immediate and practical reply in the opening of a door on the other side of the passage. A servant, with a candle, had come out of the opposite room, and in this flitting illumination I definitely recognized the man whom, an instant before, I had to the best of my belief left below in conversation with Mrs Adney. His back was half turned to me, and he bent over the table in the attitude of writing, but I was conscious that I was in no sort of error about his identity. 'I beg your pardon – I thought you were downstairs,' I said; and as the personage gave no sign of hearing me I added: 'If you're busy I won't disturb you.' I backed out, closing the door – I had been in the place, I suppose, less than a minute. I had a sense of mystification, which however deepened infinitely the next instant. I stood there with my hand still on the knob of the door, overtaken by the oddest impression of my life. Vawdrey was at his table, writing, and it was a very natural place for him to be; but why was he writing in the dark and why hadn't he answered me? I waited a few seconds for the sound of some movement, to see if he wouldn't rouse himself from his abstraction – a fit conceivable in a great writer – and call out: 'Oh, my dear fellow, is it you?' But I heard only the stillness, I felt only the starlighted dusk of the room, with the unexpected presence it enclosed. I turned away, slowly retracing my steps, and came confusedly downstairs. The lamp was still burning in the salon, but the room was empty. I passed round to the door of the hotel and stepped out. Empty too was the terrace. Blanche Adney and the gentleman with her had apparently come in. I hung about five minutes; then I went to bed.

I slept badly, for I was agitated. On looking back at these queer occurrences (you will see presently that they were queer), I perhaps suppose myself more agitated than I was; for great anomalies are never so great at first as after we have reflected upon them. It takes us some time to exhaust explanations. I was vaguely nervous – I had been sharply startled; but there was nothing I could not clear up by asking Blanche Adney, the first thing in the morning, who had been with her on the terrace. Oddly enough, however, when the morning dawned – it dawned admirably – I felt less desire to satisfy myself on this point than to escape, to brush away the shadow of my stupefaction. I saw the day would be splendid, and the fancy took me to spend it, as I had spent happy days of youth, in a lonely mountain ramble. I dressed early, partook of conventional coffee, put a big roll into one pocket and a small flask into the other, and, with a stout stick in my hand, went forth into the high places. My story is not closely concerned with the charming hours I passed there – hours of the kind that make intense memories. If I roamed away half of them on the shoulders of the hills, I lay on the sloping grass for the other half and, with my cap pulled over my eyes (save a peep for immensities of view), listened, in the bright stillness, to the mountain bee and felt most things sink and dwindle. Clare Vawdrey grew small, Blanche Adney grew dim, Lord Mellifont grew old, and before the day was over I forgot that I had ever been puzzled. When in the late afternoon I made my way down to the inn there was nothing I wanted so much to find out as whether dinner would not soon be ready. Tonight I dressed, in a manner, and by the time I was presentable they were all at table.

In their company again my little problem came back to me, so that I was curious to see if Vawdrey wouldn't look at me the least bit queerly. But he didn't look at me at all; which gave me a chance both to be patient and to wonder why I should hesitate to ask him my question across the table. I did hesitate, and with the consciousness of doing so came back a little of the agitation I had left behind me, or below me, during the day. I wasn't ashamed of my scruple, however: it was only a fine discretion. What I vaguely felt was that a public inquiry wouldn't have been fair. Lord Mellifont was there, of course, to mitigate with his perfect manner all consequences; but I think it was present to me that with these particular elements his lordship would not be at home. The moment we got up, therefore, I approached Mrs Adney, asking her whether, as the evening was lovely, she wouldn't take a turn with me outside.

'You've walked a hundred miles; had you not better be quiet?' she replied.

'I'd walk a hundred miles more to get you to tell me something.'

She looked at me an instant, with a little of the queerness that I had sought, but had not found, in Clare Vawdrey's eyes. 'Do you mean what became of Lord Mellifont?'

'Of Lord Mellifont?' With my new speculation I had lost that thread.

'Where's your memory, foolish man? We talked of it last evening.'

'Ah, yes!' I cried, recalling; 'we shall have lots to discuss.' I drew her out to the terrace, and before we had gone three steps I said to her: 'Who was with you here last night?'

'Last night?' she repeated, as wide of the mark as I had been.

343

'At ten o'clock – just after our company broke up. You came out here with a gentleman; you talked about the stars.'

She stared a moment; then she gave her laugh. 'Are you jealous of dear Vawdrey?'

'Then it was he?'

'Certainly it was.'

'And how long did he stay?'

'You have it badly. He stayed about a quarter of an hour – perhaps rather more. We walked some distance; he talked about his play. There you have it all; that is the only witchcraft I have used.'

'And what did Vawdrey do afterwards?'

'I haven't the least idea. I left him and went to bed.'

'At what time did you go to bed?'

'At what time did *you*? I happen to remember that I parted from Mr Vawdrey at ten twenty-five,' said Mrs Adney. 'I came back into the salon to pick up a book, and I noticed the clock.'

'In other words you and Vawdrey distinctly lingered here from about five minutes past ten till the hour you mention?'

'I don't know how distinct we were, but we were very jolly. *Où voulez-vous en venir?*' Blanche Adney asked.

'Simply to this, dear lady: that at the time your companion was occupied in the manner you describe, he was also engaged in literary composition in his own room.'

She stopped short at this, and her eyes had an expression in the darkness. She wanted to know if I challenged her veracity; and I replied that, on the contrary, I backed it up – it made the case so interesting. She returned that this would only be if she should back up mine; which, however, I had no difficulty in persuading her to do, after I had related to her circumstantially the incident of my quest of the manuscript – the manuscript which, at the time, for a reason I could now understand, appeared to have passed so completely out of her own head.

'His talk made me forget it – I forgot I sent you for it. He made up for his fiasco in the salon: he declaimed me the scene,' said my companion. She had dropped on a bench to listen to me and, as we sat there, had briefly cross-examined me. Then she broke out into fresh laughter ,'Oh, the eccentricities of genius!'

'They seem greater even than I supposed.'

'Oh, the mysteries of greatness!'

'You ought to know all about them, but they take me by surprise.'

'Are you absolutely certain it was Mr Vawdrey?' my companion asked.

'If it wasn't he, who in the world was it? That a strange gentleman, looking exactly like him, should be sitting in his room at that hour of the night and writing at his table *in the dark*,' I insisted, 'would be practically as wonderful as my own contention.'

'Yes, why in the dark?' mused Mrs Adney.

'Cats can see in the dark,' I said.

She smiled at me dimly. 'Did it look like a cat?'

'No, dear lady, but I'll tell you what it did look like – it looked like the author of Vawdrey's admirable works. It looked infinitely more like him than our friend does himself,' I declared.

'Do you mean it was somebody he gets to do them?'

'Yes, while he dines out and disappoints you.'

'Disappoints me?' murmured Mrs Adney artlessly.

'Disappoints *me* – disappoints everyone who looks in him for the genius that created the pages they adore. Where is it in his talk?'

'Ah, last night he was splendid,' said the actress.

'He's always splendid, as your morning bath is splendid, or a sirloin of beef, or the railway service to Brighton. But he's never rare.'

'I see what you mean.'

'That's what makes you such a comfort to talk to. I've often wondered – now I know. There are two of them.'

'What a delightful idea!'

'One goes out, the other stays at home. One is the genius, the other's the bourgeois, and it's only the bourgeois whom we personally know. He talks, he circulates, he's awfully popular, he flirts with you—'

'Whereas it's the genius *you* are privileged to see!' Mrs Adney broke in. 'I'm much obliged to you for the distinction.'

I laid my hand on her arm. 'See him yourself. Try it, test it, go to his room.'

'Go to his room? It wouldn't be proper!' she exclaimed, in the tone of her best comedy.

'Anything is proper in such an inquiry. If you see him, it settles it.'

'How charming – to settle it!' She thought a moment, then she sprang up. 'Do you mean *now*?'

'Whenever you like.'

'But suppose I should find the wrong one?' said Blanche Adney, with an exquisite effect.

'The wrong one? Which one do you call the right?'

'The wrong one for a lady to go and see. Suppose I shouldn't find – the genius?'

'Oh, I'll look after the other,' I replied. Then, as I had happened to glance about me, I added: 'Take care – here comes Lord Mellifont.'

'I wish you'd look after *him*,' my interlocutress murmured.

'What's the matter with him?'

'That's just what I was going to tell you.'

'Tell me now; he's not coming.'

Blanche Adney looked a moment. Lord Mellifont, who appeared to have emerged from the hotel to smoke a meditative cigar, had paused, at a distance from us, and stood admiring the wonders of the prospect, discernible even in the dusk. We strolled slowly in another direction, and she presently said: 'My idea is almost as droll as yours.'

'I don't call mine droll: it's beautiful.'

'There's nothing so beautiful as the droll,' Mrs Adney declared.

'You take a professional view. But I'm all ears.' My curiosity was indeed alive again.

'Well then, my dear friend, if Clare Vawdrey is double (and I'm bound to say I think that the more of him the better), his lordship there has the opposite complaint: he isn't even whole.'

We stopped once more, simultaneously. 'I don't understand.'

'No more do I. But I have a fancy that if there are two of Mr Vawdrey, there isn't so much as one, all told, of Lord Mellifont.'

I considered a moment, then I laughed out. 'I think I see what you mean!'

'That's what makes *you* a comfort. Did you ever see him alone?'

I tried to remember. 'Oh, yes; he has been to see me.'

'Ah, then he wasn't alone.'

'And I've been to see him, in his study.'

'Did he know you were there?'

'Naturally – I was announced.'

Blanche Adney glanced at me like a lovely conspirator. 'You mustn't be announced!' With this she walked on.

I rejoined her, breathless. 'Do you mean one must come upon him when he doesn't know it?'

'You must take him unawares. You must go to his room – that's what you must do.'

If I was elated by the way our mystery opened out, I was also, pardonably, a little confused. 'When I know he's not there?'

'When you know he *is*.'

'And what shall I see?'

'You won't see anything!' Mrs Adney cried as we turned round.

We had reached the end of the terrace, and our movement brought us face to face with Lord Mellifont, who, resuming his walk, had now, without indiscretion, overtaken us. The sight of him at that moment was illuminating, and it kindled a great backward train, connecting itself with one's general impression of the personage. As he stood there smiling at us and waving a practised hand into the transparent night (he introduced the view as if it had been a candidate and 'supported' the very Alps), as he rose before us in the delicate fragrance of his cigar and all his other delicacies and fragrances, with more perfections, somehow, heaped upon his handsome head than one had ever seen accumulated before, he struck me as so essentially, so conspicuously and uniformly the public character that I read in a flash the answer to Blanche Adney's riddle. He was all public and had no corresponding private life, just as Clare Vawdrey was all private and had no corresponding public one. I had heard only half my companion's story, yet as we joined Lord Mellifont (he had followed us – he liked Mrs Adney; but it was always to be conceived of him that he accepted society rather than sought it), as we participated for half an hour in the distributed wealth of his conversation, I felt with unabashed duplicity that we had, as it were, found him out. I was even more deeply diverted by that whisk of the curtain to which the actress had just treated me than I had been by my own discovery; and if I was not ashamed of my share of her secret any more than of having divided my own with her (though my own was, of the two mysteries, the more glorious for the personage involved), this was because there was no cruelty in my advantage, but on the contrary an extreme tenderness and a positive compassion. Oh, he was safe with me, and I felt moreover rich and enlightened, as if I had suddenly put the universe into my pocket. I had learned what an affair of the spot and the moment a great appearance may be. It would doubtless be too much to say that I had always suspected the possibility, in the background of his lordship's being, of some such beautiful instance; but it is at least a fact that, patronizing as it sounds, I had been conscious of a certain reserve of indulgence for him. I had secretly pitied him for the perfection of his performance, had wondered what blank face such a mask had to cover, what was left to him for the immitigable hours in which a man sits down with himself, or, more serious still, with that intenser self, his lawful wife. How was he at home and what did he do when he was alone? There was something in Lady Mellifont that gave a point to these researches – something that suggested that even to her he was still the public character and that she was haunted by similar questionings. She had never cleared them up: that was her eternal trouble. We therefore knew more than she did, Blanche Adney and I; but we wouldn't tell her for the world, nor would she probably thank us for doing so. She preferred the relative grandeur of uncertainty. She was not at home with him, so she couldn't say; and with her he was not alone, so he couldn't show her. He represented to his wife and he was a hero to his servants, and what one wanted to arrive at was what really became of him when no eye could see. He rested, presumably; but what form of rest could repair such a plenitude of presence? Lady Mellifont was too proud to pry, and as she had never looked through a keyhole she remained dignified and unassuaged.

It may have been a fancy of mine that Blanche Adney drew out our companion, or it may be that the practical irony of our relation to him at such a moment made me see him more vividly: at any rate he never had struck me as so dissimilar from what he would have been if we had not offered him a reflection of his image. We were only a concourse of two, but he had never been more public. His perfect manner had never been more perfect, his remarkable tact had never been more remarkable. I had a tacit sense that it would all be in the morning papers, with a leader, and also a secretly exhilarating one that I knew something that wouldn't be, that never could be, though any enterprising journal would give one a fortune for it. I must add, however, that in spite of my enjoyment – it was almost sensual, like that of a consummate dish – I was eager to be alone again with Mrs Adney, who owed me an anecdote. It proved impossible, that evening, for some of the others came out to see what we found so absorbing; and then Lord Mellifont bespoke a little music from the fiddler, who produced his violin and played to us divinely, on our platform of echoes, face to face with the ghosts of the mountains. Before the concert was over I missed our actress and, glancing into the window of the salon, saw that she was established with Vawdrey, who was reading to her from a manuscript. The great scene had apparently been achieved and was doubtless the more interesting to Blanche from the new lights she had gathered about its author. I judged it discreet not to disturb them, and I went to bed without seeing her again. I looked out for her betimes the next morning and, as the promise of the day was fair, proposed to her that we should take to the hills, reminding her of the high obligation she had incurred. She recognized the obligation and gratified me with her company; but before we had strolled ten yards up the pass she broke out with intensity: 'My dear friend, you've no idea how it works in me! I can think of nothing else.'

'Than your theory about Lord Mellifont?'

'Oh, bother Lord Mellifont! I allude to yours about Mr Vawdrey, who is much the more interesting person of the two. I'm fascinated by that vision of his – what-do-you-call-it?'

'His alternative identity?'

'His other self: that's easier to say.'

'You accept it, then, you adopt it?'

'Adopt it? I rejoice in it! It became tremendously vivid to me last evening.'

'While he read to you there?'

'Yes, as I listened to him, watched him. It simplified everything, explained everything.'

'That's indeed the blessing of it. Is the scene very fine?'

'Magnificent, and he reads beautifully.'

'Almost as well as the other one writes!' I laughed.

This made my companion stop a moment, laying her hand on my arm. 'You utter my very impression. I felt that he was reading me the work of another man.'

'What a service to the other man!'

'Such a totally different person,' said Mrs Adney. We talked of this difference as we went on, and of what a wealth it constituted, what a resource for life, such a duplication of character.

'It ought to make him live twice as long as other people,' I observed.

'Ought to make which of them?'

'Well, both; for after all they're members of a firm, and one of them couldn't carry on the business without the other. Moreover mere survival would be dreadful for either.'

Blanche Adney was silent a little; then she exclaimed: 'I don't know – I wish he *would* survive!'

'May I, on my side, inquire which?'

'If you can't guess I won't tell you.'

'I know the heart of woman. You always prefer the other.'

She halted again, looking round her. 'Off here, away from my husband, I *can* tell you. I'm in love with him!'

'Unhappy woman, he has no passions,' I answered.

'That's exactly why I adore him. Doesn't a woman with my history know that the passions of others are insupportable? An actress, poor thing, can't care for any love that's not all on *her* side; she can't afford to be repaid. My marriage proves that: marriage is ruinous. Do you know what was in my mind last night, all the while Mr Vawdrey was reading me those beautiful speeches? An insane desire to see the author.' And dramatically, as if to hide her shame, Blanche Adney passed on.

'We'll manage that,' I returned. 'I want another glimpse of him myself. But meanwhile please remember that I've been waiting more than forty-eight hours for the evidence that supports your sketch, intensely suggestive and plausible, of Lord Mellifont's private life.'

'Oh, Lord Mellifont doesn't interest me.'

'He did yesterday,' I said.

'Yes, but that was before I fell in love. You blotted him out with your story.'

'You'll make me sorry I told it. Come,' I pleaded, 'if you don't let me know how your idea came into your head I shall imagine you simply made it up.'

'Let me recollect then, while we wander in this grassy valley.'

We stood at the entrance of a charming crooked gorge, a portion of whose level floor formed the bed of a stream that was smooth with swiftness. We turned into it, and the soft walk beside the clear torrent drew us on and on; till suddenly, as we continued and I waited for my companion to remember, a bend of the valley showed us Lady Mellifont coming toward us. She was alone, under the canopy of her parasol, drawing her sable train over the turf; and in this form, on the devious ways, she was a sufficiently rare apparition. She usually took a footman, who marched behind her on the high-roads and whose livery was strange to the mountaineers. She blushed on seeing us, as if she ought somehow to justify herself; she laughed vaguely and said she had come out for a little early stroll. We stood together a moment, exchanging platitudes, and then she remarked that she had thought she might find her husband.

'Is he in this quarter?' I inquired.

'I supposed he would be. He came out an hour ago to sketch.'

'Have you been looking for him?' Mrs Adney asked.

'A little; not very much,' said Lady Mellifont.

Each of the women rested her eyes with some intensity, as it seemed to me, on the eyes of the other.

'We'll look for him *for* you, if you like,' said Mrs Adney.

'Oh, it doesn't matter. I thought I'd join him.'

'He won't make his sketch if you don't,' my companion hinted.

'Perhaps he will if *you* do,' said Lady Mellifont.

'Oh, I daresay he'll turn up,' I interposed.

'He certainly will if he knows we're here!' Blanche Adney retorted.

'Will you wait while we search?' I asked of Lady Mellifont.

She repeated that it was of no consequence; upon which Mrs Adney went on: 'We'll go into the matter for our own pleasure.'

'I wish you a pleasant expedition,' said her ladyship, and was turning away when I sought to know if we should inform her husband that she had followed him. She hesitated a moment; then she jerked out oddly: 'I think you had better not.' With this she took leave of us, floating a little stiffly down the gorge.

My companion and I watched her retreat, then we exchanged a stare, while a light ghost of a laugh rippled from the actress's lips. 'She might be walking in the shrubberies at Mellifont!'

'She suspects it, you know,' I replied.

'And she doesn't want him to know it. There won't be any sketch.'

'Unless we overtake him,' I subjoined. 'In that case we shall find him producing one, in the most graceful attitude, and the queer thing is that it will be brilliant.'

'Let us leave him alone – he'll have to come home without it.'

'He'd rather never come home. Oh, he'll find a public!'

'Perhaps he'll do it for the cows,' Blanche Adney suggested; and as I was on the point of rebuking her profanity she went on: 'That's simply what I happened to discover.'

'What are you speaking of?'

'The incident of the day before yesterday.'

'Ah, let's have it at last!'

'That's all it was – that I was like Lady Mellifont: I couldn't find him.'

'Did you lose him?'

'He lost *me* – that appears to be the way of it. He thought I was gone.'

'But you did find him, since you came home with him.'

'It was he who found *me*. That again is what must happen. He's there from the moment he knows somebody else is.'

'I understand his intermissions,' I said after a short reflection, 'but I don't quite seize the law that governs them.'

'Oh, it's a fine shade, but I caught it at that moment. I had started to come home. I was tired, and I had insisted on his not coming back with me. We had found some rare flowers – those

I brought home – and it was he who had discovered almost all of them. It amused him very much, and I knew he wanted to get more; but I was weary and I quitted him. He let me go – where else would have been his tact? – and I was too stupid then to have guessed that from the moment I was not there no flower would be gathered. I started homeward, but at the end of three minutes I found I had brought away his penknife – he had lent it to me to trim a branch – and I knew he would need it. I turned back a few steps, to call him, but before I spoke I looked about for him. You can't understand what happened then without having the place before you.'

'You must take me there,' I said.

'We may see the wonder here. The place was simply one that offered no chance for concealment – a great gradual hillside, without obstructions or trees. There were some rocks below me, behind which I myself had disappeared, but from which on coming back I immediately emerged again.'

'Then he must have seen you.'

'He was too utterly gone, for some reason best known to himself. It was probably some moment of fatigue – he's getting on, you know, so that, with the sense of returning solitude, the reaction had been proportionately great, the extinction proportionately complete. At any rate the stage was as bare as your hand.'

'Could he have been somewhere else?'

'He couldn't have been, in the time, anywhere but where I had left him. Yet the place was utterly empty – as empty as this stretch of valley before us. He had vanished – he had ceased to be. But as soon as my voice rang out (I uttered his name), he rose before me like the rising sun.'

'And where did the sun rise?'

'Just where it ought to – just where he would have been and where I should have seen him had he been like other people.'

I had listened with the deepest interest, but it was my duty to think of objections. 'How long a time elapsed between the moment you perceived his absence and the moment you called?'

'Oh, only an instant. I don't pretend it was long.'

'Long enough for you to be sure?' I said.

'Sure he wasn't there?'

'Yes, and that you were not mistaken, not the victim of some hocus-pocus of your eyesight.'

'I may have been mistaken, but I don't believe it. At any rate, that's just why I want you to look in his room.'

I thought a moment. 'How *can* I, when even his wife doesn't dare to?'

'She *wants* to; propose it to her. It wouldn't take much to make her. She does suspect.'

I thought another moment. 'Did he seem to know?'

'That I had missed him? So it struck me, but he thought he had been quick enough.'

'Did you speak of his disappearance?'

'Heaven forbid! It seemed to me too strange.'

'Quite right. And how did he look?'

Trying to think it out again and reconstitute her miracle, Blanche Adney gazed abstractedly up the valley. Suddenly she exclaimed: 'Just as he looks now!' and I saw Lord Mellifont stand before us with his sketch-block. I perceived, as we met him, that he looked neither suspicious nor blank: he looked simply, as he did always, everywhere, the principal feature of the scene. Naturally he had no sketch to show us, but nothing could better have rounded off our actual conception of him than the way he fell into position as we approached. He had been selecting his point of view; he took possession of it with a flourish of the pencil. He leaned against a rock; his beautiful little box of water-colours reposed on a natural table beside him, a ledge of the bank which showed how inveterately nature ministered to his convenience. He painted while he talked and he talked while he painted; and if the painting was as miscellaneous as the talk, the talk would equally have graced an album. We waited while the exhibition went on, and it seemed indeed as if the conscious profiles of the peaks were interested in his success. They grew as black as silhouettes in paper, sharp against a livid sky from which, however, there would be nothing to fear till Lord Mellifont's sketch should be finished. Blanche Adney communed with me dumbly, and I could read the language of her eyes: 'Oh, if *we* could only do it as well as that! He fills the stage in a way that beats us.' We could no more have left him than we could have quitted the theatre till the play was over; but in due time we turned round with him and strolled back to the inn, before the door of which his lordship, glancing again at his picture, tore the fresh leaf from the block and presented it with a few happy words to Mrs Adney. Then he went into the house; and a moment later, looking up from where we stood, we saw him, above, at the window of his sitting-room (he had the best apartments), watching the signs of the weather.

'He'll have to rest after this,' Blanche said, dropping her eyes on her water-colour.

'Indeed he will!' I raised mine to the window: Lord Mellifont had vanished. 'He's already reabsorbed.'

'Reabsorbed?' I could see the actress was now thinking of something else.

'Into the immensity of things. He has lapsed again; there's an *entr'acte*.'

'It ought to be long.' Mrs Adney looked up and down the terrace, and at that moment the head-waiter appeared in the doorway. Suddenly she turned to this functionary with the question: 'Have you seen Mr Vawdrey lately?'

The man immediately approached. 'He left the house five minutes ago – for a walk, I think. He went down the pass; he had a book.'

I was watching the ominous clouds. 'He had better have had an umbrella.'

The waiter smiled. 'I recommended him to take one.'

'Thank you,' said Mrs Adney; and the Oberkellner withdrew. Then she went on, abruptly: 'Will you do me a favour?'

'Yes, if you'll do *me* one. Let me see if your picture is signed.'

She glanced at the sketch before giving it to me. 'For a wonder it isn't.'

'It ought to be, for full value. May I keep it awhile?'

'Yes, if you'll do what I ask. Take an umbrella and go after Mr Vawdrey.'

'To bring him to Mrs Adney?'

'To keep him out – as long as you can.'

'I'll keep him as long as the rain holds off.'

'Oh, never mind the rain!' my companion exclaimed.

'Would you have us drenched?'

'Without remorse.' Then with a strange light in her eyes she added: 'I'm going to try.'

'To try?'

'To see the real one. Oh, if I can get at him!' she broke out with passion.

'Try, try!' I replied. 'I'll keep our friend all day.'

'If I can get at the one who does it –' and she paused, with shining eyes – 'if I can have it out with him I shall get my part!'

'I'll keep Vawdrey for ever!' I called after her as she passed quickly into the house.

Her audacity was communicative, and I stood there in a glow of excitement. I looked at Lord Mellifont's water-colour and I looked at the gathering storm; I turned my eyes again to his lordship's windows and then I bent them on my watch. Vawdrey had so little the start of me that I should have time to overtake him – time even if I should take five minutes to go up to Lord Mellifont's sitting-room (where we had all been hospitably received), and say to him, as a messenger, that Mrs Adney begged he would bestow upon his sketch the high consecration of his signature. As I again considered this work of art I perceived there was something it certainly did lack: what else then but so noble an autograph? It was my duty to supply the deficiency without delay, and in accordance with this conviction I instantly re-entered the hotel. I went up to Lord Mellifont's apartments; I reached the door of his salon. Here, however, I was met by a difficulty of which my extravagance had not taken account. If I were to knock I should spoil everything; yet was I prepared to dispense with this ceremony? I asked myself the question, and it embarrassed me; I turned my little picture round and round, but it didn't give me the answer I wanted. I wanted it to say: 'Open the door gently, gently, without a sound, yet very quickly: then you will see what you will see.' I had gone so far as to lay my hand upon the knob when I became aware (having my wits so about me) that exactly in the manner I was thinking of – gently, gently, without a sound – another door had moved, on the opposite side of the hall. At the same instant I found myself smiling rather constrainedly upon Lady Mellifont, who, on seeing me, had checked herself on the threshold of her room. For a moment, as she stood there, we exchanged two or three ideas that were the more singular for being unspoken. We had caught each other hovering, and we understood each other; but as I stepped over to her (so that we were separated from the sitting-room by the width of the hall), her lips formed the almost soundless entreaty: 'Don't!' I could see in her conscious eyes everything that the word expressed – the confession of her own curiosity and the dread of the consequences of mine. '*Don't!*' she repeated, as I stood before her. From the moment my experiment could strike her as an act of violence I was ready to renounce it; yet I thought I detected in her frightened face a still deeper betrayal – a possibility of disappointment if I should give way. It was as if she had said: 'I'll let you do it if you'll take the responsibility. Yes, with someone else I'd surprise him. But it would never do for him to think it was I.'

'We soon found Lord Mellifont,' I observed, in allusion to our encounter with her an hour before, 'and he was so good as to give this lovely sketch to Mrs Adney, who has asked me to come up and beg him to put in the omitted signature.'

Lady Mellifont took the drawing from me, and I could guess the struggle that went on in her while she looked at it. She was silent for some time; then I felt that all her delicacies and dignities, all her old timidities and pieties were fighting against her opportunity. She turned away from me and, with the drawing, went back to her room. She was absent for a couple of minutes, and when she reappeared I could see that she had vanquished her temptation; that even, with a kind of resurgent horror, she had shrunk from it. She had deposited the sketch in the room. 'If you will kindly leave the picture with me, I will see that Mrs Adney's request is attended to,' she said, with great courtesy and sweetness, but in a manner that put an end to our colloquy.

I assented, with a somewhat artificial enthusiasm perhaps, and then, to ease off our separation, remarked that we were going to have a change of weather.

'In that case we shall go – we shall go immediately,' said Lady Mellifont. I was amused at the eagerness with which she made this declaration: it appeared to represent a coveted flight into safety, an escape with her threatened secret. I was the more surprised therefore when, as I was turning away, she put out her hand to take mine. She had the pretext of bidding me farewell, but as I shook hands with her on this supposition I felt that what the movement really conveyed was: 'I thank you for the help you would have given me, but it's better as it is. If I should know, who would help me then?' As I went to my room to get my umbrella I said to myself: 'She's sure, but she won't put it to the proof.'

A quarter of an hour later I had overtaken Clare Vawdrey in the pass, and shortly after this we found ourselves looking for refuge. The storm had not only completely gathered, but it had broken at the last with extraordinary rapidity. We scrambled up a hillside to an empty cabin, a rough structure that was hardly more than a shed for the protection of cattle. It was a tolerable shelter however, and it had fissures through which we could watch the splendid spectacle of the tempest. This entertainment lasted an hour – an hour that has remained with me as full of odd disparities. While the lightning played with the thunder and the rain gushed in on our umbrellas, I said to myself that Clare Vawdrey was disappointing. I don't know exactly what I should have predicated of a great author exposed to the fury of the elements, I can't say what particular Manfred attitude I should have expected my companion to assume, but it seemed to me somehow that I shouldn't have looked to him to regale me in such a situation with stories (which I had already heard) about the celebrated Lady Ringrose. Her ladyship formed the subject of Vawdrey's conversation during this prodigious scene, though before it was quite over he had launched out on Mr Chafer, the scarcely less notorious reviewer. It broke my heart to hear a man like Vawdrey talk of reviewers. The lightning projected a hard clearness upon the truth, familiar to me for years, to which the last day or two had added transcendent support – the irritating certitude that for personal relations this admirable genius thought his second-best good enough. It *was*, no doubt, as society was made, but there was a contempt in the distinction which could not fail to be galling to an admirer. The world was vulgar and stupid, and the real man would have been a fool to come out for it when he could gossip and dine by deputy. None the less my heart sank as I felt my companion practise this economy. I don't know exactly what I wanted; I suppose I wanted him to make an exception for *me*. I almost believed he would, if he had known how I worshipped his talent. But I had never been able to translate this to him, and his application of his principle was relentless. At any rate I was more than ever sure that at such an hour his chair at home was not empty: *there* was the Manfred attitude, *there* were the responsive flashes. I could only envy Mrs Adney her presumable enjoyment of them.

The weather drew off at last, and the rain abated sufficiently to allow us to emerge from our asylum and make our way back to the inn, where we found on our arrival that our prolonged absence had produced some agitation. It was judged apparently that the fury of the elements might have placed us in a predicament. Several of our friends were at the door, and they seemed a little disconcerted when it was perceived that we were only drenched. Clare Vawdrey, for some reason, was wetter than I, and he took his course to his room. Blanche Adney was among the persons collected to look out for us, but as Vawdrey came toward her she shrank from him, without a greeting; with a movement that I observed as almost one of estrangement she turned her back on him and went quickly into the salon. Wet as I was I went in after her; on which she immediately flung round and faced me. The first thing I saw was that she had never been so beautiful. There was a light of inspiration in her face, and she broke out to me in the quickest whisper, which was at the same time the loudest cry, I have ever heard: 'I've got my *part*!'

'You went to his room – I was right?'

'Right?' Blanche Adney repeated. 'Ah, my dear fellow!' she murmured.

'He was there – you saw him?'

'He saw me. It was the hour of my life!'

'It must have been the hour of his, if you were half as lovely as you are at this moment.'

'He's splendid,' she pursued, as if she didn't hear me. 'He *is* the one who does it!' I listened, immensely impressed, and she added: 'We understood each other.'

'By flashes of lightning?'

'Oh, I didn't see the lightning then!'

'How long were you there?' I asked with admiration.

'Long enough to tell him I adore him.'

'Ah, that's what I've never been able to tell him!' I exclaimed ruefully.

'I shall have my part – I shall have my part!' she continued, with triumphant indifference; and she flung round the room with the joy of a girl, only checking herself to say: 'Go and change your clothes.'

'You shall have Lord Mellifont's signature,' I said.

'Oh, bother Lord Mellifont's signature! He's far nicer than Mr Vawdrey,' she went on irrelevantly.

'Lord Mellifont?' I pretended to inquire.

'Confound Lord Mellifont!' And Blanche Adney, in her elation, brushed by me, whisking again through the open door. Just outside of it she came upon her husband; whereupon, with a charming cry of 'We're talking of you, my love!' she threw herself upon him and kissed him.

I went to my room and changed my clothes, but I remained there till the evening. The violence of the storm had passed over us, but the rain had settled down to a drizzle. On descending to dinner I found that the change in the weather had already broken up our party. The Mellifonts had departed in a carriage and four, they had been followed by others, and several vehicles had been bespoken for the morning. Blanche Adney's was one of them, and on the pretext that she had preparations to make she quitted us directly after dinner. Clare Vawdrey asked me what was the matter with her – she suddenly appeared to dislike him. I forget what answer I gave, but I did my best to comfort him by driving away with him the next day. Mrs Adney had vanished when we came down; but they made up their quarrel in London, for he finished his play, which she produced. I must add that she is still, nevertheless, in want of the great part. I have a beautiful one in my head, but she doesn't come to see me to stir me up about it. Lady Mellifont always drops me a kind word when we meet, but that doesn't console me.

The Middle Years

I

THE APRIL DAY was soft and bright, and poor Dencombe, happy in the conceit of reasserted strength, stood in the garden of the hotel, comparing, with a deliberation in which, however, there was still something of languor, the attractions of easy strolls. He liked the feeling of the south, so far as you could have it in the north, he liked the sandy cliffs and the clustered pines, he liked even the colourless sea. 'Bournemouth as a health-resort' had sounded like a mere advertisement, but now he was reconciled to the prosaic. The sociable country postman, passing through the garden, had just given him a small parcel, which he took out with him, leaving the hotel to the right and creeping to a convenient bench that he knew of, a safe recess in the cliff. It looked to the south, to the tinted walls of the Island, and was protected behind by the sloping shoulder of the down. He was tired enough when he reached it, and for a moment he was disappointed; he was better, of course, but better, after all, than what? He should never again, as at one or two great moments of the past, be better than himself. The infinite of life had gone, and what was left of the dose was a small glass engraved like a thermometer by the apothecary. He sat and stared at the sea, which appeared all surface and twinkle, far shallower than the spirit of man. It was the abyss of human illusion that was the real, the tideless deep. He held his packet, which had come by book-post, unopened on his knee, liking, in the lapse of so many joys (his illness had made him feel his age), to know that it was there, but taking for granted there could be no complete renewal of the pleasure, dear to young experience, of seeing one's self 'just out'. Dencombe, who had a reputation, had come out too often and knew too well in advance how he should look.

His postponement associated itself vaguely, after a little, with a group of three persons, two ladies and a young man, whom, beneath him, straggling and seemingly silent, he could see move slowly together along the sands. The gentleman had his head bent over a book and was occasionally brought to a stop by the charm of this volume, which, as Dencombe could perceive even at a distance, had a cover alluringly red. Then his companions, going a little further, waited for him to come up, poking their parasols into the beach, looking around them at the sea and sky and clearly sensible of the beauty of the day. To these things the young man with the book was still more clearly indifferent; lingering, credulous, absorbed, he was an object of envy to an observer from whose connection with literature all such artlessness had faded. One of the ladies was large and mature; the other had the spareness of comparative youth and of a social situation possibly inferior. The large lady carried back Dencombe's imagination to the age of crinoline; she wore a hat of the shape of a mushroom, decorated with a blue veil, and had the air, in her aggressive amplitude, of clinging to a vanished fashion or even a lost cause. Presently her companion produced from under the folds of a mantle a limp, portable chair which she stiffened out and of which the large lady took possession. This act, and something in the movement of either party, instantly characterized the performers – they performed for Dencombe's recreation – as opulent matron and humble dependant. What, moreover, was the use of being an approved novelist if one couldn't establish a relation between such figures; the clever theory, for instance, that the young man was the son of the opulent matron, and that the humble dependant, the daughter of a clergyman or an officer, nourished a secret passion for him? Was that not visible from the way she stole behind her protectress to look back at him? – back to where he had let himself come to a full stop when his mother sat down to rest. His book was a novel; it had the catchpenny cover, and while the romance of life stood neglected at his side he lost himself in that of the circulating library. He moved mechanically to where the sand was softer, and ended by plumping down in it to finish his chapter at his ease. The humble dependant, discouraged by his remoteness, wandered, with a martyred droop of the head, in another direction, and the exorbitant lady, watching the waves, offered a confused resemblance to a flying-machine that had broken down.

When his drama began to fail Dencombe remembered that he had, after all, another pastime. Though such promptitude on the part of the publisher was rare, he was already able to draw from its wrapper his 'latest', perhaps his last. The cover of 'The Middle Years' was duly meretricious, the smell of the fresh pages the very odour of sanctity; but for the moment he went no further – he had become conscious of a strange alienation. He had forgotten what his book was about. Had the assault of his old ailment, which he had so fallaciously come to Bournemouth to ward off, interposed utter blankness as to what had preceded it? He had finished the revision of proof before quitting London, but his subsequent fortnight in bed had passed the sponge over colour. He couldn't have chanted to himself a single sentence, couldn't have turned with curiosity or confidence to any particular page. His subject had already gone from him, leaving scarcely a superstition behind. He uttered a low moan as he breathed the chill of this dark void, so desperately it seemed to represent the completion of a sinister process. The tears filled his mild eyes; something precious had passed away. This was the pang that had been sharpest during the last few years – the sense of ebbing time, of shrinking opportunity; and now he felt not so much that his last chance was going as that it was gone indeed. He had done all that he should ever do, and yet he had not done what he wanted. This was the laceration – that practically his career was over: it was as violent as a rough hand at his throat. He rose from his seat nervously, like a creature hunted by a dread; then he fell back in his weakness and nervously opened his book. It was a single volume; he preferred single volumes and aimed at a rare compression. He began to read, and little by little, in this occupation, he was pacified and reassured. Everything came back to him, but came back with a wonder, came back, above all, with a high and magnificent beauty. He read his own prose, he turned his own leaves, and had, as he sat there with the spring sunshine on the page, an emotion peculiar and intense. His career was over, no doubt, but it was over, after all, with *that*.

He had forgotten during his illness the work of the previous year; but what he had chiefly forgotten was that it was extraordinarily good. He dived once more into his story and was drawn down, as by a siren's hand, to where, in the dim underworld of fiction, the great glazed tank of art, strange silent subjects float. He recognized his motive and surrendered to his talent. Never, probably, had that talent, such as it was, been so fine. His difficulties were still there, but what was also there, to his perception, though probably, alas! to nobody's else, was the art that in most cases had surmounted them. In his surprised enjoyment of this ability he had a glimpse of a possible reprieve. Surely its force was not spent – there was life and service in it yet. It had not come to him easily, it had been backward and roundabout. It was the child of time, the nursling of delay; he had struggled and suffered for it, making sacrifices not to be counted, and now that it was really mature was it to cease to yield, to confess itself brutally beaten? There was an infinite charm for Dencombe in feeling as he had never felt before that diligence *vincit omnia*. The result produced in his little book was somehow a result beyond his conscious intention: it was as if he had planted his genius, had trusted his method, and they had grown up and flowered with this sweetness. If the achievement had been real, however, the process had been painful enough. What he saw so intensely today, what he felt as a nail driven in, was that only now, at the very last, had he come into possession. His development had been abnormally slow, almost grotesquely gradual. He had been hindered and retarded by experience, and for long periods had only groped his way. It had taken too much of his life to produce too little of his art. The art had come, but it had come after everything else. At such a rate a first existence was too short – long enough only to collect material; so that to fructify, to use the material, one must have a second age, an extension. This extension was what poor Dencombe sighed for. As he turned the last leaves of his volume he murmured: 'Ah for another go! – ah for a better chance!'

The three persons he had observed on the sands had vanished and then reappeared; they had now wandered up a path, an artificial and easy ascent, which led to the top of the cliff. Dencombe's bench was half-way down, on a sheltered ledge, and the large lady, a massive, heterogeneous person, with bold black eyes and kind red cheeks, now took a few moments to rest. She wore dirty gauntlets and immense diamond ear-rings; at first she looked vulgar, but she contradicted this announcement in an agreeable off-hand tone. While her companions stood waiting for her she spread her skirts on the end of Dencombe's seat. The young man had gold spectacles, through which, with his finger still in his red-covered book, he glanced at the volume, bound in the same shade of the same colour, lying on the lap of the original occupant of the bench. After an instant, Dencombe understood that he was struck with a resemblance, had recognized the gilt stamp on the crimson cloth, was reading 'The Middle Years', and now perceived that somebody else had kept pace with him. The stranger was startled, possibly even a little ruffled, to find that he was not the only person who had been favoured with an early copy. The eyes of the two proprietors met for a moment, and Dencombe borrowed amusement from the expression of those of his competitor, those, it might even be inferred, of his admirer. They confessed to some resentment – they seemed to say: 'Hang it, has he got it *already*? – Of course he's a brute of a reviewer!' Dencombe shuffled his copy out of sight while the opulent matron, rising from her repose, broke out: 'I feel already the good of this air!'

'I can't say I do,' said the angular lady. 'I find myself quite let down.'

'I find myself horribly hungry. At what time did you order lunch?' her protectress pursued.

The young person put the question by. 'Dr Hugh always orders it.'

'I ordered nothing today – I'm going to make you diet,' said their comrade.

'Then I shall go home and sleep. *Qui dort dîne!*'

'Can I trust you to Miss Vernham?' asked Dr Hugh of his elder companion.

'Don't I trust *you*?' she archly inquired.

'Not too much!' Miss Vernham, with her eyes on the ground, permitted herself to declare. 'You must come with us at least to the house,' she went on, while the personage on whom they appeared to be in attendance began to mount higher. She had got a little out of ear-shot; nevertheless Miss Vernham became, so far as Dencombe was concerned, less distinctly audible to murmur to the young man: 'I don't think you realize all you owe the Countess!'

Absently, a moment, Dr Hugh caused his gold-rimmed spectacles to shine at her.

'Is that the way I strike you? I see – I see!'

'She's awfully good to us,' continued Miss Vernham, compelled by her interlocutor's immovability to stand there in spite of his discussion of private matters. Of what use would it have been that Dencombe should be sensitive to shades had he not detected in that immovability a strange influence from the quiet old convalescent in the great tweed cape? Miss Vernham appeared suddenly to become aware of some such connection, for she added in a moment: 'If you want to sun yourself here you can come back after you've seen us home.'

Dr Hugh, at this, hesitated, and Dencombe, in spite of a desire to pass for unconscious, risked a covert glance at him.

What his eyes met this time, as it happened, was on the part of the young lady a queer stare, naturally vitreous, which made her aspect remind him of some figure (he couldn't name it) in a play or a novel, some sinister governess or tragic old maid. She seemed to scrutinize him, to challenge him, to say, from general spite: 'What have you got to do with us?' At the same instant the rich humour of the Countess reached them from above: 'Come, come, my little lambs, you should follow your old *bergère*!' Miss Vernham turned away at this, pursuing the ascent, and Dr Hugh, after another mute appeal to Dencombe and a moment's evident demur, deposited his book on the bench, as if to keep his place or even as a sign that he would return, and bounded without difficulty up the rougher part of the cliff.

Equally innocent and infinite are the pleasures of observation and the resources engendered by the habit of analysing life. It amused poor Dencombe, as he dawdled in his tepid air-bath, to think that he was waiting for a revelation of something at the back of a fine young mind. He looked hard at the book on the end of the bench, but he wouldn't have touched it for the world. It served his purpose to have a theory which should not be exposed to refutation. He already felt better of his melancholy; he had, according to his old formula, put his head at the window. A passing Countess could draw off the fancy when, like the elder of the ladies who had just retreated, she was as obvious as the giantess of a caravan. It was indeed general views that were terrible; short ones, contrary to an opinion sometimes expressed, were the refuge, were the remedy. Dr Hugh couldn't possibly be anything but a reviewer who had understandings for early copies with publishers or with newspapers. He reappeared in a quarter of an hour, with visible relief at finding Dencombe on the spot, and the gleam of white teeth in an embarrassed but generous smile. He was perceptibly disappointed at the eclipse of the other copy of the book; it was a pretext the less for speaking to the stranger. But he spoke notwithstanding; he held up his own copy and broke out pleadingly:

'*Do* say, if you have occasion to speak of it, that it's the best thing he has done yet!'

Dencombe responded with a laugh: 'Done yet' was so amusing to him, made such a grand avenue of the future. Better still, the young man took *him* for a reviewer. He pulled out 'The Middle Years' from under his cape, but instinctively concealed any tell-tale look of fatherhood. This was partly because a person was always a fool for calling attention to his work. 'Is that what you're going to say yourself?' he inquired of his visitor.

'I'm not quite sure I shall write anything. I don't, as a regular thing – I enjoy in peace. But it's awfully fine.'

Dencombe debated a moment. If his interlocutor had begun to abuse him he would have confessed on the spot to his identity, but there was no harm in drawing him on a little to praise. He drew him on with such success that in a few moments his new acquaintance, seated by his side, was confessing candidly that Dencombe's novels were the only ones he could read a second time. He had come the day before from London, where a friend of his, a journalist, had lent him his copy of the last – the copy sent to the office of the journal and already the subject of a 'notice' which, as was pretended there (but one had to allow for 'swagger'), it had taken a full quarter of an hour to prepare. He intimated that he was ashamed for his friend, and in the case of a work demanding and repaying study, of such inferior manners; and, with his fresh appreciation and inexplicable wish to express it, he speedily became for poor Dencombe a remarkable, a delightful apparition. Chance had brought the weary man of letters face to face with the greatest admirer in the new generation whom it was supposable he possessed. The admirer, in truth, was mystifying, so rare a case was it to find a bristling young doctor – he looked like a German physiologist – enamoured of literary form. It was an accident, but happier than most accidents, so that Dencombe, exhilarated as well as confounded, spent half an hour in making his visitor talk while he kept himself quiet. He explained his premature possession of 'The Middle Years' by an allusion to the friendship of the publisher, who, knowing he was at Bournemouth for his health, had paid him this graceful attention. He admitted that he had been ill, for Dr Hugh would infallibly have guessed it; he even went so far as to wonder whether he mightn't look for some hygienic 'tip' from a personage combining so bright an enthusiasm with a presumable knowledge of the remedies now in vogue. It would shake his faith a little perhaps to have to take a doctor seriously who could take *him* so seriously, but he enjoyed this gushing modern youth and he felt with an acute pang that there would still be work to do in a world in which such odd combinations were presented. It was not true, what he had tried for renunciation's sake to believe, that all the combinations were exhausted. They were not, they were not – they were infinite: the exhaustion was in the miserable artist.

Dr Hugh was an ardent physiologist, saturated with the spirit of the age – in other words he had just taken his degree; but he was independent and various, he talked like a man who would have preferred to love literature best. He would fain have made fine phrases, but nature had denied him the trick. Some of the finest in 'The Middle Years' had struck him inordinately, and he took the liberty of reading them to Dencombe in support of his plea. He grew vivid, in the balmy air, to his companion, for whose deep refreshment he seemed to have been sent; and was particularly ingenuous in describing how recently he had become acquainted, and how instantly infatuated, with the only man who had put flesh between the ribs of an art that was starving on superstitions. He had not yet written to him – he was deterred by a sentiment of respect. Dencombe at this moment felicitated himself more than ever on having never answered the photographers. His visitor's attitude promised him a luxury of intercourse, but he surmised that a certain security in it, for Dr Hugh, would depend not a little on the Countess. He learned without delay with what variety of Countess they were concerned, as well as the nature of the tie that united the curious trio. The large lady, an Englishwoman by birth and the daughter of a celebrated baritone, whose taste, without his talent, she had inherited, was the widow of a French nobleman and mistress of all that remained of the handsome fortune, the fruit of her father's earnings, that had constituted her dower. Miss Vernham, an odd creature but an accomplished pianist, was attached to her person at a salary. The Countess was generous, independent, eccentric; she travelled with her minstrel and her medical man. Ignorant and passionate, she had nevertheless moments in which she was almost irresistible. Dencombe saw her sit for her portrait in Dr Hugh's free sketch, and felt the picture of his young friend's relation to her frame itself in his mind. This young friend, for a representative of the new psychology, was himself easily hypnotized, and if he became abnormally communicative it was only a sign of his real subjection. Dencombe did accordingly what he wanted with him, even without being known as Dencombe.

Taken ill on a journey in Switzerland the Countess had picked him up at an hotel, and the accident of his happening to please her had made her offer him, with her imperious liberality, terms that couldn't fail to dazzle a practitioner without patients and whose resources had been drained dry by his studies. It was not the way he would have elected to spend his time, but it was time that would pass quickly, and meanwhile she was wonderfully kind. She exacted perpetual attention, but it was impossible not to like her. He gave details about his queer patient, a 'type' if there ever was one, who had in connection with her flushed obesity and in addition to the morbid strain of a violent and aimless will a grave organic disorder; but he came back to his loved novelist, whom he was so good as to pronounce more essentially a poet than many of those who went in for verse, with a zeal excited, as all his indiscretion had been excited, by the happy chance of Dencombe's sympathy and the coincidence of their occupation. Dencombe had confessed to a slight personal acquaintance with the author of 'The Middle Years', but had not felt himself as ready as he could have wished when his companion, who had never yet encountered a being so privileged, began to be eager for particulars. He even thought that Dr Hugh's eye at that moment emitted a glimmer of suspicion. But the young man was too inflamed to be shrewd and repeatedly caught up the book to exclaim: 'Did you notice this?' or 'Weren't you immensely struck with that?' 'There's a beautiful passage toward the end,' he broke out; and again he laid his hand upon the volume. As he turned the pages he came upon something else, while Dencombe saw him suddenly change colour. He had taken up, as it lay on the bench, Dencombe's copy instead of his own, and his neighbour immediately guessed the reason of his start. Dr Hugh looked grave an instant; then he said: 'I see you've been altering the text!' Dencombe was a passionate corrector, a fingerer of style; the last thing he ever arrived at was a form final for himself. His ideal would have been to publish secretly, and then, on the published text, treat himself to the terrified revise, sacrificing always a first edition and beginning for posterity and even for the collectors, poor dears, with a second. This morning, in 'The Middle Years', his pencil had pricked a dozen lights. He was amused at the effect of the young man's reproach; for an instant it made him change colour. He stammered, at any rate, ambiguously; then, through a blur of ebbing consciousness, saw Dr Hugh's mystified eyes. He only had time to feel he was about to be ill again – that emotion, excitement, fatigue, the heat of the sun, the solicitation of the air, had combined to play him a trick, before, stretching out a hand to his visitor with a plaintive cry, he lost his senses altogether.

Later he knew that he had fainted and that Dr Hugh had got him home in a bath-chair, the conductor of which, prowling within hail for custom, had happened to remember seeing him in the garden of the hotel. He had recovered his perception in the transit, and had, in bed, that afternoon, a vague recollection of Dr Hugh's young face, as they went together, bent over him in a comforting laugh and expressive of something more than a suspicion of his identity. That identity was ineffaceable now, and all the more that he was disappointed, disgusted. He had been rash, been stupid, had gone out too soon, stayed out too long. He oughtn't to have exposed himself to strangers, he ought to have taken his servant. He felt as if he had fallen into a hole too deep to descry any little patch of heaven. He was confused about the time that had elapsed – he pieced the fragments together. He had seen his doctor, the real one, the one who had treated him from the first and who had again been very kind. His servant was in and out on tiptoe, looking very wise after the fact. He said more than once something about the sharp young gentleman. The rest was vagueness, in so far as it wasn't despair. The vagueness, however, justified itself by dreams, dozing anxieties from which he finally emerged to the consciousness of a dark room and a shaded candle.

'You'll be all right again – I know all about you now,' said a voice near him that he knew to be young. Then his meeting with Dr Hugh came back. He was too discouraged to joke about it yet, but he was able to perceive, after a little, that the interest of it was intense for his visitor. 'Of course I can't attend you professionally – you've got your own man; with whom I've talked and who's excellent,' Dr Hugh went on. 'But you must let me come to see you as a good friend. I've just looked in before going to bed. You're doing beautifully, but it's a good job I was with you on the cliff. I shall come in early tomorrow. I want to do something for you. I want to do everything. You've done a tremendous lot for me.' The young man held his hand, hanging over him, and poor Dencombe, weakly aware of this living pressure, simply lay there and accepted his devotion. He couldn't do anything less – he needed help too much.

The idea of the help he needed was very present to him that night, which he spent in a lucid stillness, an intensity of thought that constituted a reaction from his hours of stupor. He was lost, he was lost – he was lost if he couldn't be saved. He was not afraid of suffering, of death; he was not even in love with life; but he had had a deep demonstration of desire. It came over him in the long, quiet hours that only with 'The Middle Years' had he taken his flight; only on that day, visited by soundless processions, had he recognized his kingdom. He had had a revelation of his range. What he dreaded was the idea that his reputation should stand on the unfinished. It was not with his past but with his future that it should properly be concerned. Illness and age rose before him like spectres with pitiless eyes: how was he to bribe such fates to give him the second chance? He had had the one chance that all men have – he had had the chance of life. He went to sleep again very late, and when he awoke Dr Hugh was sitting by his head. There was already, by this time, something beautifully familiar in him.

'Don't think I've turned out your physician,' he said; 'I'm acting with his consent. He has been here and seen you. Somehow he seems to trust me. I told him how we happened to come together yesterday, and he recognizes that I've a peculiar right.'

Dencombe looked at him with a calculating earnestness. 'How have you squared the Countess?'

The young man blushed a little, but he laughed. 'Oh, never mind the Countess!'

'You told me she was very exacting.'

Dr Hugh was silent a moment. 'So she is.'

'And Miss Vernham's an *intrigante*.'

'How do you know that?'

'I know everything. One *has* to, to write decently!'

'I think she's mad,' said limpid Dr Hugh.

'Well, don't quarrel with the Countess – she's a present help to you.'

'I don't quarrel,' Dr Hugh replied. 'But I don't get on with silly women.' Presently he added: 'You seem very much alone.'

'That often happens at my age. I've outlived, I've lost by the way.'

Dr Hugh hesitated; then surmounting a soft scruple: 'Whom have you lost?'

'Everyone.'

'Ah, no,' the young man murmured, laying a hand on his arm.

'I once had a wife – I once had a son. My wife died when my child was born, and my boy, at school, was carried off by typhoid.'

'I wish I'd been there!' said Dr Hugh simply.

'Well – if you're here!' Dencombe answered, with a smile that, in spite of dimness, showed how much he liked to be sure of his companion's whereabouts.

'You talk strangely of your age. You're not old.'

'Hypocrite – so early!'

'I speak physiologically.'

'That's the way I've been speaking for the last five years, and it's exactly what I've been saying to myself. It isn't till we *are* old that we begin to tell ourselves we're not!'

'Yet I know I myself am young,' Dr Hugh declared.

'Not so well as I!' laughed his patient, whose visitor indeed would have established the truth in question by the honesty with which he changed the point of view, remarking that it must be one of the charms of age – at any rate in the case of high distinction – to feel that one has laboured and achieved. Dr Hugh employed the common phrase about earning one's rest, and it made poor Dencombe, for an instant, almost angry. He recovered himself, however, to explain, lucidly enough, that if he, ungraciously, knew nothing of such a balm, it was doubtless because he had wasted inestimable years. He had followed literature from the first, but he had taken a lifetime to get alongside of her. Only today, at last, had he begun to *see*, so that what he had hitherto done was a movement without a direction. He had ripened too late and was so clumsily constituted that he had had to teach himself by mistakes.

'I prefer your flowers, then, to other people's fruit, and your mistakes to other people's successes,' said gallant Dr Hugh. 'It's for your mistakes I admire you.'

'You're happy – you don't know,' Dencombe answered.

Looking at his watch the young man had got up; he named the hour of the afternoon at which he would return. Dencombe warned him against committing himself too deeply, and expressed again all his dread of making him neglect the Countess – perhaps incur her displeasure.

'I want to be like you – I want to learn by mistakes!' Dr Hugh laughed.

'Take care you don't make too grave a one! But do come back,' Dencombe added, with the glimmer of a new idea.

'You should have had more vanity!' Dr Hugh spoke as if he knew the exact amount required to make a man of letters normal.

'No, no – I only should have had more time. I want another go.'

'Another go?'

'I want an extension.'

'An extension?' Again Dr Hugh repeated Dencombe's words, with which he seemed to have been struck.

'Don't you know? – I want to what they call "live".'

The young man, for good-bye, had taken his hand, which closed with a certain force. They looked at each other hard a moment. 'You *will* live,' said Dr Hugh.

'Don't be superficial. It's too serious!'

'You *shall* live!' Dencombe's visitor declared, turning pale.

'Ah, that's better!' And as he retired the invalid, with a troubled laugh, sank gratefully back.

All that day and all the following night he wondered if it mightn't be arranged. His doctor came again, his servant was attentive, but it was to his confident young friend that he found himself mentally appealing. His collapse on the cliff was plausibly explained, and his liberation, on a better basis, promised for the morrow; meanwhile, however, the intensity of his meditations kept him tranquil and made him indifferent. The idea that occupied him was none the less absorbing because it was a morbid fancy. Here was a clever son of the age, ingenious and ardent, who happened to have set him up for connoisseurs to worship. This servant of his altar had all the new learning in science and all the old reverence in faith; wouldn't he therefore put his knowledge at the disposal of his sympathy, his craft at the disposal of his love? Couldn't he be trusted to invent a remedy for a poor artist to whose art he had paid a tribute? If he couldn't, the alternative was hard: Dencombe would have to surrender to silence, unvindicated and undivined. The rest of the day and all the next he toyed in secret with this sweet futility. Who would work the miracle for him but the young man who could combine such lucidity with such passion? He thought of the fairy-tales of science and charmed himself into forgetting that he looked for a magic that was not of this world. Dr Hugh was an apparition, and that placed him above the law. He came and went while his patient, who sat up, followed him with supplicating eyes. The interest of knowing the great author had made the young man begin 'The Middle Years' afresh, and would help him to find a deeper meaning in its pages. Dencombe had told him what he 'tried for'; with all his intelligence, on a first perusal, Dr Hugh had failed to guess it. The baffled celebrity wondered then who in the world *would* guess it: he was amused once more at the fine, full way with which an intention could be missed. Yet he wouldn't rail at the general mind today – consoling as that ever had been: the revelation of his own slowness had seemed to make all stupidity sacred.

Dr Hugh, after a little, was visibly worried, confessing, on inquiry, to a source of embarrassment at home. 'Stick to the Countess – don't mind me,' Dencombe said, repeatedly; for his companion was frank enough about the large lady's attitude. She was so jealous that she had fallen ill – she resented such a breach of allegiance. She paid so much for his fidelity that she must have it all: she refused him the right to other sympathies, charged him with scheming to make her die alone, for it was needless to point out how little Miss Vernham was a resource in trouble. When Dr Hugh mentioned that the Countess would already have left Bournemouth if he hadn't kept her in bed, poor Dencombe held his arm tighter and said with decision: 'Take her straight away.' They had gone out together, walking back to the sheltered nook in which, the other day, they had met. The young man, who had given his companion a personal support, declared with emphasis that his conscience was clear – he could ride two horses at once. Didn't he dream, for his future, of a time when he should have to ride five hundred? Longing equally for virtue, Dencombe replied that in that golden age no patient would pretend to have contracted with him for his whole attention. On the part of the Countess was not such an avidity lawful? Dr Hugh denied it, said there was no contract but only a free understanding, and that a sordid servitude was impossible to a generous spirit; he liked moreover to talk about art, and that was the subject on which, this time, as they sat together on the sunny bench, he tried most to engage the author of 'The Middle Years'. Dencombe, soaring again a little on the weak wings of convalescence and still haunted by that happy notion of an organized rescue, found another strain of eloquence to plead the cause of a certain splendid 'last manner', the very citadel, as it would prove, of his reputation, the stronghold into which his real treasure would be gathered. While his listener gave up the morning and the great still sea appeared to wait, he had a wonderful explanatory hour. Even for himself he was inspired as he told of what his treasure would consist – the precious metals he would dig from the mine, the jewels rare, strings of pearls, he would hang between the columns of his temple. He was wonderful for himself, so thick his convictions crowded; but he was still more wonderful for Dr Hugh, who assured him, none the less, that the very pages he had just published were already encrusted with gems. The young man, however, panted for the combinations to come, and, before the face of the beautiful day, renewed to Dencombe his guarantee that his profession would hold itself responsible for such a life. Then he suddenly clapped his hand upon his watch-pocket and asked leave to absent himself for half an hour. Dencombe waited there for his return, but was at last recalled to the actual by the fall of a shadow across the ground. The shadow darkened into that of Miss Vernham, the young lady in attendance on the Countess; whom Dencombe, recognizing her, perceived so clearly to have come to speak to him that he rose from his bench to acknowledge the civility. Miss Vernham indeed proved not particularly civil; she looked strangely agitated, and her type was now unmistakable.

'Excuse me if I inquire,' she said, 'whether it's too much to hope that you may be induced to leave Dr Hugh alone.' Then, before Dencombe, greatly disconcerted, could protest: 'You ought to be informed that you stand in his light; that you may do him a terrible injury.'

'Do you mean by causing the Countess to dispense with his services?'

'By causing her to disinherit him.' Dencombe stared at this, and Miss Vernham pursued, in the gratification of seeing she could produce an impression: 'It has depended on himself to come into something very handsome. He has had a magnificent prospect, but I think you've succeeded in spoiling it.'

'Not intentionally, I assure you. Is there no hope the accident may be repaired?' Dencombe asked.

'She was ready to do anything for him. She takes great fancies, she lets herself go – it's her way. She has no relations, she's free to dispose of her money, and she's very ill.'

'I'm very sorry to hear it,' Dencombe stammered.

'Wouldn't it be possible for you to leave Bournemouth? That's what I've come to ask of you.'

Poor Dencombe sank down on his bench. 'I'm very ill myself, but I'll try!'

Miss Vernham still stood there with her colourless eyes and the brutality of her good conscience. 'Before it's too late, please!' she said; and with this she turned her back, in order, quickly, as if it had been a business to which she could spare but a precious moment, to pass out of his sight.

Oh, yes, after this Dencombe was certainly very ill. Miss Vernham had upset him with her rough, fierce news; it was the sharpest shock to him to discover what was at stake for a penniless young man of fine parts. He sat trembling on his bench, staring at the waste of waters, feeling sick with the directness of the blow. He was indeed too weak, too unsteady, too alarmed; but he would make the effort to get away, for he couldn't accept the guilt of interference, and his honour was really involved. He would hobble home, at any rate, and then he would think what was to be done. He made his way back to the hotel and, as he went, had a characteristic vision of Miss Vernham's great motive. The Countess hated women, of course; Dencombe was lucid about that; so the hungry pianist had no personal hopes and could only console herself with the bold conception of helping Dr Hugh in order either to marry him after he should get his money or to induce him to recognize her title to compensation and buy her off. If she had befriended him at a fruitful crisis he would really, as a man of delicacy, and she knew what to think of that point, have to reckon with her.

At the hotel Dencombe's servant insisted on his going back to bed. The invalid had talked about catching a train and had begun with orders to pack; after which his humming nerves had yielded to a sense of sickness. He consented to see his physician, who immediately was sent for, but he wished it to be understood that his door was irrevocably closed to Dr Hugh. He had his plan, which was so fine that he rejoiced in it after getting back to bed. Dr Hugh, suddenly finding himself snubbed without mercy, would, in natural disgust and to the joy of Miss Vernham, renew his allegiance to the Countess. When his physician arrived Dencombe learned that he was feverish and that this was very wrong: he was to cultivate calmness and try, if possible, not to think. For the rest of the day he wooed stupidity;

but there was an ache that kept him sentient, the probable sacrifice of his 'extension', the limit of his course. His medical adviser was anything but pleased; his successive relapses were ominous. He charged this personage to put out a strong hand and take Dr Hugh off his mind – it would contribute so much to his being quiet. The agitating name, in his room, was not mentioned again, but his security was a smothered fear, and it was not confirmed by the receipt, at ten o'clock that evening, of a telegram which his servant opened and read for him and to which, with an address in London, the signature of Miss Vernham was attached. '*Beseech you to use all influence to make our friend join us here in the morning. Countess much the worse for dreadful journey, but everything may still be saved.*' The two ladies had gathered themselves up and had been capable in the afternoon of a spiteful revolution. They had started for the capital, and if the elder one, as Miss Vernham had announced, was very ill, she had wished to make it dear that she was proportionately reckless. Poor Dencombe, who was not reckless and who only desired that everything should indeed be 'saved', sent this missive straight off to the young man's lodging and had on the morrow the pleasure of knowing that he had quitted Bournemouth by an early train.

Two days later he pressed in with a copy of a literary journal in his hand. He had returned because he was anxious and for the pleasure of flourishing the great review of 'The Middle Years'. Here at least was something adequate – it rose to the occasion; it was an acclamation, a reparation, a critical attempt to place the author in the niche he had fairly won. Dencombe accepted and submitted; he made neither objection nor inquiry, for old complications had returned and he had had two atrocious days. He was convinced not only that he should never again leave his bed, so that his young friend might pardonably remain, but that the demand he should make on the patience of beholders would be very moderate indeed. Dr Hugh had been to town, and he tried to find in his eyes some confession that the Countess was pacified and his legacy clinched; but all he could see there was the light of his juvenile joy in two or three of the phrases of the newspaper. Dencombe couldn't read them, but when his visitor had insisted on repeating them more than once he was able to shake an unintoxicated head. 'Ah, no; but they would have been true of what I *could* have done!'

'What people "could have done" is mainly what they've in fact done,' Dr Hugh contended.

'Mainly, yes; but I've been an idiot!' said Dencombe.

Dr Hugh did remain; the end was coming fast. Two days later Dencombe observed to him, by way of the feeblest of jokes, that there would now be no question whatever of a second chance. At this the young man stared; then he exclaimed: 'Why, it has come to pass — it has come to pass! The second chance has been the public's — the chance to find the point of view, to pick up the pearl!'

'Oh, the pearl!' poor Dencombe uneasily sighed. A smile as cold as a winter sunset flickered on his drawn lips as he added:

'The pearl is the unwritten – the pearl is the unalloyed, the *rest*, the lost!'

From that moment he was less and less present, heedless to all appearance of what went on around him. His disease was definitely mortal, of an action as relentless, after the short arrest that had enabled him to fall in with Dr Hugh, as a leak in a great ship. Sinking steadily, though this visitor, a man of rare resources, now cordially approved by his physician, showed endless art in guarding him from pain, poor Dencombe kept no reckoning of favour or neglect, betrayed no symptom of regret or speculation. Yet toward the last he gave a sign of having noticed that for two days Dr Hugh had not been in his room, a sign that consisted of his suddenly opening his eyes to ask of him if he had spent the interval with the Countess.

'The Countess is dead,' said Dr Hugh. 'I knew that in a particular contingency she wouldn't resist. I went to her grave.'

Dencombe's eyes opened wider. 'She left you "something handsome"?'

The young man gave a laugh almost too light for a chamber of woe. 'Never a penny. She roundly cursed me.'

'Cursed you?' Dencombe murmured.

'For giving her up. I gave her up for *you*. I had to choose,' his companion explained.

'You chose to let a fortune go?'

'I chose to accept, whatever they might be, the consequences of my infatuation,' smiled Dr Hugh. Then, as a larger pleasantry: 'A fortune be hanged! It's your own fault if I can't get your things out of my head.'

The immediate tribute to his humour was a long, bewildered moan; after which, for many hours, many days, Dencombe lay motionless and absent. A response so absolute, such a glimpse of a definite result and such a sense of credit worked together in his mind and, producing a strange commotion, slowly altered and transfigured his despair. The sense of cold submersion left him — he seemed to float without an effort. The incident was extraordinary as evidence, and it shed an intenser light. At the last he signed to Dr Hugh to listen, and, when he was down on his knees by the pillow, brought him very near.

'You've made me think it all a delusion.'

'Not your glory, my dear friend,' stammered the young man.

'Not my glory — what there is of it! It *is* glory — to have been tested, to have had our little quality and cast our little spell. The thing is to have made somebody care. You happen to be crazy, of course, but that doesn't affect the law.'

'You're a great success!' said Dr Hugh, putting into his young voice the ring of a marriage-bell.

Dencombe lay taking this in; then he gathered strength to speak once more. 'A second chance — *that's* the delusion. There never was to be but one. We work in the dark — we do what we can — we give what we have. Our doubt is our passion and our passion is our task. The rest is the madness of art.'

'If you've doubted, if you've despaired, you've always "done" it,' his visitor subtly argued.

'We've done something or other,' Dencombe conceded.

'Something or other is everything. It's the feasible. It's *you*!'

'Comforter!' poor Dencombe ironically sighed.

'But it's true,' insisted his friend.

'It's true. It's frustration that doesn't count.'

'Frustration's only life,' said Dr Hugh.

'Yes, it's what passes.' Poor Dencombe was barely audible, but he had marked with the words the virtual end of his first and only chance.

The Death of the Lion

I

I HAD SIMPLY, I suppose, a change of heart, and it must have begun when I received my manuscript back from Mr Pinhorn. Mr Pinhorn was my 'chief', as he was called in the office: he had accepted the high mission of bringing the paper up. This was a weekly periodical, and had been supposed to be almost past redemption when he took hold of it. It was Mr Deedy who had let it down so dreadfully: he was never mentioned in the office now save in connection with that misdemeanour. Young as I was I had been in a manner taken over from Mr Deedy, who had been owner as well as editor; forming part of a promiscuous lot, mainly plant and office-furniture, which poor Mrs Deedy, in her bereavement and depression, parted with at a rough valuation. I could account for my continuity only on the supposition that I had been cheap. I rather resented the practice of fathering all flatness on my late protector, who was in his unhonoured grave;

but as I had my way to make I found matter enough for complacency in being on a 'staff'. At the same time I was aware that I was exposed to suspicion as a product of the old lowering system. This made me feel that I was doubly bound to have ideas, and had doubtless been at the bottom of my proposing to Mr Pinhorn that I should lay my lean hands on Neil Paraday. I remember that he looked at me first as if he had never heard of this celebrity, who indeed at that moment was by no means in the centre of the heavens; and even when I had knowingly explained he expressed but little confidence in the demand for any such matter. When I had reminded him that the great principle on which we were supposed to work was just to create the demand we required, he considered a moment and then rejoined: 'I see; you want to write him up.'

'Call it that if you like.'

'And what's your inducement?'

'Bless my soul – my admiration!'

Mr Pinhorn pursed up his mouth. 'Is there much to be done with him?'

'Whatever there is, we should have it all to ourselves, for he hasn't been touched.'

This argument was effective, and Mr Pinhorn responded: 'Very well, touch him.' Then he added: 'But where can you do it?'

'Under the fifth rib!'

Mr Pinhorn stared. 'Where's that?'

'You want me to go down and see him?' I inquired when I had enjoyed his visible search for this obscure suburb.

'I don't "want" anything – the proposal's your own. But you must remember that that's the way we do things *now*,' said Mr Pinhorn, with another dig at Mr Deedy.

Unregenerate as I was, I could read the queer implications of this speech. The present owner's superior virtue as well as his deeper craft spoke in his reference to the late editor as one of that baser sort who deal in false representations. Mr Deedy would as soon have sent me to call on Neil Paraday as he would have published a 'holiday-number'; but such scruples presented themselves as mere ignoble thrift to his successor, whose own sincerity took the form of ringing door-bells and whose definition of genius was the art of finding people at home. It was as if Mr Deedy had published reports without his young men's having, as Pinhorn would have said, really been there. I was unregenerate, as I have hinted, and I was not concerned to straighten out the journalistic morals of my chief, feeling them indeed to be an abyss over the edge of which it was better not to peer. Really to be there this time moreover was a vision that made the idea of writing something subtle about Neil Paraday only the more inspiring. I would be as considerate as even Mr Deedy could have wished, and yet I should be as present as only Mr Pinhorn could conceive. My allusion to the sequestered manner in which Mr Paraday lived (which had formed part of my explanation, though I knew of it only by hearsay) was, I could divine, very much what had made Mr Pinhorn nibble. It struck him as inconsistent with the success of his paper that anyone should be so sequestered as that. And then was not an immediate exposure of everything just what the public wanted? Mr Pinhorn effectually called me to order by reminding me of the promptness with which I had met Miss Braby at Liverpool on her return from her fiasco in the States. Hadn't we published, while its freshness and flavour were unimpaired, Miss Braby's own version of that great international episode? I felt somewhat uneasy at this lumping of the actress and the author, and I confess that after having enlisted Mr Pinhorn's sympathies I procrastinated a little. I had succeeded better than I wished, and I had, as it happened, work nearer at hand. A few days later I called on Lord Crouchley and carried off in triumph the most unintelligible statement that had yet appeared of his lordship's reasons for his change of front. I thus set in motion in the daily papers columns of virtuous verbiage. The following week I ran down to Brighton for a chat, as Mr Pinhorn called it, with Mrs Bounder, who gave me, on the subject of her divorce, many curious particulars that had not been articulated in court. If ever an article flowed from the primal fount it was that article on Mrs Bounder. By this time, however, I became aware that Neil Paraday's new book was on the point of appearing and that its approach had been the ground of my original appeal to Mr Pinhorn, who was now annoyed with me for having lost so many days. He bundled me off – we would at least not lose another. I have always thought his sudden alertness a remarkable example of the journalistic instinct. Nothing had occurred, since I first spoke to him, to create a visible urgency, and no enlightenment could possibly have reached him. It was a pure case of professional *flair* – he had smelt the coming glory as an animal smells its distant prey.

II

I MAY AS WELL say at once that this little record pretends in no degree to be a picture either of my introduction to Mr Paraday or of certain proximate steps and stages. The scheme of my narrative allows no space for these things, and in any case a prohibitory sentiment would be attached to my recollection of so rare an hour. These meagre notes are essentially private, so that if they see the light the insidious forces that, as my story itself shows, make at present for publicity will simply have overmastered my precautions. The curtain fell lately enough on the lamentable drama. My memory of the day I alighted at Mr Paraday's door is a fresh memory of kindness, hospitality, compassion, and of the wonderful illuminating talk in which the welcome was conveyed. Some voice of the air had taught me the right moment, the moment of his life at which an act of unexpected young allegiance might most come home. He had recently recovered from a long, grave illness. I had gone to the neighbouring inn for the night, but I spent the evening in his company, and he insisted the next day on my sleeping under his roof. I had not an indefinite leave: Mr Pinhorn supposed us to put our victims through on the gallop. It was later, in the office, that the dance was set to music. I fortified myself, however, as my training had taught me to do, by the conviction that nothing could be more advantageous for my article than to be written in the very atmosphere. I said nothing to Mr Paraday about it, but in the morning, after my removal from the inn, while he was occupied in his study, as he had notified me that he should need to be, I committed to paper the quintessence of my impressions. Then thinking to commend myself to Mr Pinhorn by my celerity, I walked out and posted my little packet before luncheon. Once my paper was written I was free to stay on, and if it was designed to divert attention from my frivolity in so doing I could reflect with satisfaction that I had never been so clever. I don't mean to deny of course that I was aware it was much too good for Mr Pinhorn; but I was equally conscious that Mr Pinhorn had the supreme shrewdness of recognizing from time to time the cases in which an article was not too bad only because it was too good. There was nothing he loved so much as to print on the right occasion a thing he hated. I had begun my visit to Mr Paraday on a Monday, and on the Wednesday his book came out. A copy of it arrived by the first post, and he let me go out into the garden with it immediately after breakfast. I read it from beginning to end that day, and in the evening he asked me to remain with him the rest of the week and over the Sunday.

That night my manuscript came back from Mr Pinhorn, accompanied with a letter, of which the gist was the desire to know what I meant by sending him such stuff. That was the meaning of the question, if not exactly its form, and it made my mistake immense to me. Such as this mistake was I could now only look it in the face and accept it. I knew where I had failed, but it was exactly where I couldn't have succeeded. I had been sent down there to be personal, and in point of fact I hadn't been personal at all: what I had sent up to London was just a little finicking, feverish study of my author's talent. Anything less relevant to Mr Pinhorn's purpose couldn't well be imagined, and he was visibly angry at my having (at his expense, with a second-class ticket) approached the object of our arrangement only to be so deucedly distant. For myself, I knew but too well what had happened, and how a miracle – as pretty as some old miracle of legend – had been wrought on the spot to save me. There had been a big brush of wings, the flash of an opaline robe, and then, with a great cool stir of the air, the sense of an angel's having swooped down and caught me to his bosom. He held me only till the danger was over, and it all took place in a minute. With my manuscript back on my hands I understood the phenomenon better, and the reflections I made on it are what I meant, at the beginning of this anecdote, by my change of heart. Mr Pinhorn's note was not only a rebuke decidedly stern, but an invitation immediately to send him (it was the case to say so) the genuine article, the revealing and reverberating sketch to the promise of which – and of which alone – I owed my squandered privilege. A week or two later I recast my peccant paper, and giving it a particular application to Mr Paraday's new book, obtained for it the hospitality of another journal, where, I must admit, Mr Pinhorn was so far justified that it attracted not the least attention.

III

I WAS FRANKLY, at the end of three days, a very prejudiced critic, so that one morning when, in the garden, Neil Paraday had offered to read me something I quite held my breath as I listened. It was the written scheme of another book – something he had put aside long ago, before his illness, and lately taken out again to reconsider. He had been turning it round when I came down upon him, and it had grown magnificently under this second hand. Loose, liberal, confident, it might have passed for a great gossiping, eloquent letter – the overflow into talk of an artist's amorous plan. The subject I thought singularly rich, quite the strongest he had yet treated; and this familiar statement of it, full too of fine maturities, was really, in summarized splendour, a mine of gold, a precious, independent work. I remember rather profanely wondering whether the ultimate production could possibly be so happy. His reading of the epistle, at any rate, made me feel as if I were, for the advantage of posterity, in close correspondence with him – were the distinguished person to whom it had been affectionately addressed. It was high distinction simply to be told such things. The idea he now communicated had all the freshness, the flushed fairness of the conception untouched and untried: it was Venus rising from the sea, before the airs had blown upon her. I had never been so throbbingly present at such an unveiling. But when he had tossed the last bright word after the others, as I had seen cashiers in banks, weighing mounds of coin, drop a final sovereign into the tray, I became conscious of a sudden prudent alarm.

'My dear master, how, after all, are you going to do it?' I asked. 'It's infinitely noble, but what time it will take, what patience and independence, what assured, what perfect conditions it will demand! Oh for a lone isle in a tepid sea!'

'Isn't this practically a lone isle, and aren't you, as an encircling medium, tepid enough?' he replied, alluding with a laugh to the wonder of my young admiration and the narrow limits of his little provincial home. 'Time isn't what I've lacked hitherto: the question hasn't been to find it, but to use it. Of course my illness made a great hole, but I daresay there would have been a hole at any rate. The earth we tread has more pockets than a billiard-table. The great thing is now to keep on my feet.'

'That's exactly what I mean.'

Neil Paraday looked at me with eyes – such pleasant eyes as he had – in which, as I now recall their expression, I seem to have seen a dim imagination of his fate. He was fifty years old, and his illness had been cruel, his convalescence slow. 'It isn't as if I weren't all right.'

'Oh, if you weren't all right I wouldn't look at you!' I tenderly said.

We had both got up, quickened by the full sound of it all, and he had lighted a cigarette. I had taken a fresh one, and, with an intenser smile, by way of answer to my exclamation, he touched it with the flame of his match. 'If I weren't better I shouldn't have thought of *that*!' He flourished his epistle in his hand.

'I don't want to be discouraging, but that's not true,' I returned. 'I'm sure that during the months you lay here in pain you had visitations sublime. You thought of a thousand things. You think of more and more all the while. That's what makes you, if you will pardon my familiarity, so respectable. At a time when so many people are spent you come into your second wind. But, thank God, all the same, you're better! Thank God, too, you're not, as you were telling me yesterday, "successful". If *you* weren't a failure, what would be the use of trying? That's my one reserve on the subject of your recovery – that it makes you "score", as the newspapers say. It looks well in the newspapers, and almost anything that does that is horrible. "We are happy to announce that Mr Paraday, the celebrated author, is again in the enjoyment of excellent health." Somehow I shouldn't like to see it.'

'You won't see it; I'm not in the least celebrated – my obscurity protects me. But couldn't you bear even to see I was dying or dead?' my companion asked.

'Dead – *passe encore*; there's nothing so safe. One never knows what a living artist may do – one has mourned so many. However, one must make the worst of it; you must be as dead as you can.'

'Don't I meet that condition in having just published a book?'

'Adequately, let us hope; for the book is verily a master-piece.'

At this moment the parlour-maid appeared in the door that opened into the garden: Paraday lived at no great cost, and the frisk of petticoats, with a timorous 'Sherry, sir?' was about his modest mahogany. He allowed half his income to his wife, from whom he had succeeded in separating without redundancy of legend. I had a general faith in his having behaved well, and I had once, in London, taken Mrs Paraday down to dinner. He now turned to speak to the maid, who offered him, on a tray, some card or note, while agitated, excited, I wandered to the end of the garden. The idea of his security became supremely dear to me, and I asked myself if I were the same young man who had come down a few days before to scatter him to the four winds. When I retraced my steps he had gone into the house, and the woman (the second London post had come in) had placed my letters and a newspaper on a bench. I sat down there to the letters, which were a brief business, and then, without heeding the address, took the paper from its envelope. It was the journal of highest renown, *The Empire* of that morning. It regularly came to Paraday, but I remembered that neither of us had yet looked at the copy already delivered. This one had a great mark on the 'editorial' page, and, uncrumpling the wrapper, I saw it to be directed to my host and stamped with the name of his publishers. I instantly divined that *The Empire* had spoken of him, and I have not forgotten the odd little shock of the circumstance. It checked all eagerness and made me drop the paper a moment. As I sat there conscious of a palpitation I think I had a vision of what was to be. I had also a vision of the letter I would presently address to Mr Pinhorn, breaking as it were with Mr Pinhorn. Of course, however, the next minute the voice of *The Empire* was in my ears.

The article was not, I thanked heaven, a review; it was a 'leader', the last of three, presenting Neil Paraday to the human race. His new book, the fifth from his hand, had been but a day or two out, and *The Empire*, already aware of it, fired, as if on the birth of a prince, a salute of a whole column. The guns had been booming these three hours in the house without our suspecting them. The big blundering newspaper had discovered him, and now he was proclaimed and anointed and crowned. His place was assigned him as publicly as if a fat usher with a wand had pointed to the topmost chair; he was to pass up and still up, higher and higher, between the watching faces and the envious sounds – away up to the daïs and the throne. The article was a date; he had taken rank at a bound – waked up a national glory. A national glory was needed, and it was an immense convenience he was there. What all this meant rolled over me, and I fear I grew a little faint – it meant so much more than I could say 'yea' to on the spot. In a flash, somehow, all was different; the tremendous wave I speak of had swept something away. It had knocked down, I suppose, my little customary altar, my twinkling tapers and my flowers, and had reared itself into the likeness of a temple vast and bare.

When Neil Paraday should come out of the house he would come out a contemporary. That was what had happened: the poor man was to be squeezed into his horrible age. I felt as if he had been overtaken on the crest of the hill and brought back to the city. A little more and he would have dipped down the short cut to posterity and escaped.

IV

WHEN HE CAME out it was exactly as if he had been in custody, for beside him walked a stout man with a big black beard, who, save that he wore spectacles, might have been a policeman, and in whom at a second glance I recognized the highest contemporary enterprise.

'This is Mr Morrow,' said Paraday, looking, I thought, rather white: 'he wants to publish heaven knows what about me.'

I winced as I remembered that this was exactly what I myself had wanted. 'Already?' I exclaimed, with a sort of sense that my friend had fled to me for protection.

Mr Morrow glared, agreeably, through his glasses: they suggested the electric headlights of some monstrous modern ship, and I felt as if Paraday and I were tossing terrified under his bows. I saw that his momentum was irresistible. 'I was confident that I should be the first in the field,' he declared. 'A great interest is naturally felt in Mr Paraday's surroundings.'

'I hadn't the least idea of it,' said Paraday, as if he had been told he had been snoring.

'I find he has not read the article in *The Empire*,' Mr Morrow remarked to me. 'That's so very interesting – it's something to start with,' he smiled. He had begun to pull off his gloves, which were violently new, and to look encouragingly round the little garden. As a 'surrounding' I felt that I myself had already been taken in; I was a little fish in the stomach of a bigger one. 'I represent,' our visitor continued, 'a syndicate of influential journals, no less than thirty-seven, whose public – whose publics, I may say – are in peculiar sympathy with Mr Paraday's line of thought. They would greatly appreciate any expression of his views on the subject of the art he so brilliantly practises. Besides my connection with the syndicate just mentioned, I hold a particular commission from *The Tatler*, whose most prominent department, "Smatter and Chatter" – I daresay you've often enjoyed it – attracts such attention. I was honoured only last week, as a representative of *The Tatler*, with the confidence of Guy Walsingham, the author of "Obsessions". She expressed herself thoroughly pleased with my sketch of her method; she went so far as to say that I had made her genius more comprehensible even to herself.'

Neil Paraday had dropped upon the garden-bench and sat there at once detached and confused; he looked hard at a bare spot in the lawn, as if with an anxiety that had suddenly made him grave. His movement had been interpreted by his visitor as an invitation to sink sympathetically into a wicker chair that stood hard by, and as Mr Morrow so settled himself I felt that he had taken official possession and that there was no undoing it. One had heard of unfortunate people's having 'a man in the house', and this was just what we had. There was a silence of a moment, during which we seemed to acknowledge in the only way that was possible the presence of universal fate; the sunny stillness took no pity, and my thought, as I was sure Paraday's was doing, performed within the minute a great distant revolution. I saw just how emphatic I should make my rejoinder to Mr Pinhorn, and that having come, like Mr Morrow, to betray, I must remain as long as possible to save. Not because I had brought my mind back, but because our visitor's last words were in my ear, I presently inquired with gloomy irrelevance if Guy Walsingham were a woman.

'Oh yes, a mere pseudonym; but convenient, you know, for a lady who goes in for the larger latitude. "Obsessions, by Miss So-and-so" would look a little odd, but men are more naturally indelicate. Have you peeped into "Obsessions"?' Mr Morrow continued sociably to our companion.

Paraday, still absent, remote, made no answer, as if he had not heard the question: a manifestation that appeared to suit the cheerful Mr Morrow as well as any other. Imperturbably bland, he was a man of resources – he only needed to be on the spot. He had pocketed the whole poor place while Paraday and I were woolgathering, and I could imagine that he had already got his 'heads'. His system, at any rate, was justified by the inevitability with which I replied, to save my friend the trouble: 'Dear, no; he hasn't read it. He doesn't read such things!' I unwarily added.

'Things that are *too* far over the fence, eh?' I was indeed a godsend to Mr Morrow. It was the psychological moment; it determined the appearance of his notebook, which, however, he at first kept slightly behind him, even as the dentist, approaching his victim, keeps the horrible forceps. 'Mr Paraday holds with the good old proprieties – I see!' And thinking of the thirty-seven influential journals, I found myself, as I found poor Paraday, helplessly gazing at the promulgation of this ineptitude. 'There's no point on which distinguished views are so acceptable as on this question – raised perhaps more strikingly than ever by Guy Walsingham – of the permissibility of the larger latitude. I have an appointment, precisely in connection with it, next week, with Dora Forbes, the author of "The Other Way Round", which everybody is talking about. Has Mr Paraday glanced at "The Other Way Round"?' Mr Morrow now frankly appealed to me. I took upon myself to repudiate the supposition, while our companion, still silent, got up nervously and walked away. His visitor paid no heed to his withdrawal; he only opened out the notebook with a more motherly pat. 'Dora Forbes, I gather, takes the ground, the same as Guy Walsingham's, that the larger latitude has simply got to come. He holds that it has got to be squarely faced. Of course his sex makes him a less prejudiced witness. But an authoritative word from Mr Paraday – from the point of view of *his* sex, you know – would go right round the globe. He takes the line that we *haven't* got to face it?'

I was bewildered: it sounded somehow as if there were three sexes. My interlocutor's pencil was poised, my private responsibility great. I simply sat staring, however, and only found presence of mind to say: 'Is this Miss Forbes a gentleman?'

Mr Morrow hesitated an instant, smiling. 'It wouldn't be "Miss" – there's a wife!'

'I mean is she a man?'

'The wife?' – Mr Morrow, for a moment, was as confused as myself. But when I explained that I alluded to Dora Forbes in person he informed me, with visible amusement at my being so out of it, that this was the 'pen-name' of an indubitable male – he had a big red moustache. 'He only assumes a feminine personality because the ladies are such popular favourites. A great deal of interest is felt in this assumption, and there's every prospect of its being widely imitated.' Our host at this moment joined us again, and Mr Morrow remarked invitingly that he should be happy to make a note of any observation the movement in question, the bid for success under a lady's name, might suggest to Mr Paraday. But the poor man, without catching the allusion, excused himself, pleading that, though he was greatly honoured by his visitor's interest, he suddenly felt unwell and should have to take leave of him – have to go and lie down and keep quiet. His young friend might be trusted to answer for him, but he hoped Mr Morrow didn't expect great things even of his young friend. His young friend, at this moment, looked at Neil Paraday with an anxious eye, greatly wondering if he were doomed to be ill again; but Paraday's own kind face met his question reassuringly, seemed to say in a glance intelligible enough: 'Oh, I'm not ill, but I'm scared: get him out of the house as quietly as possible.' Getting news-papermen out of the house was odd business for an emissary of Mr Pinhorn, and I was so exhilarated by the idea of it that I called after him as he left us:

'Read the article in *The Empire*, and you'll soon be all right!'

V

'DELICIOUS MY having come down to tell him of it!' Mr Morrow ejaculated. 'My cab was at the door twenty minutes after *The Empire* had been laid upon my breakfast-table. Now what have you got for me?' he continued, dropping again into his chair, from which, however, the next moment he quickly rose. 'I was shown into the drawing-room, but there must be more to see – his study, his literary sanctum, the little things he has about, or other domestic objects or features. He wouldn't be lying down on his study-table? There's a great interest always felt in the scene of an author's labours. Sometimes we're favoured with very delightful peeps. Dora Forbes showed me all his table-drawers, and almost jammed my hand into one into which I made a dash! I don't ask that of you, but if we could talk things over right there where he sits I feel as if I should get the keynote.'

I had no wish whatever to be rude to Mr Morrow, I was much too initiated not to prefer the safety of other ways; but I had a quick inspiration and I entertained an insurmountable, an almost superstitious objection to his crossing the threshold of my friend's little lonely, shabby, consecrated workshop. 'No, no – we shan't get at his life that way,' I said. 'The way to get at his life is to— But wait a moment!' I broke off and went quickly into the house; then, in three minutes, I reappeared before Mr Morrow with the two volumes of Paraday's new book. 'His life's here,' I went on, 'and I'm so full of this admirable thing that I can't talk of anything else. The artist's life's his work, and this is the place to observe him. What he has to tell us he tells us with *this* perfection. My dear sir, the best interviewer's the best reader.'

Mr Morrow good-humouredly protested. 'Do you mean to say that no other source of information should be open to us?'

'None other till this particular one – by far the most copious – has been quite exhausted. Have you exhausted it, my dear sir? Had you exhausted it when you came down here? It seems to me in our time almost wholly neglected, and something should surely be done to restore its ruined credit. It's the course to which the artist himself at every step, and with such pathetic confidence, refers us. This last book of Mr Paraday's is full of revelations.'

'Revelations?' panted Mr Morrow, whom I had forced again into his chair.

'The only kind that count. It tells you with a perfection that seems to me quite final all the author thinks, for instance, about the advent of the "larger latitude".'

'Where does it do that?' asked Mr Morrow, who had picked up the second volume and was insincerely thumbing it.

'Everywhere – in the whole treatment of his case. Extract the opinion, disengage the answer – those are the real acts of homage.'

Mr Morrow, after a minute, tossed the book away. 'Ah, but you mustn't take me for a reviewer.'

'Heaven forbid I should take you for anything so dreadful! You came down to perform a little act of sympathy, and so, I may confide to you, did I. Let us perform our little act together. These pages overflow with the testimony we want: let us read them and taste them and interpret them. You will of course have perceived for yourself that one scarcely does read Neil Paraday till one reads him aloud; he gives out to the ear an extraordinary quality, and it's only when you expose it confidently to that test that you really get near his style. Take up your book again and let me listen, while you pay it out, to that wonderful fifteenth chapter. If you feel that you can't do it justice, compose yourself to attention while I produce for you – I think I can! – this scarcely less admirable ninth.'

Mr Morrow gave me a straight glance which was as hard as a blow between the eyes; he had turned rather red, and a question had formed itself in his mind which reached my sense as distinctly as if he had uttered it: 'What sort of a damned fool are

The Death of the Lion

you?' Then he got up, gathering together his hat and gloves, buttoning his coat, projecting hungrily all over the place the big transparency of his mask. It seemed to flare over Fleet Street and somehow made the actual spot distressingly humble: there was so little for it to feed on unless he counted the blisters of our stucco or saw his way to do something with the roses. Even the poor roses were common kinds. Presently his eyes fell upon the manuscript from which Paraday had been reading to me and which still lay on the bench. As my own followed them I saw that it looked promising, looked pregnant, as if it gently throbbed with the life the reader had given it. Mr Morrow indulged in a nod toward it and a vague thrust of his umbrella. 'What's that?'

'Oh, it's a plan – a secret.'

'A secret!' There was an instant's silence, and then Mr Morrow made another movement. I may have been mistaken, but it affected me as the translated impulse of the desire to lay hands on the manuscript, and this led me to indulge in a quick anticipatory grab which may very well have seemed ungraceful, or even impertinent, and which at any rate left Mr Paraday's two admirers very erect, glaring at each other while one of them held a bundle of papers well behind him. An instant later Mr Morrow quitted me abruptly, as if he had really carried something off with him. To reassure myself, watching his broad back recede, I only grasped my manuscript the tighter. He went to the back-door of the house, the one he had come out from, but on trying the handle he appeared to find it fastened. So he passed round into the front garden, and by listening intently enough I could presently hear the outer gate close behind him with a bang. I thought again of the thirty-seven influential journals and wondered what would be his revenge. I hasten to add that he was magnanimous: which was just the most dreadful thing he could have been. *The Tatler* published a charming, chatty, familiar account of Mr Paraday's 'Home-life', and on the wings of the thirty-seven influential journals it went, to use Mr Morrow's own expression, right round the globe.

VI

A WEEK LATER, early in May, my glorified friend came up to town, where, it may be veraciously recorded, he was the king of the beasts of the year. No advancement was ever more rapid, no exaltation more complete, no bewilderment more teachable. His book sold but moderately, though the article in *The Empire* had done unwonted wonders for it; but he circulated in person in a manner that the libraries might well have envied. His formula had been found – he was a 'revelation'. His momentary terror had been real, just as mine had been – the overclouding of his passionate desire to be left to finish his work. He was far from unsociable, but he had the finest conception of being let alone that I have ever met. For the time, however, he took his profit where it seemed most to crowd upon him, having in his pocket the portable sophistries about the nature of the artist's task. Observation too was a kind of work and experience a kind of success; London dinners were all material and London ladies were fruitful toil. 'No one has the faintest conception of what I'm trying for,' he said to me, 'and not many have read three pages that I've written; but I must dine with them first – they'll find out why when they've time.' It was rather rude justice, perhaps; but the fatigue had the merit of being a new sort, and the phantasmagoric town was probably after all less of a battle-field than the haunted study. He once told me that he had had no personal life to speak of since his fortieth year, but had had more than was good for him before. London closed the parenthesis and exhibited him in relations; one of the most inevitable of these being that in which he found himself to Mrs Weeks Wimbush, wife of the boundless brewer and proprietress of the universal menagerie. In this establishment, as everybody knows, on occasions when the crush is great, the animals rub shoulders freely with the spectators and the lions sit down for whole evenings with the lambs.

It had been ominously clear to me from the first that in Neil Paraday this lady, who, as all the world agreed, was tremendous fun, considered that she had secured a prime attraction, a creature of almost heraldic oddity. Nothing could exceed her enthusiasm over her capture, and nothing could exceed the confused apprehensions it excited in me. I had an instinctive fear of her which I tried without effect to conceal from her victim, but which I let her perceive with perfect impunity.

Paraday heeded it, but she never did, for her conscience was that of a romping child. She was a blind, violent force, to which I could attach no more idea of responsibility than to the creaking of a sign in the wind. It was difficult to say what she conduced to but to circulation. She was constructed of steel and leather, and all I asked of her for our tractable friend was not to do him to death. He had consented for a time to be of india-rubber, but my thoughts were fixed on the day he should resume his shape or at least get back into his box. It was evidently all right, but I should be glad when it was well over. I had a special fear – the impression was ineffaceable of the hour when, after Mr Morrow's departure, I had found him on the sofa in his study. That pretext of indisposition had not in the least been meant as a snub to the envoy of *The Tatler* – he had gone to lie down in very truth. He had felt a pang of his old pain, the result of the agitation wrought in him by this forcing open of a new period. His old programme, his old ideal even had to be changed. Say what one would, success was a complication and recognition had to be reciprocal. The monastic life, the pious illumination of the missal in the convent cell were things of the gathered past. It didn't engender despair, but it at least required adjustment. Before I left him on that occasion we had passed a bargain, my part of which was that I should make it my business to take care of him. Let whoever would represent the interest in his presence (I had a mystical prevision of Mrs Weeks Wimbush), I should represent the interest in his work – in other words in his absence. These two interests were in their essence opposed; and I doubt, as youth is fleeting, if I shall ever again know the intensity of joy with which I felt that in so good a cause I was willing to make myself odious.

One day, in Sloane Street, I found myself questioning Paraday's landlord, who had come to the door in answer to my knock. Two vehicles, a barouche and a smart hansom, were drawn up before the house.

'In the drawing-room, sir? Mrs Weeks Wimbush.'

'And in the dining-room?'

'A young lady, sir – waiting: I think a foreigner.'

It was three o'clock, and on days when Paraday didn't lunch out he attached a value to these subjugated hours. On which days, however, didn't the dear man lunch out? Mrs Wimbush, at such a crisis, would have rushed round immediately after her own repast. I went into the dining-room first, postponing the pleasure of seeing how, upstairs, the lady of the barouche would, on my arrival, point the moral of my sweet solicitude. No one took such an interest as herself in his doing only what was good for him, and she was always on the spot to see that he did it. She made appointments with him to discuss the best means of economizing his time and protecting his privacy. She further made his health her special business, and had so much sympathy with my own zeal for it that she was the author of pleasing fictions on the subject of what my devotion had led me to give up. I gave up nothing (I don't count Mr Pinhorn) because I had nothing, and all I had as yet achieved was to find myself also in the menagerie. I had dashed in to save my friend, but I had only got domesticated and wedged; so that I could do nothing for him but exchange with him over people's heads looks of intense but futile intelligence.

VII

THE YOUNG LADY in the dining-room had a brave face, black hair, blue eyes, and in her lap a big volume. 'I've come for his autograph,' she said when I had explained to her that I was under bonds to see people for him when he was occupied. 'I've been waiting half an hour, but I'm prepared to wait all day.' I don't know whether it was this that told me she was American, for the propensity to wait all day is not in general characteristic of her race. I was enlightened probably not so much by the spirit of the utterance as by some quality of its sound. At any rate I saw she had an individual patience and a lovely frock, together with an expression that played among her pretty features like a breeze among flowers. Putting her book upon the table, she showed me a massive album, showily bound and full of autographs of price. The collection of faded notes, of still more faded 'thoughts', of quotations, platitudes, signatures, represented a formidable purpose.

'Most people apply to Mr Paraday by letter, you know,' I said.

'Yes, but he doesn't answer. I've written three times.'

'Very true,' I reflected; 'the sort of letter you mean goes straight into the fire.'

'How do you know the sort I mean?' My interlocutress had blushed and smiled, and in a moment she added: 'I don't believe he gets many like them!'

'I'm sure they're beautiful, but he burns without reading.' I didn't add that I had told him he ought to.

'Isn't he then in danger of burning things of importance?'

'He would be, if distinguished men hadn't an infallible nose for nonsense.'

She looked at me a moment – her face was sweet and gay. 'Do *you* burn without reading, too?' she asked; in answer to which I assured her that if she would trust me with her repository I would see that Mr Paraday should write his name in it.

She considered a little. 'That's very well, but it wouldn't make me see him.'

'Do you want very much to see him?' It seemed ungracious to catechize so charming a creature, but somehow I had never yet taken my duty to the great author so seriously.

'Enough to have come from America for the purpose.'

I stared. 'All alone?'

'I don't see that that's exactly your business; but if it will make me more appealing I'll confess that I'm quite by myself. I had to come alone or not come at all.'

She was interesting; I could imagine that she had lost parents, natural protectors – could conceive even that she had inherited money. I was in a phase of my own fortune when keeping hansoms at doors seemed to me pure swagger. As a trick of this bold and sensitive girl, however, it became romantic – a part of the general romance of her freedom, her errand, her innocence. The confidence of young Americans was notorious, and I speedily arrived at a conviction that no impulse could have been more generous than the impulse that had operated here. I foresaw at that moment that it would make her my peculiar charge, just as circumstances had made Neil Paraday. She would be another person to look after, and one's honour would be concerned in guiding her straight. These things became clearer to me later; at the instant I had scepticism enough to observe to her, as I turned the pages of her volume, that her net had, all the same, caught many a big fish. She appeared to have had fruitful access to the great ones of the earth; there were people moreover whose signatures she had presumably secured without a personal interview. She couldn't have worried George Washington and Friedrich Schiller and Hannah More. She met this argument, to my surprise, by throwing up the album without a pang. It wasn't even her own; she was responsible for none of its treasures. It belonged to a girl-friend in America, a young lady in a western city. This young lady had insisted on her bringing it, to pick up more autographs: she thought they might like to see, in Europe, in what company they would be. The 'girl-friend', the western city, the immortal names, the curious errand, the idyllic faith, all made a story as strange to me, and as beguiling, as some tale in *The Arabian Nights*. Thus it was that my informant had encumbered herself with the ponderous tome; but she hastened to assure me that this was the first time she had brought it out. For her visit to Mr Paraday it had simply been a pretext. She didn't really care a straw that he should write his name; what she did want was to look straight into his face.

I demurred a little. 'And why do you require to do that?'

'Because I just love him!' Before I could recover from the agitating effect of this crystal ring my companion had continued: 'Hasn't there ever been any face that you've wanted to look into?'

How could I tell her so soon how much I appreciated the opportunity of looking into hers? I could only assent in general to the proposition that there were certainly for everyone such hankerings, and even such faces; and I felt that the crisis demanded all my lucidity, all my wisdom. 'Oh, yes, I'm a student of physiognomy. Do you mean,' I pursued, 'that you've a passion for Mr Paraday's books?'

'They've been everything to me and a little more beside – I know them by heart. They've completely taken hold of me. There's no author about whom I feel as I do about Neil Paraday.'

'Permit me to remark then,' I presently rejoined, 'that you're one of the right sort.'

'One of the enthusiasts? Of course I am!'

'Oh, there are enthusiasts who are quite of the wrong. I mean you're one of those to whom an appeal can be made.'

'An appeal?' Her face lighted as if with the chance of some great sacrifice.

If she was ready for one it was only waiting for her, and in a moment I mentioned it. 'Give up this crude purpose of seeing him. Go away without it. That will be far better.'

She looked mystified; then she turned visibly pale. 'Why, hasn't he any personal charm?' The girl was terrible and laughable in her bright directness.

'Ah, that dreadful word "personal"!' I exclaimed; 'we're dying of it, and you women bring it out with murderous effect. When you encounter a genius as fine as this idol of ours, let him off the dreary duty of being a personality as well. Know him only by what's best in him, and spare him for the same sweet sake.'

My young lady continued to look at me in confusion and mistrust, and the result of her reflection on what I had just said was to make her suddenly break out: 'Look here, sir – what's the matter with him?'

'The matter with him is that, if he doesn't look out, people will eat a great hole in his life.'

She considered a moment. 'He hasn't any disfigurement?'

'Nothing to speak of!'

'Do you mean that social engagements interfere with his occupations?'

'That but feebly expresses it.'

'So that he can't give himself up to his beautiful imagination?'

'He's badgered, bothered, overwhelmed, on the pretext of being applauded. People expect him to give them his time, his golden time, who wouldn't themselves give five shillings for one of his books.'

'Five? I'd give five thousand!'

'Give your sympathy – give your forbearance. Two-thirds of those who approach him only do it to advertise themselves.'

'Why, it's too bad!' the girl exclaimed with the face of an angel. 'It's the first time I was ever called crude!' she laughed.

I followed up my advantage. 'There's a lady with him now who's a terrible complication, and who yet hasn't read, I am sure, ten pages that he ever wrote.'

My visitor's wide eyes grew tenderer. 'Then how does she talk—?'

'Without ceasing. I only mention her as a single case. Do you want to know how to show a superlative consideration? Simply avoid him.'

'Avoid him?' she softly wailed.

'Don't force him to have to take account of you; admire him in silence, cultivate him at a distance and secretly appropriate his message. Do you want to know,' I continued, warming to my idea, 'how to perform an act of homage really sublime?' Then as she hung on my words: 'Succeed in never seeing him at all!'

'Never at all?' she pathetically gasped.

'The more you get into his writings the less you'll want to; and you'll be immensely sustained by the thought of the good you're doing him.'

She looked at me without resentment or spite, and at the truth I had put before her with candour, credulity, pity. I was afterwards happy to remember that she must have recognized in my face the liveliness of my interest in herself. 'I think I see what you mean.'

'Oh, I express it badly; but I should be delighted if you would let me come to see you – to explain it better.'

She made no response to this, and her thoughtful eyes fell on the big album, on which she presently laid her hands as if to take it away. 'I did use to say out West that they might write a little less for autographs (to all the great poets, you know) and study the thoughts and style a little more.'

'What do they care for the thoughts and style? They didn't even understand you. I'm not sure,' I added, 'that I do myself, and I daresay that you by no means make me out.' She had got up to go, and though I wanted her to succeed in not seeing Neil Paraday I wanted her also, inconsequently, to remain in the house. I was at any rate far from desiring to hustle her off. As Mrs Weeks Wimbush, upstairs, was still saving our friend in her own way, I asked my young lady to let me briefly relate, in illustration of my point, the little incident of my having gone down into the country for a profane purpose and been converted on the spot to holiness. Sinking again into her chair to listen, she showed a deep interest in the anecdote. Then thinking it over gravely, she exclaimed with her odd intonation:

'Yes, but you do see him!' I had to admit that this was the case; and I was not so prepared with an effective attenuation as I could have wished. She eased the situation off, however, by the charming quaintness with which she finally said: 'Well, I wouldn't want him to be lonely!' This time she rose in earnest, but I persuaded her to let me keep the album to show to Mr Paraday. I assured her I would bring it back to her myself. 'Well, you'll find my address somewhere in it, on a paper!' she sighed resignedly, at the door.

VIII

I BLUSH TO confess it, but I invited Mr Paraday that very day to transcribe into the album one of his most characteristic passages. I told him how I had got rid of the strange girl who had brought it — her ominous name was Miss Hurter, and she lived at an hotel; quite agreeing with him moreover as to the wisdom of getting rid with equal promptitude of the book itself. This was why I carried it to Albemarle Street no later than on the morrow. I failed to find her at home, but she wrote to me and I went again: she wanted so much to hear more about Neil Paraday. I returned repeatedly, I may briefly declare, to supply her with this information. She had been immensely taken, the more she thought of it, with that idea of mine about the act of homage: it had ended by filling her with a generous rapture. She positively desired to do something sublime for him, though indeed I could see that, as this particular flight was difficult, she appreciated the fact that my visits kept her up. I had it on my conscience to keep her up; I neglected nothing that would contribute to it, and her conception of our cherished author's independence became at last as fine as his own conception. 'Read him, read him,' I constantly repeated; while, seeking him in his works, she represented herself as convinced that, according to my assurance, this was the system that had, as she expressed it, weaned her. We read him together when I could find time, and the generous creature's sacrifice was fed by our conversation. There were twenty selfish women, about whom I told her, who stirred her with a beautiful rage. Immediately after my first visit her sister, Mrs Milsom, came over from Paris, and the two ladies began to present, as they called it, their letters. I thanked our stars that none had been presented to Mr Paraday. They received invitations and dined out, and some of these occasions enabled Fanny Hurter to perform, for consistency's sake, touching feats of submission. Nothing indeed would now have induced her even to look at the object of her admiration. Once, hearing his name announced at a party, she instantly left the room by another door and then straightway quitted the house. At another time, when I was at the opera with them (Mrs Milsom had invited me to their box) I attempted to point Mr Paraday out to her in the stalls. On this she asked her sister to change places with her, and while that lady devoured the great man through a powerful glass, presented, all the rest of the evening, her inspired back to the house. To torment her tenderly I pressed the glass upon her, telling her how wonderfully near it brought our friend's handsome head. By way of answer she simply looked at me in charged silence, letting me see that tears had gathered in her eyes. These tears, I may remark, produced an effect on me of which the end is not yet. There was a moment when I felt it my duty to mention them to Neil Paraday; but I was deterred by the reflection that there were questions more relevant to his happiness.

These questions indeed, by the end of the season, were reduced to a single one – the question of reconstituting, so far as might be possible, the conditions under which he had produced his best work. Such conditions could never all come back, for there was a new one that took up too much place; but some perhaps were not beyond recall. I wanted above all things to see him sit down to the subject of which, on my making his acquaintance, he had read me that admirable sketch. Something told me there was no security but in his doing so before the new factor, as we used to say at Mr Pinhorn's, should render the problem incalculable. It only half reassured me that the sketch itself was so copious and so eloquent that even at the worst there would be the making of a small but complete book, a tiny volume which, for the faithful, might well become an object of adoration. There would even not be wanting critics to declare, I foresaw, that the plan was a thing to be more thankful for than the structure to have been reared on it. My impatience for the structure, none the less, grew and grew with the interruptions. He had, on coming up to town, begun to sit for his portrait to a young painter, Mr Rumble, whose little game, as we also used to say at Mr Pinhorn's, was to be the first to perch on the shoulders of renown. Mr Rumble's studio was a circus in which the man of the hour, and still more the woman, leaped through the hoops of his showy frames almost as electrically as they burst into telegrams and 'specials'. He pranced into the exhibitions on their back; he was the reporter on canvas, the Van Dyck up to date, and there was one roaring year in which Mrs Bounder and Miss Braby, Guy Walsingham and Dora Forbes proclaimed in chorus from the same pictured walls that no one had yet got ahead of him.

Paraday had been promptly caught and saddled, accepting with characteristic good-humour his confidential hint that to figure in his show was not so much a consequence as a cause of immortality. From Mrs Wimbush to the last 'representative' who called to ascertain his twelve favourite dishes, it was the same ingenuous assumption that he would rejoice in the repercussion. There were moments when I fancied I might have had more patience with them if they had not been so fatally benevolent. I hated, at all events, Mr Rumble's picture, and had my bottled resentment ready when, later on, I found my distracted friend had been stuffed by Mrs Wimbush into the mouth of another cannon. A young artist in whom she was intensely interested, and who had no connection with Mr Rumble, was to show how far he could make him go. Poor Paraday, in return, was naturally to write something somewhere about the young artist. She played her victims against each other with admirable ingenuity, and her establishment was a huge machine in which the tiniest and the biggest wheels went round to the same treadle. I had a scene with her in which I tried to express that the function of such a man was to exercise his genius – not to serve as a hoarding for pictorial posters. The people I was perhaps angriest with were the editors of magazines who had introduced what they called new features, so aware were they that the newest feature of all would be to make him grind their axes by contributing his views on vital topics and taking part in the periodical prattle about the future of fiction. I made sure that before I should have done with him there would scarcely be a current form of words left me to be sick of; but meanwhile I could make surer still of my animosity to bustling ladies for whom he drew the water that irrigated their social flower-beds.

I had a battle with Mrs Wimbush over the artist she protected, and another over the question of a certain week, at the end of July, that Mr Paraday appeared to have contracted to spend with her in the country. I protested against this visit; I intimated that he was too unwell for hospitality without a *nuance*, for caresses without imagination; I begged he might rather take the time in some restorative way. A sultry air of promises, of ponderous parties, hung over his August, and he would greatly profit by the interval of rest. He had not told me he was ill again – that he had had a warning; but I had not needed this, and I found his reticence his worst symptom. The only thing he said to me was that he believed a comfortable attack of something or other would set him up; it would put out of the question everything but the exemptions he prized. I am afraid I shall have presented him as a martyr in a very small cause if I fail to explain that he surrendered himself much more liberally than I surrendered him. He filled his lungs, for the most part, with the comedy of his queer fate: the tragedy was in the spectacles through which I chose to look. He was conscious of inconvenience, and above all of a great renouncement; but how could he have heard a mere dirge in the bells of his accession? The sagacity and the jealousy were mine, and his the impressions and the anecdotes. Of course, as regards Mrs Wimbush, I was worsted in my encounters, for was not the state of his health the very reason for his coming to her at Prestidge? Wasn't it precisely at Prestidge that he was to be coddled, and wasn't the dear Princess coming to help her to coddle him? The dear Princess, now on a visit to England, was of a famous foreign house, and, in her gilded cage, with her retinue of keepers and feeders, was the most expensive specimen in the good lady's collection. I don't think her august presence had had to do with Paraday's consenting to go, but it is not impossible that he had operated as a bait to the illustrious stranger. The party had been made up for him, Mrs Wimbush averred, and everyone was counting on it, the dear Princess most of all. If he was well enough he was to read them something absolutely fresh, and it was on that particular prospect the Princess had set her heart. She was so fond of genius, in *any* walk of life, and she was so used to it, and understood it so well; she was the greatest of Mr Paraday's admirers, she devoured everything he wrote. And then he read like an angel. Mrs Wimbush reminded me that he had again and again given her, Mrs Wimbush, the privilege of listening to him.

I looked at her a moment. 'What has he read to you?' I crudely inquired.

For a moment too she met my eyes, and for the fraction of a moment she hesitated and coloured. 'Oh, all sorts of things!'

I wondered whether this were an imperfect recollection or only a perfect fib, and she quite understood my unuttered comment on her perception of such things. But if she could orget Neil Paraday's beauties she could of course forget my rudeness, and three days later she invited me, by telegraph, to join the party at Prestidge. This time she might indeed have had a story about what I had given up to be near the master. I addressed from that fine residence several communications to a young lady in London, a young lady whom, I confess, I quitted with reluctance and whom the reminder of what she herself could give up was required to make me quit at all. It adds to the gratitude I owe her on other grounds that she kindly allows me to transcribe from my letters a few of the passages in which that hateful sojourn is candidly commemorated.

IX

'I SUPPOSE I ought to enjoy the joke of what's going on here,' I wrote, 'but somehow it doesn't amuse me. Pessimism on the contrary possesses me and cynicism solicits. I positively feel my own flesh sore from the brass nails in Neil Paraday's social harness. The house is full of people who like him, as they mention, awfully, and with whom his talent for talking nonsense has prodigious success. I delight in his nonsense myself; why is it therefore that I grudge these happy folk their artless satisfaction? Mystery of the human heart – abyss of the critical spirit! Mrs Wimbush thinks she can answer that question, and as my want of gaiety has at last worn out her patience she has given me a glimpse of her shrewd guess. I am made restless by the selfishness of the insincere friend – I want to monopolize Paraday in order that he may push me on. To be intimate with him is a feather in my cap; it gives me an importance that I couldn't naturally pretend to, and I seek to deprive him of social refreshment because I fear that meeting more disinterested people may enlighten him as to my real motive. All the disinterested people here are his particular admirers and have been carefully selected as such. There is supposed to be a copy of his last book in the house, and in the hall I come upon ladies, in attitudes, bending gracefully over the first volume. I discreetly avert my eyes, and when I next look round the precarious joy has been superseded by the book of life. There is a sociable circle or a confidential couple, and the relinquished volume lies open on its face, as if it had been dropped under extreme coercion. Somebody else presently finds it and transfers it, with its air of momentary desolation, to another piece of furniture. Everyone is asking everyone about it all day, and everyone is telling everyone where they put it last. I'm sure it's rather smudgy about the twentieth page. I have a strong impression too that the second volume is lost – has been packed in the bag of some departing guest; and yet everybody has the impression that somebody else has read to the end. You see therefore that the beautiful book plays a great part in our conversation. Why should I take the occasion of such distinguished honours to say that I begin to see deeper into Gustave Flaubert's doleful refrain about the hatred of literature? I refer you again to the perverse constitution of man.

'The Princess is a massive lady with the organization of an athlete and the confusion of tongues of a *valet de place*. She contrives to commit herself extraordinarily little in a great many languages, and is entertained and conversed with in detachments and relays, like an institution which goes on from generation to generation or a big building contracted for under a forfeit. She can't have a personal taste any more than, when her husband succeeds, she can have a personal crown, and her opinion on any matter is rusty and heavy and plain – made, in the night of ages, to last and be transmitted. I feel as if I ought to pay someone a fee for my glimpse of it. She has been told everything in the world and has never perceived anything, and the echoes of her education respond awfully to the rash footfall – I mean the casual remark – in the cold Valhalla of her memory. Mrs Wimbush delights in her wit and says there is nothing so charming as to hear Mr Paraday draw it out. He is perpetually detailed for this job, and he tells me it has a peculiarly exhausting effect. Everyone is beginning – at the end of two days – to sidle obsequiously away from her, and Mrs Wimbush pushes him again and again into the breach. None of the uses I have yet seen him put to irritate me quite so much. He looks very fagged, and has at last confessed to me that his condition makes him uneasy – has even promised me that he will go straight home instead of returning to his final engagements in town. Last night I had some talk with him about going today, cutting his visit short; so sure am I that he will be better as soon as he is shut up in his lighthouse. He told me that this is what he would like to do; reminding me, however, that the first lesson of his greatness has been precisely that he can't do what he likes. Mrs Wimbush would never forgive him if he should leave her before the Princess has received the last hand. When I say that a violent rupture with our hostess would be the best thing in the world for him he gives me to understand that if his reason assents to the proposition his courage hangs woefully back. He makes no secret of being mortally afraid of her, and when I ask what harm she can do him that she hasn't already done he simply repeats: "I'm afraid, I'm afraid! Don't inquire too closely," he said last night; "only believe that I feel a sort of terror. It's strange, when she's so kind! At any rate, I would as soon overturn that piece of priceless Sèvres as tell her that I must go before my date." It sounds dreadfully weak, but he has some reason, and he pays for his imagination, which puts him (I should hate it) in the place of others and makes him feel, even against himself, their feelings, their appetites, their motives. It's indeed inveterately against himself that he makes his imagination act. What a pity he has such a lot of it! He's too beastly intelligent. Besides, the famous reading is still to come off, and it has been postponed a day, to allow Guy Walsingham to arrive. It appears that this eminent lady is staying at a house a few miles off, which means of course that Mrs Wimbush has forcibly annexed her. She's to come over in a day or two – Mrs Wimbush wants her to hear Mr Paraday.

'Today's wet and cold, and several of the company, at the invitation of the Duke, have driven over to luncheon at Bigwood. I saw poor Paraday wedge himself, by command, into the little supplementary seat of a brougham in which the Princess and our hostess were already ensconced. If the front glass isn't open on his dear old back perhaps he'll survive. Bigwood, I believe, is very grand and frigid, all marble and precedence, and I wish him well out of the adventure. I can't tell you how much more and more *your* attitude to him, in the midst of all this, shines out by contrast. I never willingly talk to these people about him, but see what a comfort I find it to scribble to you! I appreciate it – it keeps me warm; there are no fires in the house. Mrs Wimbush goes by the calendar, the temperature goes by the weather, the weather goes by God knows what, and the Princess is easily heated. I have nothing but my acrimony to warm me, and have been out under an umbrella to restore my circulation. Coming in an hour ago, I found Lady Augusta Minch rummaging about the hall. When I asked her what she was looking for she said she had mislaid something that Mr Paraday had lent her. I ascertained in a moment that the article in question is a manuscript, and I have a foreboding that it's the noble morsel he read me six weeks ago. When I expressed my surprise that he should have bandied about anything so precious (I happen to know it's his only copy – in the most beautiful hand in all the world) Lady Augusta confessed to me that she had not had it from himself, but from Mrs Wimbush, who had wished to give her a glimpse of it as a salve for her not being able to stay and hear it read.

'"Is that the piece he's to read," I asked, "when Guy Walsingham arrives?"

'"It's not for Guy Walsingham they're waiting now, it's for Dora Forbes," Lady Augusta said. "She's coming, I believe, early tomorrow. Meanwhile Mrs Wimbush has found out about *him*, and is actively wiring to him. She says he also must hear him."

'"You bewilder me a little," I replied; "in the age we live in one gets lost among the genders and the pronouns. The clear thing is that Mrs Wimbush doesn't guard such a treasure as jealously as she might."

'"Poor dear, she has the Princess to guard! Mr Paraday lent her the manuscript to look over."

'"Did she speak as if it were the morning paper?"

'Lady Augusta stared – my irony was lost upon her. "She didn't have time, so she gave me a chance first; because unfortunately I go tomorrow to Bigwood."

'"And your chance has only proved a chance to lose it?"

'"I haven't lost it. I remember now – it was very stupid of me to have forgotten. I told my maid to give it to Lord Dorimont – or at least to his man."

'"And Lord Dorimont went away directly after luncheon."

'"Of course he gave it back to my maid – or else his man did," said Lady Augusta. "I daresay it's all right."

'The conscience of these people is like a summer sea. They haven't time to "look over" a priceless composition; they've only time to kick it about the house. I suggested that the "man", fired with a noble emulation, had perhaps kept the work for his own perusal; and her ladyship wanted to know whether, if the thing didn't turn up again in time for the session appointed by our hostess, the author wouldn't have something else to read that would do just as well. Their questions are too delightful! I declared to Lady Augusta briefly that nothing in the world can ever do so well as the thing that does best; and at this she looked a little confused and scared. But I added that if the manuscript had gone astray our little circle would have the less of an effort of attention to make. The piece in question was very long – it would keep them three hours.

'"Three hours! Oh, the Princess will get up!" said Lady Augusta.

'"I thought she was Mr Paraday's greatest admirer."

'"I daresay she is – she's so awfully clever. But what's the use of being a Princess—"

'"If you can't dissemble your love?" I asked, as Lady Augusta was vague. She said, at any rate, that she would question her maid; and I am hoping that when I go down to dinner I shall find the manuscript has been recovered.'

X

'IT HAS NOT been recovered,' I wrote early the next day, 'and I am moreover much troubled about our friend. He came back from Bigwood with a chill and, being allowed to have a fire in his room, lay down awhile before dinner. I tried to send him to bed, and indeed thought I had put him in the way of it; but after I had gone to dress Mrs Wimbush came up to see him, with the inevitable result that when I returned I found him under arms and flushed and feverish, though decorated with the rare flower she had brought him for his button-hole. He came down to dinner, but Lady Augusta Minch was very shy of him. Today he's in great pain, and the advent of *ces dames* – I mean of Guy Walsingham and Dora Forbes – doesn't at all console me. It does Mrs Wimbush, however, for she has consented to his remaining in bed, so that he may be all right tomorrow for the listening circle. Guy Walsingham is already on the scene, and the doctor, for Paraday, also arrived early. I haven't yet seen the author of "Obsessions", but of course I've had a moment by myself with the doctor. I tried to get him to say that our invalid must go straight home – I mean tomorrow or next day; but he quite refuses to talk about the future. Absolute quiet and warmth and the regular administration of an important remedy are the points he mainly insists on. He returns this afternoon, and I'm to go back to see the patient at one o'clock, when he next takes his medicine. It consoles me a little that he certainly won't be able to read – an exertion he was already more than unfit for. Lady Augusta went off after breakfast, assuring me that her first care would be to follow up the lost manuscript. I can see she thinks me a shocking busybody and doesn't understand my alarm, but she will do what she can, for she's a good-natured woman. "So are they all honourable men." That was precisely what made her give the thing to Lord Dorimont and made Lord Dorimont bag it. What use *he* has for it God only knows. I have the worst forebodings, but somehow I'm strangely without passion – desperately calm. As I consider the unconscious, the well-meaning ravages of our appreciative circle I bow my head in submission to some great natural, some universal accident; I'm rendered almost indifferent, in fact quite gay (ha-ha!) by the sense of immitigable fate. Lady Augusta promises me to trace the precious object and let me have it, through the post, by the time Paraday is well enough to play his part with it. The last evidence is that her maid did give it to his lordship's valet. One would think it was some thrilling number of *The Family Budget*. Mrs Wimbush, who is aware of the accident, is much less agitated by it than she would doubtless be were she not for the hour inevitably engrossed with Guy Walsingham.'

Later in the day I informed my correspondent, for whom indeed I kept a sort of diary of the situation, that I had made the acquaintance of this celebrity and that she was a pretty little girl who wore her hair in what used to be called a crop. She looked so juvenile and so innocent that if, as Mr Morrow had announced, she was resigned to the larger latitude, her superiority to prejudice must have come to her early. I spent most of the day hovering about Neil Paraday's room, but it was communicated to me from below that Guy Walsingham, at Prestidge, was a success. Towards evening I became conscious somehow that her superiority was contagious, and by the time the company separated for the night I was sure that the larger latitude had been generally accepted. I thought of Dora Forbes and felt that he had no time to lose. Before dinner I received a telegram from Lady Augusta Minch. *'Lord Dorimont thinks he must have left bundle in train – inquire.'* How could I inquire – if I was to take the word as command? I was too worried and now too alarmed about Neil Paraday. The doctor came back, and it was an immense satisfaction to me to feel that he was wise and inter-ested. He was proud of being called to so distinguished a patient, but he admitted to me that night that my friend was gravely ill. It was really a relapse, a recrudescence of his old malady. There could be no question of moving him: we must at any rate see first, on the spot, what turn his condition would take. Meanwhile, on the morrow, he was to have a nurse. On the morrow the dear man was easier, and my spirits rose to such cheerfulness that I could almost laugh over Lady Augusta's second telegram: *'Lord Dorimont's servant been to station – nothing found. Push inquiries.'* I did laugh, I am sure, as I remembered this to be the mystic scroll I had scarcely allowed poor Mr Morrow to point his umbrella at. Fool that I had been: the thirty-seven influential journals wouldn't have destroyed it, they would only have printed it. Of course I said nothing to Paraday.

When the nurse arrived she turned me out of the room, on which I went downstairs. I should premise that at breakfast the news that our brilliant friend was doing well excited universal complacency, and the Princess graciously remarked that he was only to be commiserated for missing the society of Miss Collop. Mrs Wimbush, whose social gift never shone brighter than in the dry decorum with which she accepted this fizzle in her fireworks, mentioned to me that Guy Walsingham had made a very favourable impression on her Imperial Highness. Indeed I think everyone did so, and that, like the money-market or the national honour, her Imperial Highness was constitutionally sensitive. There was a certain gladness, a perceptible bustle in the air, however, which I thought slightly anomalous in a house where a great author lay critically ill. '*Le roy est mort – vive le roy*': I was reminded that another great author had already stepped into his shoes. When I came down again after the nurse had taken possession I found a strange gentleman hanging about the hall and pacing to and fro by the closed door of the drawing-room. This personage was florid and bald; he had a big red moustache and wore showy knickerbockers – characteristics all that fitted into my conception of the identity of Dora Forbes. In a moment I saw what had happened: the author of 'The Other Way Round' had just alighted at the portals of Prestidge, but had suffered a scruple to restrain him from penetrating further. I recognized his scruple when, pausing to listen at his gesture of caution, I heard a shrill voice lifted in a sort of rhythmic, uncanny chant. The famous reading had begun, only it was the author of

'Obsessions' who now furnished the sacrifice. The new visitor whispered to me that he judged something was going on that he oughtn't to interrupt.

'Miss Collop arrived last night,' I smiled, 'and the Princess has a thirst for the *inédit*.'

Dora Forbes lifted his bushy brows. 'Miss Collop?'

'Guy Walsingham, your distinguished *confrère* – or shall I say your formidable rival?'

'Oh!' growled Dora Forbes. Then he added: 'Shall I spoil it if I go in?'

'I should think nothing could spoil it!' I ambiguously laughed.

Dora Forbes evidently felt the dilemma; he gave an irritated crook to his moustache. '*Shall* I go in?' he presently asked.

We looked at each other hard a moment; then I expressed something bitter that was in me, expressed it in an infernal 'Do!' After this I got out into the air, but not so fast as not to hear, when the door of the drawing-room opened, the disconcerted drop of Miss Collop's public manner: she must have been in the midst of the larger latitude. Producing with extreme rapidity, Guy Walsingham has just published a work in which amiable people who are not initiated have been pained to see the genius of a sister-novelist held up to unmistakable ridicule; so fresh an exhibition does it seem to them of the dreadful way men have always treated women. Dora Forbes, it is true, at the present hour, is immensely pushed by Mrs Wimbush, and has sat for his portrait to the young artists she protects, sat for it not only in oils but in monumental alabaster.

What happened at Prestidge later in the day is of course contemporary history. If the interruption I had whimsically sanctioned was almost a scandal, what is to be said of that general dispersal of the company which, under the doctor's rule, began to take place in the evening? His rule was soothing to behold, small comfort as I was to have at the end. He decreed in the interest of his patient an absolutely soundless house and a consequent break-up of the party. Little country practitioner as he was, he literally packed off the Princess. She departed as promptly as if a revolution had broken out, and Guy Walsingham emigrated with her. I was kindly permitted to remain, and this was not denied even to Mrs Wimbush. The privilege was withheld indeed from Dora Forbes; so Mrs Wimbush kept her latest capture temporarily concealed. This was so little, however, her usual way of dealing with her eminent friends that a couple of days of it exhausted her patience, and she went up to town with him in great publicity. The sudden turn for the worse her afflicted guest had, after a brief improvement, taken on the third night raised an obstacle to her seeing him before her retreat; a fortunate circumstance doubtless, for she was fundamentally disappointed in him. This was not the kind of performance for which she had invited him to Prestidge, or invited the Princess. Let me hasten to add that none of the generous acts which have characterized her patronage of intellectual and other merit have done so much for her reputation as her lending Neil Paraday the most beautiful of her numerous homes to die in. He took advantage to the utmost of the singular favour. Day by day I saw him sink, and I roamed alone about the empty terraces and gardens. His wife never came near him, but I scarcely noticed it: as I paced there with rage in my heart I was too full of another wrong. In the event of his death it would fall to me perhaps to bring out in some charming form, with notes, with the tenderest editorial care, that precious heritage of his written project. But where *was* that precious heritage, and were both the author and the book to have been snatched from us? Lady Augusta wrote me that she had done all she could and that poor Lord Dorimont, who had really been worried to death, was extremely sorry. I couldn't have the matter out with Mrs Wimbush, for I didn't want to be taunted by her with desiring to aggrandize myself by a public connection with Mr Paraday's sweepings. She had signified her willingness to meet the expense of all advertising, as indeed she was always ready to do. The last night of the horrible series, the night before he died, I put my ear closer to his pillow.

'That thing I read you that morning, you know.'

'In your garden that dreadful day? Yes!'

'Won't it do as it is?'

'It would have been a glorious book.'

'It *is* a glorious book,' Neil Paraday murmured. 'Print it as it stands — beautifully.'

'Beautifully!' I passionately promised.

It may be imagined whether, now that he is gone, the promise seems to me less sacred. I am convinced that if such pages had appeared in his lifetime the Abbey would hold him today. I have kept the advertising in my own hands, but the manuscript has not been recovered. It's impossible, and at any rate intolerable, to suppose it can have been wantonly destroyed. Perhaps some hazard of a blind hand, some brutal ignorance has lighted kitchen-fires with it. Every stupid and hideous accident haunts my meditations. My undiscourageable search for the lost treasure would make a long chapter. Fortunately I have a devoted associate in the person of a young lady who has every day a fresh indignation and a fresh idea, and who maintains with intensity that the prize will still turn up. Sometimes I believe her, but I have quite ceased to believe myself. The only thing for us, at all events, is to go on seeking and hoping together; and we should be closely united by this firm tie even were we not at present by another.

The Altar of the Dead

I

H E HAD A MORTAL dislike, poor Stransom, to lean anniversaries, and he disliked them still more when they made a pretence of a figure. Celebrations and suppressions were equally painful to him, and there was only one of the former that found a place in his life. Again and again he had kept in his own fashion the day of the year on which Mary Antrim died. It would be more to the point perhaps to say that the day kept *him*: it kept him at least, effectually, from doing anything else. It took hold of him year after year with a hand of which time had softened but had never loosened the touch. He waked up to this feast of memory as consciously as he would have waked up to his marriage-morn. Marriage had had, of old, but too little to say to the matter: for the girl who was to have been his bride there had been no bridal embrace. She had died of a malignant fever after the wedding-day had been fixed, and he had lost, before fairly tasting it, an affection that promised to fill his life to the brim.

Of that benediction, however, it would have been false to say this life could really be emptied: it was still ruled by a pale ghost, it was still ordered by a sovereign presence. He had not been a man of numerous passions, and even in all these years no sense had grown stronger with him than the sense of being bereft. He had needed no priest and no altar to make him for ever widowed. He had done many things in the world – he had done almost all things but one: he had never forgotten. He had tried to put into his existence whatever else might take up room in it, but he had never made it anything but a house of which the mistress was eternally absent. She was most absent of all on the recurrent December day that his tenacity set apart. He had no designed observance of it, but his nerves made it all their own. They always drove him forth on a long walk, for the goal of his pilgrimage was far. She had been buried in a London suburb, in a place then almost natural, but which he had seen lose one after another every feature of freshness. It was in truth during the moments he stood there that his eyes beheld the place least. They looked at another image, they opened to another light. Was it a credible future? Was it an incredible past? Whatever it was, it was an immense escape from the actual.

It is true that if there were not other dates than this there were other memories; and by the time George Stransom was fifty-five such memories had greatly multiplied. There were other ghosts in his life than the ghost of Mary Antrim. He had perhaps not had more losses than most men, but he had counted his losses more; he had not seen death more closely, but he had, in a manner, felt it more deeply. He had formed little by little the habit of numbering his Dead: it had come to him tolerably early in life that there was something one had to do for them. They were there in their simplified, intensified essence, their conscious absence and expressive patience, as personally there as if they had only been stricken dumb. When all sense of them failed, all sound of them ceased, it was as if their purgatory were really still on earth: they asked so little that they got, poor things, even less, and died again, died every day, of the hard usage of life. They had no organized service, no reserved place, no honour, no shelter, no safety. Even ungenerous people provided for the living, but even those who were called most generous did nothing for the others. So, on George Stransom's part, there grew up with the years a determination that he at least would do something, do it, that is, for his own, and perform the great charity without reproach. Every man had his own, and every man had, to meet this charity, the ample resources of the soul.

It was doubtless the voice of Mary Antrim that spoke for them best; at any rate, as the years went on, he found himself in regular communion with these alternative associates, with those whom indeed he always called in his thoughts the Others. He spared them the moments, he organized the charity. How it grew up he probably never could have told you, but what came to pass was that an altar, such as was after all within everybody's compass, lighted with perpetual candles and dedicated to these secret rites, reared itself in his spiritual spaces. He had wondered of old, in some embarrassment, whether he had a religion; being very sure, and not a little content, that he had not at all events the religion some of the people he had known wanted him to have. Gradually this question was straightened out for him: it became clear to him that the religion instilled by his earliest consciousness had been simply the religion of the Dead. It suited his inclination, it satisfied his spirit, it gave employment to his piety. It answered his love of great offices, of a solemn and splendid ritual, for no shrine could be more bedecked and no ceremonial more stately than those to which his worship was attached. He had no imagination about these things save that they were accessible to everyone who should ever feel the need of them. The poorest could build such temples of the spirit – could make them blaze with candles and smoke with incense, make them flash with pictures and flowers. The cost, in the common phrase, of keeping them up fell entirely on the liberal heart.

II

HE HAD THIS YEAR, on the eve of his anniversary, as it happened, an emotion not unconnected with that range of feeling. Walking home at the close of a busy day, he was arrested in the London street by the particular effect of a shop-front which lighted the dull brown air with its mercenary grin and before which several persons were gathered. It was the window of a jeweller whose diamonds and sapphires seemed to laugh, in flashes like high notes of sound, with the mere joy of knowing how much more they were 'worth' than most of the dingy pedestrians staring at them from the other side of the pane. Stransom lingered long enough to suspend, in a vision, a string of pearls about the white neck of Mary Antrim, and then was kept an instant longer by the sound of a voice he knew. Next him was a mumbling old woman, and beyond the old woman a gentleman with a lady on his arm. It was from him, from Paul Creston, the voice had proceeded: he was talking with the lady of some precious object in the window. Stransom had no sooner recognized him than the old woman turned away; but simultaneously with this increase of opportunity he became aware of a strangeness which stayed him in the very act of laying his hand on his friend's arm. It lasted only a few seconds, but a few seconds were long enough for the flash of a wild question. Was *not* Mrs Creston dead? – the ambiguity met him there in the short drop of her husband's voice, the drop conjugal, if it ever was, and in the way the two figures leaned to each other. Creston, making a step to look at something else, came nearer, glanced at him, started and exclaimed – a circumstance the effect of which was at first only to leave Stransom staring, staring back across the months at the different face, the wholly other face the poor man had shown him last, the blurred, ravaged mask bent over the open grave by which they had stood together. Creston was not in mourning now; he detached his arm from his companion's to grasp the hand of the older friend. He coloured as well as smiled in the strong light of the shop when Stransom raised a tentative hat to the lady. Stransom had just time to see that she was pretty before he found himself gaping at a fact more portentous. 'My dear fellow, let me make you acquainted with my wife.'

Creston had blushed and stammered over it, but in half a minute, at the rate we live in polite society, it had practically become, for Stransom, the mere memory of a shock. They stood there and laughed and talked; Stransom had instantly whisked the shock out of the way, to keep it for private consumption. He felt himself grimacing, he heard himself exaggerating the usual, but he was conscious that he had turned slightly faint. That new woman, that hired performer, Mrs Creston? Mrs Creston had been more living for him than any woman but one. This lady had a face that shone as publicly as the jeweller's window, and in the happy candour with which she wore her monstrous character there was an effect of gross immodesty. The character of Paul Creston's wife thus attributed to her was monstrous for reasons which Stransom could see that his friend perfectly knew that he knew. The happy pair had just arrived from America, and Stransom had not needed to be told this to divine the nationality of the lady. Somehow it deepened the foolish air that her husband's confused cordiality was unable to conceal. Stransom recalled that he had heard of poor Creston's having, while his bereavement was still fresh, gone to the United States for what people in such predicaments call a little change. He had found the little change indeed, he had brought the little change back; it was the little change that stood there and that, do what he would, he couldn't, while he showed those high front-teeth of his, look like anything but a conscious ass about. They were going into the shop Mrs Creston said, and she begged Mr Stransom to come with them and help to decide. He thanked her, opening his watch and pleading an engagement for which he was already late, and they parted while she shrieked into the fog, 'Mind now you come to see me right away!' Creston had had the delicacy not to suggest that, and Stransom hoped it hurt him somewhere to hear her scream it to all the echoes.

He felt quite determined, as he walked away, never in his life to go near her. She was perhaps a human being, but Creston oughtn't to have shown her without precautions, oughtn't indeed to have shown her at all. His precautions should have been those of a forger or a murderer, and the people at home would never have mentioned extradition. This was a wife for foreign service or purely external use; a decent consideration would have spared her the injury of comparisons. Such were the first reflections of George Stransom's amazement; but as he sat alone that night – there were particular hours that he always passed alone – the harshness dropped from them and left only the pity. *He* could spend an evening with Kate Creston, if the man to whom she had given everything couldn't. He had known her twenty years, and she was the only woman for whom he might perhaps have been unfaithful. She was all cleverness and sympathy and charm; her house had been the very easiest in all the world and her friendship the very firmest. Without accidents he had loved her, without accidents everyone had loved her: she had made the passions about her as regular as the moon makes the tides. She had been also of course far too good for her husband, but he never suspected it, and in nothing had she been more admirable than in the exquisite art with which she tried to keep everyone else (keeping Creston was no trouble) from finding it out. Here was a man to whom she had devoted her life and for whom she had given it up – dying to bring into the world a child of his bed; and she had had only to submit to her fate to have, ere the grass was green on her grave, no more existence for him than a domestic servant he had replaced. The frivolity, the indecency of it made Stransom's eyes fill; and he had that evening a rich, almost happy sense that he alone, in a world without delicacy, had a right to hold up his head. While he smoked, after dinner, he had a book in his lap, but he had no eyes for his page: his eyes, in the swarming void of things, seemed to have caught Kate Creston's, and it was into their sad silences he looked. It was to him her sentient spirit had turned, knowing that it was of her he would think. He thought, for a long time, of how the closed eyes of dead women could still live – how they could open again, in a quiet lamp-lit room, long after they had looked their last. They had looks that remained, as great poets had quoted lines.

The newspaper lay by his chair – the thing that came in the afternoon and the servants thought one wanted; without sense for what was in it he had mechanically unfolded and then dropped it. Before he went to bed he took it up, and this time, at the top of a paragraph, he was caught by five words that made him start. He stood staring, before the fire, at the 'Death of Sir Acton Hague, K.C.B.', the man who, ten years earlier, had been the nearest of his friends and whose deposition from this eminence had practically left it without an occupant. He had seen him after that catastrophe, but he had not seen him for years. Standing there before the fire he turned cold as he read what had befallen him. Promoted a short time previous to the governorship of the Westward Islands, Acton Hague had died, in the bleak honour of this exile, of an illness consequent on the bite of a poisonous snake. His career was compressed by the newspaper into a dozen lines, the perusal of which excited on George Stransom's part no warmer feeling than one of relief at the absence of any mention of their quarrel, an incident accidentally tainted at the time, thanks to their joint immersion in large affairs, with a horrible publicity. Public indeed was the wrong Stransom had, to his own sense, suffered, the insult he had blankly taken from the only man with whom he had ever been intimate; the friend, almost adored, of his University years, the subject, later, of his passionate loyalty: so public that he had never spoken of it to a human creature, so public that he had completely overlooked it. It had made the difference for him that friendship too was all over, but it had only made just that one. The shock of interests had been private, intensely so; but the action taken by Hague had been in the face of men. Today it all seemed to have occurred merely to the end that George Stransom should think of him as 'Hague' and measure exactly how much he himself could feel like a stone. He went cold, suddenly and horribly cold, to bed.

III

THE NEXT DAY, in the afternoon, in the great grey suburb, he felt that his long walk had tired him. In the dreadful cemetery alone he had been on his feet an hour. Instinctively, coming back, they had taken him a devious course, and it was a desert in which no circling cabman hovered over possible prey. He paused on a corner and measured the dreariness; then he became aware in the gathered dusk that he was in one of those tracts of London which are less gloomy by night than by day, because, in the former case, of the civil gift of light. By day there was nothing, but by night there were lamps, and George Stransom was in a mood which made lamps good in themselves. It wasn't that they could show him anything; it was only that they could burn clear. To his surprise, however, after a while, they did show him something: the arch of a high doorway approached by a low terrace of steps, in the depth of which – it formed a dim vestibule – the raising of a curtain, at the moment he passed, gave him a glimpse of an avenue of gloom with a glow of tapers at the end. He stopped and looked up, making out that the place was a church. The thought quickly came to him that since he was tired he might rest there; so that after a moment he had in turn pushed up the leathern curtain and gone in. It was a temple of the old persuasion, and there had evidently been a function – perhaps a service for the dead; the high altar was still a blaze of candles. This was an exhibition he always liked, and he dropped into a seat with relief. More than it had ever yet come home to him it struck him as good that there should be churches.

This one was almost empty and the other altars were dim; a verger shuffled about, an old woman coughed, but it seemed to Stransom there was hospitality in the thick sweet air. Was it only the savour of the incense, or was it something larger and more guaranteed? He had at any rate quitted the great grey suburb and come nearer to the warm centre. He presently ceased to feel an intruder – he gained at last even a sense of community with the only worshipper in his neighbourhood, the sombre presence of a woman, in mourning unrelieved, whose back was all he could see of her and who had sunk deep into prayer at no great distance from him. He wished he could sink, like her, to the very bottom, be as motionless, as rapt in prostration. After a few moments he shifted his seat; it was almost indelicate to be so aware of her. But Stransom subsequently lost himself altogether; he floated away on the sea of light. If occasions like this had been more frequent in his life he would have been more frequently conscious of the great original type, set up in a myriad temples, of the unapproachable shrine he had erected in his mind. That shrine had begun as a reflection of ecclesiastical pomps, but the echo had ended by growing more distinct than the sound. The sound now rang out, the type glazed at him with all its fires and with a mystery of radiance in which endless meanings could glow. The thing became, as he sat there, his appropriate altar, and each starry candle an appropriate vow. He numbered them, he named them, he grouped them – it was the silent roll-call of his Dead. They made together a brightness vast and intense, a brightness in which the mere chapel of his thoughts grew so dim that as it faded away he asked himself if he shouldn't find his real comfort in some material act, some outward worship.

This idea took possession of him while, at a distance, the black-robed lady continued prostrate; he was quietly thrilled with his conception, which at last brought him to his feet in the sudden excitement of a plan. He wandered softly about the church, pausing in the different chapels, which were all, save one, applied to a special devotion. It was in this one, dark and ungarnished, that he stood longest – the length of time it took him fully to grasp the conception of gilding it with his bounty. He should snatch it from no other rites and associate it with nothing profane; he would simply take it as it should be given up to him and make it a masterpiece of splendour and a mountain of fire. Tended sacredly all the year, with the sanctifying church around it, it would always be ready for his offices. There would be difficulties, but from the first they presented themselves only as difficulties surmounted. Even for a person so little affiliated the thing would be a matter of arrangement. He saw it all in advance, and how bright in especial the place would become to him in the intermissions of toil and the dusk of afternoons; how rich in assurance at all times, but especially in the indifferent world. Before withdrawing he drew nearer again to the spot where he had first sat down, and in the movement he met the lady whom he had seen praying and who was now on her way to the door. She passed him quickly, and he had only a glimpse of her pale face and her unconscious, almost sightless eyes. For that instant she looked faded and handsome.

This was the origin of the rites more public, yet certainly esoteric, that he at last found himself able to establish. It took a long time, it took a year, and both the process and the result would have been – for any who knew – a vivid picture of his good faith. No one did know, in fact – no one but the bland ecclesiastics whose acquaintance he had promptly sought, whose objections he had softly overridden, whose curiosity and sympathy he had artfully charmed, whose assent to his eccentric munificence he had eventually won, and who had asked for concessions in exchange for indulgences. Stransom had of course at an early stage of his inquiry been referred to the Bishop, and the Bishop had been delightfully human, the Bishop had been almost amused. Success was within sight, at any rate, from the moment the attitude of those whom it concerned became liberal in response to liberality. The altar and the small chapel that enclosed it, consecrated to an ostensible and customary worship, were to be splendidly maintained; all that Stransom reserved to himself was the number of his lights and the free enjoyment of his intention. When the intention had taken complete effect the enjoyment became even greater than he had ventured to hope. He liked to think of this effect when he was far from it – he liked to convince himself of it yet again when he was near. He was not often, indeed, so near as that a visit to it had not perforce something of the patience of a pilgrimage; but the time he gave to his devotion came to seem to him more a contribution to his other interests than a betrayal of them. Even a loaded life might be easier when one had added a new necessity to it.

How much easier was probably never guessed by those who simply knew that there were hours when he disappeared and for many of whom there was a vulgar reading of what they used to call his plunges. These plunges were into depths quieter than the deep sea-caves, and the habit, at the end of a year or two, had become the one it would have cost him most to relinquish. Now they had really, his Dead, something that was indefeasibly theirs; and he liked to think that they might, in cases, be the Dead of others, as well as that the Dead of others might be invoked there under the protection of what he had done. Whoever bent a knee on the carpet he had laid down appeared to him to act in the spirit of his intention. Each of his lights had a name for him, and from time to time a new light was kindled. This was what he had fundamentally agreed for, that there should always be room for them all. What those who passed or lingered saw was simply the most resplendent of the altars, called suddenly into vivid usefulness, with a quiet elderly man, for whom it evidently had a fascination, often seated there in a maze or a doze; but half the satisfaction of the spot for this mysterious and fitful worshipper was that he found the years of his life there, and the ties, the affections, the struggles, the submissions, the conquests, if there had been such, a record of that adventurous journey in which the beginnings and the endings of human relations are the lettered mile-stones. He had in general little taste for the past as a part of his own history; at other times and in other places it mostly seemed to him pitiful to consider and impossible to repair; but on these occasions he accepted it with something of that positive gladness with which one adjusts one's self to an ache that is beginning to succumb to treatment. To the treatment of time the malady of life begins at a given moment to succumb; and these were doubtless the hours at which that truth most came home to him. The day was written for him there on which he had first become acquainted with death, and the successive phases of the acquaintance were each marked with a flame.

The flames were gathering thick at present, for Stransom had entered that dark defile of our earthly descent in which someone dies every day. It was only yesterday that Kate Creston had flashed out her white fire; yet already there were younger stars ablaze on the tips of the tapers. Various persons in whom his interest had not been intense drew closer to him by entering this company. He went over it, head by head, till he felt like the shepherd of a huddled flock, with all a shepherd's vision of differences imperceptible. He knew his candles apart, up to the colour of the flame, and would still have known them had their positions all been changed. To other imaginations they might stand for other things – that they should stand for something to be hushed before was all he desired; but he was intensely conscious of the personal note of each and of the distinguishable way it contributed to the concert. There were hours at which he almost caught himself wishing that certain of his friends would now die, that he might establish with them in this manner a connection more charming than, as it happened, it was possible to enjoy with them in life. In regard to those from whom one was separated by the long curves of the globe such a connection could only be an improvement: it brought them instantly within reach. Of course there were gaps in the constellation, for Stransom knew he could only pretend to act for his own, and it was not every figure passing before his eyes into the great obscure that was entitled to a memorial. There was a strange sanctification in death, but some characters were more sancti- fied by being forgotten than by being remembered. The greatest blank in the shining page was the memory of Acton Hague, of which he inveterately tried to rid himself. For Acton Hague no flame could ever rise on any altar of his.

IV

EVERY YEAR, the day he walked back from the great graveyard, he went to church as he had done the day his idea was born. It was on this occasion, as it happened, after a year had passed, that he began to observe his altar to be haunted by a worshipper at least as frequent as himself. Others of the faithful, and in the rest of the church, came and went, appealing sometimes, when they disappeared, to a vague or to a particular recognition; but this unfailing presence was always to be observed when he arrived and still in possession when he departed. He was surprised, the first time, at the promptitude with which it assumed an identity for him – the identity of the lady whom, two years before, on his anniversary, he had seen so intensely bowed, and of whose tragic face he had had so flitting a vision. Given the time that had elapsed, his recollection of her was fresh enough to make him wonder. Of himself she had of course no impression, or rather she had none at first: the time came when her manner of transacting her business suggested to him that she had gradually guessed his call to be of the same order. She used his altar for her own purpose – he could only hope that, sad and solitary as she always struck him, she used it for her own Dead. There were interruptions, infidelities, all on his part, calls to other associations and duties; but as the months went on he found her whenever he returned, and he ended by taking pleasure in the thought that he had given her almost the contentment he had given himself. They worshipped side by side so often that there were moments when he wished he might be sure, so straight did their prospect stretch away of growing old together in their rites. She was younger than he, but she looked as if her Dead were at least as numerous as his candles. She had no colour, no sound, no fault, and another of the things

about which he had made up his mind was that she had no
fortune. She was always black-robed, as if she had had a succes-
sion of sorrows. People were not poor, after all, whom so many
losses could overtake; they were positively rich when they had
so much to give up. But the air of this devoted and indifferent
woman, who always made, in any attitude, a beautiful, accidental line, conveyed somehow to Stransom that she had known
more kinds of trouble than one.

He had a great love of music and little time for the joy of it;
but occasionally, when workaday noises were muffled by
Saturday afternoons, it used to come back to him that there
were glories. There were moreover friends who reminded him
of this and side by side with whom he found himself sitting out
concerts. On one of these winter evenings, in St James's Hall, he
became aware after he had seated himself that the lady he had so
often seen at church was in the place next him and was evidently
alone, as he also this time happened to be. She was at first too
absorbed in the consideration of the programme to heed him,
but when she at last glanced at him he took advantage of the
movement to speak to her, greeting her with the remark that he
felt as if he already knew her. She smiled as she said 'Oh yes, I
recognize you'; yet in spite of this admission of their long
acquaintance it was the first time he had ever seen her smile.
The effect of it was suddenly to contribute more to that acquaintance than all the previous meetings had done. He hadn't 'taken
in', he said to himself, that she was so pretty. Later, that evening
(it was while he rolled along in a hansom on his way to dine out)

he added that he hadn't taken in that she was so interesting. The next morning, in the midst of his work, he quite suddenly and irrelevantly reflected that his impression of her, beginning so far back, was like a winding river that had at last reached the sea.

His work was indeed blurred a little, all that day, by the sense of what had now passed between them. It wasn't much, but it had just made the difference. They had listened together to Beethoven and Schumann; they had talked in the pauses and at the end, when at the door, to which they moved together, he had asked her if he could help her in the matter of getting away. She had thanked him and put up her umbrella, slipping into the crowd without an allusion to their meeting yet again and leaving him to remember at leisure that not a word had been exchanged about the place in which they frequently met. This circumstance seemed to him at one moment natural enough and at another perverse. She mightn't in the least have recognized his warrant for speaking to her; and yet if she hadn't he would have judged her an underbred woman. It was odd that when nothing had really ever brought them together he should have been able successfully to assume that they were in a manner old friends — that this negative quantity was somehow more than they could express. His success, it was true, had been qualified by her quick escape, so that there grew up in him an absurd desire to put it to some better test. Save in so far as some other improbable accident might assist him, such a test could be only to meet her afresh at church. Left to himself he would have gone to church the very next afternoon, just for the curiosity of seeing if he should find her there. But he was not left to himself, a fact he discovered quite at the last, after he had virtually made up his mind to go. The influence that kept him away really revealed to him how little to himself his Dead ever left him. They reminded him that he went only for them – for nothing else in the world.

The force of this reminder kept him away ten days: he hated to connect the place with anything but his offices or to give a glimpse of the curiosity that had been on the point of moving him. It was absurd to weave a tangle about a matter so simple as a custom of devotion that might so easily have been daily or hourly; yet the tangle got itself woven. He was sorry, he was disappointed: it was as if a long, happy spell had been broken and he had lost a familiar security. At the last, however, he asked himself if he was to stay away for ever from the fear of this muddle about motives. After an interval neither longer nor shorter than usual he re-entered the church with a clear conviction that he should scarcely heed the presence or the absence of the lady of the concert. This indifference didn't prevent his instantly perceiving that for the only time since he had first seen her she was not on the spot. He had now no scruple about giving her time to arrive, but she didn't arrive, and when he went away still missing her he was quite profanely and consentingly sorry. If her absence made the tangle more intricate, that was only her fault. By the end of another year it was very intricate indeed; but by that time he didn't in the least care, and it was only his cultivated consciousness that had given him scruples. Three times in three months he had gone to church without finding her, and he felt that he had not needed these occasions to show him that his suspense had quite dropped. Yet it was, incongruously, not indifference, but a refinement of delicacy that had kept him from asking the sacristan, who would of course immediately have recognized his description of her, whether she had been seen at other hours. His delicacy had kept him from asking any question about her at any time, and it was exactly the same virtue that had left him so free to be decently civil to her at the concert.

This happy advantage now served him anew, enabling him when she finally met his eyes – it was after a fourth trial – to determine without hesitation to wait till she should retire. He joined her in the street as soon as she had done so, and asked her if he might accompany her a certain distance. With her placid permission he went as far as a house in the neighbourhood at which she had business: she let him know it was not where she lived. She lived, as she said, in a mere slum, with an old aunt, a person in connection with whom she spoke of the engrossment of humdrum duties and regular occupations. She was not, the mourning niece, in her first youth, and her vanished freshness had left something behind which, for Stransom, represented the proof that it had been tragically sacrificed. Whatever she gave him the assurance of she gave it without references. She might in fact have been a divorced duchess, and she might have been an old maid who taught the harp.

V

THEY FELL at last into the way of walking together almost every time they met, though, for a long time, they never met anywhere save at church. He couldn't ask her to come and see him, and, as if she had not a proper place to receive him, she never invited him. As much as himself she knew the world of London, but from an undiscussed instinct of privacy they haunted the region not mapped on the social chart. On the return she always made him leave her at the same corner. She looked with him, as a pretext for a pause, at the depressed things in suburban shop-fronts; and there was never a word he had said to her that she had not beautifully understood. For long ages he never knew her name, any more than she had ever pronounced his own; but it was not their names that mattered, it was only their perfect practice and their common need.

These things made their whole relation so impersonal that they had not the rules or reasons people found in ordinary friendships. They didn't care for the things it was supposed necessary to care for in the intercourse of the world. They ended one day (they never knew which of them expressed it first) by throwing out the idea that they didn't care for each other. Over this idea they grew quite intimate; they rallied to it in a way that marked a fresh start in their confidence. If to feel deeply together about certain things wholly distinct from themselves didn't constitute a safety, where was safety to be looked for? Not lightly nor often, not without occasion nor without emotion, any more than in any other reference by serious people to a mystery of their faith; but when something had happened to warm, as it were, the air for it, they came as near as they could come to calling their Dead by name. They felt it was coming very near to utter their thought at all. The word 'they' expressed enough; it limited the mention, it had a dignity of its own, and if, in their talk, you had heard our friends use it, you might have taken them for a pair of pagans of old alluding decently to the domesticated gods. They never knew — at least Stransom never knew — how they had learned to be sure about each other. If it had been with each a question of what the other was there for, the certitude had come in some fine way of its own. Any faith, after all, has the instinct of propagation, and it was as natural as it was beautiful that they should have taken pleasure on the spot in the imagination of a following. If the following was for each but a following of one, it had proved in the event to be sufficient. Her debt, however, of course, was much greater than his, because while she had only given him a worshipper, he had given her a magnificent temple. Once she said she pitied him for the length of his list (she had counted his candles almost as often as himself) and this made him wonder what could have been the length of hers. He had wondered before at the coincidence of their losses, especially as from time to time a new candle was set up. On one occasion some accident led him to express this curiosity, and she answered as if she was surprised that he hadn't already understood. 'Oh, for me, you know, the more there are the better – there could never be too many. I should like hundreds and hundreds – I should like thousands; I should like a perfect mountain of light.'

Then of course, in a flash, he understood. 'Your Dead are only One?'

She hesitated as she had never hesitated. 'Only One,' she answered, colouring as if now he knew her innermost secret. It really made him feel that he knew less than before, so difficult was it for him to reconstitute a life in which a single experience had reduced all others to nought. His own life, round its central hollow, had been packed close enough. After this she appeared to have regretted her confession, though at the moment she spoke there had been pride in her very embarrassment. She declared to him that his own was the larger, the dearer possession – the portion one would have chosen if one had been able to choose; she assured him she could perfectly imagine some of the echoes with which his silences were peopled. He knew she couldn't: one's relation to what one had loved and hated had been a relation too distinct from the relations of others. But this didn't affect the fact that they were growing old together in their piety. She was a feature of that piety, but even at the ripe stage of acquaintance in which they occasionally arranged to meet at a concert or to go together to an exhibition she was not a feature of anything else. The most that happened was that his worship became paramount. Friend by friend dropped away till at last there were more emblems on his altar than houses left him to enter. She was more than any other the friend who remained, but she was unknown to all the rest. Once when she had discovered, as they called it, a new star, she used the expression that the chapel at last was full.

'Oh no,' Stransom replied, 'there is a great thing wanting for that! The chapel will never be full till a candle is set up before which all the others will pale. It will be the tallest candle of all.'

Her mild wonder rested on him. 'What candle do you mean?'

'I mean, dear lady, my own.'

He had learned after a long time that she earned money by her pen, writing under a designation that she never told him in magazines that he never saw. She knew too well what he couldn't read and what she couldn't write, and she taught him to cultivate indifference with a success that did much for their good relations. Her invisible industry was a convenience to him; it helped his contented thought of her, the thought that rested in the dignity of her proud, obscure life, her little remunerated art and her little impenetrable home. Lost, with her obscure relative, in her dim suburban world, she came to the surface for him in distant places. She was really the priestess of his altar, and whenever he quitted England he committed it to her keeping. She proved to him afresh that women have more of the spirit of religion than men; he felt his fidelity pale and faint in comparison with hers. He often said to her that since he had so little time to live he rejoiced in her having so much; so glad was he to think she would guard the temple when he should have ceased. He had a great plan for that, which of course he told her too, a bequest of money to keep it up in undiminished state. Of the administration of this fund he would appoint her superintendent, and if the spirit should move her she might kindle a taper even for him.

'And who will kindle one even for me?' she gravely inquired.

VI

SHE WAS ALWAYS in mourning, yet the day he came back from the longest absence he had yet made her appearance immediately told him she had lately had a bereavement. They met on this occasion as she was leaving the church, so that postponing his own entrance he instantly offered to turn round and walk away with her. She considered, then she said: 'Go in now, but come and see me in an hour.' He knew the small vista of her street, closed at the end and as dreary as an empty pocket, where the pairs of shabby little houses, semi-detached but indissolubly united, were like married couples on bad terms. Often, however, as he had gone to the beginning, he had never gone beyond. Her aunt was dead – that he immediately guessed, as well as that it made a difference; but when she had for the first time mentioned her number he found himself, on her leaving him, not a little agitated by this sudden liberality. She was not a person with whom, after all, one got on so very fast: it had taken him months and months to learn her name, years and years to learn her address. If she had looked, on this reunion, so much older to him, how in the world did he look to her? She had reached the period of life that he had long since reached, when, after separations, the dreadful clockface of the friend we meet announces the hour we have tried to forget. He couldn't have said what he expected as, at the end of his waiting, he turned the corner at which, for years, he had always paused; simply not to pause was a sufficient cause for emotion. It was an event, somehow; and in all their long acquaintance there had never been such a thing. The event grew larger when, five minutes later, in the faint elegance of her little drawing-room, she quavered out some greeting which showed the measure she took of it. He had a strange sense of having come for something in particular; strange because, literally, there was nothing particular between them, nothing save that they were at one on their great point, which had long ago become a magnificent matter of course. It was true that after she had said 'You can always come now, you know,' the thing he was there for seemed already to have happened. He asked her if it was the death of her aunt that made the difference; to which she replied: 'She never knew I knew you. I wished her not to.' The beautiful clearness of her candour – her faded beauty was like a summer twilight – disconnected the words from any image of deceit. They might have struck him as the record of a deep dissimulation; but she had always given him a sense of noble reasons. The vanished aunt was present, as he looked about him, in the small complacencies of the room, the beaded velvet and the fluted moreen; and though, as we know, he had the worship of the Dead, he found himself not definitely regretting this lady. If she was not in his long list, however, she was in her niece's short one, and Stransom presently observed to his friend that now, at least, in the place they haunted together, she would have another object of devotion.

'Yes, I shall have another. She was very kind to me. It's that that makes the difference.'

He judged, wondering a good deal before he made any motion to leave her, that the difference would somehow be very great and would consist of still other things than her having let him come in. It rather chilled him, for they had been happy together as they were. He extracted from her at any rate an intimation that she should now have larger means, that her aunt's tiny fortune had come to her, so that there was henceforth only one to consume what had formerly been made to suffice for two. This was a joy to Stransom, because it had hitherto been equally impossible for him either to offer her presents or to find contentment in not doing so. It was too ugly to be at her side that way, abounding himself and yet not able to overflow – a demonstration that would have been a signally false note. Even her better situation too seemed only to draw out in a sense the loneliness of her future. It would merely help her to live more and more for their small ceremonial, at a time when he himself had begun wearily to feel that, having set it in motion, he might depart. When they had sat a while in the pale parlour she got up and said: 'This isn't *my* room: let us go into mine.' They had only to cross the narrow hall, as he found, to pass into quite another air. When she had closed the door of the second room, as she called it, he felt that he had at last real possession of her. The place had the flush of life – it was expressive; its dark red walls were articulate with memories and relics. These were simple things – photographs and water-colours, scraps of writing framed and ghosts of flowers embalmed; but only a moment was needed to show him they had a common meaning. It was here that she had lived and worked; and she had already told him she would make no change of scene. He saw that the objects about her mainly had reference to certain places and times; but after a minute he distinguished among them a small portrait of a gentleman. At a distance and without their glasses his eyes were only caught by it enough to feel a vague curiosity. Presently this impulse carried him nearer, and in another moment he was staring at the picture in stupefaction and with the sense that some sound had broken from him. He was further conscious that he showed his companion a white face when he turned round on her with the exclamation: 'Acton Hague!'

She gave him back his astonishment. 'Did you know him?'

'He was the friend of all my youth – my early manhood. And *you* knew him?'

She coloured at this, and for a moment her answer failed; her eyes took in everything in the place, and a strange irony reached her lips as she echoed: 'Knew him?'

Then Stransom understood, while the room heaved like the cabin of a ship, that its whole contents cried out with him, that it was a museum in his honour, that all her later years had been addressed to him and that the shrine he himself had reared had been passionately converted to this use. It was all for Acton

Hague that she had kneeled every day at his altar. What need had there been for a consecrated candle when he was present in the whole array? The revelation seemed to smite our friend in the face, and he dropped into a seat and sat silent. He had quickly become aware that she was shocked at the vision of his own shock, but as she sank on the sofa beside him and laid her hand on his arm he perceived almost as soon that she was unable to resent it as much as she would have liked.

VII

HE LEARNED IN that instant two things: one of them was that even in so long a time she had gathered no knowledge of his great intimacy and his great quarrel; the other was that in spite of this ignorance, strangely enough, she supplied on the spot a reason for his confusion. 'How extraordinary,' he presently exclaimed, 'that we should never have known!'

She gave a wan smile which seemed to Stransom stranger even than the fact itself. 'I never, never spoke of him.'

Stransom looked about the room again. 'Why then, if your life had been so full of him?'

'Mayn't I put you that question as well? Hadn't your life also been full of him?'

'Anyone's, everyone's life was who had the wonderful experience of knowing him. I never spoke of him,' Stransom added in a moment, 'because he did me – years ago – an unforgettable wrong.' She was silent, and with the full effect of his presence all about them it almost startled her visitor to hear no protest escape from her. She accepted his words; he turned his eyes to her again to see in what manner she accepted them. It was with rising tears and an extraordinary sweetness in the movement of putting out her hand to take his own. Nothing more wonderful had ever appeared to Stransom than, in that little chamber of remembrance and homage, to see her convey with such exquisite mildness that as from Acton Hague any injury was credible. The clock ticked in the stillness – Hague had probably given it to her – and while he let her hold his hand with a tenderness that was almost an assumption of responsibility for his old pain as well as his new, Stransom after a minute broke out: 'Good God, how he must have used *you*!'

She dropped his hand at this, got up and, moving across the room, made straight a small picture to which, on examining it, he had given a slight push. Then turning round on him with her pale gaiety recovered: 'I've forgiven him!' she declared.

'I know what you've done,' said Stransom; 'I know what you've done for years.' For a moment they looked at each other across the room, with their long community of service in their eyes. This short passage made, to Stransom's sense, for the woman before him, an immense, an absolutely naked confession; which was presently, suddenly blushing red and changing her place again, what she appeared to become aware that he perceived in it. He got up. 'How you must have loved him!' he cried.

'Women are not like men. They can love even where they've suffered.'

'Women are wonderful,' said Stransom. 'But I assure you I've forgiven him too.'

'If I had known of anything so strange I wouldn't have brought you here.'

'So that we might have gone on in our ignorance to the last?'

'What do you call the last?' she asked, smiling still.

At this he could smile back at her. 'You'll see – when it comes.'

She reflected a moment. 'This is better perhaps; but as we were – it was good.'

'Did it never happen that he spoke of me?' Stransom inquired.

Considering more intently, she made no answer, and he quickly recognized that he would have been adequately answered by her asking how often he himself had spoken of their terrible friend. Suddenly a brighter light broke in her face, and an excited idea sprang to her lips in the question: 'You *have* forgiven him?'

'How, if I hadn't, could I linger here?'

She winced, for an instant, at the deep but unintended irony of this; but even while she did so she panted quickly: 'Then in the lights on your altar——?'

'There's never a light for Acton Hague!'

She stared, with a great visible fall. 'But if he's one of your Dead?'

'He's one of the world's, if you like – he's one of yours. But he's not one of mine. Mine are only the Dead who died possessed of me. They're mine in death because they were mine in life.'

'*He* was yours in life then, even if for a while he ceased to be. If you forgave him you went back to him. Those whom we've once loved—'

'Are those who can hurt us most,' Stransom broke in.

'Ah, it's not true – you've *not* forgiven him!' she wailed with a passion that startled him.

He looked at her a moment. 'What was it he did to you?'

'Everything!' Then abruptly she put out her hand in farewell. 'Good-bye.'

He turned as cold as he had turned that night he read of the death of Acton Hague. 'You mean that we meet no more?'

'Not as we have met – not *there*!'

He stood aghast at this snap of their great bond, at the renouncement that rang out in the word she so passionately emphasized. 'But what's changed – for you?'

She hesitated, in all the vividness of a trouble that, for the first time since he had known her, made her splendidly stern. 'How can you understand now when you didn't understand before?'

'I didn't understand before only because I didn't know. Now that I know, I see what I've been living with for years,' Stransom went on very gently.

She looked at him with a larger allowance, as if she appreciated his good-nature. 'How can I, then, with this new knowledge of my own, ask you to continue to live with it?'

'I set up my altar, with its multiplied meanings,' Stransom began; but she quickly interrupted him.

'You set up your altar, and when I wanted one most I found it magnificently ready. I used it, with the gratitude I've always shown you, for I knew from of old that it was dedicated to Death. I told you, long ago, that my Dead were not many. Yours were, but all you had done for them was none too much for *my* worship! You had placed a great light for Each – I gathered them together for One!'

'We had simply different intentions,' Stransom replied. 'That, as you say, I perfectly knew, and I don't see why your intention shouldn't still sustain you.'

'That's because you're generous – you can imagine and think. But the spell is broken.'

It seemed to poor Stransom, in spite of his resistance, that it really was, and the prospect stretched grey and void before him. All, however, that he could say was: 'I hope you'll try before you give up.'

'If I had known you had ever known him I should have taken for granted he had his candle,' she presently rejoined. 'What's changed, as you say, is that on making the discovery I find he never has had it. That makes *my* attitude –' she paused a moment, as if thinking how to express it, then said simply – 'all wrong.'

'Come once again,' Stransom pleaded.

'Will you give him his candle?' she asked.

He hesitated, but only because it would sound ungracious; not because he had a doubt of his feeling. 'I can't do that!' he declared at last.

'Then good-bye.' And she gave him her hand again.

He had got his dismissal; besides which, in the agitation of everything that had opened out to him, he felt the need to recover himself as he could only do in solitude. Yet he lingered – lingered to see if she had no compromise to express, no attenuation to propose. But he only met her great lamenting eyes, in which indeed he read that she was as sorry for him as for anyone else. This made him say: 'At least, at any rate, I may see you here.'

'Oh, yes, come if you like. But I don't think it will do.'

Stransom looked round the room once more; he felt in truth by no means sure it would do. He felt also stricken and more and more cold, and his chill was like an ague in which he had to make an effort not to shake. 'I must try on my side, if you can't try on yours,' he dolefully rejoined. She came out with him to the hall and into the doorway, and here he put to her the question that seemed to him the one he could least answer from his own wit. 'Why have you never let me come before?'

'Because my aunt would have seen you, and I should have had to tell her how I came to know you.'

'And what would have been the objection to that?'

'It would have entailed other explanations; there would at any rate have been that danger.'

'Surely she knew you went every day to church,' Stransom objected.

'She didn't know what I went for.'

'Of me then she never even heard?'

'You'll think I was deceitful. But I didn't need to be!'

Stransom was now on the lower door-step, and his hostess held the door half closed behind him. Through what remained of the opening he saw her framed face. He made a supreme appeal. 'What *did* he do to you?'

'It would have come out – *she* would have told you. That fear, at my heart – that was my reason!' And she closed the door, shutting him out.

VIII

HE HAD RUTHLESSLY abandoned her – that, of course, was what he had done. Stransom made it all out in solitude, at leisure, fitting the unmatched pieces gradually together and dealing one by one with a hundred obscure points. She had known Hague only after her present friend's relations with him had wholly terminated; obviously indeed a good while after; and it was natural enough that of his previous life she should have ascertained only what he had judged good to communicate. There were passages it was quite conceivable that even in moments of the tenderest expansion he should have withheld. Of many facts in the career of a man so in the eye of the world there was of course a common knowledge; but this lady lived apart from public affairs, and the only period perfectly clear to her would have been the period following the dawn of her own drama. A man, in her place, would have 'looked up' the past – would even have consulted old newspapers. It remained singular indeed that in her long contact with the partner of her retrospect no accident had lighted a train; but there was no arguing about that; the accident had in fact come: it had simply been that security had prevailed. She had taken what Hague had given her, and her blankness in respect of his other connections was only a touch in the picture of that plasticity Stransom had supreme reason to know so great a master could have been trusted to produce.

This picture, for a while, was all that our friend saw: he caught his breath again and again as it came over him that the woman with whom he had had for years so fine a point of contact was a woman whom Acton Hague, of all men in the world, had more or less fashioned. Such as she sat there today, she was ineffaceably stamped with him. Beneficent, blameless as Stransom held her, he couldn't rid himself of the sense that he had been the victim of a fraud. She had imposed upon him hugely, though she had known it as little as he. All this later past came back to him as a time grotesquely misspent. Such at least were his first reflections; after a while he found himself more divided and only, as the end of it, more troubled. He imagined, recalled, reconstituted, figured out for himself the truth she had refused to give him; the effect of which was to make her seem to him only more saturated with her fate. He felt her spirit, in the strange business, to be finer than his own in the very degree in which she might have been, in which she certainly had been, more wronged. A woman, when she was wronged, was always more wronged than a man, and there were conditions when the least she could have got off with was more than the most he could have to endure. He was sure this rare creature wouldn't have got off with the least. He was awestruck at the thought of such a surrender – such a prostration. Moulded indeed she had been by powerful hands, to have converted her injury into an exaltation so sublime. The fellow had only had to die for everything that was ugly in him to be washed out in a torrent. It was vain to try to guess what had taken place, but nothing could be clearer than that she had ended by accusing herself. She absolved him at every point, she adored her very wounds. The passion by which he had profited had rushed back after its ebb, and now the tide of tenderness, arrested for ever at flood, was too deep even to fathom. Stransom sincerely considered that he had forgiven him; but how little he had achieved the miracle that she had achieved! His forgiveness was silence, but hers was mere un-uttered sound. The light she had demanded for his altar would have broken his silence with a blare; whereas all the lights in the church were for her too great a hush.

She had been right about the difference – she had spoken the truth about the change: Stransom felt before long that he was perversely but definitely jealous. *His* tide had ebbed, not flowed; if he had 'forgiven' Acton Hague, that forgiveness was a motive with a broken spring. The very fact of her appeal for a material sign, a sign that should make her dead lover equal there with the others, presented the concession to Stransom as too handsome for the case. He had never thought of himself as hard, but an exorbitant article might easily render him so. He moved round and round this one, but only in widening circles – the more he looked at it the less acceptable it appeared. At the same time he had no illusion about the effect of his refusal; he perfectly saw that it was the beginning of a separation. He left her alone for many days; but when at last he called upon her again this conviction acquired a depressing force. In the interval he had kept away from the church, and he needed no fresh assurance from her to know she had not entered it. The change was complete enough: it had broken up her life. Indeed it had broken up his, for all the fires of his shrine seemed to him suddenly to have been quenched. A great indifference fell upon him, the weight of which was in itself a pain; and he never knew what his devotion had been for him till, in that shock, it stopped like a dropped watch. Neither did he know with how large a confidence he had counted on the final service that had now failed: the mortal deception was that in this abandonment the whole future gave way.

These days of her absence proved to him of what she was capable; all the more that he never dreamed she was vindictive or even resentful. It was not in anger she had forsaken him; it was in absolute submission to hard reality, to crude destiny. This came home to him when he sat with her again in the room in which her late aunt's conversation lingered like the tone of a cracked piano. She tried to make him forget how much they were estranged; but in the very presence of what they had given up it was impossible not to be sorry for her. He had taken from her so much more than she had taken from him. He argued with her again, told her she could now have the altar to herself; but she only shook her head with pleading sadness, begging him not to waste his breath on the impossible, the extinct. Couldn't he see that in relation to her private need the rites he had established were practically an elaborate exclusion? She regretted nothing that had happened; it had all been right so long as she didn't know, and it was only that now she knew too much and that from the moment their eyes were open they would simply have to conform. It had doubtless been happiness enough for them to go on together so long. She was gentle, grateful, resigned; but this was only the form of a deep immutability. He saw that he should never more cross the threshold of the second room, and he felt how much this alone would make a stranger of him and give a conscious stiffness to his visits. He would have hated to plunge again into that well of reminders, but he enjoyed quite as little the vacant alternative.

After he had been with her three or four times it seemed to him that to have come at last into her house had had the horrid effect of diminishing their intimacy. He had known her better, had liked her in greater freedom, when they merely walked together or kneeled together. Now they only pretended; before they had been nobly sincere. They began to try their walks again, but it proved a lame imitation, for these things, from the first, beginning or ending, had been connected with their visits to the church. They had either strolled away as they came out or gone in to rest on the return. Besides, Stransom now grew weary; he couldn't walk as of old. The omission made everything false; it was a horrible mutilation of their lives. Our friend was frank and monotonous; he made no mystery of his remonstrance and no secret of his predicament. Her response, whatever it was, always came to the same thing – an implied invitation to him to judge, if he spoke of predicaments, of how much comfort she had in hers. For him indeed there was no comfort even in complaint, for every allusion to what had befallen them only made the author of their trouble more present. Acton Hague was between them, that was the essence of the matter; and he was never so much between them as when they were face to face. Stransom, even while he wanted to banish him, had the strangest sense of desiring a satisfaction that could come only from having accepted him. Deeply disconcerted by what he knew, he was still worse tormented by really not knowing. Perfectly aware that it would have been horribly vulgar to abuse his old friend or to tell his companion the story of their quarrel, it yet vexed him that her depth of reserve should give him no opening and should have the effect of a magnanimity greater even than his own.

He challenged himself, denounced himself, asked himself if he were in love with her that he should care so much what adventures she had had. He had never for a moment admitted that he was in love with her; therefore nothing could have surprised him more than to discover that he was jealous. What but jealousy could give a man that sore, contentious wish to have the detail of what would make him suffer? Well enough he knew indeed that he should never have it from the only person who, today, could give it to him. She let him press her with his sombre eyes, only smiling at him with an exquisite mercy and breathing equally little the word that would expose her secret and the word that would appear to deny his literal right to bitterness. She told nothing, she judged nothing; she accepted everything but the possibility of her return to the old symbols. Stransom divined that for her too they had been vividly individual, had stood for particular hours or particular attributes — particular links in her chain. He made it clear to himself, as he believed, that his difficulty lay in the fact that the very nature of the plea for his faithless friend constituted a prohibition; that it happened to have come from *her* was precisely the vice that attached to it. To the voice of impersonal generosity he felt sure he would have listened; he would have deferred to an advocate who, speaking from abstract justice, knowing of his omission without having known Hague, should have had the imagination to say: 'Oh, remember only the best of him; pity him; provide for him.' To provide for him on the very ground of having discovered another of his turpitudes was not to pity him, but to glorify him. The more Stransom thought the more he made it out that this relation of Hague's, whatever it was, could only have been a deception finely practised. Where had it come into the life that all men saw? Why had he never heard of it, if it had had the frankness of an attitude honourable? Stransom knew enough of his other ties, of his obligations and appearances, not to say enough of his general character, to be sure there had been some infamy. In one way or another the poor woman had been coldly sacrificed. That was why, at the last as well as the first, he must still leave him out.

IX

AND YET THIS was no solution, especially after he had talked again to his friend of all it had been his plan that she should finally do for him. He had talked in the other days, and she had responded with a frankness qualified only by a courteous reluctance, a reluctance that touched him, to linger on the question of his death. She had then practically accepted the charge, suffered him to feel that he could depend upon her to be the eventual guardian of his shrine; and it was in the name of what had so passed between them that he appealed to her not to forsake him in his old age. She listened to him now with a sort of shining coldness and all her habitual forbearance to insist on her terms; her deprecation was even still tenderer, for it expressed the compassion of her own sense that he was abandoned. Her terms, however, remained the same, and scarcely the less audible for not being uttered; although he was sure that, secretly, even more than he, she felt bereft of the satisfaction his solemn trust was to have provided for her. They both missed the rich future, but she missed it most, because after all it was to have been entirely hers; and it was her acceptance of the loss that gave him the full measure of her preference for the thought of Acton Hague over any other thought whatever. He had humour enough to laugh rather grimly when he said to himself: 'Why the deuce does she like him so much more than she likes me?' – the reasons being really so conceivable. But even his faculty of analysis left the irritation standing, and this irritation proved perhaps the greatest misfortune that had ever overtaken him. There had been nothing yet that made him so much want to give up. He had of course by this time well reached the age of renouncement; but it had not hitherto been vivid to him that it was time to give up everything.

Practically, at the end of six months, he had renounced the friendship that was once so charming and comforting. His privation had two faces, and the face it had turned to him on the occasion of his last attempt to cultivate that friendship was the one he could look at least. This was the privation he inflicted; the other was the privation he bore. The conditions she never phrased he used to murmur to himself in solitude: 'One more, one more – only just one.' Certainly he was going down; he often felt it when he caught himself, over his work, staring at vacancy and giving voice to that inanity. There was proof enough besides in his being so weak and so ill. His irritation took the form of melancholy, and his melancholy that of the conviction that his health had quite failed. His altar moreover had ceased to exist; his chapel, in his dreams, was a great dark cavern. All the lights had gone out – all his Dead had died again. He couldn't exactly see at first how it had been in the power of his late companion to extinguish them, since it was neither for her nor by her that they had been called into being. Then he understood that it was essentially in his own soul the revival had taken place, and that in the air of this soul they were now unable to breathe. The candles might mechanically burn, but each of them had lost its lustre. The church had become a void; it was his presence, her presence, their common presence, that had made the indispensable medium. If anything was wrong every-thing was – her silence spoiled the tune.

Then when three months were gone he felt so lonely that he went back; reflecting that as they had been his best society for years his Dead perhaps wouldn't let him forsake them without doing something more for him. They stood there, as he had left them, in their tall radiance, the bright cluster that had already made him, on occasions when he was willing to compare small things with great, liken them to a group of sea-lights on the edge of the ocean of life. It was a relief to him, after a while, as he sat there, to feel that they had still a virtue. He was more and more easily tired, and he always drove now; the action of his heart was weak and gave him none of the reassurance conferred by the action of his fancy. None the less he returned yet again, returned several times, and finally, during six months, haunted the place with a renewal of frequency and a strain of impatience. In winter the church was unwarmed, and exposure to cold was forbidden him, but the glow of his shrine was an influence in which he could almost bask. He sat and wondered to what he had reduced his absent associate and what she now did with the hours of her absence. There were other churches, there were other altars, there were other candles; in one way or another her piety would still operate; he couldn't absolutely have deprived her of her rites. So he argued, but without contentment; for he well enough knew there was no other such rare semblance of the mountain of light she had once mentioned to him as the satisfaction of her need. As this semblance again gradually grew great to him and his pious practice more regular, there was a sharper and sharper pang for him in the imagination of her darkness; for never so much as in these weeks had his rites been real, never had his gathered company seemed so to respond and even to invite. He lost himself in the large lustre, which was more and more what he had from the first wished it to be – as dazzling as the vision of Heaven in the mind of a child. He wandered in the fields of light; he passed, among the tall tapers, from tier to tier, from fire to fire, from name to name, from the white intensity of one clear emblem, of one saved soul, to another. It was in the quiet sense of having saved his souls that his deep, strange instinct rejoiced. This was no dim theological rescue, no boon of a contingent world; they were saved better than faith or works could save them, saved for the warm world they had shrunk from dying to, for actuality, for continuity, for the certainty of human remembrance.

By this time he had survived all his friends; the last straight flame was three years old, there was no one to add to the list.

Over and over he called his roll, and it appeared to him compact and complete. Where should he put in another, where, if there were no other objection, would it stand in its place in the rank? He reflected, with a want of sincerity of which he was quite conscious, that it would be difficult to determine that place. More and more, besides, face to face with his little legion, reading over endless histories, handling the empty shells and playing with the silence – more and more he could see that he had never introduced an alien. He had had his great compassions, his indulgences – there were cases in which they had been immense; but what had his devotion after all been if it hadn't been fundamentally a respect? He was, however, himself surprised at his stiffness; by the end of the winter the responsibility of it was what was uppermost in his thoughts. The refrain had grown old to them, the plea for just one more. There came a day when, for simple exhaustion, if symmetry should really demand just one more he was ready to take symmetry into account. Symmetry was harmony, and the idea of harmony began to haunt him; he said to himself that harmony was of course everything. He took, in fancy, his composition to pieces, redistributing it into other lines, making other juxtapositions and contrasts. He shifted this and that candle, he made the spaces different, he effaced the disfigurement of a possible gap. There were subtle and complex relations, a scheme of cross-reference, and moments in which he seemed to catch a glimpse of the void so sensible to the woman who wandered in exile or sat where he had seen her with the portrait of Acton Hague.

Finally, in this way, he arrived at a conception of the total, the ideal, which left a clear opportunity for just another figure. 'Just one more — to round it off; just one more, just one,' continued to hum itself in his head. There was a strange confusion in the thought, for he felt the day to be near when he too should be one of the Others. What, in this case, would the Others matter to him, since they only mattered to the living? Even as one of the Dead, what would his altar matter to him, since his particular dream of keeping it up had melted away? What had harmony to do with the case if his lights were all to be quenched? What he had hoped for was an instituted thing. He might perpetuate it on some other pretext, but his special meaning would have dropped. This meaning was to have lasted with the life of the one other person who understood it.

In March he had an illness during which he spent a fortnight in bed, and when he revived a little he was told of two things that had happened. One was that a lady, whose name was not known to the servants (she left none) had been three times to ask about him; the other was that in his sleep, and on an occasion when his mind evidently wandered, he was heard to murmur again and again: 'Just one more — just one.' As soon as he found himself able to go out, and before the doctor in attendance had pronounced him so, he drove to see the lady who had come to ask about him. She was not at home; but this gave him the opportunity, before his strength should fail again, to take his way to the church. He entered the church alone; he had declined, in a happy manner he possessed of being able to decline effectively, the company of his servant or of a nurse. He knew now perfectly what these good people thought; they had discovered his clandestine connection, the magnet that had drawn him for so many years, and doubtless attached a significance of their own to the odd words they had repeated to him. The nameless lady was the clandestine connection – a fact nothing could have made clearer than his indecent haste to rejoin her. He sank on his knees before his altar, and his head fell over on his hands. His weakness, his life's weariness overtook him. It seemed to him he had come for the great surrender. At first he asked himself how he should get away; then, with the failing belief in the power, the very desire to move gradually left him. He had come, as he always came, to lose himself; the fields of light were still there to stray in; only this time, in straying, he would never come back. He had given himself to his Dead, and it was good: this time his Dead would keep him. He couldn't rise from his knees; he believed he should never rise again; all he could do was to lift his face and fix his eyes upon his lights. They looked unusually, strangely splendid, but the one that always drew him most had an unprecedented lustre. It was the central voice of the choir, the glowing heart of the brightness, and on this occasion it seemed to expand, to spread great wings of flame. The whole altar flared – it dazzled and blinded; but the source of the vast radiance burned clearer than the rest, it gathered itself into form, and the form was human beauty and human charity – it was the far-off face of Mary Antrim. She smiled at him from the glory of Heaven – she brought the glory down with her to take him. He bowed his head in submission, and at the same moment another wave rolled over him. Was it the quickening of joy to pain? In the midst of his joy at any rate he felt his buried face grow hot as with some communicated knowledge that had the force of a reproach. It suddenly made him contrast that very rapture with the bliss he had refused to another. This breath of the passion immortal was all that other had asked; the descent of Mary Antrim opened his spirit with a great compunctious throb for the descent of Acton Hague. It was as if Stransom had read what her eyes said to him.

After a moment he looked round him in a despair which made him feel as if the source of life were ebbing. The church had been empty – he was alone; but he wanted to have something done, to make a last appeal. This idea gave him strength for an effort; he rose to his feet with a movement that made him turn, supporting himself by the back of a bench. Behind him was a prostrate figure, a figure he had seen before; a woman in deep mourning, bowed in grief or in prayer. He had seen her in other days – the first time he came into the church, and he slightly wavered there, looking at her again till she seemed to become aware he had noticed her. She raised her head and met his eyes: the partner of his long worship was there. She looked across at him an instant with a face wondering and scared; he saw that he had given her an alarm. Then quickly rising, she came straight to him with both hands out.

'Then you *could* come? God sent you!' he murmured with a happy smile.

'You're very ill – you shouldn't be here,' she urged in anxious reply.

'God sent me too, I think. I was ill when I came, but the sight of you does wonders.' He held her hands, and they steadied and quickened him. 'I've something to tell you.'

'Don't tell me!' she tenderly pleaded; 'let me tell you. This afternoon, by a miracle, the sweetest of miracles, the sense of our difference left me. I was out – I was near, thinking, wandering alone, when, on the spot, something changed in my heart. It's my confession – there it is. To come back, to come back on the instant – the idea gave me wings. It was as if I suddenly saw something – as if it all became possible. I could come for what you yourself came for: that was enough. So here I am. It's not for my own – that's over. But I'm here for *them*.' And breathless, infinitely relieved by her low, precipitate explanation, she looked with eyes that reflected all its splendour at the magnificence of their altar.

'They're here for you,' Stransom said, 'they're present tonight as they've never been. They speak for you – don't you see? – in a passion of light – they sing out like a choir of angels. Don't you hear what they say? – they offer the very thing you asked of me.'

'Don't talk of it – don't think of it; forget it!' She spoke in hushed supplication, and while the apprehension deepened in her eyes she disengaged one of her hands and passed an arm round him, to support him better, to help him to sink into a seat.

He let himself go, resting on her; he dropped upon the bench, and she fell on her knees beside him with his arm on her shoulder. So he remained an instant, staring up at his shrine. 'They say there's a gap in the array – they say it's not full, complete. Just one more,' he went on, softly – 'isn't that what you wanted? Yes, one more, one more.'

'Ah, no more – no more!' she wailed, as if with a quick, new horror of it, under her breath.

'Yes, one more,' he repeated, simply; 'just one!' And with this his head dropped on her shoulder; she felt that in his weakness he had fainted. But alone with him in the dusky church a great dread was on her of what might still happen, for his face had the whiteness of death.

A Note on the Texts

The texts of the tales in this selection are taken from their original magazine publications (or in the case of 'The Altar of the Dead' its publication in James's 1895 collection *Terminations*), and not from the amended versions James prepared for the New York edition of his works:

'The Author of *Beltraffio*' (*English Illustrated Magazine*, June–July 1884); 'Sir Edmund Orme' (*Black and White*, December 1891); 'Brooksmith' (*Harper's Weekly*, May 1891); 'Owen Wingrave' (*The Graphic*, December 1892); 'The Visits' (*Black and White*, May 1892); 'Collaboration' (*English Illustrated Magazine*, December 1892); 'Nona Vincent' (*English Illustrated Magazine*, February–March 1892); 'The Real Thing' (*Black and White*, April 1892); 'The Private Life' (*The Atlantic*, 1892); 'The Middle Years' (*Scribner's Magazine*, May 1893); 'The Death of the Lion' (*The Yellow Book*, 1894); 'The Altar of the Dead' (*Terminations*, 1895).